THE
LOOM
OF
CRIME

I0666247

FootSteps Press

© Shänne Sands 2015

The right of Shänne Sands to be identified as the author
of this work has been asserted in accordance with
sections 77 and 78 of the Copyright Designs and Patents
Act 1988.

The Loom Of Crime

Footsteps Press First Edition
Published in the United Kingdom

Typeset by Daniel Nanavati

ISBN 978-1-908867-88-9

Cover images Bodmin Prison, Cornwall
© Emily Whitfield Wicks 2015

The right of Emily Whitfield Wicks to be identified as the
photographer of the cover to this work has been asserted
in accordance with sections 77 and 78 of the Copyright
Designs and Patents Act 1988.

In this work of Fiction the characters, places and events
are either the product of the author's imagination or they
are used entirely fictitiously. Therefore any resemblance
to persons living or dead is coincidental.

THE
LOOM
OF
CRIME

by

Shänne Sands

Foreword

I considered it important to put in writing what I knew of the lives of these children who seemed to be the outcasts of England.

I am not praising these boys, they are rogues, but I will leave them to the judgment to my readers.

Shänne Sands, June 2013.

To
My
Mother

Chapters

Birth

Every few seconds, against the bedroom window of a high, narrow, three-storey, east-end Victorian house, a freezing gust of wind blew its bleak draughts through the ageing wooden framework until the curtains shook.

It was just past midnight on November 7th 1909. An icy, cold rain drizzled down the window panes leaving a pretty pattern of winter raindrops in spite of London grime that fouled the glass.

Like the rest of the house the bedroom was square and indifferent, as if the builder had always known only the poor would ever inhabit it, or if it had at any time in its history seen better days, this house showed no signs of it.

A double iron bedstead was made up with a featherbed and feather quilt in eastern European style. A washstand, a chair, a heavy chest of drawers took their place in each corner and a jet of gaslight from the one lamp against the faded wallpaper set shadow phantoms in grotesque and humorous shapes across the ceiling with its damp patches and peeling paint.

Rifka Myersavitch felt her time had nearly come. For the fifth baby preparation was not difficult. Sarah from Quaker Street would come, if she was needed. Sarah was getting old but she knew about babies. Babies were her special knowledge,

'Everyone has a special knowledge,' Sarah

always said as she dipped honey cake into her glass of tea in Rifka's front room on the afternoons all the women gossiped together. After all, the Community had to pray together and had to stay together. Praying together was Reuben Myersavitch's special knowledge. He was Reuben the scholar. Reuben the *Zaddik¹*. His knowledge was all the prayers and benedictions of over thirty centuries of his people. Ah, Reuben, wonderful Reuben, wonderful, kind, bearded Reuben with Slavic eyes and a bear hug that told people,

"I love you – I love you. Life is a joy. Life is a gift from our everlasting Father in Heaven, blessed be his name."

Maybe old Sarah wouldn't be needed. It was only birth. Rifka was a female cat-woman. Her babies gave little bother. The pain was soon forgotten.

She folded her bed quilt with great care. It was her comforter in a cold hour. In her most private meditations, when her children were asleep and Reuben was away talking about his vision of the Promised Land to his devout group of followers, Rifka would lie in the feather bed and pull the quilt around her small body and dare to dream, such dreams! If Reuben knew he'd die of a million doubts. But no one knew of Rifka's dreams, only the feather quilt, and sometimes she would hum to herself the words of an ancient song, '*Only God and myself know what is in my heart*.' She placed the quilt on top of the chest of drawers and held her hands to her aching back.

She then spread brown paper over her mattress. Rifka always collected brown paper. So much brown paper stained with the her blood had been burnt in England. It was too late to call Sarah, Reuben would have to cut the cord. It would be alight, didn't he cut

1 Righteous man (Heb.)

Benjamin's cord? And Benjamin was five years old, God bless him.

"My first-born. My Benjamin with blue eyes. Reuben wasn't keen on those blue eyes, until I said,

'Tell me Reuben Myersavitch how to change them? These things happen. And besides, you know something?'

'What?' he asked.

'I, his mother have blue eyes. And underneath this *sheitel*[2] I have blond hair. Have you forgotten because I am now a married lady, I had long fair plaits and you used to twine them around your neck and say, 'Rifka, mine, we are betrothed,' remember Reuben?'

'Then how we laughed at Benjamin's blue eyes and the Cossack ancestor who most likely shone through them. Although we banished him to hell and circumcised our son into the safety of the Covenant. Anyway, when we stopped laughing Reuben said,

'Next time I want a son with deep brown eyes,' and we laughed and danced all over the house."

In the next bedroom, on another double, iron bedstead her children slept together, their tiny pale shapes cuddled together in the warmth of each other and their feather quilt. Their brown curls tossed on the pillows, their sleeping heads full of the land of night fairies and huge giants.

Rifka could hear their breathing through the thin walls. The pains in her back were bad. She lay on the brown paper, her head supported by a pillow covered in a white, linen pillow case. The cool cloth soothed her head as she drifted into the first contractions of labour and her mind tried to leave the pain behind as her hands gripped the iron bedstead above her head and her body heaved into long, sad moans that came from the depth of her being. Birth

---

2 Wig

had begun.

Sometimes during labour as her mind cleared for a moment she could hear Reuben praying, softly singing his prayers backwards and forwards, his body rocked towards the Holy Land. Forwards and backwards to her heart, soothing her pains,

"Thank God we men were not born women," he sang softly, "Children are always a blessing."

Pray hard Reuben Myersavitch. Pray hard that the birth will soon be over and have a little wine ready!

She lay in agony but did not scream. Reuben came into the room many times with an enamel basin with warm water to wipe her face. Suddenly old Sarah appeared with hot water in another enamel basin muttering to herself,

"The way we poor have our babies is not right. It's not right! You will kill your Rifka next time, Reuben Myersavitch, you will kill her. Do you hear? Five babies! She is only twenty two! Animals! Disgusting animals that is what you are," she muttered on and on. Her eyes glaring at poor Reuben every time Rifka bit her lips and moaned.

"My husband tried to kill me with babies but, thank God, one morning he fell under a coach. That was freedom! I lived for the first time. I didn't walk, I floated like a queen. Bah, to babies! A blessing indeed! When did you last pay the rent man, Reuben Myersavitch, eh?" She rubbed Rifka's back. She muttered on,

"I made a knowledge of babies. I help deliver them now. I stopped having them myself!"

Reuben didn't hear a word. He had left the bedroom. The brown paper was now bloodstained. Rifka's legs were wide apart and her knees almost touched her chin. She pushed, with her insides being torn and stretched and it seemed there was no more breath in her lungs. The waters broke and the universe exploded inside her, like the Big Bang which had sent fragments of worlds into dark and secret space. Her dilated womb rushed pain into her belly, down to her groin. Pain opened her up hurting her to her very soul – as the infant's dark head came into existence for the first time. Old Sarah, with blood over her hands and down the front of her long, white apron, spat at Reuben,

"Another Myersavitch to drive the neighbourhood mad!" Then she pulled the baby clear out of its mother's body.

Rifka slumped to the side of the mattress. She was wet with sweat and blood. Her hands sore from being clenched too tightly. On the floorboards a crumpled heap of brown paper was ready to be thrown away. Reuben brushed with extreme tenderness, the damp hair from his wife's forehead.

"We have another son Rifka. Sleep now and I will sing the prayers for the blessing of a safe birth."

He poured red wine across Rifka's lips. It slithered down the side of her chin. She had passed out. In his ignorance and poverty he said to the tired midwife,

"See, she sleeps. My Rifka sleeps."

The first birth cries came from the new born boy. The wind continued to batter the Victorian house as the other children slept on, unaware of their new brother or bed-bugs that crawled over their small, white legs.

Above the tenement, above the yellow gaslights, above the icy November pavements and the sleeping East-end poor and the awake poor still roaming the unforgiving city streets emigrants call home; a grey, winter sky held above all their souls, a pale, distant moon. A piece of gleaming light shone out into all this greyness. The Evening Star. Every emigrant who had ever crossed a hostile sea seeking a new shore, a new Promised Land, had loved this star, this precious Venus. The single light in the dark night sky. As the infant boy sucked in the first oxygen of life outside his mother's womb the moon and the Evening Star shone just a little brighter,

'Hope, little brother,' they said. 'Always reach up high and try to touch our glitter.'

The children would wake soon and see their new brother,

"Welcome little Abraham."

Even the inhospitable wind seemed to say,

'Welcome!'

Prophecy

Koppel Ginsberg's other name was Koppel the soothsayer. He didn't look like a miracle worker, but his eyes held a knowing gaze and his black eyebrows arched above them with the right brow raised slightly, giving Koppel's face the look that goes with magic and bumps in the night.

Koppel worked at a little bit of this, a little bit of that. He came from the same village in Eastern Europe as the family Myersavitch. The same fears and hopes were his. Their struggles in a new land were his. His wife had given him five mouths to feed and telling of spirits perhaps assuaged some of his sorrows in a foreign environment.

Koppel's special knowledge was the well of wonder and superstition which villages have always traded upon. Stories woven like a huge oriental rug on dark nights in old cottages in forgotten villages surrounded by deep, pine woods where wolves howled and owls hooted and the thousand creatures of the night scuttled and flew, whilst secret spirits plundered the souls of stupid, unsuspecting humans! Koppel the soothsayer knew of such happenings.

Rifka and her friends liked to listen to his stories. The women grew pale and agitated with awe as he told of cunning spirits who crept underneath a man's skin and lodged in his kneecap if he wasn't home before six stars were in the sky. And if a stray dog looked beseechingly for a bone or crust – beware!

It carried the spirit of twenty demons. Kick it at your peril, give it a crust even if you go hungry. Then runaway fast and never, never gaze into its eyes – for staring back at you will be the eyes of ...

"Enough, Koppel! Enough! Before one of us has a fit. We are all scared stiff," laughed Rifka. The other women were all so scared they could hardly move.

Soon after the circumcision of little Abraham, Koppel the soothsayer visited Rifka Myersavitch with news of the new born boy's horoscope chart and a bag of bagels.

"Here, take the chart Rifka and hide it with the others."

"Thank you Koppel. I know it is against our Law, but I enjoy knowing about the stars."

"This baby you will not enjoy knowing about." The right eyebrow went up and Rifka felt disturbed. "This baby is a Scorpio."

"So? What is so terrible about Scorpio?" Rifka smiled. "Have a glass of tea, Koppel. My little Abraham is a fine son." Koppel Ginsberg shook his head from side-to-side, refused the glass of tea and stroked his beard.

"If he had been born when the sun was high success would also have been high. But he was born after midnight, no sun all was black and the storm was terrible."

"When is the sun ever high in England, I would like to know Koppel Ginsberg. You were in a bad mood when you cast Abraham's chart."

"Don't believe me, Rifka Myersavitch, but you will see. The stars don't lie. This boy is born to trouble, born to be frustrated."

Rifka folded the chart and put it down her blouse front where she also kept a purse.

"Perhaps I have bought bad luck on my own child."

"What is written is written," Koppel Ginsberg said as he smoothed the baby's cheek with one, tubby finger. "Anyway Rifka when he is older watch this one and tell him to be careful. The gentile world is harsh."

"For all of us, Koppel, but God is good. A good star will guide my little Abraham away from your prophecy."

"I hope so, Rifka Myersavitch."

"Better still, a good angel will guide him. Every soul has a good angel. Here Koppel, take a penny for the chart. If I pay for it maybe the luck will change."

The conversation went on in Rifka's kitchen till the baby boy became restless. Koppel put the penny into his purse, picked up some *yiddish*[3] books he had brought with him,

"A blessing on your house, Rifka. Next time don't give birth to a Scorpio after midnight."

Reuben didn't approve of Koppel Ginsberg. He rarely went to *schul*[4] and old village ways clung to him like stale sweat. Reuben felt men hanging around women were an abomination. Men should have better things to do then sit in kitchens all day. Koppel Ginsberg's last visit irked Reuben Myersavitch to an anger he rarely showed.

"Koppel the *dybbuk-monger*[5]! Koppel the Satan worshipper! Koppel of the evil eye"

Rifka made the movements with her mouth of a slight spitting on her baby's head to keep of the terrible evil eye which haunted all of them.

"So you don't like Koppel Ginsberg," Rifka said in her quietest voice, "but he means well."

"He means ill," Reuben's raised voice shouted

3   Language of the Jewish people of Eastern Europe
4   Synagogue   5   Mother of a bad spirit

back at the tiny woman with the new born pulling at her nipple. "Wait till your milk turns sour. Wait, Rifka Myersavitch till calamity falls down the chimney."

"Who's superstitious now? Listen to you! You sound worse than Koppel the soothsayer."

"I need a ritual bath every time I see that man. To think such men came to London with us! He should still be under his mother's straw roof."

"Hush! Reuben, hush. The baby will have colic from your shouting."

"The baby! The baby! This house is all babies."

"Anyway Reuben Myersavitch, who suddenly hates his children, shouts and screams at his wife. The Ginsbergs are going to New York."

"An abomination on their house!" Reuben cursed pushing his skull-cap into place.

He sat down at the large, brown table in corner of the old kitchen where a volume of the *Gemorah*[6] lay open. 'The dear, sweet sanity in this house,' he said to himself, 'The blessed hope in our exile.'

---

6   Part of the 'Talmud' – holy books.

Sister-in-Law

The third storey of the old house had two rooms in the front and one small back-room. On the east wall of this room hanged the *mizrach*, a sacred picture showing the direction a Jew faced and prayed. Where in his mind's eye the glory of the Temple shone. An eternal patience glowed from Jerusalem sunlight and showed its beauty in the eyes and devotions of the devout. Looking down from the sash-cord window a yard could just about be seen. A solitary mulberry tree grew from a patch of muddy earth. A lean cat waited and watched longing to kill a sparrow having a mud bath by the tree's starved roots.

From the top back-room Reuben's only sister Peshe Fischelson looked down at the yard. She shared the house with Rifka and Reuben, her son was being raised with theirs. For Peshe there would be no more births she was a widow. Her hair covered with a 'kerchief was the colour of Mulberry berries in autumn. Unlike Rifka she did not wear a *sheitel* and she often felt alone like the lonely Mulberry tree growing in a patch of poor soil. Her sad eyes so young and so like Reuben's would look at the mizrach on its eastern wall and feel comfort in a heart hurting with memories.

Mendel Fischelson was a cantor. His voice had belonged to an angel first. The angel had seen Mendel at midnight prayer and said 'Mendel Fischelson shall sing the Psalms and all Heaven shall rejoice.' His singing was a joy to the congregation.

"What a cantor! What a voice! Why, a *takif*[7] could not afford him. He is beyond price!" They would say to each other. Then the angel said, 'A divine voice must belong to the divine,' and the angel came and took Mendel Fischelson to Heaven.

Peshe loved the delicate musician with intense early love that widowhood had matured into a soft remembering. A handful of earth from Israel had been placed under Mendel's head as he lay dying and went into the coffin with him. Peshe said,

"I keep my heart for my children, my head to teach me how to survive but my soul lies with Mendel my husband, the cantor from Cracow."

So Peshe the young widow who sewed clothes for a living in the back room, looked out of the window where suddenly a London blackbird started to sing. Pity the poor widow. Do not forsake her children in their hour of need. A down draft blew black smuts of soot into the room covering the pieces of cloth she sewed for a living into long, black skirts, with ugly spots. She blew them off then raked the coal. It smouldered like the anger in her eyes for all their poverty. But in a gentle voice she called to her small son Joseph, who had been playing at her feet with his cousin Benjamin,

"Come. It is time to make a lemon tea for Rifka and see little Abraham."

A staircase went from landing to landing. Its dark, brown bannister and worn treads holding together despite the shaky foundations of age, dry rot and woodworm. The stairs ended on the ground floor where a narrow hallway smelled of dust and cooking. The family ate in the ground floor room where the Mulberry tree came nearer into view. A fire burned

7   Influential man

in a grate, the chief pleasure winter and summer of a draughty house. The scullery offered a sink with a cold water tap. From the scullery a damp cellar was reached down a flight of six, stone steps. A faded bottle-green, heavy door lead to the back yard. The Mulberry tree stood triumphant in front of a door hanging on its last hinge. The other side of this door a lavatory, with a cracked basin and newspaper on a string gave out a purulent warning.

Down in the cellar with whatever coal or wood Reuben could afford, a shuffle of feet could be heard. Sometimes a whistle. The feet and the whistle belonged to the outsider in the house. Cockney Jim lit the *shabbas*[8] fire, put on the *shabbas* gas lights, carried the *shabbas* coals.

Coming into the house and leaving it, everyone would kiss the *mezuzah*[9] hung in the right-hand corner of the sunken street door. A light kiss placed on the finger tips then with affection given to the prayer held within the *mezuzah*. A melancholy street of poor houses stretched on either side of the family Myersavitch. The East-end cradle of Russian, Polish Jewry, the food of the poor gave out its odours. Smells of cabbage with a few raisins, bean soup to fill the children up with a slice of black bread and the emigrant mother singing a lullaby;

'Babyla, Babyla,
The winds of sorrow will not blow on you
Whilst I hold you close.
Babyla – Babyla –'

The lullaby echoed with the rhythm of the house itself. Abraham's circumcision and Rifka's ritual bath. Peshe preparing the *Shabbas cholent*[10]. Reuben's arms and forehead bound each morning

8   Sabbath   9   Blessing inside container
10 Cold Sabbath food

with phylacteries saying his *tefillin*[11]. Poverty was not their imprisonment. Poverty was the guardian of their ambition.

The seed growing within their small children's brains. The seed that would grow into realms beyond East-end tenements on harsh, winter days. The seed that was not within reach of the mighty Czar of all the Russias. The seed the Philistine could not crush. There was no shame in poverty only be ashamed if you did not nourish this precious, precious seed. An old mystical man in a long gabardine walked back and forth, up and down these harsh, East-end streets and to every house showing the mezuzah, his mission was to stop, mutter a prayer and from his pocket take a handful of seeds and scatter them.

"The days of the Messiah are not yet come but may your strength increase," prayed the old, mystical man as he walked on.

---

11 The phylacteries

Alas Poor Thing

As Rifka's long, black skirt took on again a balloon-like shape, as the last three buttonholes on her white blouse could no longer fasten the pearl buttons together, bube Kosminski smiled at her daughter-in-law Chayah. Chayah Kosminski thought a smile from *bube*[12] Kosminski rare.

"What are you smiling for mother-in-law? Have you seen Reb Kosminski, God rest-his-soul, in a dream?"

"No Chayah, I was looking at Rifka Myersavitch in the yard hanging washing."

"And that's something to smile about already? Was her *sheitel* crooked?"

"Now why should Rifka's *sheitel* be crooked, God forbid I should smile at such thing!"

"If the mood took you mother-in-law you would not only smile you would shake with laughter."

"So, Chayah, why do you think I was smiling?"

"So, mother-in-law, I am not a mind reader this morning I don't know ask me tomorrow by tomorrow I may have become one. Maybe you've got wind. Wind makes babies smile."

"And already you think I'm in second childhood because you've made me a *bube* six times over since I gave you my Moshe."

"You gave me nothing *bube* Kosminski I came with good *gelt*[13]. Besides my Moshe is no great

12 Grandmother   13 Money

metsiah[14]. With glasses and ginger hair who wanted him?"

"You did Chayah, you did."

"I was brainwashed. I could have been a *rebbitsin*[15]."

"You a *rebbitsin*! Give me a drop of schnapps to get over such a thought."

"If there is any schnapps in this house it was bought with the *gelt* my father gave!"

"Your father! Your father, he stole it from your mother!"

"Leave my poor mother out of this *bube* Kosminski."

"By the *mezuzah*[16] on the door, by the *mizrach* on the wall, by the *menorah*[17] ..."

"Yes, yes mother-in-law and by the *Midrash*[18] and by all the Commentaries of the Torah I know, I know but I should catch smallpox, God forbid, before you will talk of my mother! My mother was a queen!"

"Your mother was a pauper who sold herrings."

"Such a pauper! I came with *gelt* to the *chuppah*[19]."

"She borrowed from the marriage society."

"God forgive you mother-in-law."

"God is good, it is only the truth I speak."

"Truth! Truth! Wait till I tell my Moshe how you've upset me today. I'll give you truth. He'll send you back to Slonin."

"Ah, please Lord send me strength I'd walk back to Slonin to be rid of you Chayah and your wicked tongue."

"Don't walk *bube*, don't run, let me throw you!"

"You only wait Chayah soon the ten days of penitence will make you tremble!"

"So, I'll tremble, but I'll still throw you back to Slonin."

14	Blessing	15	Rabbi's Wife
16	Prayer	17	Candelabra
18	Commentaries	19	Bridal canopy

"Come home quickly Moshe, your wife is killing me, she will poison me, she will murder my grandchildren, I am tearing my clothes in agony Moshe, my first born. Why did you bring this terrible creature to the family Kosminski."

"Why? I'll tell you why he loves me and hates you. You stink of prune pudding and goose fat. You horrible old woman."

"To think we thought in Slonin the Czar was evil may nobody have a daughter-in-law like you. I am cursed, I am *kaput*[20]."

"Shut up mother-in-law the baby is crying, where is Rachel? Rachel Kosminski what are you doing? If you are playing with those Myersavitch's it will be trouble for you. Where is Hankel, Leah, Yenta, help me with supper. Your father works like a slave for our few flat cakes and a piece of goose flesh. Give me the baby *bube* Kosminski you look tired."

"Yes I am tired daughter-in-law please God Moshe will come home for supper."

"Of course mother-in-law, of course. Soon, soon."

"I made a *strudl*."

"A *strudl bube*, wonderful, what luxury! Is that why you were smiling?"

"No I saw Rifka from next-door in the yard."

"So?"

"Well I hadn't noticed before."

"Noticed what?"

"Well a few months ago Reuben Myersavitch didn't go to midnight prayers."

"He didn't? What a terrible thing! Tell me how do you know?"

"Because Rifka is pregnant again."

"Again so soon after Abbie she has one in her stomach, one in her arms, one at her feet.

"I told Moshe six is enough after six we stop."

"Achi Nabbich daughter-in-law."

"Yes bube have a flat cake lets have a *nash*[21], a glass of tea maybe."

"Maybe daughter-in-law, maybe."

"You know mother-in-law you are always right. That family Myersavitch is pathetic. All prayers, all babies no money achi nebbich, alas poor things."

The Weeper

Spring seduced by hope arrived. A melancholy sun warmed in small moments Samuel Yitzchok's broad back. He walked slowly by the dockside making out shapes here and there. Sammy was very short sighted it took a few moments for the shapes to become dockers, the long, black patches, barges. The moving, grey water the great and noble Thames. He smiled to himself, tugged at his short, black beard – he liked the shapes. In early spring in his new country he felt not that his shoe-leather was too thin, that he could speak only a few English words, hardly enough to make a sentence, a pauper-alien wearing a shabby coat – he felt full of well being because he was 'The Weeper.'

Sammy was boarded with Reuben when he arrived from Europe. His poor sight made it difficult to find a trade for him – the furriers, the tailors didn't want to know,

'Haven't we enough trouble without Samuel Yitzchok?' was a chorus whenever Reuben tried to find him work. But the decrees of life and death are sealed by God and a place for Sammy there must be. Even the hawkers and peddlers in The Lane called him an unlucky person, a *schlemihl*[22]. His awkward height seemed to oppress them, his short sight aggravated them because to make a living you had to be quick and Sammy was always slow!

Reuben felt a deep warmth for Sammy. The

children loved him, Rifka and Peshe were used to
new arrivals staying awhile then finding their feet
and leaving but they sensed Sammy was different.
He wouldn't leave in a hurry.

The family adopted him as if a strange cat or
dog had come to sit by the fire in bad weather or sit
by an open window in springtime.

Reuben became aware of Samuel Yitzchok's
strange gift on the 17th of *Tammuz²³* which begins
three weeks of mourning for the destruction of the
Temple. Shrouded in his prayer shawl a solemn chant
of pain coming from the prayers of Lamentation.
Samuel Yitzchok began his weeping. With ash on his
forehead.

'And the Romans took Jerusalem and the hills
and valleys echoed with their evil noise and the
women and children were humiliated with slavery
and capture and torment and the best of men were
slain. And the High Priests were ridiculed and the
High Altar plundered and stone by stone king Herod's
Temple was torn apart, stripped and desecrated and
in a small unnoticed corner of a lost city, covered
with his mother's blood a small boy wept. 'I shall
ever be the spirit of lamentation' a voice cried within
the child, 'whosoever weeps with me weeps for the
land of Israel.'

And one by one the living gathered strength
and kissed the fallen Temple stones."

So Samuel wept and the congregation wept
and *Reb* Reuben Myersavitch looked up to heaven
and thanked God.

"You have sent the weeper to our *schul*! The
days of the Messiah have not yet come but God bless
Samuel The Weeper!"

Ever since that day Rifka, when she could

afford it, made an extra portion of *gafullte*[24] fish
with sugar not pepper for Samuel The Weeper and
Bertha Rosenfeld wanted to marry him which
brought laughter to the community.

---

24   Pickled fish

Betrothal

As the fragrance of stored sweet corn-cobs drifted from house to house and sheets of *matzos*[25] hanging from low ceiling beams were blown gently to and fro, Rifka's mother walked with her by the towpath of a broad, grey flowing river. Fertile grain fields stretched flat and far touching distant Russian soil – Rifka was seventeen.

Ahead of them walked her father Jacob Sholdovsky, the innkeeper, with his long, red beard like a flame and her brother who now walked with the men. Reuben's mother looked on with approval at her son walking with his father *Reb* Myersavitch, although she wished he was going to marry a *Reb's* daughter and not an innkeeper's.

Half the village walked behind the two families. The voices were voices of celebration, of wine, of merriment and teasing for this day the wedding contract for Reuben and Rifka had been signed.

From the high balcony in their *schul* the married women, young girls and children had thrown sweets onto the families soon to be joined by marriage, calling out with pleasure,

"*Mazzol tov*[26], *mazzol tov*."

The old pious Jews with their velvet skullcaps smiled as they cast their eyes downward to the hems of their caftans, lest evil thoughts came into their heads as they glimpsed such a throng of laughing

---

25   Flat bread   26   Good luck

young wives and lovely girls.

On the walk back to their homes they teased Reuben the enlightened scholar, for asking the hand of the innkeeper's daughter. They looked forward to the wedding feast where a little *narischkeit*[27] mingled with tears and the best food would be good for all of them. Thus the betrothal was blessed by religious fellowship and 'increase and multiply' echoed along the river's bank.

From their high nest-tops the storks looked down on Rifka and Reuben. Storks were an omen of great luck. A rooftop without a stork's nest could mean misfortune which was never far away so everyone took pride in the special nests above their heads.

Handfuls of almonds and raisins were given to all the children and on the wooden porch that surrounded *Reb* Myersavitch's house the joined families sat talking and drinking warm lemon tea with snacks of sweet, honeyed prunes, with creamed cheese and honey-cake. Rifka sat close to her mother her blonde hair shining with youth, her eyes blue and tender full of love for Reuben and the wonder of it all.

Friends and neighbours showered affection on the young lovers with simple gifts of food and wine; water melons and loaves of freshly baked bread. Even a *shabbas cholent* was given and always for the betrothed, feather pillows and chickens with beautiful feathers. *Yeshiva*[28] boys came and danced for them whilst two fiddlers filled the air with loving melancholy. Tears touched Rifka's cheeks because tears always came with the music. Gentle steam from the samovar misted their faces as in a dream.

Mendel the matchmaker stroked Chontche's hand and said,

27 Foolishness   28   Acolytes

"Please God by you, I'll go soon to talk to your father." Chontche joked,

"He knows my mother has cutlets Friday night. The moment he smells them he forgets about weddings."

The night of the betrothal her mother came to her and held her close.

"My daughter will soon be a woman with children of her own. Whatever happens child of my heart take this gift from me, it will be with you always."

When Rifka looked for the gift there was nothing to see – her mother's arms tightened around her. She knew wherever Reuben took her, her mother's arms would be holding her.

With essence of pine on the breeze from the pinewoods filling her bedroom she climbed into bed with the story of her grandparents' wedding feast, where the scissor dance and the snapps were all perfection, where Isaac the jester made them laugh and cry and where fifty poor Jews came for potato-and-borscht soup. The cantor danced the kozotsky with such zeal both his hats fell off!

Now that was a wedding!

The Escape

A lupine awareness seemed to engulf the atmosphere. A chilly yet still friendly breeze swayed the pine-tree tops and settled into a still, silent mist across the marshes.

Summer was over.

A few miles from the village the small whitewashed synagogue with its low rooftop and five, maybe six, square, wooden-shuttered windows was in no way provocative.

The Community drew close inside this simple structure. Next to it, in a wooden, taller house with large airy windows, also drab in colour, lived their Rabbi with his family. Visiting *maggid*[29] often stayed.

In a corner of the synagogue the *sofer*[30] with his pure white beard and covered head sat with a Torah scroll unrolled before him. His ink bottle filled to the brim with black ink and his long-handled pen in his spotlessly clean hand.

A spiritual leadership was theirs and the small Community was grateful.

Their traditions, their piety, their very souls were safe-and-sound.

If social conflict happened outside they drew down the shutters, closed the door on hostile faces and prayed.

Today a *maggid* from a *yeshivot*[31] in the Ukraine had come to preach. Many young, loud voices could be heard as *yeshiva* boys began to arrive

29 Preacher   30   Scribe
31 Religious School

to spend a long day and evening listening and questioning the scholar. They brought food and drink and high spirits but soon quietened as the *maggid* began his discourse. Rising and falling his deep, serious voice speaking sometimes in Hebrew to the Yiddish speaking students could be heard outside. He told them in every detail about the *Mizrahi* – the orthodox Zionist movement which had been formed in 1902 to keep religious identity from being damaged in any way by political Zionism. He told them a Jewish homeland was their birthright. He told them to fill their Jewish consciousness with the dream of a return to Zion.

"Make it your reality, my students," he said. He told them societies were formed everywhere Jews gathered – students, intellectuals, the orthodox were moving mountains in Eastern Europe and they would win.

Then after prayers and food he talked on about ethical instruction.

"Everyone in whom God delights, he crushes with suffering. This is called *y'surin shel ahavah* – suffering of love."

He concluded his long, long day with a hand waving above their heads,

"You are the pride of Jacob, *ya'akov*, take your places each of you. Teach yourselves, then please God in time your children. For so it has always been. And may God bless you."

His wisdom melted into the young students and shone from their eyes. The *maggid* was always adored.

One-by-one the horses and carts came to collect the students and take them home to the villages scattered along the woodland route. The boys were still in furious discussion with each other about the sermon they had been listening to. Candlelight flickered across each face as they collected their holy books and shook soot-specks from their skullcaps. They stood around the wood burning stove to warm their hands before the cold ride. One of them with shy gratitude gave the *maggid* a small gift of marzipan to thank him for coming to their *schul.*

Rabbi Myersavitch, hearing the last horses moving off, seeing to the safety of the candles and stove took a lantern and led the *maggid* along the pathway to his house. The *rebbetsin* had laid the solid, oval table with supper places for each man. Her sons, Reuben and Shepsul, were also eating with their father, Mendel the *cantor,* who led the congregation in prayer and was married to Peshe the Rabbi's only daughter, and their guest the *maggid.*

Every important decision in the Myersavitch family had been talked through around this table covered with a pure-white linen table cloth.

The *rebbetsin* served hot soup and black bread as a pregnant Peshe sat quietly by a log fire watching her husband who was often ill. The Rabbi showed no surprise when Reuben told his father that very soon he and Shepsul would leave the village for good.

The *maggid* went on eating his supper and wiping soup spills from his beard.

Mendel's eyes caught his wife's gaze the way lovers do.

The *rebbetsin* brought wine to the table and flat, sweet biscuits.

Reuben filled the wine glasses. Shepsul, although a year older than his brother, was smaller with tight, black curls and broad shoulders. His black beard curled around his face as if cuddling him. The affectionate name 'Shepsul' meaning little lamb. It was Shepsul who said,

"Papa, the secret police have been seen in Lomza."

"Shepsul, are secret police news to us? Here they are all informers for the secret police. If you had a corn on your toe, the secret police would know an hour before your foot!" The *maggid* smiled and said,

"Spying is their hobby, just a hobby, take no notice of what others have seen."

"No Papa, this is serious not a joke. Reuben and I must leave. You know Papa we are members of the *Mizrahi* and our military deferment has ended. Soon the recruitment sergeant will come for us."

Mendel with his wistful face said, in almost a whisper,

"Ah, the Czar's armies know nothing of the *Mizrahi.*"

"Then I must be serious and listen to my sons."

"Yes, indeed yes," agreed the *maggid*, who felt so warm and welcome within the comfort of the wooden house, evil spirits did not exist. But that was the illusion of fire-glow and family.

Outside the streets of towns and dust-tracks of villages were a burden of stress to the Jews. Only prayer and patience made living bearable in an Eastern Europe with pogrom mania.

"If we do not go Papa," continued Reuben, "the secret police will send an agent to demand taxes from you. Even if you have paid a thousand times over they will drain the *schul* of every penny. When you have nothing left they will list you as unproductive Jew and tighten their grip even harder. No, Papa we must leave this country."

"Oy!" said Rabbi Myersavitch.

"Oy! oy!" said the *maggid*.

Shepsul again filled the glasses.

The *rebbetsin* took the empty soup dishes to the scullery.

Before Mendel led the family in evening prayers it was decided that the sons would tell their plans. Rabbi Myersavitch lifted a wine glass high, "To the *Mizrahi*!" he toasted.

"To the *Mizrahi*!" they sang in one voice and then broke the glasses beneath their defiant feet.

The two days of *Succot* which ended the year's reading of the Law, *Simchat Torah*, was a festival celebrated with love and loyalty for their *Torah* from Genesis to the end of Deuteronomy – a time for rejoicing.

Rabbi Myersavitch walked with Shepsul and Reuben towards the schul they had known since childhood.

Their faces showed no stress.

However strange to rejoice when a family is losing two sons this was a day of merry making. The Rabbi smiled and called to the people gathered outside their *schul*. Every child dressed in their best clothes waved little home-made flags painted with Biblical pictures.

Once inside led by Rabbi Myersavitch and cantor Mendel they marched seven times around the *bimah*[32] with scrolls of the Law in their hands. That coming evening they would do the same.

One-by-one they took their place in reading the Law and in the coming evening they would do the same.

As the *hattan bereshit*, the groom of the beginning of the Torah, read his portion the joy expressed by the children running in and out of the legs of the scholars became hilarious. Their mothers and grandmothers clapped and sang, not a second of solemnity was allowed. Then the greatest scholar in their congregation, the *hattan Torah*, groom of the *Torah* read the closing portion.

Amid such rejoicing Shepsul and Reuben Myersavitch said farewell to all the families they loved.

Cholera, typhus, smallpox were diseases known too well with many other evils of the flesh that left villages with more graves than people.

Smallpox had very recently taken its toll and pain and grief were felt by everyone. Dreaded by Jew and gentile these vicious plagues had no mercy. Hundreds of faces showed the unsightly pock-marked skins which left the prettiest women plain and scarred.

So when the land agent sent word with a servant to inform the police that Rabbi Myersavitch's house was under smallpox quarantine no suspicion was suspected.

The village community inspector was a lenient Russian, more than a bit of a simpleton. Given his vodka bottle and his over-large wife to sleep with, Jews and smallpox were his least concern. The icon and the Czar's portrait hanging In his house would protect him and his own from illness. He shut the door on the servant's thin back and did not give the matter of smallpox another thought.

A week passed.

Members of the burial society brought two coffins to the Rabbi's wooden house. The family in the deepest gloom did not speak to each other very much but showed understanding and affection to the heartbroken *rebbetsin.*

Another week passed. The countryside took on a mysterious blue-grey light. The sky showed signs of snow. The wind blew red and orange leaves everywhere. The sons now prepared themselves for their Journey. Uncles and aunts came to say goodbye. Prayers and blessings were said over their heads.

Rabbi Myersavitch prayed in silence. To lose two sons is not easy, not even unto Zion.

The brothers had shaved their beards. Both wore Russian dress. Both held heavy woollen blankets against damp and cold.

"The decrees of life and death are sealed by God," sang Mendel the *cantor.* Rabbi Myersavitch kindled two, long, white candles. A bright flame touched the darkness.

After early morning service, the brothers ate a meal of oats to help calm their nerves. Each was given a draft of meadow-sweet to drink to stop indigestion. They kissed their sister Peshe and mother and father and stooped to stroke the dog's head. He wagged his tail as if this was a wonderful game.

Then to begin the longest wagon-ride of their lives, Mendel helped first Shepsul and then Reuben climb inside two specially prepared coffins.

The burial grounds lay on a wooded-slope where at this time of the year red rowan berries were massed against tall, slender almost white birches. Here the Jewish dead rested in peace several miles from the *schul.*

The snow fell so gently that soon would be deep, hard and cold. Fieldfare thrushes were ready for their own flight to more hospitable lands to spend the winter months. The mock funeral procession began. No women were allowed at burials they stayed with covered heads, behind closed shutters.

As the strong, chestnut horse pulled the wagon

slowly away with two coffins holding her sons, the rebbetsin and her daughter wept away the anguish with burning tears. Hidden behind a group of dark green, feathered conifers a second wagon stood. Its driver wrapped in a heavy top-coat and wearing a fur hat, was alert to every unknown sound. But all seemed calm, the sky showing nothing but snow clouds.

Suddenly two tired, young men were behind the driver, lying flat and well out of sight. Not a word was spoken. All that could be heard was a quickened clip-clop of two impatient horses.

Devout and devoted members of the *Mizrahi* gave refuge to young men leaping from the clutches of the Czar's conscription orders.

After at least travelling for thirty-six hours the first stage of the journey had ended. Beneath a bare glimpse of moonlight the tired horses halted at the first safe house.

The brothers were exhausted but warmed with hot food and schnapps to ease the cold from their bones began to relax. There remained little of the night for sleep and for the first time since the ordeal began Reuben spoke to his brother.

"You know Shepsul there are wolves in the forest and bears . My Rifka is frightened of them."

"She is a foolish girl Reuben. Do you think she would like a wolf, of course not, your Rifka loves her geese. The wolves take them – Rifka hates that."

"Do you think, Shepsul, mama is asleep?"

"Maybe but maybe she is waiting up for papa if he went to midnight prayers. You know mama can't rest without papa."

"The *shtetl*[33] will be snow bound in a few weeks."

"They are used to it."

33   Village

"The cocks will crow soon and Dosha will just be waking up. Do you love Dosha, Shepsul?"

"Yes I love her."

"Will she leave to join us?"

"She will leave with Rifka."

"Please God I'll dance at your wedding."

"I'm the greatest catch Reuben, we'll all dance again."

"I'm proud you are my brother Shepsul."

"And I'm proud of you Reuben Myersavitch."

A week later and two hundred and fifty kilometres from their journey's beginning the brothers reached the Prussian port of Danzig. Yet another *Mizrahi* member gave each of them letters to be handed to society members in England, the country of their destination. The letters would bring them money and shelter in a new land.

Polish crew manned the boats called onion boats by refuge seekers. The crew took almost no notice of the passengers, The boats often held strange cargo and the captain was well paid. Crowded together the immigrants talked together with excited, Yiddish voices.

"Where are you going grandfather?" Shepsul asked an old, wrinkled Jew wrapped in a black velvet shawl that looked older than him.

"Going?" He shrugged his shoulders, "I'm going. It is enough to go."

The brothers felt the heave of the vessel as it raised anchor. Danzig harbour raced away from them. They watched Eastern Europe disappear from their lives – forever.

The *shammos*[34] wearing his best, long gabardine made his way to Rabbi Myersavitch's wooden house. He was greeted with pleasure in a home where the hearts felt heavy, The eyes sad. He told his Rabbi in a few words information had come about Shepsul and Reuben.

"Your sons sailed from Danzig with other Jews – they are safe."

Rabbi Myersavitch grasped the shammos tenderly by both hands,

"The Almighty is merciful," was all he said.

Years later when Rifka's growing children began to learn their family history they would chorus to their mother,

"Tell us about the escape, mama, tell us about the escape!"

And ending the story Rifka Myersavitch would tell the children,

"The Czar was mighty but God is Almighty," then smiling she always added, "Do you know my children there are wolves and bears in the forests!"

Rifka and Peshe and Dosha

The spring sky above Reuben's head was
sapphire-blue – beautiful, simply beautiful. In the
month of *Nisan*[35], just after *Pesach*[36], walking with
Shepsul in Stoke Newington the empty, depressed
feelings that ached inside them were giving place to
a slow release of philosophical thought patterns. The
leadership ideal for the Community they had come to
serve would become action!

The synagogue Reuben had just founded under
the sanction of Chief Rabbi Dr.Nathan Marcus Adler
was in Casenove Road between Stamford Hill and
Upper Clapton Road. The brothers stood at its
entrance for a few moments then quietly opened the
door. Spring's delicate sunlight came in beams of
pale gold through the high windows.

Blue the colour of truth glinted from tall
candles and spring flowers.

A quorum was at prayer the stripes in their
prayer shawls the blue of hope. A calming and
healing had taken the place of pogrom misery.

Their pride gave way to prayer for entering the
synagogue,

'As for me in the abundance of Thy
lovingkindness will I come into Thy
house: I will worship toward Thy holy
Temple in the fear of Thee. Into the house
of God we will walk with the throng.

35   March/April   36   Passover

How goodly are thy tents O Jacob, thy
dwelling places O Israel!'
And so the brothers prayed.

It was hard for the brothers with energy in their limbs to wait with patience for the arrival of the young girls who with God's blessing would stand beneath the Chuppah in this very new synagogue. Reuben smoked too much and Shepsul drank as many glasses of lemon tea as Mrs. Ida Sirkes would give him. Until their brides came over Mrs. Sirkes their landlady, understood their smoking and drinking in her kitchen. She hoped by the feast of *Omer* the brothers would have news. And every morning if the post came for them she would ask,

"So, are they coming yet?"

As a great laugh came suddenly from Reuben and Shepsul became a juggler with a dish of fruit on the breakfast table Mrs. Sirkes knew the brides-to-be would soon arrive in Britain.

Rifka with her eyes the blue of cornflowers, Dosha with her eyes the brown of good earth, would be united in marriage to Reuben and Shepsul Myersavitch.

Euston station echoed with train noises, hissing steam, hundreds of mingled voices, pigeons cooing and wing flapping and stamping hooves as the horses waited with drivers who tried to be as courteous as possible in case a quality fare hired their hansom.

The evening train bringing the travellers to London could be heard in the near distance. Reuben and Shepsul waited and watched for their loved ones. The train came to a slow halt and for a brief second a strange silence lingered and vanished the way it does when a train arrives after a long journey.

The porters smelling of sweat came from

nowhere in dozens rushing to open carriage doors, pick up cases and boxes trying not to fall over their own feet. Yellow gas-light gave the scene a rather sad and urgent look.

Almost immediately Shepsul saw them.

"Reuben they are here!"

"Where? Where?"

"Walking from the very end of the platform. That must be the cheap end."

"Are you sure? It may just look like them."

"What am I an idiot or something? If I tell you it is them, it is them."

"Shepsul you are right it is them."

"What are we standing here for? Show the platform tickets and come and carry their things."

"What things?"

"Their bits and pieces. You know young women always have bits and pieces."

The brothers' thoughts had been so occupied with longing for their future wives and sister and nephew to be with them that seeing them all walking the length of the platform with other travellers did not seem quite real. Eventually Reuben quickened his steps and Shepsul broke into a run as the shadowy shapes came closer and closer.

As if all the jewels of heaven had fallen on Euston station, Rifka, Dosha and Peshe and baby Joseph with smiles and tears were gathered into the brothers' arms. Their long skirts and short woollen jackets, their heads covered in scarves, baby Joseph wrapped in a woollen rug; everyone carrying bundles of their few possessions.

Dosha's father and elderly aunt had chaperoned the young women. All their faces showed tired but excited expressions the way travellers faces do. Dosha's father, Jascha Bloch, a powerful bodied man with distinctive Jewish looks gripped each brother's shoulders in warm greetings,

"This is London. Foggy, foggy London."

At last Rifka looked at Reuben and her gentle laugh came with a,

"So many pigeons Dosha!"

"Come its a long platform and Peshe looks worn out. The baby is heavy."

"We'll talk later," Shepsul called above the noise around them, "Follow me."

The women walk behind their men folk unaware of the crowds around them. A secret harmony held them close as the hansom was piled with bundles and Reuben's deep voice gave the driver in broken English Ida Sirkes' address. How clever Reuben is, Rifka thought, he speaks English already. Then the station was gone and the streets of London offered a history and a new life to these serious Rabbinic Jews.

Ida Sirkes

A twist and a turn off the Mile End Road, Jubilee Street stretched long and narrow. Small terraced houses showed pocket sized front gardens or were paved from the curb's edge with one step leading to the front doors. A group of evergreens hid from view a synagogue.

With their son Eli, Ida and Monty Sirkes lived in the house at the end of the terrace. Middle-age found Ida a plump, smiling lady with amazing energy, her silver curls covered with a 'kerchief, usually blue. Her friends called her the 'Silver Queen'. Everyone liked her. Eli worked with his father in their Kosher butcher's shop just off The Lane. Ida was totally committed to devoting hours to Jewish Care in the Community. She worked for the Jewish Welfare Board and many anxious, weary east and central European arrivals to the East-end were given Ida's address.

She greeted them in *Yiddish*. In her front parlour they drank hot, sweet tea. Their children ate a piece of fruit or maybe a handful of raisins or a cup of milk. The elderly rested.

Looking at the homely things on the Victorian sideboard, sepia photographs of her mother and father; her wedding photographs in a special frame and their silver, polished *menorah*, made lonely emigrants feel comfortable, able to cope.

If anyone mocked the newcomers, laughing at

their strange dress and foreign voices, if anyone dared call out, "Greenhorn", Ida would raise an eyebrow, point a chubby forefinger and shout back,

"You feel a big-shot because you've been in London six months!"

Without too much trouble Ida could help some of their needs. Boots for the children, coal for warmth. Finding rooms, was a 'big' if. The East-end tenements were stinking places, fourteen to a room, sleeping in hallways on stairs, most in doorways and under archways. *Matzos* for Pesach gave small joy if your home was a pavement in a rat infested alleyway.

She could ask the 'Jewish Shelter for poor Jews' for their temporary charity. In a year four thousand people fleeing pogroms were given a roof over their heads, for a fortnight or longer for the sick.

Finding work was not easy. Even if in Jewish Law it is permitted to be a *schnorrer*[37], nobody in their right mind wanted to be one. Ida always said,

"My Jews are not poverty stricken, they just need work, so give them work."

She would then read her list to the employers of labour.

"I have a young tailor's apprentice. What do you mean it's overcrowded, an occupation is an occupation. He's twelve sit him in a corner, you won't notice him, but his mother will buy bread."

"For you Ida I'll do it but don't bring me anymore alright!"

"Alright. We'll see. We'll see. Remember he is twelve! No sweat shop and pay him money not promises."

"Ida, go go I have suits to finish. My children must also eat. Do me a favour, Ida go. I'll sit the boy over there."

"All right I'm going already. He's a good-

37 Beggar

looking boy, at twenty not only will you have a tailor you might have a son-in-law!"

Ida would read her list to cabinet makers, shoe and boot makers, glove makers, all the East-end trades. The soup kitchens of Spitalfields rarely saw Ida's families. She found work, even health checks and despite the odds which were overwhelming, did not defeat her or bow the families down.

To share a Friday night meal Ida and Monty invited the brothers and their brides. It was custom that a young girl might only kindle the *shabbat* candle when a bride. Dosha had already kindled the candles the Friday that had passed and now Ida asked Rifka to honour the custom. Rifka, her hair covered, sang the blessing as the flame of *shabbat* graced two candles.

Ida noticed during the simple meal, the young women were pale and quiet. Perhaps for brides this is not unusual, and these young women had come through so much. A sad dejection, seemed to weigh them down. Even little Joseph had a restless, miserable gaze. Strain showed on the men's faces, no one was eating.

"Is something wrong Reuben have you heard bad news?"

"No, Ida no believe me nothing is wrong."

Suddenly tears fell into Rifka's soup. Dosha began to weep, then Peshe, then Joseph. All cried bitter tears.

Reuben tried to comfort everyone at once. But it was too much for him when Shepsul cradled his head in his hands on the table, with his shoulders shaking with sorrow.

Ida and Monty had seen it all before – with other families, yet Ida had such a lump in her throat, she could hardly speak. Monty, not used to seeing his wife speechless tried to humour the tearful ones around his *shabbat* table.

"What is this? Is the fowl no good, we are only a small butchers. Next time, if business picks up, I'll bring a goose home."

"Shut up Monty, let them have a good cry. It settles their emotions."

Reuben could take it no longer,

"Enough all of you, is this good in front of Ida and Monty our first real friends in a new land." At the mention of a new land the young women wept even more.

"Don't worry, I understand you are all very homesick." Ida spoke softly as the candles flickered a gentle light around the room. "It will pass. Even for a bad country we grieve if our loved ones are still there."

Monty smiled at his wife,

"She's right. It will pass, I swear on my life you will all be fine in London. You'll like it just give it time. There's no place like London."

"Look Rifka, the candles are bright and beautiful, all your tears didn't put the flames out. Peshe feed your son, he must be starving. Eat everyone, eat."

With eyelids red from weeping they ate their nearly cold soup, their chicken and potatoes. A bowl of fruit gradually emptied. The wet cheeks dried, the pale faces showed the strain of homesickness. Reuben blessed the wine. Shepsul sang the evening prayers. Joseph fell asleep!

"Peshe and Joseph stay here tonight," Ida called from the kitchen, "It's too far to walk and carrying a sleeping little one in the street. Shepsul can come for them tomorrow."

Peshe was glad to stay. She thought Ida was a

golden treasure in a strange country and Monty was a funny, loveable man.

After they had said their good night and thanks the brides and their very new husbands were silent, each lost for a while in their own thoughts. Reuben glanced at his wife's face, she was tired but always lovely to him. He saw in Dosha a quiet hope life would be kind to them. Across his brother's features he saw the haunting quality that might or might not go away. The haunting memory of Jews having to walk over the other side of a street from gentiles. Of Jews having to ask a gentile Russian or Pole to collect payment for goods sold them as they had no contact with the Jew. It would fade, no doubt this haunting.

The silence was broken by an old cockney passing them on the pavement calling,

"Night, night me old cock-sparras, mind 'ow you go."

Reuben took his wife's hands,

"No walking behind me Rifka this is a new land, new customs."

"Yes," said Shepsul with his black curls falling into his eyes, "Did you hear that Dosha? Our Rabbi said no walking behind me!"

Esther Starr

The brightest golden-leafed trees of autumn, could not cheer the greyness of East-end pavements. Littered with drunks, public-houses jutting out from every corner, the smell of dirty, ragged clothes, sour beer and cheap gin attacked the nostrils.

Drooping women sang vulgar songs to vulgar men. Against the walls of narrow back lanes 'the sixpence a time' girls worked their trade. The barrel-organ played on and on as the chestnut-vendor turning his hot-cinders shouted,

"'ot chestnuts, six for a farthin'."

In 1908 Lloyd George with the suspicion of a wise Welshman that the gin bottle was near to becoming England's ruin, closed public houses all over the country.

Just before the public bathhouse and tea factory off Goldstone Street, 'The Three-penny Bit and Whistle' pub was run by Flo' and Albert Kneebone. Flo' a tall, thin energy-packed woman who saw things were done quickly; whilst 'bert needed a drink to start his day and more than one to finish it and his red, thick nose gave proof of this. Their pub motto was, 'come in for a knees-up not a punch-up'. If black eyes and bloody knuckles provoked the crowd, well good luck to 'em, but not on yer life in the 'The Three-penny Bit and Whistle!

"If that ain't the last straw, closing our pub.

Who does 'e bleedin' think 'e is! An' 'im not even an Englishman, I ask yer – 'taint right tellin' the likes of us what to do!"

"Now don't take on so – it won't last – them laws hain't worth a light. 'The Three-penny Bit and Whistle' will open its doors as usual right soon, take it from me."

"Defend our rights, that's what I says, defend our rights. Life is 'ard enough without 'im takin' our livin' away. I tell yer 'bert as the good Lord be my judge, I'll give an ale to the reg'lar who comes rawnd the back yard, gawd 'elp us, so I will, you see if I don't 'bert. Lloyd bleedin' George or no!"

"Cors you will Flo', cors you will. It'll be business as usual at 'The Three-penny Bit and Whistle', or our name hain't Kneebone."

"Maisie! Maisie! Where's she gorn naw? I told 'er we was goin' to the lyin' in rooms to pay Esther a visit. She was delivered of a gal 'bert ain't that rich, Esther's a ma – Maisie! You up there?"

Flo' pierced her over-large velvet black hat with an even larger hat-pin, placed a worn out fur tie around her neck and once more shouted up the stairs for her daughter Maisie.

"Who does that gal take after, not me I'm sure! Your ma 'bert, yus your ma, muver Kneebone ain't never ready on time even your 'ead came out 'for she was ready. She told me the yarn of your arrival more times than I cares to remember. "

Albert knew when to keep his mouth shut. Flo' and her hat pin could be a difficult match for a feeble bloke who needed a pint.

"I ain't comin' ma."

"What yer mean yer ain't comin'?"

"I 'ate 'ospitals."

"We ain't goin' to no 'ospital, we is goin' to the

lyin' in rooms."

"Ain't no different, they all smell 'orrible, it makes me come over all unnecessary – nan says you see too much of them Jews so she does."

"None of your lip my gal. I've 'ad enough of Lloyd George today without you startin'. Now before I gives you what for put on yer 'at an' put on yer coat."

"Do as yer ma says, Maisie or yer get a clip from me for good measure, Esther's 'er mate ain't she."

"Nan says ... "

"Maisie yer 'at an' coat, if you please."

"I ain't goin' into that place ma, yer can't make me neither. Just see if I am! If nan don't like Jews, I don't like 'em neither."

"Yer need yer mouth washed out with green soap."

"Leave the gal be Flo' she listens to talk. Take no notice of our Maisie's lip she ain't a bad gal at 'eart. Esther's a good sort Jew or no – best 'urry up old duck or visits will be done. Give Esther me best. We'll wet the baby's 'ead with milk stout when Esther's back at the buildin's."

"That we will 'bert. Maisie carry them flowers an' straigh'en yer face – it's looks would give a fright to a ghost. Not comin' indeed, where is it gorna end? That's what I ask meself, where is it gorna end? 'bert polish them brasses 'fore you tipple an' wash down the yard – it will be late when I gets in. Madam Battia's callin' up the dear depart'd over at Ivy's."

"She better watch out Flo', Lloyd George will close her down next – spirits is spirits."

Flo's laughter as the door closed echoed along the narrow passage of 'The Three-penny Bit and Whistle'.

"Poor Flo'," Albert muttered to himself "she takes everythin' to 'eart so bad an' Maisie shows us up terrible."

The lying in rooms at Commercial Road where a short walk from the pub. Flo' and Maisie had argued all the way there. Esther Starr heard Flo's loud voice before she saw her. Flo' greeted the new mother from the door with a,

"'allo my old duck, 'ow ar' yer?"

Maisie clutching the by now limp flowers put them on the bed without a word.

"Take no notice of our Maisie, she's a saucy cow. Can't think why I brung 'er! Well, blind me I was tickled to 'ear yer Solly say yer was confined of a gal. Nurse, nurse lets 'ave an eyeful of Mrs. Starr's baby if yer will oblige."

An Irish helper carried the baby in swamped in flannel, Flo' chuckled,

"That'll learn yer to keep yer 'at on a windy day," she joked and roared with laughter. A tired Esther smiled,

"I won't 'alf be glad to go 'ome, Flo' – I'm fed-up to my eye balls in 'ere."

"Make the most of the rest my gal, once yer on them feet agin it's no rest for the wicked. Ain't that the truth ladies?" she called, to three other mothers in the room. They chorused back,

"Rest ain't for the likes of us."

They all agreed when someone said,

"Bloody men, its oats for them and comin' in 'ere for us." They all laughed as their newborns were brought in for a feed.

"Gawd what a life Flo'!"

"Na, 'taint that bad, we're 'avin you on like. Yer Solly's a fair bloke not like some I knows of – if walls could talk - eh."

"Can we go now? Ma, I feels sick."

"Best be goin' Esther this mare is a rod on me back, so she is. Tootle-oo muvers, see yer at 'The Three-penny Bit and Whistle'."

"Ta for comin' Flo' an' you Maisie, ta for the flowers ever so."

"If Madam Battia 'as a message for yer Esther I'll give Solly an earful."

"You an' yer spirits Flo', one day they'll put the wind up yer proper."

"Maisie straigh'en yer 'at. By the by Esther, 'fore I goes, yer won't believe what Lloyd George been an gorn an' done. The old sod closed the pubs."

"Never."

"On my true oath all over England."

Esther's humour suddenly bubbled up,

"Well Flo' yer back yard ain't 'alf gorna be packed out, ain't it just."

Flo left Esther's bedside with an irritable Maisie looking sick and declaring,

"I ain't 'avin' no babies ma."

Esther Starr was born in the heart of The Lane, in the same dwelling where Phoebe Harris birthed all her children and where she herself had been born and her mother before her. The house had belonged to her family for at least a hundred and fifty years. The stair-treads had the feel of ancestors in the wood, nothing unkind could be sensed in the small, poorly furnished rooms.

Henry Harris sat quietly. His feet soaking in a white enamel basin of soapy water, Phoebe adding a trickle of hot water now and again then testing it with her finger.

"Your bad feet 'enry will be yer death. What will yer Phoebe do without yer? Standin' at the stall in all weathers – ain't right for yer 'enry. Yer must pack it in. Yer just ain't up to it no more. Now sip yer cuppa an' them feet won't 'urt so much. I'm goin' over the buildin's with Sophie to do a bit of clearing up. Can't expect Solly to 'ave it nice. Not 'im. Wouldn't know 'ow to boil a kettle. I wish our Esther 'ad married a different boy. She could 'ave 'ad the pick of Mile End an' no mistake. No, it 'as to be Solly Starr, truth it did, well more fool our Esther that's what I says."

"Solly will settle down Phoebe – we all do when we 'as to. Give 'im a chance for gawd sake. Now you tell me who would do for our Esther in yer eyes? Ma's 'ate son-in-laws. Son-in-laws 'ate ma-in-laws. Top up me tea cup an' don't upset yerself. Our gal's a married lady with a child she's grown an' she's gorn to her own place."

"I knows yer right, 'enry. Any rate as I was sayin', Solly gorn to bring our Esther and the blessed angel. Did I go for 'er when she says to me, 'ma Solly will be sorry I've 'ad a gal.' That's an 'andsome baby you 'ave my gal just put yer 'ands together an' thank the Almighty – are you listenin' 'enry? And do me a favour if she don't then says, 'well she's ugly' and I replies, I do 'enry, I replies that blessed infant is a doll-face. But our gal will 'ave the last word for then she says the baby was born with a grey skin all over 'er face. The midwife tells 'er give it to a sailor and 'e'll not drown. That's right true I tells 'er. Give it to our Alfie an' it will preserve him from 'arm and perils of the deep. She's got the birth miseries alright, I've 'ad that a few times ain't I 'enry? I remember our Rachel's birth like it were yesterday."

Henry Harris put his pipe down on the table covered with a deep red chenille tablecloth that in turn was covered with a white linen one, and began drying his swollen, sore toes one-by-one in front of the warm stove his gentle features showed pain but he did not complain.

"'as our new granddaughter been named then?"

"She 'as indeed she's Klara – after Solly's Ma."

His only words before replacing his pipe where, "I'll call her little Cora."

"That's lovely – little Cora will be the pride of the place, just like all our gals was 'enry."

Phoebe arrived at Stepney Green buildings to see her youngest daughter Sophie waving down to her from the top floor landing. Nine years old and tall for her age with a boyish body full of fun her auburn curls match the autumn leaves and her face bright with happiness.

As Phoebe climbed the iron staircases that led from one landing to the next, neighbours called out,

"'ow's Esther, Phoebe?"

"Esther's well my dears. Ta for askin' – Solly's gorn to fetch 'er and my granddaughter 'ome."

"*Mazzol tov, mazzol tov*," echoed up the stairs.

"Ta again," Phoebe called out.

"You can see loads of places up 'ere Ma, it ain't 'alf a sight. Not as smoky as the street."

"Best watch out my gal or yer fall over the top."

"I ain't a daft-date ma am I? I won't fall over will I? Sniff up ma you can smell all the suppers. Can we go soon I'm starvin'?"

"We'll goes when I am right and ready to go, look at this scullery. Solly ain't cleaned a plate for weeks! Sophie tidy the parlour – whilst I scrub this lot, Esther ain't used to dirt – I'll give Solly what for you sees if I don't."

"There's loads of baby clothes in this drawer ma. Fit my doll they would."

"Cora will soon be out of 'em – babies grow

fast as bean-stalks – then Esther's next one will 'ave 'em. I 'ad a feeling she'd 'ave a daughter when I knitted them pink booties. Beckie did a grand shawl it was a picture, yus all 'er sisters made them clothes. Good as gold them gals."

At last Phoebe was satisfied the two roomed and scullery home was fit for Esther to come back to. She went on the landing for some fresh air. Shaking her black shawl free of dust she looked across the East-end rooftops.

"Well I must say it's 'igh up alright. I 'ope she'll manage them stairs. Sophie stop larkin' about an' wash yer hands."

"Ma, is our Esther a woman now?"

"Indeed she is, but none of that talk from you my lady."

"Well, you always says no gal is a woman till she 'as a baby."

"Your trouble Sophie Harris is you listens too much to what is no business of yours, now take 'old of this basket whilst I fix me shawl and lock-up. Mrs. Cohen underneath is takin' the key to give to Solly – I was goin' over Dinah's for a jaw but it's too late – never mind I'll goes in the mornin'. Don't tread in them peelin's! There are those who throw their rubbish anywhere. They make you sick."

On the kerb side old Mrs. Jacobs was standing with her sweet barrow,

"Boiled sweets an' toffee apples," she sang out.

"'ere you are Soph', don't eat them before supper."

As Sophie went to buy her two-farthings-worth of sweets Phoebe fingered her thick, Victorian wedding band knowing by Friday night it would be pawned for food – she would roll cigar for the Dutch to earn enough to claim it back, with her bed sheets which were pawned for rent money last week!

Ten days later Esther and Phoebe went together to Bevis-Marks Synagogue where Esther offered thanksgiving to God for a safe delivery.

Klara was hidden amid a dozen white beribboned shawls and pretty bonnet. A delicate wrist band of scarlet silk could just be seen tied by her grandmother Phoebe the day she was born.

Esther stood in the beauty of young motherhood – a Spanish Sephardic Jewess whose face told the history of Princes. Whose ancestry told the history of King David's glory.

Side-by-side Phoebe and Esther prayed.

Hidden courtiers and Hebrew poets of three thousand years ago sang a harmonious blessing on their heads.

Solly

Resting her head on a feather pillow propped against the back of the double iron bedstead, her baby tugging and sucking at her swollen nipple, Esther watched Solly at his morning shave.

Her husband was a good looking man. His oval face, his black silky hair and the smile of a man whom women would fancy and men would like as a man's man. His body was toned and strong from hard work. Esther admired her husband's hands – his long tapered fingers with filbert shaped nails and his almost perfect teeth. No doubt about it her Solly was as handsome as a man can be.

'If they was rich,' Esther thought as she watched Solly, 'if they was rich he'd be somethin' Solly would. 'e'd strut an' pose with the best of 'em. As it was nobody would take much notice of 'im or 'er as it 'appens an' maybe it was best left at tha'.'

A regret struggled within her as she gazed at Klara with tiny milk bubbles on her delicate cheeks – a regret of special mothering, deep feeling edged with sorrow that her little girl was born to their poorness.

'Rothschild friend to the poor. No' in this 'ome – why even a widow wait'd 'alf a year for a shillin' an' a bag of coal an' be lucky to see that much.'

Her thoughts were broken as Solly took his razor to a leather strop and with quick strokes back and forth sharpened the blade.

"Yer slice yer cheek orf one of these mornin's.

That's villainous that razor – once Klara's up an' doin' yer best watch it safe somewhere."

"Do yer think Esther I'd let my Klara 'urt 'erself?"

"Well don't forgets yer a father now."

"My darlin' wife, if I forgets, remind me."

"I will Sol, I will. I can't forgets I'm a ma, my nipples are red raw. I'll 'ave to asks ma what I should be rub on 'em."

"Never mind yer tits Esther, drink this 'ot tea and eat yer toast, whilst I learn abou' national insurance."

"'ow can the government take anythin' orf us, we 'ardly making ends meet!"

"Yus, bu' when I starts to do well I'll knows what to do, won't I? We'll 'ave loads of money Esther, wait an' see."

"Don't worry I will an' we'll live out somewhere nice an' I'll 'ave crystal vases in every room of our 'ouse filled out with real red carnations Solly, no' paper one's all dyed up like them gypsies hawk."

"Yus an' I'll buy vases wholesale from Archie's pawn shop to show 'em orf."

Laughing together Esther rubbed Klara's back before putting her to the other breast.

"Old Solly sent a sovereign for 'er."

"Yer didn't tell me."

"Well I'm telling' yer now."

"It must 'ave killed 'im."

"Nahh, my father ain't bad, my mother gets on 'is nerves, she says we are to go over Friday night to share the fried fish."

"Ain't that the way always, women gets on the man's nerves. Yer pa's a tyrant, all the Starr men is tyrants even you Solly 'ave that' streak runnin' through yer."

"Then why did yer marry me? "

"Why do we marry anyone? 'cause we ain't got no sense 'ave we. Yer ma's a saint to bear the old sheikh an' 'is dogs! Any odds wha' time is 'e comin' with the wagon?"

"Abou' seven O'clock I'll pack the stuff soon an' start for The Lane."

"My poor pa's at Spitalfields before three O'clock in the mornin'."

"'e should give up being a coster an' go into second-'ands with Dinah – to save 'is feet."

"Nahh, 'e don't get on too well with Monty."

"That's our trouble always rowin' it's a wonder to me anyone talks to anyone."

"Troubles make you irritable, don't they?"

"Troubles, all I ever 'ears 'is troubles. Don't fret yerself Esther none of us is starvin', gawd-forbid, we are respectable, 'ard-workin' an' on a good day 'ave rooves over our 'eads. An' that's wha' counts I can tell yer. No bread tickets for us, eh Klara? Tha' baby's so full of milk she'll sleep all day."

"I'm goin' over my Ma's to roll cigars with 'er. I like it over Cox Street an' them Dutch pay."

"Gawd 'elp yer if yer make a mistake – them mean bastards will give you peanuts."

"You can't stand the Dutch Sol."

"I 'ate 'em with their bloody cigars an' 'errings."

"It buys our supper."

"I knows old cock, bu' them and those *froomers*[38] you can keep."

"Don't be a date Solly, we are all Jews, Russian, Dutch, Pole what's the difference?"

"They're all Bolsheviks."

"Wat all of 'em?"

"Yus, all of 'em an' yer mark my words, they will bring troubles to us English Jews. Then yer

38   Religious (slang)

knows wat trouble is!"

"Don't be wicked Sol, its 'ard for newcomers – give 'em a chance. They 'ave come 'ere from awful places."

"We didn't exactly come from 'eaven."

"That was centuries past it ain't bad for a us now is it?"

"Nahh, it ain't bad, but all of 'em is *schnorrers* – try sellin' one of 'em a shirt – it's murder – they want our goods for piss-all, they argue for 'alf-an-'our for sixpence bloody paupers an' they stink of pickled cucumbers."

"Cor-blimey listen to your pa Klara, 'e sounds worse than the *goyyim*[39], so 'e do! "

"I think I'll buy our Klara a piana an' when we are old and worn-ou' she can play a tune an' cheer us up!"

"A piana will go well with 'er napkins, I ain't bin young yet an' now yer on abou' us bein' grey-'eads. The wagons are on the move Sol, your pa will turn up any second – there 'e is shoutin' up for you now. Put yer coat on and wear yer cap – I'll go on the landin' an' tell 'im yer on the way down."

Solly put his empty mug in the scullery sink, tiptoed up to his daughter and gently kissed her.

"Nothin' like a proud family man, Esther – I was 'opin' for a kiss and a cuddle before work."

"Not on your life Solly Starr that's 'ow I got sore tits in the first place – 'urry up the 'orse gets fed up. Solly, where's the sovereign?"

"Esther, there ain't a grain of romance in your dark soul."

"Never mind romance, I'll 'ave Klara's sovereign or I'll brain yer. I know you with a bit of money it will go on the nags."

Solly dug into his trouser pocket and produced

---

39   Nations – used here to mean non-Jews

the golden coin.

"I'll toss yer for it Esther 'eads or tails? "

"Solly give us Klara's money."

"'eads or tails?"

"'eads, 'eads, 'eads."

"Ya lost my gal, its tails."

"Yer bleedin' cheat, you would rob yer own daughter!"

"See you later, keep our 'appy home tidy an' I just might give yer the sovereign when I comes back."

Esther was never sure if Solly was joking, as he could tease the life out of you – she called after him as he reached the outside landing,

"Solly."

"Wat yer want now?"

"Don't forgets the piana! – what a pair we are yer ma and pa." Klara was sound asleep.

As Esther was making-up their bed underneath the feather pillow glittered the sovereign.

"What a pair we are!"

By half past eight Solly and old Solomon had laid out neatly white shirts and men's underwear on their stall. Hanging on a rail working men's trousers and overalls and a few second-hand suits for best wear. The noise of stall holders had already started – shouting their wares with eyes in the backs on their heads for the abundant thieves and instant smiles for anyone who might buy their goods!

Cockney voices and *yiddish* voices selling food, china-ware, materials, boots – straining on their throats to be heard and throwing covers over everything if it began to rain – pigeons pecked at mostly nothing around their feet – women shoved each other to buy bread – the eel stall with hot small pies was surrounded and the *kosher*[40] butchers sold pieces and halves of fowls for soup. Here and there cafes offered a bacon roll and a mug of tea for a penny and on a cold day hot potatoes to put inside gloves to warm the hands for a farthing. The crowds idled along staring at it all and in corners groups of Indian seamen sat on the ground smoking.

The public-house still closed by order stood silent and sullen men were moved on by a policeman who seemed to come out of nowhere. Urchins sang the music-hall favourite *'Lloyd George knew my Father'* as the policeman moved them on.

Old Solomon could be overbearing – he ordered his poor wife Sarah about and his children. Sometimes the passer-by caught his eye,

"Do ya want these trousers or don't ya want these trousers?"

Solly tapped his father's shoulder,

"Pa, their priests collectin' for charity."

"So, they don't wear trousers?"

"Yur they wear trousers Pa, but they have to buy 'em from the Pope or they wouldn't be 'oly would they?"

Old Solomon called over to the priests,

"Good mornin' gentlemen, welcome to The Lane this fine mornin'. My son an' myself trust yer 'ave come to buy an' not to preach. So allow me gentlemen to interest yer both in this smart, black two-piece suit of clothes cut by tailors to the Pope!"

The priests smiled and one said,

"God bless you and good mornin' to you." Then walked on.

"Ah! wat do they know abou' suits of clothes. Nothin' I tells you, nothin'. Plenty abou' prayin',

40   Religiously acceptable

about suits nothin'."

Solly, busy shouting to the crowd, holding up white shirts,

"Buy these bargains now – whilst our sale lasts, only Solly Starr's stall is the sale gen-u-ine – wat yer laughin' at yer saucy buggars, a gen-u-ine sale it is an' to prove my word 'ere take these winter long-johns better than the King wears 'imself for 'alf-a-dollar a pair and I swears on my life yer be toast warm. Come orn ladies, dear ladies, would yer see yer nearest and dearest freezing cold in the snow – pure wool trousers, dip into your purses now before I pack 'em up! 'ere arf-a-sovereign an' me pa an' me's out of pocket – gen-u-ine sale, buy from Solly Starr – Starr quality, that's our family motto. Wat, ain't yer got a family motto? Well yer should 'ave, an' by the look of them trousers yer standin' in yer could do with a new pair. 'ere pa, wat yer think of 'is trousers?"

"I pity him, 'is trousers is a disgrace."

The banter continued to the day's end. Piles of litter lay around their feet, hot mugs of tea were drunk as the willow baskets kept under the stall were brought out to be filled with goods. Solly shook off dust specks, carefully counting the garments for loss against thieving. The day's takings were kept in a leather pouch worn on Solly's thick belt.

The collies, Charlie and Bear, cocked their legs up a lamp-post then jumped on the wagon.

The narrow streets took hold of the crowd as the horse slowly moved the wagon away.

The Lane was left to vagabonds, lean cats and grey London pigeons. In dark corners rats waited to for the night sky. Old newspaper blown here and there looked in the half shadows of twilight like forlorn ghosts searching the broken down atmosphere for a haunting retreat.

The real East End ghosts had long ago found it.

New Boots for Old

"My feet 'urt me ma."

With half an ear Phoebe listened to Sophie's complaint.

"Think yerself lucky my gal to 'ave new boots. There are those out there on them very streets who goes barefoot summer an' winter an' well yer knows it."

"Bare-feet is be'er than these 'ere boots. I 'ate 'em!"

"Yer are off school for *Rosh Hashanah*[41] and old enough to know we gets new boots an' if we are fortunate new clothes for *yom tov*[42]. Now stop moanin' 'round me legs, learn to be grateful. If Dinah didn't 'ave a pair in, yer would 'ave gorn without an' then how would you feel, with everyone wearing new boots?"

"Comfortable."

"Wear them in – them boots will stretch."

Sophie was unimpressed with her ma's argument and went on talking back.

"Well Fanny Michaels said them goods of Dinah's is all nicked, so wat yer make of that ma?"

"'er ma bin at the gossip-shop again – just yer wait till I sees tha' woman, she's all mouth an' no sense. I shall give Mrs Michaels a peace of my mind an' no mistake. Talk like that from 'er gossip could cause yer sister no end of trouble. She makes an 'onest livin' she do. Mrs Michaels indeed! Why 'er old

41 New Year   42 A good day

man ain't done an 'ands turn of work in 'is life, lazy ain't the word. Yer mark my words Sophie, Fanny Michaels with 'er Ma will up at the board of charity with their pleading faces askin' for more than new boots. I 'ope their feet drops orf – nicked clothes – bleedin' liberty!"

Sophie regretted upsetting her mother with gossip but she would not give in about her painful toes.

"Well our boots is cast-orfs ma, we never gets new stuff – ever."

"With the coppers yer pa puts in me purse after standin' in all weathers, rain or shine to feed us, 'ow do yer think I can buy new clothes. Why yer sisters make dresses new as new, but they ain't cobblers who can stitch boots are they? You look a picture in yer white apron an' yer polished boots so wat more do yer want? Any rate thank gawd in *schul* we can stand up with the best of 'em. You should be ashamed for naggin' so yer should."

Sophie went quiet, sensing she had provoked her mother enough.

"Tell yer what Soph, if yer wears in 'em boots like a good gal, when pa 'as 'is feet soakin' come night, yer can soak them feet in the same water - 'ow's that? An' fer good measure yer ma will bake a biscuit for yer."

"Ta ma, but 'ow will I knows me own biscuit?"

"'cause I will put a big 's' for my Sophie on the dough, won't I."

"Ma."

"Wat do yer want now?"

"Let's give yer a kiss."

"Gawd 'elp us the child's lost 'er 'ead."

"Nahh I ain't."

"Well wat yer waitin' for?"

Sophie kissed her mother very tenderly. Phoebe's hard life did not shower her with kisses, and this affection from her youngest child was a glad moment.

"Ma I'm gorna save, save, save till I'm rich, rich, rich. Then when you an' pa is very old I will buy yer a brand new boots with pearl buttons up the sides an' fer pa leather as soft as bu'er so as 'is toes don't ache. Real pearl buttons ma an' a silk blue shawl for the back of yer chair as I've seen in books and another one fer yer shoulders – fit fer a Duchess ma, the whole lot, fit fer a Duchess."

"That's right noble of yer Soph, an' no more than I expects from a daughter of mine. Watch the grate, don't let the fire go low. The *schuls* coal fer *yom tov* stops a bit of worry fer yer pa. Now I'm orf to the grounds."

"Why can't I come?"

"Children are not allowed down the grounds."

"Why – I'm almost grown ain't I?"

"Yer endless questions will bring on one of me 'eadaches, tha' school teaches yer to ask too many questions. They ain't allowed an' that's that."

"Why are yer goin'?"

"To pay my respects to our ancestors that first came 'ere to live. Its tradition ain't it? An' the rabbi said it was fer our 'spiritual reflection.'"

"Cor ma, thems the biggest words yer 'ave ever said."

"Well yer never knew 'ow clever yer ma was, did yer my gal."

"I swear I never did ma. Who is goin' with yer?"

"Esther and Dinah, Rachel is at the stall with pa an' Becky's gorn for 'is brown mixture, Katie is in Southend. Now if yer ask me one more question I'll

brain yer. Fetch me the button-'ook an' 'elp me on
with these boots – gawd they are as stiff as a poker."
   "Now yer knows 'ow I 'urts."
   After much pulling and stretching the black
books were on,
   "There ain't no pleasure without pain."
   Phoebe hobbled to the door and Sophie hobbled
to the grate to rake the coals. Their boots squeaked
and ached.
   "Well yer can't help laughin' can yer Soph?"
   Poor little Sophie, with sore toes like her pa did
not agree, only thought how rich she was going to be
when she grew up and made her fortune.
   That evening Henry was in a unusually
talkative mood. Phoebe who always had much to say
was occupied with her cooking for the *Rosh Hashanah*
meal. She quietly listened to her husband as he
soaked his sore feet and Sophie waited for her turn
hoping the water wasn't stone cold.
   With scrupulous care Phoebe counted the
potatoes to be peeled, the onions and carrots for her
soup and each piece of fowl, to be sure enough food
on every plate made the feast special. Her daughters
each brought an oil-cloth bag of vegetables or fruit
and fresh bread. The table to Sophie's eyes was
wonderful and her biscuit with its 's' in the middle
golden with butter – and smelled of cinnamon.
Phoebe held up a long string of potato peeling, peeled
in a continuous string. Sophie laughed and wore it
for a necklace. Ma was good at making toys from
peelings.
   "Any rate Phoeb, there was this geezer shoutin'
at the top of 'is voice 'All fer 1/ and a kick the lot.
Come an' buy, me lovlies. Fresh as a daisy,' when
from behin' comes this ruffian, a right bastard he
looked, I can tell yer an' 'e kicks the poor coster

right-up, right-up Phoeb, I'd seen it with me own eyes."

"Wat 'appened next pa."

"Shut up Soph let yer pa talk."

"Well, there was a rumpus an' 'ow, runnin', shoutin'. The ruffian gorn fast as yer like an' the coster's barrow-load all over the show. Anyways Sammy Cohen, yer know 'im Phoeb, 'e married one of them Segal gals from Mile End an' 'e asks me,

'Yer all right 'enry? Did 'e grab any veg orf yer?'

'Nahh,' says I, 'I only 'ad a few onions left.'

'Them thievin' rats its their old lark. A menace all right, but thank gawd they leave us alone, am I right or no?'

'Right as right is,' I says to Sammy.

'Well good *yom tov* to yer an' yours 'enry.'

'Good *yom tov* Sammy,' I says an' pushes me barra 'ome.'

"The streets are full of 'em, but maybe 'e was 'ungry."

"Don't be soft Phoebe. Who gives us?"

"The Almighty, blessed be his name."

"I wish 'e give us a bit more!"

"Don't be saucy Soph an' dry yer feet the both of yer, water all over the floor – I ain't clearin' up no more."

All was ready by sun-down. Phoebe had brushed Sophie's hair till it glittered in the soft light. Her best dress was covered with a new white apron with a starched frill and huge bow at her back. Phoebe wore her best black silk and around her shoulders a Spanish shawl hung in folds of lace. Henry was suited and shirted and polished till he could hardly move. A white linen table cloth covered the table, gas lights flickered on the candle sticks and fruit and flowers lay in the centre of all. The fireside was warm and Phoebe felt happy to be ready and waiting for the family.

Esther and Solly arrived first with Klara in her arms and Solly with a box of food. Phoebe had eyes only for her grandchild. Klara was smothered with kisses and held close.

"Good *yom tov*, good *yom tov* pa an' Sophie."

"Come in, warm yerselves I'll make a cup of tea."

"Sit down ma, no rush, it's an 'oliday."

"I'll make the tea."

Solly gave Henry a bottle of brandy. Esther unpacked their box of food – some small cakes, fruit, butter and sweets for Sophie. Becky and Rachel came together tired but looking forward to the family get-together.

"Good *yom tov* ma an' pa."

They hugged ad kissed everyone.

By the time Dinah, Monty and Becky, their six year old arrived, the meal was ready.

"Wat an 'ouse full we are – 'enry, its like when our gals was all small. 'ow I wish our Alf an' Joey were 'ome as well."

Henry said the prayers as he broke the bread. He lit the *yom tov* candles and Phoebe served the soup.

With relief the family stretched their toes – underneath the table a pile of leather boots lay in a stiff heap!

Eli

Sukkoth[43] and *Passover* are favourite times for weddings.

"Please God my bride will go to the *mikvah*[44] by the coming Passover."

Eli's thoughts were on such things. Occasionally doubts came, he banished them with a wave of his hand.

That very morning in an old piece of guttering on the side of the house, Eli had sighted a blackbird sitting on her nest, when she left it for a few seconds he peeped in to find two blue eggs fragile and beautiful. 'Eggs have magical properties and blue is our eternal colour, it must be meant!'

The shop was closed. The day was his. He bathed and dressed with care. He chose a blue shirt, a suit with not a speck of dust on it, his black shoes polished, his hair brushed and oiled. He glanced at himself in the wardrobe mirror, smiled with satisfaction and left the house humming a music-hall tune.

"Wish me luck blackbird," he called.

The afternoon was warm. He walked in a dreamy style. The drab streets looked welcoming. He stopped to buy some sweets and a cake topped with almonds. The drum beat of love in his head found him at Rifka's front door.

From outside he could hear children and when Rifka opened the door children seemed to engulf

43 Tabernacles   44   Ritual bath

him. They led him in a laughing procession to the front room where Eli shared the sweets with them and Rifka took the cake.

"Eli is it good to see you. How smart you look. How is your mother? How is your father? Is the shop closed today?"

"Rifka to all your questions my mother is well, thank God, my father is well, thank God and the shop is closed."

"This house is full of women and children it's good to see a man!"

"Where is Reuben?"

"He's gone with Shepsul to a town in Scotland."

"Why Scotland?"

"We have a community there. They talk about Zionism, you know – it's important."

"Scotland is freezing and miles away."

"True, true but who will talk if Reuben is silent and who will visit the bedridden and sick if Shepsul didn't. They are isolated, poor Jews nobody cares about them."

"They are good men Rifka."

"They are better than good. Enough talk, I will make you a glass of tea. I must tell you Eli the children are teaching me English. Every time I say a word they laugh. Anyway I like *Yiddish*, it's a warn tongue, no Eli?"

"You will learn Rifka it all takes time."

"Ah! time, soon, it will be time for this one to come." She stroked her belly.

Eli saw yet another birth, but said nothing.

"Dosha and Peshe are upstairs they will soon be down. They're hemming skirts - it's a living, no?"

With the glass of sweet lemon tea and almond cake, with the sun warming the room, with the noisy children and Rifka's chat Eli had almost forgotten why he was there until the drumbeat reminded him.

At last Peshe came down with several skirts over here arm. Dosha followed also carrying some garments.

"Hallo Eli, you look well."

"Hallo Eli how are your parents?"

Eli felt almost defeated, three women and an army of children were almost too much for the quiet butcher! Somehow he heard himself saying,

"Peshe I would like to talk with you."

Everybody looked at everyone else. Eli felt sick.

"So talk Eli, I'm here. Do you want to place an order?"

"Do I look as if I wear a skirt?"

"Maybe for you mother, my work is good ask Rifka."

"No Peshe I want to talk to you alone."

"Come Dosha, Eli will not share his secret with us."

Dosha couldn't wait for Peshe to tell them the secret, but with their tea and cake they left Peshe and Eli together.

"Eli is this some English game or something?"

"No, Peshe, this is not a game. I want to marry you."

The silence in the room was unbearable. Eli wanted to run for his life, he continued,

"I love you Peshe – Stand under the *chuppah* with me. You are young and beautiful – You must marry again – It is not right for you sewing-up skirts all day. I will look after you – The children will have free meat every day. Say yes Peshe and let us have a *Passover* wedding – I love you."

Eli felt the house swallow him up he, Eli Sirkes had proposed to lovely Peshe – he was brave beyond words.

Peshe did not reply. She smiled gently at Eli picked up her empty glass and plate. Eli sat looking at nothing.

"The blackbird laid two blue eggs in a nest in our guttering; that's a sign, no Peshe, of great joy!"

"Goodbye Eli, thank you for coming."

'I am simpleton – she thinks I'm mad. I am mad. I will be a laughing stock, Rifka will never let me into the house again!'

Eli left the room and quickly walked from the house. The drumbeat of love was now a headache!

"Eli's gone mama."

"What, without a goodbye. Peshe what happened in there?"

Dosha saw the funny side of Peshe being so quiet.

"Tell us, tell us Peshe what is Eli's secret?"

"When Shepsul comes home I will ask him to send a *shadchan*[45] to Ida's place. Eli needs a wife! Now where are the children? They are running wild. Dosha come with me to find the children."

Rifka and Dosha both decided to keep quiet, but Dosha simply had to say,

"It's that time of the year, I remember Shepsul."

"I remember Reuben. Men are funny creatures. Peshe will never tell us."

"She will when I tickle her feet. It's the only way to make Peshe talk. Shepsul told me."

"Dosha you are impossible. But hurry up, I'm longing to know!"

Just before the *Passover* that year an invitation to a wedding arrived from Ida and Monty.

Eli was to marry Gertie Sugarman.

---

45 Matchmaker

If Cissy had been a Flower

If Cissy had been a flower it would have been a lily. Slender, pale, white, delicate, in a house spilling-over with small boys with amazing energy, Cissy was special. Seven years old with her mother's blond, fair-light hair and blue eyes, her child's voice calling her brothers to order, when Rifka had run out of patience. As she learnt to read she would read the stories to her younger brothers sitting in a circle around her on the floor.

Benjamin thought her stories stupid and would run off after untying her apron, treading on all their toes, crying,

"Mother goose! mother goose!"

The small ones began to yell, Rifka would come running, shouting at the top of her voice,

"Wait till papa comes, he will bang all your heads together!"

The children ran in all directions, Cissy would gather her story-books and retreat to her aunt Peshe's rooms at the top of the house.

"I try auntie Peshe, I try,"

Peshe would cuddle her, drape her in material and with a kiss promise to sew her a new dress when she had time.

"Brothers are always a torment. When you are grown up, then you will be friends."

"I will never be friends with Benjamin, never, never."

"Sure you will – just as I love your papa and Shepsul. We had fights with handfuls of corn. The corn used to tangle our hair, half choking us, mama went crazy, the dogs would bark, papa would threaten to lock us away forever for wasting precious grain. Ah! yes Cissy, brothers are demons sent to annoy their sisters. Shepsul could not stay away from water. Mama always said he was a fish. Shepsul would say, 'I am Shepsul your son, do I look like a fish?' Mama laughed,

'Not exactly, but when you play by the river you smell like a fish.'

So to aggravate Shepsul we'd call him 'fishy' all day. By bed time we were worn out with trying to climb up to the stork's nest and fighting, it's a wonder we lived."

"Didn't you have to go to school auntie Peshe?"

"No. Papa taught us everything he thought we should know. Jews did not go to Russian schools."

"Why?"

"Because they hated us like poison and would have killed us."

"That is wicked auntie."

"Yes, Cissy, that is wicked – you go to the Jewish Free School because it is different here for us."

"Papa teaches us Hebrew and it's so difficult."

"You are just seven darling, you will learn, papa is a great teacher."

"Papa said he would bring presents for us when he comes home, do you think he will auntie?"

"Sure he will, papa never says what he doesn't mean. What would you like?"

"I want a skipping-rope mama won't let me skip outside, but in the yard is alright."

"Well she worries about you."

"Benjamin wants a ball, Yossel would like a ball also, and Aaron would like a surprise – Isaac said papa would bring sweets because Jews have to study not play around. But Uncle Shepsul might bring a surprise, no auntie?"

"We'll see, we'll see, anyway you have all new clown costumes for *Purim*[46] and papa has little *gelt* to spare."

"Will we ever be rich auntie?"

"We will be rich, you will marry a prince because you are my princess and I will sew you a wonder dress covered with all the stars heaven can hold. And everyone will say 'princess Cissy is the world's most beautiful bride.' Now what do you say to that?"

"I love you auntie Peshe, but first I would like a skipping-rope."

"I can smell the *cholent* cooking. I must go down to make sure your mama has cooked enough for the schnorrer, one is bound to turn up!"

"Why do we feed *schnorrers*?"

"Because nobody else will and it's our duty as a family of rabbis."

"But we are poor and mama worries."

"They are poorer and perhaps have no mama, so that is even more reason to share."

"You are wise auntie Peshe."

"And you are my Cissy princess."

The Amulet

Tomfoolery was in the air.

After weeks of colds and chicken-pox the children were well and bursting with fun after many hot bowls of Rifka's soups. Rifka felt worn down and without Peshe's help felt she could have slept forever.

"Will we go back to school now mama?"

"Of course."

"Why, I hate school, send Benjamin back he likes school. Benjamin is clever mama. I am a *schlemihl*[47]."

"My amiable Ezra, a *schlemihl* – who called you such a name?"

"Uncle Shepsul."

"Uncle Shepsul called you a *schlemihl!*"

"I swear it mama, and everyone laughed at me, Benjamin said I couldn't spell my name and Aaron said a *schlemiel* in our family of *rabbonim* was a disgrace – am I a disgrace mama?"

Rifka could not help smiling at her son's crestfallen face.

"They were teasing you Ezra – uncles and brothers always do – Ezra, tell me, can you spell your name?"

"Sometimes."

"What do you mean sometimes, either you can spell your name or you can't."

"I forget. I hate school, I like home."

"Home doesn't make a living, when you are a

man."

"All right, mama, I will learn to spell my name when I grow up, but I am a boy and it gives me a headache."

"*Oy vey*, what am I going to do with you – listen Ezra, when Benjamin, God bless my first born, calls his brother a *schlemihl* it's a joke. When uncle Shepsul says you are like Samuel Kosminski it's a joke, but when your mama calls you a *schlemihl* it's no joke."

"It's not?"

"It's not. So my Ezra will go to school, my Ezra, God keep you safe always, will learn to spell his name and my Ezra will become a great man."

"You think mama?"

"I don't think, I know. Tell me Ezra, can Jossel write his name?"

"Nope mama, Jossel's a *schlemihl*."

"*Tzimmus*[48], I must cook plenty of *tzimmus*, my sons are backward, at their *mitzvim*[49] they will all be idiots."

"If you wait a while I'll help you cook it."

"Dosha, I didn't see you there. I was thinking aloud, the boys are domineering everyone. They are fed up being at home – Ezra doesn't want to attend school. Thank God they are all better and not a mark left on their skins. I was worried about my Cissy's lovely face, but all is well. Better still when our men come – I indulge the children, Peshe ruins them, only Reuben is strict. Dosha you are dressed up. Are you going somewhere special perhaps?"

"No, not special, I needed to cheer myself up."

"Ah! You miss Shepsul, I told you to stay with us, you will sit and brood in your room."

"You have enough here without me, and our little place would be dusty and not aired if I stayed

48   Carrots, pudding, potatoes
49   Coming of age ceremonies

away."

"So you care about dust! It's a waste of time – Peshe and I fight the dust, the bugs. We dread the children having fleas, then what happens, we both suffer terrible headaches – now I say fresh air is more important and soon we'll have a nicer house."

"I'll make tea, Rifka, you rest – it can't be long now before the confinement."

"Not even days. I think this one will see daylight before my Reuben is back. I long for another daughter – Cissy is overcrowded with brothers – she says, 'I want a sister mama,' I told her I'll do my best – three of us in this street are expecting any second, it's a race to who's first."

"It won't be me, Rifka, it wont be me!"

"You have a lifetime Dosha darling, to have children, some of us take longer – take one of mine, with pleasure."

"You wouldn't part with one of your family – you'd die first."

"Yes, but I'm tired, worn-out. I hardly remember being young, yet we are all still so young – I day-dream still, do you day-dream Dosha?"

"I day-dream about our village – I pretend we still live with my geese and storks and my family – that the hatred didn't happen and we lived happy people with the *goyim*."

"Believe me Dosha, that is a day-dream. It can never be – at least for a while here it's not bad, but who can tell!"

"My day-dreams protect me against not having a child – every month when my period comes I weep – Shepsul, God bless him, understands, but it's sad for him also – no son yet, no daughter. Enough talk you have your own problems – only I think we were under an illusion – marriage is a burden to us – it burns up our emotions – I was happy with my geese."

"Dosha, you were fourteen, fifteen then – it was another place – life moves on – womanhood is interwoven with despairs, but the world is beautiful my Dosha – you and Shepsul will mould each other into sunshine – wait – free yourself from desire and worry and the babies will come – then you will feel like me!"

"Living with Reuben you have wisdom."

"Its also made me mama to more boys than names I can remember – now tell me, what are you up to, where are you going?"

"I'm going to see Koppel Ginsberg."

"Koppel? Why? Reuben loathes him."

"I know, don't tell anyone, not even Peshe – his wife will sit between us, but I want an amulet – he will have one."

"Dosha, why, that is not for us – such things are bad – he tells me about the birthdays, but it's different – an amulet is ... is ..."

"No, Rifka, don't put me off, it's something I want to do."

"What if Shepsul finds out?"

"We'll have a row, then we'll make up and he'll buy me flowers."

"Flowers, rows, an amulet, Koppel – Dosha are you ill?"

"On the way back, do you want me to bring anything from The Lane"

"No. There is no need, just take care – it's not good for you to go alone."

"I'll be all right, Koppel will walk back with me and tonight I'll stay with you and Peshe."

"Wonderful – Peshe is cooking – Cissy has learnt how to cook dumplings – don't refuse trying one!"

❀

Koppel's wife greeted Dosha with,

"Come Dosha we won't eat you, you looked scared out of your wits."

"No, no Rachel, I looked forward to being here, I just feel uncomfortable alone on the streets."

"So you should, the *goyim's* boys pull our men's beards and try and knock our *sheitels* off - Koppel carries a stick everywhere - may the synagogue warm our hearts, Dosha - I'll tell Koppel you've come - go in and see the children, the chicken-pox is over."

"I know, Rifka's had an awful time."

"Dear Rifka, she's carrying again no? I must go and visit - Reuben hates Koppel, it makes things awkward - but I will go, yes when my children are at school I will go."

"Dosha how kind of you to see us - sit down, drink tea with us - tell us your news."

"Hello Koppel - I've come for something special."

"Special I don't have - 'Rachel bring the sugar', Rachel is a good wife, but every day I call Rachel bring the sugar and Rachel calls 'it makes you too fat' - listen."

A voice came from the scullery,

"Koppel, it makes you too fat."

Dosha laughed and relaxed.

Rachel brought sugar, the children came carrying small cakes and fruit. After the pleasant tea-time Rachel sent the children to play - sitting between Koppel and Dosha she asked what troubled her.

"Koppel, please give me an amulet - I want a charm to wear - I need help."

"Dosha this is no small request – it is serious. Why do you want a magic charm?"

"I cannot conceive."

Dosha's eyes softened with tears. Her head ached. She felt so alone and lost and looked so helpless both Koppel and Rachel fell silent until the moment passed.

"Just because you have not yet experienced motherhood, that does not mean you are unable to conceive – sometimes it may take years then God Almighty the blessed one, looks down upon you and you become a mother. Be patient Dosha."

"I am barren – I feel so."

"Don't mention the word it's unlucky – you will bring it upon yourself, fruit trees do not bear fruit all in a year. Time, Dosha, time. You are a child yet in years."

"Please Koppel, on my knees, on my mother's life, on my grandmother's soul, I beg you to help me with an amulet."

"Koppel, come, what harm is in it? Dosha is in torment, the charm will ease her mind. She'll feel more content and the babies will come."

Koppel's eyebrows went up, first one, then the other. He stroked his beard. He tapped the side of the chair. He walked up; he walked down.

"If Reuben find out I'll be locked out of schul. Shepsul will walk past me – I'll be a nobody to everybody."

"Koppel it's a small amulet the young wife is asking for, not for you to build the Temple!"

"Please Koppel, please!"

"There are charms and charms Dosha. Some are very powerful, some simple. Most are ancient in dusty books and it is impossible to find the recipes anymore. Some are unpleasant - you would not like them."

"Tell me."

"Take the brains of a raven and arsenic and saffron. Mix them together and hang them around your neck for forty days – or wear the brains and fat of a white dove in your womb all day – or take the skin of a fox and burn it to dust then drink the ashes in water for three days."

"They sound horrible. I couldn't do any of those things – I only need a charm."

"Horrible indeed, but it was long ago – so what shall I give Dosha?"

Koppel opened a huge, black book, turned a few pages until he found 'Fruit Charms'.

"This is for you Dosha, simple and pleasant.

Take five almonds
Five Apricot pips
One Nutmeg
Equal amounts of anise
Pound it all together
Boil in wine
And drink it at night in a pure state.

You must do this several times."

"Koppel I can do that one."

"Good, it's better than a walnut in a lizard with three flies and chalk, worn around your neck in a piece of linen."

"No, no! Shepsul would never forgive me!"

"Or you may search high and low for an egg which contains another egg and drink the inner egg whilst standing in your ritual bath. Eggs are strong magic."

"Koppel, where is she going to find the egg."

"Ah! That's the secret."

Up went the eyebrow.

"No your charm Dosha shall be fruit – I shall write it out for you and you may collect it anytime – I shall also make your amulet – but you must give me your oath, you will never open the small piece of linen and read the Hebrew. Your word Dosha."

"I swear Koppel, on my life."

"Good – all is settled – now we will have a fresh glass of tea with plenty of sugar, eh, Rachel? Then I will walk you to Rifka's place. Wear blue Dosha, blue is pure. Drape your bed with a blue spread."

Dosha felt her mission out alone had proved successful – no matter what everybody said she liked Koppel – she would wear the amulet when it was ready and would collect all the fruits she needed for her drink. Maybe next time she cracked an egg it would hold another.

It was evening of magic – but never would she burn a fox, God forbid, or eat brains. Her Hebrew charm would bring her child – she clung to the hope as ancient women clung to the apple tree or worshipped the moon fairies.

Dinah's Old Clothes Shop

Willows swayed by gentle summer breeze touched the Thames. Swans seemed to sway with the water towards the green banks. On a passive London day only the plane trees and grey patches of sky showed signs of rain.

The mile walk to her sister's shop cheered-up Esther. Three months pregnant and suffering from sickness. The air cleared her head. Klara slept in her pram, sparrows and pigeons were in harmony, not a quarrelsome sound could be heard.

Nearing the shop Esther could hear her sister singing at the top of her voice,

"I can't marry you today –

My wife, won't let me!"

"Someone is 'appy today, yer found a guinea or somethin'? They can 'ear yer in Whitechapel!"

"Well, its a day for singing ain't it gal – beside 'our Marie' ain't a patch on me! Did yer come by tram?"

"Nahh, we walked me an' my Klara. I'm as sick as a dog with this one. The tram turns me stomach over."

"Early days, always the same. Babies don't come easy. Take the weight orf yer feet an' I'll give yer a glass of lemonade with a bit of ginger – Klara my angel will also 'ave a taste. I always keeps a bit for Monty. 'is stomach is not too strong, nothin' like a bit of ginger to settle it. Mind yer, peppermint will also do the trick."

"Ta, I felt low, bu' the river is a picture – 'ard to believe the dirt of the East-end is everywhere. Solly's good as gold – 'e spends 'alf 'is time 'olding me over the sink. 'Cor, gal,' 'e says, 'yer wasn't like this with our Klara!' Funny ain't it Dinah, I thought it was the first one made yer sick!"

"Always different, every time, ma says. I ain't goin' in for another one. Becky is enough for me. I tells Monty if 'e wants a son 'e can adopt one, children ain't up my street. I likes me shop – an' Abdul of course!"

"Yer still believe in them spirits, one of these days that lot will 'aunt the daylights out of yer an' won't yer 'ave a scream then, don't say I didn't warn yer!"

"Abdul is my faithful an' lovin' spirit-guide an' 'e told me as true as I'm standin' 'ere, 'Dinah, no more children,' an' I'll tell yer a secret Esther, not a word to anyone of I'll brain yer, I'm learnin' 'ow to go into a trance an' receive messages from the 'otherside' – the dear departed talk to me – now don't make a face; I goes right orf an' I 'ear voices in me 'ead, an' they tell me messages, don't they?"

"I don't bleedin' know what they tells you – bu' I do know them that 'ear voices in their 'eads are most likely orf their 'eads! Ma thinks yer a right scatty cow an' pa says yer drink too much of Flo's pale-ale, it's turning yer brain 'round the wrong way. Solly says every family 'as its nut-case!"

"What a load yer all 'ave to say about me. Just yer wait till I 'ave a real true message for yer. Then it will be 'our Dinah's a real card ain't she,' anyway wat yer come for to see yer mad sister, for a jaw or 'ave yer come to buy?"

"Both – I needs a winter coat, wat's come in?"

"A few things – coats go fast. Take a look. Dresses an' skirts on the right rail an' everythin' else on the left. Boots underneath an' a pile of 'ats an' odds an' ends in the corner bin."

"Where's Becky? – cor, 'ow do I find a coat amongst this lot?"

"Becky's with ma. She's under my feet in 'ere – besides ain't right for a child to be with old clothes all day makes her sneeze terrible, our Becky is a sensitive soul. Watch out them rails don't fall on yer. They're top 'eavy, like you in a few months!"

"Don't remind me, that's why I want to try a coat on now, it don't show yet. I ain't goin' to any lyin'-in-rooms neither. This one is seeing daylight in me own bed, please God. Solly ain't keen on the idea, still I've made me mind up."

"Good luck to yer Esther. It's them suffragettes given us courage to stand-up for wat we want. Yer want to lie-in at 'ome, an' that's that, ain't it."

"Brave ain't they, on 'unger strike an' all that."

"Women 'ave always bin brave. Our women are up there with the best of 'em. We marched for forty years in the desert an' 'ad our babies on the way. An' then we marched around the world to find a place to call 'ome!"

"An' look where it landed us – old clothes shops, stalls in dirty markets an' not tuppence between us an' the poor 'ouse!"

"Look at it this way Esther, we 'ave more than ma an' pa, my Monty travels with 'is goods an' yer Solly does well most days. Our children will do even better – it takes time, don't it?"

"Yus it do – it's 'ard waitin' bu' we 'ave been trodden under foot for centuries, it's a miracle we're still 'ere."

"Just think, little Klara, bless 'er for a 'undred

years, will be able to vote!"

"An' I bet it's for a lousy Government, that lot don't change!"

"'old on, someone comin' – 'allo Bessie 'ow are yer."

"Going on nicely, can't grumble. Me ma's bunions are bad, but all in all life ain't bad."

"Can I 'elp yer Bessie, wat yer lookin' for?"

"I want an 'at wiv a feava for goin' up West with me bloke, them 'ats are the rage."

"'old on I'll 'ave a look to see wat's 'ere."

"It's good weather ain't it Esther? Ain't Klara grown, there be no 'olding 'er soon."

"I know Bessie. They grow as yer watch 'em – my Klara's been such a good baby."

"'ere you are Bessie, 'ows abouts this for a grand 'at? With this 'at yer can go anywhere!"

"Well I ain't goin' anywhere, am I? I'm goin' up West an' that's special ain't it? An' I don't like this 'at Dinah, it's moth eaten right thru' the bleedin' crown."

"That ain't moths, Bessie, its where the feather goes, come 'ere an' try it on – there wat did I tell yer, it was made for yer, a bob with the feather."

"Give over for gawds sake, I can't see daylight – it's over me face!"

"Try this one – I ain't 'ad any 'ats in for a while maybe next week."

"Next week! I won't need an 'at next week, I'll sell it back to yer won't I."

"If yer ain't pawned it. Why don't yer 'ave a summer dress an' forget the 'at?"

"Na, me bloke likes me dress 'e doesn't care for me 'at."

"Do you like yer 'at?"

"As a ma'er of fact, yus. It's a right comfortable 'at. I wears it at funerals."

"Then be strong Bessie like them votes for women marchers an' go up West in yer old 'at."

"My bloke will leave me. 'e's got 'is eye on Ivy at the eel stall."

"Then find a knew bloke in yer old 'at. A good lookin' gal like yerself will 'ave 'em fallin' at yer feet. 'ow about this black skirt, smart ain't it?"

"Na, I 'ave changed me mind. I don't want nuffin'. Good day to yer Esther an' yerself Dinah an' ta very much. I'll go rou' the Good Samaritans clothin' club."

"No trouble Bessie, my pleasure to serve yer."

"I could 'ave laughed when the 'at fell over 'er ears."

"Bessie drives me mad, she ain't ever bought a piece orf me yet. Feathers, who wears feathers, no one since 1903."

"What do they know."

"I ain't taken sixpence all week – if things don't buck up I'll pack it in."

"No yer won't Dinah, bu' yer should get the rag an' bone man to take some of them old dresses, they're past it."

"Yus, yer right, an' I'll give my Klara the goldfish. I've 'ad enough today Esther, 'urry up an' take a coat yer fancy an' we'll go to my place for a nice cup-a-tea an' some 'ot toast with a slice of cheese."

"Sounds lovely, I'll 'ave some as well."

"Where did yer come from, why ain't yer workin'?"

"Well give us a chance to catch me breath an' I'll tell yer, won't I. Nice to see our Klara, ain't she a beauty then, Esther yer don't look well what's up?"

"Mornin' sickness, it's an 'orrible feelin'."

"Thank gawd it ain't me – all the wives 'round

'ere are always carryin' – I'll put it orf as long as possible."

"It 'appens to the best of us, yer won't escape."

"I will, I will."

"Shut up jawin' about babies an' tell us what 'appened at work!"

"Well it was like this – I've been workin' me notice out since last week, bu' didn't tell ma 'cos she worries – I 'ad enough of that Mr. Joseph to last me a lifetime – an' I says to meself, Rachel, the poor 'ave to fight their corner, else the bosses will sweat us into the ground – my fingers were bleedin' with button-'olin' an' finishin', my eyes was killin' me 'e keeps the room so dark, an' the gals were coughing an' miserable; the place should be shut down – then when I 'ands in my notice the sod says,

'What's up Rachel, I am a lenient, good employer?'

Lenient, says I, yer don't know the meanin' of the word.

'Yer won't find any work 'round 'ere an' yer makin' my workers discontented'

'Good, says I, they should all quit now!"

"Wha' abou' yer wages?"

"I'll 'ave me wage-packet Friday, 'e 'as to make it up."

"I 'ope 'e gives it yer Rachel."

"I'll take the law 'round there is 'e don't. I ain't going back to tailoring, I may try me luck with me own stall an' give pa a rest. Any odds, I'm ready for that cuppa Dinah."

"Yer be fine Rachel, none of us gals are simpletons – them sweaters should all drop dead – vicious men the lot of 'em!"

"I'll take the old 'at an' feather to ma's for Sophie, she likes dressing-up an' doin' a music 'all turn – yer laugh tears watchin' 'er do a knees-up!"

"I won't bother with a coat Dinah, I'll wait till more come in I don't feel up to it."

"All right, my angel, I'll save yer a nice warm coat – come on Rachel stop moochin' 'elp Esther with Klara, yer can see she looks green."

"I'm comin', bu' I likes this skirt, keep it till I gets me wages."

"If it fits yer, yer can 'ave it – take it while I'm in a good mood, or I'll change me mind."

"Ah, yer a good sister, Dinah, the best of the best."

"Stop *smoozing*⁵⁰ – take the bleedin' skirt an' lets all 'ave a breath of air."

The Harris sisters had a sylishness about them as they strolled towards Dinah's small home for tea. Their backs straight, their black hair shining in the late afternoon haze – no timidity showed in their bearing. They were resolute in all their actions. No wonder Phoebe loved her daughters. The jostling crowds of the East-end, symbolic of poverty, did not menace the sisters. Isolated in their poorness they might be but a scrupulous caring about each other and the comfortable feeling each one of them had about a better future, took them with ease along the street. Baby Klara's angelic features already showed the same spirit of life.

---

50   Flattery

The Row

From her sitting-room window, Phoebe could see, passers-by, all the coming and going of carts on route to The Lane and anyone who was on a visit to 3, Cox Street.

Coming down the street with a face angry with itself, kicking up dust with agitated footsteps, encouraging no pleasant feelings, Solly's sister Kitty was nearing the front door.

Kitty had such a pretty name and a fine, shapely body with the worst of quarrelling natures!

Although Phoebe saw her she was in no hurry to answer the door and when Kitty knocked, calling-out at the same time,

"Yer at 'ome Phoebe?"

Phoebe with the slowness of someone about to be burdened with the caller least welcome, opened the door. She pretended to be surprised to see Kitty.

"Took yer long enough to answer the door!"

"'allo Kitty, come in. I was doin' me potato's for dinner. Don't 'ave many visitors this time of day. 'ow yer keepin' anyway?"

"I'm well enough but I ain't come to be sociable."

"Yer ain't?"

"No, I ain't "

"Wat yer come for then?"

"I 'ave com' Phoebe for the photographs."

"Wat photographs would they be then?"

"Don't give me that, yer knows well enough the photographs I mean."

"'ave yer by any chance come to Cox Street to 'ave a row, my instinct tells me yer 'ave."

"I ain't come on the purpose to 'ave a row, I 'ave come for the photographs bu' if it takes a row to lay me 'ands on 'em, then I'll 'ave a bleedin row won't I?"

"It beats me tha' a pretty gal like yerself 'as nothin' nicer to do on a pleasant day, than row. Now yer best calm down an' tell me wat photographs I 'ave that yer want so bad."

"Our Solly's weddin' photographs thats wat! Ma says Phoebe took the lot an' we Starrs ain't been give none."

"Well Kitty, that ain't my fault, do yer realise our Esther's carryin' 'er second an' yer come for photographs taken at the wedding!"

"Right, we've bin waitin'."

"Waitin' for wat? If yer wanted 'em, yer should 'ave ordered 'em like I did."

"Ma says yer took orders.

"Don't be daft 'ow could I take orders I ain't a photographer. I just abouts saved enough money to afford the few of our Esther's wedding. On the sideboard they are, an' I ain't any more."

"Well, Phoebe 'arris I don't believe yer."

"Are yer calling me a liar in me own sitting-room Kitty?"

"Yus I am. Not one of the 'arris brood would know 'ow to tell the truth if it were right under their noses."

"Yer a sour creature Kitty Starr, a sour, miserable gal who 'ates to see others 'appy. Sarah indulges yer too much. Wat yer needs is a man to sort yer bile out. Tho' mind yer I pity the poor sod as gets yer!"

"Leave me out of this, I've come 'round for wat is rightly ours nothin' more."

"Kitty my gal yer go 'ome an' tell yer ma, I ain't 'ad 'er photographs an' I'll tell yer wats more, if yer come to Cox Street again an' call me a liar an' into the bargain insult my good, 'ard workin' family, I'll throw yer out on the pavement on yer arse, gawd 'elp me I will."

"Lay one 'and on me an' I scream the 'ouse down an' take yer to court ."

"Leave orf the magistrate would take one look at yer face an' 'ave yer locked-up for frightening 'im."

"Oh yus, an' are yer such an oil-painting?"

"Nahh, I ain't bu' I knows me place I do. I respect others an' not go upsettin' 'em. I knows 'ow to show tenderness in an' 'ard life an' I won't 'ave the likes of yer pointing an accusin' finger at me or mine. I won't 'ave it I tells yer Kitty, an' yer best make yerself scarce. Wait my gal till I tell my Esther abou' this! The whole bleedin' family will 'ave a row with the lot of yer."

"All we ever hears is yer Esther. I'll 'ave yer remember my brother Solly wed yer Esther an' my brother Solly is the father of yer grandchildren."

"Leave me gal ou' of this, as for Solly I don't know wat she saw in 'im, never 'ave."

"She saw a good provider, that's wat. We Starrs know 'ow to make the shillings an' yer 'enry barely makes tuppence a week, an' that's a good week! We knows my dear all pawning yer weddin' ring an' sheets, don't yer worry Phoebe, we knows all right. Yer ought to be ashamed pawning sheets. It's a disgrace."

"'ow much longer do I 'ave to put up with this

Kitty, I 'ave just abou' 'ad enough an' I want yer out of the 'ouse. Yer a pain in the neck to all yer relatives. A viper's tongue – all yer do is cause rows. If it wasn't the photographs it would be somethin' else. Now yer know where me street-door is. Do me a favour – use it!"

"I ain't ever, in this life, comin' 'ere again Phoebe 'arris an' I intend to tell everyone yer thieved our photographs."

"Good, good, do tha', an' please gawd almighty, I never set eyes on yer again."

"Don't worry yer won't. I'll take bets all yer draws are stuffed up with pinched things!"

"Good day Kitty, don't break yer neck on the way out!"

Kitty muttered along the small hallway and with a bang that rattled the teacups shut the street door.

The unpleasant scene had worn poor Phoebe out. She sat in her chair staring at Kitty's back as her angry strides took her away from Cox Street.

When Sophie came in from school Phoebe asked her to make her a strong pot of tea.

"I've one of me headaches," was all she said.

As the family came home later-on from their work-places Sophie called out before a foot had barely touched the mat,

"Keep yer noise down ma's 'ead is bad."

"Tst, tst, what's up with my Phoebe then?" Henry soothed his wife and the couple sat quietly sipping tea. Sipping tea did not satisfy Rachel,

"Not like you ma, what's up then, come on out with it, what's turned yer quiet as a mouse?"

"She's a bad 'eadache, I told yer," piped Sophie.

"Am I askin' yer Sophie, shut-up."

"Now don't start for gawd's sake, I've 'ad

enough today."

"Enough of wat ma, wats upset yer?" Becky asked with concern for her mother who was frail at the best of times. If they loved anyone in the world it was their mother. If she hurt, they hurt .

"Someone bin 'ere today 'cause best cups are on the drainin' board, wat 'appened ma, 'oo was it came?" Rachel had that determined look and Phoebe smiled at her gals an' joked,

"Well it were't the bailiffs, 'cause our best china is still 'ere an' if yer must know I'll tell yer then I'll 'ave some peace, Kitty Starr came 'round."

"Kitty Starr, that face-ache, wat she want with us?" Becky looked puzzled.

"She claims we 'ave the photographs of Esther's weddin' that belong to 'er family an' we nicked 'em. Called us all thieves and liars an' I don't know wat an' we 'ad a right row an' I showed 'er the door. There, satisfied, nows yer know!"

"Rachel, put yer coat on. You an' me goin' out."

"Where yer goin, it's dinner-time!"

"Keep it 'ot ma, Rachel an' me will settle this once an' for all."

"Don't go upsettin' our Esther, she is due any minute."

Henry too was upset.

"*Rosh Hashanah* is any day an' the family rowin' is terrible. We 'ave to sit with 'em in *schul* an' it will be a right tight-lipped lot for sure."

"Can't be 'elped pa. Can't 'ave ma upset an' then 'avin' one of 'er turns an' we can't 'ave Kitty mouthing we are thieving their stuff all over Whitechapel."

"Sit quiet with ma, we won't be long, bu' its about time the Starr family 'ad a shake-up."

By the time Becky and Rachel arrived at old

Solomon's dwelling they had worked themselves into a fury – all the way there it was,

"Call ma a thief, call us liars, come to Cox Street an' make ma ill. Esther's to blame, standin' under the *chuppah* with that Solly. Ma's always bin right abou' tha' lot with their dogs an' money, think they're bleedin' royalty.

Sarah Starr in actual fact was a lovely lady who spoiled her huge family with love, food and every manner of pleasant, pleasing comfort she could shower upon them.

Sarah did not go out very much. She was small, far too fat and her home was her sanctuary from an outside that told her to lose weight and to stop spoiling her children.

"'oo shall I spoil then?" she would ask, "An' I'm old and old ladies are usually fat."

Old Solomon led her a dance with his commanding way and the dogs. The dogs came before Sarah, at least Sarah claimed so. Sarah welcomed Rachel and Becky with warm smiles,

"'ow nice a *yom tov* visit where's yer ma and pa?"

"This ain't a *yom tov* visit Sarah an' ma an' pa ain't 'ere."

"'as somethin' bad 'appened? Is it bad news yer bring us?"

"It ain't bad news, it's Kitty we 'ave come to 'ave a word with. Is she 'ome?"

The moment they asked for Kitty Sarah knew it meant trouble – she kept smiling.

"I'll tell 'er to come, she is 'elping me mix a cake for the 'oliday."

"That's more than she did for our ma – all ma 'ad from 'er is a bad 'ead!"

"Kitty 'as bin to Cox Street. She never said a

word."

"I bet she didn't," both girls almost said it together.

"Kitty, Kitty wash the flour 'orf yer 'ands. We 'ave company."

Kitty turned slightly pale in front of Becky and Rachel, but she asked in her usual bossy voice, which was copied from old Solomon,

"Wha' you two doin' 'ere then?"

"Now Kitty the likes of yer can tell Rachel an' meself what yer said to our ma this afternoon an' if yer not quick abou' it, I'll swipe yer one across yer miserable face."

"Are yer goin' to let 'er talk to me like that ma?"

"Well why did yer go to Cox Street. Yer didn't tell me. Why 'ave yer upset Phoebe?"

Kitty didn't say a word. She sat down by the window and stared like a sphinx with a sullen look at the street.

"Ma says yer sent 'er for Esther's weddin' photographs. Ma says Kitty claimed we pinched all yours an' she called all our family liars an' thieves."

"I must sit down. My 'eart beats quick when everyone rows. I 'ate rows."

"'ow do yer think our ma liked it then, when Kitty set on 'er. Ma is frail an' she was alone."

"Kitty is a menace when 'er mood is bad - I don't know what came over 'er - Kitty 'ave yer got yer period? She is always bad with it - always, every month a scene. I don't know 'ow I stand it - please gawd she will be married soon."

"Some chance."

"Shut up Becky, we didn't come 'ere to talk abou' Kitty's marriage or 'er periods. We came Sarah to tell yer daughter if she don't say sorry to our ma there will be trouble."

"Listen, we all 'ave a nice cuppa tea, a piece of cake, a chat, it's a storm over nothin', nothin' I tell yer. Sit awhile, sit an' talk, it's almost *yom tov*. Photographs, photographs, 'oo cares it's a nonsense."

Kitty silent, Becky and Rachel upset but too fond of Sarah to shout anymore glared at Kitty with contempt and refused any tea.

"Ta Sarah, ma's keepin' our dinner warm. We won't 'ave any tea. Keep your Kitty away from Cox Street an' we'll all be much 'appier. Good evenin' Sarah."

Sarah took them to the door,

"Ah, your nice gals, photographs I can see my Solly anytime withou' photographs."

Nevertheless as the women in their best clothes and ever tight shoes stood in their groups in the gallery looking down at their men praying during the evening *Rosh Hashanah* prayers the Starrs looked daggers at the Harrises and the Harrises showed eyes of fury to every Starr they spied. Suddenly Esther sat down with a deep, low moan,

"Ma," she called, "Ma."

"Gawd 'elp us Esther's goin' into labour. Becky 'elp me out of 'ere with 'er, before she faints!"

The women huddled round Esther. All with a worried look. The men glanced upwards, but did not leave their prayers. The journey to Esther's place was impossible and the midwife was called to Cox Street. Little Phoebe was born there on *yom tov* in the midst of a row.

A few days passed and a knock at the door found Kitty walking away – she had left flowers and a sovereign. Phoebe sighed,

"Families what can yer do with relatives," as she took the gift to Esther.

Myersavitch Bros. - Cabinet Makers

Above the workshop in bold lettering the sign stood out,

Myersavitch Bros, Cabinet Makers

Reuben and Shepsul stood back to the curbside to look at the sign.

"We may not be master tailors Reuben. I look at it like this, a cabinet is a good, solid piece of craft. It is noble. We have to earn. I say our hands are finer than machines. Machines are for women!"

"Don't let Peshe hear you say that!"

"Tell me who wants to make button-holes all day? Yes, our decision was right. To use the trade we learnt at home. Papa always said, 'bread sometimes grows by a miracle, but don't count on it,' remember?"

"I remember every detail about papa. If he disliked somebody, which wasn't often, he would say 'that man doesn't think he schemes' mama added, 'and he's a *spieler*[51].' Papa would reply 'of course he is – the family is lost, lost I tell you!'"

"Shespul why are we talking about our parents as if they're dead?"

"It feels like a dream we ever knew them. So many years, what is one to say?"

"We say, raise a glass of schnapps to Myersavitch Brothers, kiss our wives and pray for customers. Come my brother open the workshop up."

---

51   Gambler

Shepsul opened the creaking workshop-door with a huge key,

"Such a key Reuben look!"

"Never mind the key open the door wider I can't move."

Inside against the wall a high pile of wooden planks in various sizes and shapes. On a long workbench all the work tools for cabinet making were neatly laid out. Mallets, saws, a couple of vices rather rusty from damp and all the glues and polishes. Rented to them from Abe Silverberg, who failed in the business, and generously left the working rabbis two aprons, clean and ironed by Mrs. Silverberg, also pencils, planes, sandpaper and squares. With a good luck message.

On seeing the pile of planks Reuben looked at his brother with a surprised and comical face,

"Now that is what I call a large pile of wood."

Its the finest quality, Silverberg said, he only bought the best, and made the best. Come to think of it, funny he went bust."

"Shepsul where did you learn that expression – bust?"

"It's American."

"See here is our order book. Date, name of customer, goods required, delivery date, cost – very good, business like. Maybe by *Chanukah* the Lord willing, we'll have *Chanukah gelt*."

"Ah! Reuben, you'll be a *takif* yet!"

"Never with nine children and soon another."

Shepsul always became quiet when children were mentioned. His beloved Dosha suffered such longing for motherhood. He shared her pain and felt helpless. Reuben hugged his brother saying only,

"*Oy vey*, what a pile of planks. I wonder what our first customer will order?"

"We'll soon find out. A family needs this and that. The orange box days have nearly gone. Dosha wants a footstool."

"A footstall? Interesting!"

"What did papa teach you to craft, Reuben?"

"I made a long, brown broom handle for mama's yard-broom and signed my name at the tip. What did you make?"

"I carved a piece of wood and polished it till it shone. Papa asked me pulling his beard, 'Shepsul what is that?' I remember saying, 'papa can't you tell, it's a perfectly crafted piece of wood.' 'My sons the cabinet makers will be rabbis, thank God' was all he said."

"Did you make anything else?"

"No, I lost interest."

"Why did cabinet-making seem an excellent idea round the kitchen table?"

"Because you have nine children to feed and a thin purse."

"That reminds me, Rifka wants me to buy a few cloves for a *yom tov* pudding. Also sweets for the *cheder*[52]-boys *schul* party. *Oy vey*! What a pile of planks."

"Reuben I'm taking a cheder-class the boys will be waiting outside the door, you never know some *goyyim* may start with them so I'll hurry there. Stay here, a customer may come."

"It smells damp in here. With so much wood a kerosene stove would be dangerous. Never mind the work will warm us up."

"Reuben put your apron on, it looks professional."

"Don't nag me, I must become used to the workshop. I can't make a cabinet by noon today."

"True but if you stand staring at the wood-pile

52   Hebrew School

and don't move about you'll be stiff as a poker by noon. Sweep-up, Silverberg left too many wood-shavings. I'm going, I'll see you at evening prayers, maybe sooner."

"Wasn't there a story about a long piece of wood that held a *dybbuk*[53] in the grain for a thousand years?"

"No, Reuben there is an old tale about a Rabbi, a pile of planks and a floor of wood-shavings."

"Maybe I should have become a *badchan*[54]. Rifka and Peshe laugh at my jokes."

"Reuben, sweep-up!"

"Reuben? Am I seeing this, what are you doing with a broom?"

"Rifka, what are you doing here? You'll tire yourself. Are you alone? Rifka you walked here alone! What are you carrying?"

"No, I flew here. Besides carrying our baby I've brought you a *nash*. When you stop walking round me in circles like a *meshuggene*[55] maybe you'll tell me, why the broom?"

"Wood-shavings, I'm sweeping them up, they could blow into people's eyes."

"Already, what's been made?"

"Nothing, it's from Silverberg."

"So why didn't Silverberg sweep up? A rabbi should sweep-up it's unheard of."

"Shepsul said it would look better."

"Shepsul said? Where is he?"

"At the *cheder*."

"All the children are in school, is he teaching a wall?"

"Rifka, sit down. Questions, questions. This is a business, I need to do things."

"You need your head examined – a Rabbi

---

53   Spirit
54   jester   55   mad

doesn't make cabinets, a rabbi doesn't sweep-up, a rabbi ..."

"No, a rabbi starves, his wife wears rags, his children grow thin – Rifka I must work at some other work as well as my mission for Zion. The community barely keeps itself alive let alone us."

"We are not paupers. I manage. Peshe and Dosha cope. Our children are well thank-God. This is all for nothing. Its damp in here. Sniff-up. You will both catch colds. The children will catch colds. All of us ill, why? Because papa and uncle Shepsul have the sense of chickens."

"Wait till I bring home *gelt* and you buy a goose – then we'll see my Rifka laughing and maybe, just maybe keeping her mouth shut!"

"Reuben eat your food."

"I need to wash my hands – I eat at home."

"I brought a bottle of water, hold out your hands, there, now eat."

"All this way my wife carries water. She then calls me a *meshuggene.*"

"Reuben, good day, Rifka, Rifka I have not seen you for I don't know how long, thank-God you are well. Reuben I heard on the grapevine about your workshop. So I said to myself, I must go and wish Reuben and Shepsul *mazzol tov.* My it's nice in here but damp, air, the place needs airing, no Rifka?"

"Yenta, good morning. Thank you, we all need *mazzol.* Nice of you to come. What can I do for you?"

"Well it's like this, I was thinking to myself, Reuben and his brother Shepsul make cabinets which is wonderful. A good living is always wonderful, no Rifka? I should know my husband may his soul rest, never earned more than pennies, believe me, pennies,. Anyway the other cabinet-maker I know is at the end of nowhere. Miles from here. I can never find it as I have no sense of direction. But as luck would have it, this streets I knew already."

"Very lucky for us, so, the order. Wait I'll find my order book."

"My Sprintza is to be confined about the same tine as you Rifka, amazing, so I want to order a cradle. The finest you make!"

"A cradle, the finest we make. Yenta the sign above the workshop, have you read it?"

"Nahh, Reuben, I can't read English."

"Well it says we make cabinets, would you like maybe a cabinet with rockers?"

"You are both so clever of course you can make a cradle."

"Yenta, how about a solid drawer. Our babies sleep soundly in a drawer with warm covers. Cradles are for the rich we live simple lives."

"I should put my *eynikl*[56], my prince in a drawer!"

"You know already it's a grandson?"

"Of course, a *bube*[57] knows."

"How about a broomstick with his name carved by hand in out best wood?"

"Reuben Myersavitch, I want a cradle!"

"Rifka, Yenta wants a cradle."

"Good, then when you've made Yenta's cradle, I want a carved table, ours is old, with six chairs, also a bed for the children, a set of stools and I'll take an order from Peshe later on."

"Yenta, don't listen to my wife she likes to joke. When Shepsul comes in the morning he'll take your order."

"Good, good. I could talk all day, but I am busy – so busy I can't tell you."

"Yenta, don't lose your way, thank you for your

56   Grandchild   57   Grandmother

custom."

"It was a pleasure. Don't forget air, it needs air. Goodbye Rifka."

"Goodbye Yenta."

"What did you think is funny Rifka?"

"It's more than funny. The children will laugh for years. When papa and uncle Shepsul became cabinet-makers, have you heard the story? They'll ask everyone. Come on Reuben, my husband the woodworker up with those tools – a cradle has to be made for a prince!"

"Rifka what are you doing here?"

"All day long I am asked, 'Rifka what are you doing here?' I am beginning to feel I'm not wanted. Anyway what is with you Dosha, what are you doing here?"

"Rifkala don't be upset, but you are heavy now, it is unwise. I have brought *nash* for the cabinet-makers. Where is Shepsul?"

"He'll be back soon. He has a cheder class."

"Funny, he didn't say a word this morning. I would have put the books out."

"I'm not surprised he didn't remember the *cheder-kinder*[58] till he saw the planks."

"What does Shepsul, may goodness always shine on is head, know about wood? It's damp in here, you'll catch colds. Both crazy. Rabbis cabinet-makers. Shepsul cannot cut bread, so all of a sudden, a miracle, he can make a cabinet.

"Papa, I want to saw wood also, I'll make a boat, won't I Cissy?"

"Abe you should be in school, Cissy why no school?"

"They stayed with me last night, this morning Abe's head felt hot and his throat is sore so Cissy

58   School children

stayed with him."

"Reuben has so many children he doesn't know when two spend the night with their aunt."

"Abe, open your mouth, wide, say 'ah'. Wider I can't see. No red throat. No warm head! Rifka at home give Abe a salt gargle."

"Papa it'll will be better by then."

"Papa thinks it's better already – none of my sons wants to study. Abe you are five years old. School tomorrow, do you understand? You too Cissy, no nonsense – school."

"Yes papa."

"Papa, before then I'll saw wood with you."

"Abe don't touch the planks if they fall on us splinters will hurt us. That is all I'm short of this morning – a pile of falling wood God forbid!"

"Good morning everyone, what a gathering – an opening party."

"Ida, good morning, wonderful to see you, we don't see enough of our 'silver-lady' how's the family?"

"Monty hasn't been too good, but I can't grumble. I help in the shop a couple of days a week now, Monty's feeling middle-age strain!"

"Ida, what can I do for you? It can't be a cabinets. Your home is a picture, just perfect, no need for more, Rifka and I should be so lucky, eh Rifka?"

"Reuben, quiet, let Ida catch her breath. Ida darling friend, sit down, find a place, have a slice of something. Dosha and I both brought *nash*."

"No thanks Rifka, I've eaten, I need a favour. I went to the house and Peshe told me you were here; by the way Reuben, may you have *mazzol* for the work – it's a pity rabbis need a business, there, what can one do – life is a struggle. The ends just about meet for all of us!"

"Yes, Ida a pity, but the favour, how can we help?"

"Reuben, Rifka, I have a small boy."

"Don't ask me to take him on Ida, the workshop has just opened."

"No ,No, I'm not a fool. I need to find a home for this child."

"Ida, we have a house full of children. From top to bottom, every room. You should know already how much we need a small boy."

"It's a sad story."

"Tell us a Jewish story that isn't sad."

"Reuben, these days not many come for my help. Those I speak to tell of troubles in Europe, bad troubles. Have you are heard of the 'Warsaw cafe'?"

"A little. It is for anarchists, no, I keep away from such places. They spell disaster."

"Gossips call them anarchists, trouble-makers – you name it. In truth they are frightened men in a strange land and everyone to them is the secret-police because that's all they've ever known! Anyway they end up fighting, then it's arrest, custody, prison. The boy's father's in prison, locked-up for years, perhaps, and yesterday, his mother died in hospital of lung disease. There is not a soul for the boy. I work all hours and ... "

"Bring him to me Ida, no more story, just bring him."

"Dosha you are all good."

"No, just childless, he is welcome to stay with us. Rifka has enough to cope with. Peshe works all day, does he know Yiddish?"

"Yes and Russian, not a word of English."

"Don't worry, he'll be all right, we only have two words of English between us – what's his name?"

"I should have said, Yo'sef, you won't regret it Dosha, he's a clean, sweet boy, missing his mama. Now there is war talk – the Jews may be trapped – who knows what will happen!"

"Ida, this is a pleasant occasion, no more sad talk. War, war, who said, mere talk – *shtetl* talk. All-day they sip lemon-tea and frightened the life out of each other. This is England, when an Englishman says it, I'll believe it."

"Yes, Reuben you are right. I become an idiot with all the sorrow I listened to."

"Reuben good day and *mazzol tov* to you and Shepsul. Rifka how are you? Now you live in Victoria Park Road, I miss you – Dosha you look pale it would be better maybe if you moved – your name I don't remember, no matter, who can remember names? Reuben I want you should make a door!"

"Bube Kosminski, good morning. We don't hear you these days."

"Yes, yes Rifka I scream, I shout, I weep bitter tears. That daughter-in-law is killing me. Not slowly you understand quickly Oy! So quickly, you should only know – she is evil, I tell everybody, a witch, but all they say bube sit quietly, sit, sit – don't call me bube I shout, I am not old. Only the vicious woman I live with turned me white – so I think, Reuben the reb who now makes cabinets with Shepsul, good, good, a rabbi grows shabby, now a cabinet-maker I can look up to no – be proud Rifka, proud – please God protect me from my daughter-in-law a door, a door is what I need. To shut her out! A vision it was Reuben, a vision floating towards me, a door – paint it blue, blue keeps off the evil-eye, believe me it's a fact. My son will pay you, sometime, don't ask when. Money I don't have. They give me food and aggravation. Oy! I can't tell you."

"Bube Kosminski, Shepsul is the one who makes doors. Come in the morning, he will take your kind order, sit a while with us, catch your breath."

"Sit down he says. Come in the morning."

"It's a ten-minute walk, it's nothing."

"Nothing, *oy vey*! Nothing he says. It almost killed me."

"Alright, I'll write the order in my book, don't fret."

"Good, and Reuben don't use damp wood – it's damp in here, Rifka smell, damp, no – may you all prosper and be only well. A blue door Reuben, don't forget. Now my door will protect me from that women – my son would have been better off with a *shiksah*[59]– God forbid. Goodbye to you."

"Is she mad, papa? "

"Nahh, Cissy, just old and poor – tomorrow she'll forget all about her blue door while she cooks cabbage and raisins."

"Papa, will I be mad when I'm an old man?"

"Abe, apple-face, if you go to school like a rabbi's son should, you will never be mad, you will be a good kind man."

"Good, mama tomorrow I go to school to become rich."

"I'm glad, then you can keep us Abe don't forget."

"No mama I won't forget. I'll buy you a carpet."

"What a morning, the community come one-by-one – it's like the ark already."

"Papa, that's two-by-two."

"Give them time Cissy they'll bring the whole family and their cats!"

"Its an outing for them, they have few places to visit."

---

59   Non-Jewess

"At last Shepsul, you've arrived, do I know this gentleman?"

"Reuben, I've brought Mr. Mendoza to meet you."

"Ah! A Sephardi! We do not meet many Sephardi, they never come near us, eh Rifka? My wife Rifka, my sister-in-law Dosha, our dear friend Ida and for good measure a couple of our children. Cissy and Abe – at home we have a house full, but bring them out two at a time – it saves on shoe-leather."

"Take no notice Mr. Mendoza my husband is a clown today, it's near *Purim*. Our children are at school."

"Pleased to meet yer all. Nahh yer right an all about my community. They don't trust outsiders much, keep a safe distance they do – bu' never mind eh, it will come right in the wash, as we say."

"Good, I'm glad to hear you say that. We Jews need each other, what can I do for you Mr. Mendoza? To place an order today is too late already. Soon my brother and I go to evening prayers. We must lock-up and see our family home."

"Nahh! It's no order, it's like this ain't it – I buy wood for my business – I'm in the trade meself ain't I. Used to do a bit of the French-polishing bu' me lungs almost packed-up, on my life. I tell yer it's a bleedin' punishment that work, devil's work an' no mistake, nahh, I've come to buy yer planks."

"You've come to buy the planks?"

"Yus. From what I see 'ere. I'll make yer a fair offer of five sovereigns the load."

"Five sovereigns the load?"

"Papa take it!"

"Abe hush, no nonsense!"

"Shepsul kindly explain what this is about?"

"I didn't take cheder, I went to Whitechapel. I ask this one and that one I meet tell me please is there a wood-buyer near here? I met Mr. Mendoza at his workshop and we strike a deal."

"You strike a deal?"

"Everything my brother repeats. It's a Rebs habit. Take no notice."

"Reuben its late, we are tired. Abe is restless. Rifka needs a glass of tea. Accept the gentleman's offer."

"Mr. Mendoza after careful consideration I have decided to take your most generous offer for the planks."

"Shake on it. Five sovereigns I said, five sovereigns I give. Anytime yer want to sell wood remember me name, Bernie Mendoza, the best in the land buys me cabinets – I collect at 8.30 tomorra please God."

"Sammy our helper will come and pack for you – he's half blind but he'll pick-up the planks and take them outside."

"See yer then, good night all."

The brothers gazed at the money and suddenly danced round the workshop singing '*Purim gelt, Purim gelt*', Abe skipping behind and the women clapping.

Mr. Mendoza collected the planks on the dot of eight thirty. Sammy walked into the walls. Shepsul paid Mr. Silverberg his rent and wood money. Outside the workshop a notice read,

This Business Is Now Closed

Reuben and Shepsul sat round the kitchen table talking.

"What's so funny?"

"Funny, Reuben it's hilarious!"

"Did you ever see such a pile of planks. The

Jews of Chodorow would have built a synagogue and study hall."

"Shame, if we had come from Chodorow we'd still be in business!"

Purim is a Happy Time

"Good *yom tov.*

Family and friends we the *Purim* players are happy to present our *Purim* show for you. Please enjoy."

"Hallo, hallo. I am clown Svenk. You knew that already. Never mind, I've told you again. How did I make this funny face, with mama's borscht-beetroot. Koppel Ginsberg looks like this always. He saw a ghost, had a fright, and turned red – believe me – You thought I would say he turned white, ha! fooled you. I fooled old Chaim. It wasn't hard, anyone can fool old Chaim. Spin the *dreidl*[60] old Chaim and win a prize."

Old Chaim spun the *dreidl.*

"I've won, I've won, give me my surprise."

"The prize is – nothing!"

"Nothing!"

"Yes, that's the surprise!

"I bet you can't guess why old Chaim's wife isn't here this evening? Simple, old Chaim isn't married. Old Chaim's not here either, for one day he's had enough of my *chine*[61]."

"Who are you?"

"Me? I am the one and only clown Popov and I am going to bang your head with my wooden hammer. Take that and that and that ..."

"Ouch! Ouch! You are pushing me off the stage."

---

60   Game   61   Playful humour

"I, clown Ferfel-face will save clown Svenk – watch!"

"Oh! Clown Popov a beautiful lady is at the door waiting for a kiss."

"I, the one and only clown Popov will do her a favour and kiss her – when I return I'll bang both your heads."

"There, he's locked out, the beautiful lady at the door is Jim sweeping up. Popov will have a fit – ha, ha."

"My thanks to you clown Ferfel-Face – what can I do for you?"

"Tell me a good joke."

"I should tell you a joke."

"Sure, I want a good laugh."

"But you are called clown Ferfel-Face pincher of jokes."

"I won't pinch your joke."

"I know you won't clown Ferfel-Face. I'm not telling you one ha ha."

"Ha ha to you. Take that, bang bang, I won't save you again clown Svenk ... out with you."

"Ouch!"

"Out with you."

"Here comes Leah Kosminski to sing an old Yiddish song - sing Leah."

"Ah! Like a bird she sings, from here I notice a big tear on mama's cheek! Never mind Benjamin, our brilliant brother, (he can read Hebrew already) will cheer you up – Benjamin take the stage please!"

"Oy! vat a day!

My name is Ike Moses
And I keeps a tailor's shop
I live in de city of London

Mit my name upon the top –

De other day a man comes in
A suit of clothes to buy
I showed him a suit for 12/6
Try it on, says I –

He tried it on, it very well fit
And he goes to valk away –
I tapped him on the shoulder saying
The money he's gotta pay –

(Everybody clap and sing)

My name is Ike Moses ..."

Dancing the *kozotsky* as best they could, Yossel, Ezra and Aaron leapt about Benjamin's feet. As Yo'sef found a tune in a battered fiddle.

"Hallo, hallo I'm back. Ha! You can't be rid of clown Svenk. Don't make too much noise – clown Popov will throw water over me – a little rhyme in English ...

"Little Boy Blue come blow up your horn
The cow's in the meadow, the sheep's in the corn
Where is the little boy who looks after sheep?
He's under the haystack, eating *hammentatchen*[62]."

"For mama and all mamas an old yiddish proverb:

God could not be everywhere
So he made mamas."

---

62   Sweets

"Another joke to keep you smiling about Old Chaim. Old Chaim how old are you?"

"A year older than I was last year."

"So how old were you last year?"

"A year younger than I am this year!"

"Oy!

We hope you enjoyed the Purim players. Please throw your sweets – now!"

1914

Children used to a monotonous wait as their mothers drank inside the pub played hopscotch on the warm pavements, boys leaned against the beery smelling, urine stained pub walls, shouting rude names at the girls sitting on the curb-side, holding siblings.

Moonlight glints tipped the transparent wings of moths. The 'Three-penny Bit and Whistle' pub sign creaked.

"Gawd if I don't open them doors to fresh'n the air 'round 'ere I will melt, see if I don't. 'umid August nights are 'ot enough to grow bananas in the yard."

"Won't make no diff'rent Flo', just as well shut them doors, there ain't no air."

"If there ain't 'ow come yer breathin' Albert Kneebone, or do yer think our best ale is wot does yer breathin'?"

"I ain't daft, am I, I know me lungs do me breathin'."

"Thank-gawd, we set'led that' then, an' by the by Albert Kneebone talkin' of no diff'rent. It won't make no diff'rent to our pub sign. Since the great storm of June '12 that sign 'as creaked. Can Albert Kneebone oil the bleedin' sign, nahh, 'e's too lazy ain't 'e?"

"In me own time I'll fix it, won't I?"

"Yus, when the moon turns blue an' fish fly. Cor wha' with this 'eat an' Maisie, wha' a family, I don't knows 'ow I put up with it in truth I don't."

"Nice to see yer Ivy, same as usual gal?"

"Yus, if yer please Albert. I 'ates this weather me dress is stickin' to me skin. There's some likes the 'eat, bu' give us a good downpour, eh Flo'?"

"Righ' an all Ive, a good downpour be just the job. Albert Kneebone 'ere wants rain 'cause in the wet like 'e won't 'ave to fix the pub sign. All I 'ears day an' nigh' is tha' bleedin' sign creakin'!"

"'taint bad Flo' yer nerves is playing up, when me and Bill 'ears it creakin' Bill 'e says, 'soon 'ave me blessed pint ducks,' makes me laugh it do."

"Don't take much to make our Ivy laugh, anythin' creakin' I comes over all queer. Reminds me of Madam whats'er name an' 'er predictions. 'ave yer been lately Flo'?"

"Nahh Vi me angel, too much to do 'ere."

"Tha' *Joanna*[63] ain't 'alf quiet. When we gorna 'ave a tinkle?"

"Soon as Freddie's 'ere yer can sing yer 'eart out Vi."

"I likes yer singin' Vi, yer ought ta be in a church choir."

"Tha' a be the day I sings in church, mind yer I likes a nice choir meself, brings tears to me eyes."

"Best watch out Vi, when Freddie's 'ere. Yer might 'ave wha' yer least expected!"

"An' wha' might tha' be Ethel Backhurst?"

"If yer don't know I haint sayin', any rate yer might like it!"

"I might an' all."

"No Esther then Flo'?"

"Solly don't like 'er commin' 'ere nights."

"Why, too much temptation to fall orf the straight an narrow? Gawd anyone think we was gorna eat 'er."

63   Piano

"Well that Solly's a right guv'nor an' no mistake. My old man 'ave an earful if 'e kept me 'ome."

"'e's glad to be rid of yer if I'm a judge."

"Gawd 'elp the country if yer was a beak. Yer mob would be on the rounds before yer took yer wig orf."

"If I knows Esther Starr she can speak up for 'erself. 'er mouf is as big as 'er nose."

"Now then none of yer lip Ethel."

"Nahh offence meant Flo', just me lit'le joke."

"Nahh offence taken Ethel, bu' I noticed for the first time the size of yer feet an' yer ears stick out. Albert Kneebone go an' give our Maisie an 'and. The bar is crowded up."

"'allo Jessie, ow's our Jess this 'ot nigh'?"

"Bleeding' 'eat worse than Africa. Makes me real edgy it do. Thunder any minute – under the table I goes – storms don't do my nerves good – nothin' like a good glass of stout for yer nerves I says – nothin'."

"Albert Kneebone still haint picked one tile up from the yard. A pile of 'em fell orf the roof durin' last storm an' now dogs are doin' yer knows wha' all over 'em – stinkin' them tiles are an' does 'e care – nahh!"

"Your Albert's bet'er than some I knows Flo' 'e's a kind gent I likes 'im."

"'ow would yer know Jessie, yer ain't wed. After all it's Flo' 'as to put up with 'im."

"I knows things don' I."

"Oo! Jess knows things gals."

"Come on Jessie love, tell us wha' yer knows an' I will treat yer to a stout."

"I knows abou' them pocuwer women, don't I."

"'orrible cows them are Jessie, evil 'earts they

'ave. Mind out they don' catch yer unawares like."

"Nahh! I'm too old, twelve an' thirteen is wat brings in the money my ma says, so she do."

"'orrible, bleedin' 'orrible."

"'ere gals 'ave yers 'eard the lat'st, 'bout Maudie Brown?"

"Nahh, we ain't, 'urry up an' tell us."

"Well it was like this it were, I was standin' jawin' an' this 'ackney pulls up don't it, outside 'er ma's door. Out me lady muck comes, painted like yer ain't seen in yer life, with 'er fancy man. Yer could smell the scent in 'ackney marshes."

"That's not all yer can small on 'er, she always were a lairy minx – any odds wat goes into 'er don't go into us – do it."

"Nahh! All 'er family 'ave been on the game. Me gran says in 'er young days Maudie's gran kept a brothel."

"Against the law that."

"Were the law that used it most."

"Our Ivy is a right card tonight an' we ain't 'ad out sing-song yet. Give us a tune Ivy yer don't need no music."

"Come on gals, 'My old man said follow the van, don't dilly dally on the way eee -'"

"'ere's Freddie now, where yer bin Fred, yer look as if a blinkin' spook frightened the life out of yer."

"Flo' ain't yer 'eard the news?"

"What news yer talkin' abou'? We 'eard abou' Maudie Brown's new fancy man."

"Nahh, sod Maudie Brown, the country's at war."

"War! yer orf yer perch Freddie boy? 'ave a brandy."

"War I tells yer. We gorna fight the Kaiser."

"Well I never did, an' us boozin' and' singin' the nigh' away an' there a bleedin' war declared."

"They should 'ave shot the old git Kaiser when tha' other foreigner coped it."

A crescendo of laughter suddenly ended. Quietly the women drank the last few drops of the glasses.

"Best be orf Flo'."

"Nigh', nigh' Ivy."

"Me an' all Flo'. See yer tomorra eh?"

"Nigh', nigh' Jessie ducks, mind 'ow yer go."

"It's this 'eat upsetting everyone ain't it Flo'."

"Yus Vi, puts yer out of sorts don' it, nigh',nigh' me gal, best to ma an' pa."

"Ma,"

"Yus Maisie."

"Ma, it's a joke, ain't it?"

"Best ask the bleedin' Kaiser Maisie. Albert! Albert Kneebone."

"Pa's with the lads outside."

"Come on let's sniff a breather, it's like an oven in 'ere. Gawd Maisie look at tha' moon. Funny I ain't ever noticed 'ow beau'iful it is. Gerroff 'ome the lot of yers. No more hopin' an' scotchin', don't yer know there's a war on!"

II

Troops on leave, before departure for France, were light-hearted. Joking with their families and friends. They agreed the Kaiser would be sent running after one or two battles with the British Royal navy. The greatest navy in the world,

To enlist and wear the khaki, fight for king and country, no slackers and the devil take the Hun.

The Spanish ambassador said, "It was not

serious". Nobody, it seemed as the August sun shone on countryside and city, dare imagine the momentous crisis.

"'ow d'ya like pa's new suit Klara?"

"Pa's nice, likkle Klara want one."

"Nahh yer don' Dolly-face. Me likkle Klara will 'ave a new summer dress all covered with daisy-flow'rs, won' she ma?"

"She migh' if she be'aves 'erself. Torments Phoebe all day she do."

"My likkle Klara is always good, ain't yer me angel?"

"Yus, I ain't a ba' gal pa. Phoebe pulls me 'air an' 'urts likkle Klara. Bu' granny give me cherri's."

"Yus an' now tell pa 'ow yer 'ad the runs all day."

"Yer ma spoils 'er rot'en. So 'ow does me wife like me new outfit then?"

"I've seen better."

"Don't be like that Esther, it ain't tha' bad. Once I gets used to 'ow rough the cloth is on me legs, a tuck 'ere an' there an' a good pressin'. It will look like Manny Cohen made it. Come orn gal give Solly a big smile then, bein' gloomy brings the rain."

"None of us 'arris' 'ave smilin' faces an' I ain't the flag wavin' sort. Wha' with me 'usband gawd knows where in France an' two small ones to fend for I 'ardly feels like doin' a turn – I asks yer Sol, France, yer ain't bin tha' far in yer life."

"Well look at it this way, I'll 'ave an adventure won' I. An' I can jaw abou' it fer the rest of me life."

"Just mind who yer 'ave yer adventure with I knows abou' them French gals."

"Me 'ands will be too busy with me 'orses an' me 'eart is me Esther's, French gals indeed – wha' yer take me for?"

"It ain't yer 'ands an' yer 'eart I'm worried abou'!"

"Flo' will go green with envy when she finds out yer old mans in the cavalry."

"Don't fool yerself Solly, Flo ain't a dope, she knows all the Jewish boys are in the stables."

"Yus, that's true enough, give me the 'orses any day, best place to be. We'll win the war for 'em us boys. Yer ought ta see the riff-raff tha' enlist for a pair of boots."

"Yer can't blame 'em, poor sods ain't 'ad a square meal in their lives or lain on a mattress."

"Gawd wha' an up'eaval the nations 'as on their 'ands, bu' you're a prac'ical woman Esther nothin' will beat yer down. As yer pa says - 'The Lord our God is 'igh, bu' 'e looks low an' takes care of 'is own."

"Tha' sounds like pa, wha' I'd do without ma, pa an' me sisters I dread ta think."

"In me knap-sack I 'ave me photographs, a seedy cake from me ma, a tin of sweets from me sisters an' almond cake from yer ma, me bleedin' teeth will fall out before I gets orf the boat – an' a copy of David Copperfield from our Sophie."

"I'd like to see France."

"When I comes 'ome I'll takes yer."

"I'll believe it when it 'appens. Flo says it will be over by Christmas an' when they see Albert Kneebone 'oldin' a rifle the enemy will all die laughin'."

"If Albert Kneebone is kill'd Flo will be sorry an' 'ow for 'er treatment of tha' poor man. Yer never know Esther his majesty migh' give me a pension for bein' an 'ero."

"Yer a daft date Solly, bu' at least yer strong with good, muscular limbs. An' thank-Gawd, with marchin' an 'orses tha' will be an advantage, won't it?"

"I'll be alrigh', I gives yer me word – me beau'iful Phoebe is sound asleep, bless 'er. Don' yer let 'er forget 'er pa."

"Cors I won'."

"Klara, come an' give pa a big kiss."

"Pa, I wants to go with yer."

"Not this time Klara, bu' when I comes 'ome I'll take yer everywhere, won' I? It's time to be orf Esther."

"Are yer sailin' today?"

"Nahh, we'll end up in military camps all of us. Bu' the likes of us ain't told nothin'."

"Will yer be allowed to write?"

"Cors I will, the army ain't prison. Come on Esther Starr gives us a cuddle before I goes to war. I want to 'old yer close an' smell yer 'air. I loves yer Esther. I always 'ave an' I always will."

"Solly, gawd keep yer safe. Don' lose yer *Magen Dovid*[64] – I loves yer Sol."

"Well ain't that rich. I 'ave to go to bleedin' war to 'ear me wife say she loves me."

The women wept and cheered. The children waved paper flags – the men of London marched to war singing at the tops of their voices,

"God 'elp Kaiser Bill."

---

64   Star of David

Grey is a Slow Colour

Grey is a slow colour.

Slow as an ancient tortoise showing its shell after winter.

Shade loving grey of leaf, of early morning March skies. London's slow grey quietness of wartime amid much noise. The white-grey beating wings of pigeons. The blue-greyness of afternoon as the skies clear.

Little or no attention was given to the hearse holding the small, unadorned coffin of *bube* Kosminski. Slowly dragged along by a tired horse. The terrible daughter-in-law could upset her no more. Her cracking, old voice full of curses and aggravation towards her family, without protest faded into the greyness of death.

Circles of grey cigarette smoke around their dry lips, disabled soldiers rough with pain stared into nothing. Rifka missed the shuffle of feet, his music-hall whistle, as Cockney-Jim moved about the house.

"Soon as I gets 'ome I'll be rahnd. Lads, best be'ave or Jim will tan yer 'ides. Don' go messin' abou' in me cellar or else. An' say yer prayers good an' loud like, so as me an' me mates can 'ear 'em."

The sky-monster zeppelin dropped three bombs over the city and Thames on the morning of October 13th at 9.30 am. If Londoners felt terror they did not display it.

Suffering finds a capacity of depth, of staying power in people more durable than cheap zeppelin metal. One poor Jewish woman was killed; the only fatality. 'She came here to feel safe' was her brief epitaph.

At the beginning of the war Dosha and Shepsul with Yo'sef, came to live with everybody at Victoria Park Road. Rifka was so glad the family were together. The closeness was important to her.

The women lavished kindness, even if only with smiles. House-work, laundry, cooking, they coped.

The tensions war brings brought back memories to them of cruelty in their old villages to Jews. Rifka shouted at her children. Peshe went into a long silence. Dosha dusted with fury.

Usually by dinner-time humour returned.

Now Londoners were being bombed Reuben insisted the youngest children with their mother and aunts slept in the cellar. To the small ones with their few toys and three cats it was a game. Dosha took turns with Peshe of telling fairy-tales.

"Mama will Silky have her kittens soon?"

"Stop squeezing her, the kittens will choke."

"Cissy, don't tell them such things."

"Papa says kittens are in Silky's belly, is that true mama?"

"Oy! Papa, papa, tells his children too much."

"Ezra said a bomb will blow our roof off."

"That was to keep you quiet. It was a joke."

"Aaron said only heathens blow you up."

"Papa said *Gehenna*[65] is too good for them."

"Do you know what mama says? Mama says no more talk, go to sleep."

Cissy listened to the women and sitting on the cellar steps Samuel Yitzchok heard the fairy-tales

---

65   Hell

and remembered them from long ago. He brushed a cobweb away from the wall and joined the men upstairs.

"Koppel told me to take precautions, the eclipse is to blame, this was foretold by the stars."

"What doesn't Koppel blame on the sky I should like to know."

"Even a partial eclipse is something to believe in."

"No, it's bad. There are reasons for war. Not pleasing reasons. The world is a soiled place. Koppel is tiresome with his nonsense."

"He said there'd be mass hysteria."

"The only one having hysterics is Koppel."

"You're hard on him Peshe. He's harmless, a simple soul really."

"The man gets on my nerves."

"He's an outlaw like Rifka."

"So that's what you think of me!"

"It doesn't show, but I agree with Dosha, an outlaw is longing to jump out of your spirit and catch us unawares."

"With eleven children to look after you will both have a long wait before that happens."

"Did you know the majority of zeppelin raids are on Sundays?"

"I hadn't thought about it, horrible savages."

"Just before the war Chontche and Baruch made aliyah. I had hoped they would come here. Chonchte was my best friend."

"I remember Chontche, her plaits were the longest in the village. I wonder if she is happy."

"Baruch sounds like a good husband."

"Lets hope so. The land of Israel is austere and very hot."

"Here it's austere and cold."

"War isn't saffron and cloves, but we still have the samovar."

"It purrs like the cats."

"Don't mention cats, soon kittens will be everywhere. If I give one away the children will not forgive me."

"Nether will I. Silky's kittens will be lovely."

"We must be the only house without mice."

"The men have gone to midnight prayers I heard them shut the street-door."

"Reuben will go come what may!"

"We must sleep soon. I have a shop to open in the morning. I'll try and bring home some butter but it's hard to find any."

"Everything is going to need a ticket – rationing is fair after all – sugar, cheese, bread, tea, milk, meat, even candles and matches."

"We are used to making little go a long way – it will be over one day, thank God we live in a civilised country now."

"I hope the children don't catch colds down here."

"Rifka don't worry, they're tough only we ache in the morning."

"Any day Ida's daughter-in-law Leah is going to be confined, she was heartbroken when Eli enlisted."

"We'll pray for her. It's a sad time, but the baby will give such joy to Ida and Monty."

"Peshe say the *Shema*[66] and lets sleep. We've talked the night away."

"And the roof is still on."

Peshe softly sang the *Shema Yisroel* as the cats lay between the sleeping children.

---

66   Prayer – Hear O! Israel

1918

The corners of a city, where low life characters tread are not serene.

Many East-end *back-doubles*[67] give a sense of heavy fear, an atmosphere of dark mystery. Footsteps lingered, footsteps hurried away. Even in wartime these men of secret lives clung to the streets as if carved into the decay of old walls.

Towards Mile End, pavements widen. A thin faced crowd symbolic of war filtered with women munition, night-shift workers in shapeless factory clothes on their way home for breakfast, troops, stall-holders shouting whatever was available in days of rationing. A good-natured cockney crowd with tongue-in-cheek smiles.

A black suited man with slow undertaker paces went up and down the long pavement, with a doom-and-gloom placard hung from his shoulders proclaiming in huge black print,

THE END OF THE WORLD IS NIGH, REPENT SINNERS BEFORE IT IS TOO LATE, JESUS SAVES.

Marching tunes boomed out from a barrel-organ as a monkey dressed like a soldier held out his master's cap for the odd farthing. Laughter from the music-hall echo'd around the tree tops, for awhile the people left their anxieties behind.

Trying to make himself heard over the din a

67   Side street

comic shouted at the top of his voice,

"Mrs, give 'er a poke in 'er ribs she's in 'ere for a kip. Now if yers shut-up I'll tell a joke. A boy asks a cobbler,

'Do us a favour mister, stretch these boots for father.'

'Where do they pinch sonny?'

'Where was they pinched? Why from next door's lodger.'

Cobblers to yerself mate. Wha' dirty minds the lot of yer 'aves. Before I does me song an' dance, 'ere's a nice un I 'eard down the pub.

A soldier boy startin' for Solonica see, an' 'is old lady told 'er neighbour, 'cause the wives tell the neighbours everythin', don' say yer don' 'cause I knows yer do – well as I was sayin' she says, me 'ubby 'ad an inflated waistcoat.'

'Dear me' says 'er neighbour, 'I 'opes tha' don' mean an operation!'

"Wha' yer mean me jokes are lousy. No' 'alf as lousy as yerself, gor blimey I haint playin' this 'all no more, 'oo shouted good? I'll see yer later yer cheeky buggar – outside.

'ere a song for me poor Irish muvver, shut yer mouth up there, I 'ave an Irish muvver if yer likes it or no, an', me pa wears a kilt, wha' yer laugin' at if yer don' be'ave I'll play me bagpipes to teach yer a lesson, bein' rude abou' me ma an' pa, wha' a disgrace. Now remember them true 'earted 'eros at the front an' keep knittin' them socks an' scarves 'cause the winter is rawnd the corner an' we must do our bit to keep them lads warm; good luck an' god bless our boys, three cheers for our troops, the best in the whole-wide world."

Laughter and cheers helped ease the heartache of a bitter war.

On her way to Cox Street Esther stopped to buy bunches of violets and a single red carnation from the flower seller.

"Good luck dearie. Dip the 'eads in wa'er soon as yer gets in, them blooms will last a good while yet."

"Ta, for tellin' me. I wish I knew as much abou' flowers as yerself."

"Ah! We gypsy-folk 'ave all the secret knowledge. We knows everythin' for thousands of years."

"When will the war be over so me 'usband can come 'ome then?"

"Yer 'ave a kind face lady so give us another three penny piece an' I'll read yer palm and tell yer."

"Another three penny piece an' the War Office will tell me!"

"As yer like, dearie, as yer like."

A smiling Esther walked on, the fragrant violets lifting her spirits.

"Mummy's 'ome granny, le' me open the door. Ruthie broke grandpa's pipe, Phoebe ate a carrot an' I 'elped granny with breakfast."

"Yer mother needs to catch 'er breath Klara an' none of yer tales. Fill up the kettle like I showed yer, then 'elp me lay the table. Our toast will be stone cold. I can't be doin' with cold toast."

"Take these ma, our *Shavuot* posies. The but'on-'ole is for pa, 'e likes a nice red carnation."

"Ain't they grand, pretty as a picture. A fair bit gorn west on them Esther. We could 'ave shared a couple of bunches."

"We goes short enough. Put 'em in a dish of fresh wa'er till we needs 'em, smell ma' wine for yer soul."

"My parlour smells like I imagine 'eaven

smells."

"Nothin' like a posie of violets, goes well in 'eaven with kippers!"

"'ow was I to know yer was buyin' violets. Soon as pa an' the gals gets in they'll be done. Smell don' last long. Pa's gorn for 'is bath. Nice an' early this mornin', the children an' me 'ad ours. La'er on its 'ot an' crowded. Squeak-clean tha's us. Klara's a right madam, an' no mistake. First she asks for more wa'er, a bit of 'ot and a bit of cold, then if yer don' mind a white towel. I tells 'er the attendant will come any minute an' give yer a clip rawnd the ear-ole. So madam says, 'mummy lets me and Phoebe wash 'er back, can I wash yours granny please?'

'I ain't yer mother and yer can't.' Poor Phoebe can't get a word in edgeways with Klara."

"My Klara likes nice things, 'oo knows she might grow-up to 'ave a rich 'usband."

"Don' fool yerself Esther some rich 'usbands yer can do withou' their wives 'ate 'em."

"Wat would I do withou' yer ma, everyday yer should 'ave somethin' lovely. Gawd if I don' ever see another shell-case it won't be too soon. Fancy gettin' one straight through yer 'ead."

"Them war-mongers deserve all the bullets tha' strike 'em, causin' all this misery an' death. Yer two brovers an' yer 'usband in uniform please gawd almighty we see 'em 'ome again. After we eat, 'ave a nice sleep. Forgits abou' schul, yer needs yer rest. Nigh' work is a strain on workers."

"I'm alrigh' ma, don' worry. It ain't a long service. Yer gets used to nights. The war can't last forever. Wat 'ave me daugh'ers been up to?"

"Them picture faces, good as gold."

"Wat abou' grandpa's pipe granny?"

"Klara Starr, yer mouth is bigger than yer

feet!"

"Nahh it ain't granny."

"Yus it is, an' every time yer tells tales on yer sisters yer feet will turn green. And wats more if yer fib it will be writ large righ' across yer for'ead. So there my gal, tha's somethin' to think abou'"

"It ain't true is it mummy, granny is foolin' ain't she, Klara is a fibber ain't on my for'ead?"

"If granny said its true, then its true."

"Bu' Ruthie broke grandpa's pipe I seen 'er she threw it ou' the win'ow an' Phoebe eats everythin'."

"Ruthie is only lit'le ain't she, when you was a lit'le 'un yer was breakin' all me stuff minute yer 'ands were on it."

"I'm fed up with sisters they bothers me, Ruthie pulls me 'air an' Phoebe is stupid. I likes Sophie best. Phoebe can look after Ruthie."

"Klara, don' be saucy go an' wash yer 'ands an' take yer sisters, breakfast is ready. Gawd 'oo'd 'ave children. Was it a good pipe ma?"

"Nahh, an old clay thin' pa 'as loads of 'em abou' the place, an' with 'is cough 'e puffs too much baccy, bu' 'e ain't much comfort my 'enry with 'is feet an' all, I don' nag 'im abou' 'is pipe. They say rationin' is 'ere for years. No' an egg for love or money, black-market gets 'em. Wat a disgrace , them crooks needs a good 'iding. At least I buys bread withou' any trouble."

"Bread ain't no good ma, its bulk'd up with chalk an' tea's messed up with wood – ain't worth thinkin' abou' wat goes on with the rest of our food!"

"Bread-un-tea tha's all the poor lives on, no wonder babies are ill. Never righ' is it? Open the window Esther, kippers are smellin' us out – freshen the 'ouse up – we 'ave to eat wat the market 'as. I asks 'ow many kippers can I 'ave an' the fish monger 'e says,

'Mrs, 'as I stand 'ere an' yer standin' there, 'ave three.' I says,

'I 'ave a family to feed.'

'There's a war on Mrs, three kippers an' a sprat,' 'e says,

'Keep the sprat an' wrap them kippers before yer change yer mind.' Any odds it's a change from our cheese ration, a mouthful an' its gorn."

"Where's Sophie ma?"

"Gorn to Dinah's, we'll mee' at schul la'er. Nothin' fits 'er, she ain't 'arf tall. I 'opes Dinah gives 'er a dress for this 'ot weather."

"Dinah will fit 'er up with an outfit, an' Sophie will dress up to the nines with everythin' in the shop."

"She don't open much, there ain't the business, with bombs an' all people can't be fussin' with clothes, 'oo can blame 'em."

"Phoebe 'ave yer washed yer 'ands?"

"Yus, mummy look."

"Tha's my gal an' my dolly-face Ruthie show me yer 'ands an' give us a big kiss."

"Mummy can I call yer ma, like yer call granny?"

"Phoebe me an' yer aunts 'ave no manners bu' me daugh'ers will be proper ladies, so its 'mummy' me gal."

"Mummy 'as me for'ead go' words on it like Klara's?"

"Nahh, not yet at any rate, if yer fib tho' writ large, Phoebe Starr's a fibber, righ' across it."

"See Phoebe, I told yer, so there."

"Be quiet with yer questions, givin' me an 'eadache both of yer."

"Cor wat a pong it goes down Cox Street,

everyone's sniffin'-up."

"'allo Becky, ma bought three kippers we'll all 'ave a taste, where's Rachel an' pa?"

"Pa's jawin' to a coster 'e knows, Rachel 'as never bin on time in 'er life, bu' she likes it up there in your place. So do I. She wants me an' 'er to move to a couple rooms of our own till we find 'usbands. With the war I doubt any will be left for us."

"Pa'll 'ave a fit if yer mention movin' out. It'll upset 'im somethin' terrible."

"I know ma needs our money, bu' a load of gals are livin'-out now, sorta freedom come with the war. Funny ain't it."

"Don't be daft Becky. Most of 'em are in service slavin' for their bet'ers, some freedom, I don' think. Gals on their own ain't as alone as you thinks, at least every 'alf 'our they 'ave payin' company. Gals from good families wouldn't dream of takin' rooms."

"Esther, wat a way to think!"

"Yer won' go far wrong me sister, if yer listens to me, Rachel is always scatty, tomorro' she'll 'ave another idea."

"A chap at the factory is sellin' soldiers luminous watches for 15 bob each, pa wouldn't 'alf 'ave a treat with one."

"'ave yer 15 bob to spare? Sounds fishy to me."

"Nah, it ain't crooked. Army surplice stuff. Between us Rachel an' me could only spare 10 bob, bu' 'e wouldn't sell for less."

"Never mind, it's the thought tha' counts."

"I'm fed up with sayings."

"Klara me angel is fed-up with sisters, I'm fed up to me eyeballs with shell-cases, it must be tha' kind of mornin'."

"If I could spare the odd bob yer could 'ave it Becky, bu' the children an' ma takes all I earn. Old

Solomon always says we 'aves lit'le or nothin' to begins with bu' we ends up with a lot."

"Gawd another sayin'. 'e 'as a lot for sure, pity 'e don' give 'is daugh'er-in-law some, them Starrs are stingy."

"My Solly ain't, bu' old Solomon is tight, Sarah squeezes a few pence ou' of 'im for shoppin', then takes the rest ou' 'is pocket."

"If my husband turns out mean, I'll leave the sod."

"Nahh yer won', yer'll pinch from 'is pocket."

"'oo's 'avin' kippers then?"

"Flo' Kneebone, wha' yer doin' down our way?"

"Yer fron'-door was op'n so I took the liberty of walkin' in."

"Becky left it op'n for pa."

"I pass'd 'im as I came in, jawin' nine-to-the dozen."

"Ma, look 'oo's come to visit."

"Well I never, Flo', down Cox Street, 'ow are yer? Sit yerself down an' 'ave a cuppa."

"Mornin' Phoebe, I ain't lost me way. I was right fed-up with the stink of beer. Me arms is achin' from 'eavy shiftin' of goods when they is available like."

"'ere's another one fed-up. Yer come to the right 'ouse Flo', we're all fed-up 'ere, except ma, an' she's a saint."

"My Alf did all the 'eavy stuff, didn't 'e, true, I nagged 'im till 'e got rawnd to it, Maisie's at the munitions or moonin' over some soldier-boy she 'as a fancy for, so I'm on me own. Strong men is at the front, or on sick-leave, the poor lot tha' come in the pub for work ain't an arm or a leg between 'em. I gives 'em ale on the 'ouse an' me till is near em'ty. Wot yer tryin' to work for, I ask 'em. Ask the bleedin'

War Office for pensions they sen' yer ou' there to ge' all maim'd for life."

"Well it's their pride ain't it?"

"Yus, right proud they are, so Flo', I says to meself, Flo' old gal, take yerself for a stroll to Phoebe's place, the 'Three Penny Bit and Whistle' will be 'ere when yer gets back."

"Take the weigh' orf yer feet, it's a pleasure to see yer, 'ows yer ma these days?"

"Don' ask Phoebe, she gets on me nerves. 'er legs is bad see an 'urt 'er awful, 'go to the 'ospital ma', I says, 'yer won' be scared with me.' I ain't a doctor what do I know abou' 'er legs.

'I'd be obliged Flo' if yer don' talk abou' 'ospitals', she says! Worse than Maisie me ma, 'er corns need do'n' an' she sits an' moans at me starin' at nothin'."

"Are 'er feet green?"

"Cors they ain't Klara."

"Granny says if yer tell tales yer feet turns green."

"In tha' case ducks me ma's feet is green as grass."

"'enry! Kipp'rs ready this 'alf 'our an' me 'usband jawin' away."

"Mornin' Flo nice to see yer."

"Mornin' 'enry nothin' like a sunny mornin' eh?"

"Grandpa, Ruthie broke yer pipe, an' now me feets turn green, so there."

"My Cora go' green feet, Well fancy tha'."

"Flo', wan' a taste of kipp'r on a slice-a-bread?"

"Nahh, Phoebe, ta just the same, enjoy yer food, its 'ard enough to come by. Wat a war, 'enry no' a whiff of peace. I sees 'em readin' the lists of missin' an' dead an' I feels sick in me insides. I told our

Maisie, no 'arm will come to yer father, 'es such a tiddler the bleedin' 'un won' see 'im. Ent it a life?"

"It is tha' Flo, think when peace do come an' yer gets yer pearlies out, wha' a knees-up yer all 'ave."

"I 'opes they fit me. Some'ow af'er this war our lives won' be the same."

"The day'll be a long time comin' tha' us cockneys forgits our knees-up, I lay bets with yer Flo', momen' armistice comes, please gawd, knees-up Muvver Browns'll be 'eard from 'ere to Bow."

"Listen to me 'enry layin' bets, 'e ain't a sixpence from 'is pocket to 'is 'and. Best be careful with thin 'airy bones, gets stuck in yer throat else, Klara, Phoebe, eat slowly, its mash'd up nice for yer, Esther, Ruthie 'as bread an' milk in 'er bowl. 'ave yer tasted tha' margarine stuff Flo', its 'orrible."

"'orrible ain't the word, Maisie won' touch it. Poison tastes bet'er."

"Tha' grease 'as pu' us 'orf but'er for life."

"We won' 'alf be thirsty all day af'er fish."

"Don' grumble 'enry, wa'ers in the tap. Yer ain't eaten enough to make yer thirsty. If Rachel don' turn up soon 'er portion goes to poor Gertie. Tha' cat 'as no tit-bits these days. Mice is all she gets."

"'er nine lives will keep 'er goin' ma. Them streets is runin' alive. Rachel 'as no sense of time, yer sees 'er when she feels like it."

"Ma Kneebone is just the same, waitin' for 'er an' Maisie is bad for me nerves. I 'ate goin' anywhere with 'em."

"Granny."

"Wat me angel."

"Can I 'ave a cup-of-tea?"

"Best ask yer muver."

"Nahh Klara drink yer milk, tea ain't no good

for children, 'ow many times do I 'ave to tell yer."

"Can I 'ave a sip of yours auntie Becky?"

"Cors yer can, be careful its 'ot."

"Gor on, Becky ruin me children. They'll be playin' rummy next."

"Leave 'em alone, they're only young once."

"Wait me gal, till yer 'ave yer own an' I ruins 'em."

"Spoil'n me nieces is an aunts priv'lege, ain't it."

"Phoebe wats all yer finery 'angin' up for, goin' to a weddin' are yer?"

"Our festival of *Shevuot*, ain't it, we're orf to schul la'er."

"Amazin' 'ow many festivals you Jews 'ave, always dressin' up, we only 'as Easter and Christmas, the odd weddin' an' funerals. Mind yer I do enjoys a nice weddin' an' a gloomy funeral with a good breakfast. An' I likes me Christmas."

"Fancy comin' to schul then Flo?"

"Nahh don' be daft, best to keep to wat yer knows, 'sides its all double-Dutch to me."

"Its all double-Dutch to us an' all."

"Years ago my Alber' watch'd one of yer weddin's an' real upset he was, when 'e sees them break a glass, wat a waste of a good glass, 'e says. My Alber' can't bear waste."

"In a few months we go to schul again to remember the destruction of our temple."

"Wat for, ain't that thousands of years ago?"

"Yus, we never forgets, never."

"Daft if yer asks me all them years gorn."

"You pray to Jesus an' 'es bin gorn a thousand years or more ain't 'e?"

"Yus, but that's different ain't it, 'im bein' the one true god like."

"Flo' 'as yer know righ' well, tha' ain't our belief, we keeps our laws."

"Before the both of yers gits 'ot under the collar, I'll make a fresh po'-a-tea."

"None for me Esther, I must be goin', ta for yer 'ospitali'y Phoebe, I 'opes to see yer an' 'enry down the pub. 'alf me reg'lars are dead and gorn. Never will fam'lies be as they was, never, an' wat for I asks yer. Enjoy yer outin'. 'ere are Klara, share it with yer sisters."

"I'll see yer out Flo', ta for yer company."

"My pleasure, Esther, Madam Battia 'avin' a meetin' Thursday 8 O'clock me back parlour as usual. If yer likes I'll ask if she 'as any messages for yer, a florin a go."

"If its all the same Flo', I ain't a liken for a seance."

"Our Dinah's bound to turn up she'll 'ave enough messages for everyone."

"Such a shame yer ain't go' a fondness for the spirits, Madam Battia is the best I can tell yer, makes all the 'airs on the back of me neck stand up. Vibrations she said, The 'Threepenny Bit and Whistle' 'ad vibrations. Wat yer think of that? An' auma'ic writin' comes ou' the air."

"Takes all sorts Flo'. Mind the step, see yer soon dear."

"Esther can I borrow yer blue 'at. Goes nice with me dress."

"Yus, bu' no' too many 'at pins, its delicate."

"Flo give me a bob, mummy, look."

"Tha's very nice of 'er indeed, work it ou' 'ow much yer sister's share is."

"Its too 'ard."

"I though' yer were good at yer figures, well yer can 'ave four pence each, ain't yer lucky today."

"Cor tha's a load of money."

"'ow yer goin' to spend it?"

"Well – a penny for me money box, a penny for Grandpa so's 'e can take granny to see Charlie."

"'ow kind my Cora is, growin' up a lovely gran'-daugh'er, she knows the value of 'er money. Charlie will be a nice treat."

"Klara you still have tuppence left over."

"I ain't partin' with it. I likes it in me pocket."

"Yer migh' lose it."

"Money is a worry ain't it mummy."

"It's a bother, pu' it in yer box an' save it."

"I'll thin' abou' it. I migh' buy a book."

"Alrigh' darlin' 'ave a think, wat abou' my Phoebe 'ow yer goin' to spend yer fortune?"

"A penny for yer shoppin' mummy and a penny for a ball."

"Don' yer break winders with it."

"Are yer goin' to save yer tuppence."

"Nahh I like spendin' tuppence."

"Mummy keeps Ruthie's till we goes shoppin', eh Ruthie?"

"Yus mummy keep Ruthie's four pence."

"Good gal."

"Auntie's 'ome granny."

"Sorry I'm late ma, met Sadie Jacobs an' we wanted to 'ave a look at some remnants 'er ma 'ad. A nice piece enough for yer winter dress ma."

"I won' bother this winter I'll makes do with me old 'un."

"I'll buy it for yer ma yer needs a dress an' Dinah will stitch it up won't cost yer nothin'."

"Nahh 'taint worth it Rachel, pa needs boots more important than me dress, don' 'e?"

"Shame to let someone else 'ave it. I'll buy it just the same an' decide then oo'll 'ave a dress."

"Now sit down an' eat."

"I ain't 'ungry ma, I 'ad a sandwich with Sadie, I didn't like to say no. I think I'll 'ave a kip I'm dead tired."

"I ain't keepin' food warn for you no more Rachel, late is yer second name."

"I said I was sorry, bu' I can't eat if I ain't 'ungry."

"I'll wash-up ma, 'ave a rest yer never sit down."

"Soak 'em Esther, else the cutlery will smell fishy – pa's dozed orf I think I 'ave a doze me self."

"Gor on ma, I'll wake yer in time to get ready."

"Ta doll, it ain't 'alf bin a long mornin'."

A few hours later the family left Cox Street to walk to the *Shevuot* service. Phoebe holding Henry's arm. Esther with Ruthie, the daughter Solly was yet to see, Becky holding Klara's hand and Rachel holding Phoebe's hand. The children in white muslin with blue bows of ribbon for their hair. Each with a posy of violets carefully pinned on their frocks. Becky all in blue wearing Esther's blue hat, Rachel in a soft lilac silk to match her violets, Phoebe in her black silk and Henry his suit without a crease to be seen, his button-hole red carnation bright as the sunshine. Phoebe smiled with pride.

Passing a building with a sign reading '*Mission to the Jews*' looking straight ahead, the family turned into a side street away from the crowds and entered the synagogue, their house of prayer.

Armistice

"*Sholem Aleichem*[68] Shepsul Myersavitch."

"*Aleichem Sholem* are you new to London? The service is over."

"Don't you recognise me? Of course you know me, we age, today I feel already seventy. I knew Shepsul, the curls a little grey, no matter the boy is still in your face."

"I thought I knew you, I'm not sure, if you've come to live with our community, welcome."

"I'm Shlomo Zisman, your sister Peshe was best friends with my sister Chaya."

"Zisman, from our *shtetl*. Shlomo Zisman, I can't believe it, my bother Reuben fought with your brother Shmuel more than once. Am I right?"

"More than right."

"A friend from our past. What are you doing here, why so long in coming to see us?"

"Such a story for the rest of my life, God willing, free soup I will eat to tell my story."

"So tell."

"I came to visit my family."

"You have family in London?"

"Nah, Scotland."

"Scotland!"

"My sister-in-law's cousin."

"Your sister-in-law's cousin."

"On the other side of the family, true. A relation is a relation is a relation. I had an address. Such a

68   Peace be upon you

journey, it should only happen to my enemies. What do I know of politics. The Tzars politics, I know, mean trouble, English politics I have no knowledge. Before I look around this Scotland war comes, they lock me up. I can't leave, a bad dream is better."

"They lock you up in Scotland?"

"They lock me up. A man says a speech, I can't understand a word, so a Yiddish speaker they get, music could not sound sweeter."

"Then what happened?"

"Then I wait, when you are locked up you wait. They gave me brown bread thick as four fingers with a mug of tea. My sister-in-laws cousin's cousin comes. I hear shouting,

'A harmless man and you lock him up. He's my wife's cousin. The Yiddish speaker tells the Scotsman what he said,

"Prove it."

"I should prove it. I should prove he's not a German. We know such things. We don't need proof about a cousin. Does he look like a German?'

A headache I have from the shouting, indigestion from the bread. Then all of a sudden the cell's unlocked, I am a free man. My relative takes me to his place. He tells me war is no joke. They lock up aliens. How lucky he was not to have his family in a cell. Between you and me Shepsul he's claustrophobic, a cell would kill him. He puts me to work in his small factory. All day I pack rubbish. Who buys this stuff I wonder. God-forbid I offend my sister-in-law's cousin. His temper roars like a lion and before him I choose the lion. I didn't like him or his wife. They put up with me because after all where can they send me?

Shepsul, what a funny thing, here they lock Jews up to keep them in a country, it's the other way round in our history, they unlock us and throw us out! Thinking aloud I say, this is a good island country, I think I'll stay.

'Drink your lemon tea' his wife calls, this means I should shut up, because I talk too much. I like to talk. To be silent all day I may as well die already. Every time she is fed up the lemon tea comes. I ask myself, where does she buy so many lemons in Scotland!"

"When you find out tell me my Dosha can't find any."

"To continue with my story, I make up my mind to go to London. Packing rubbish I can do anywhere. I'm grateful for their help, but to be treated like a *nishtikeit*[69] is bad for the health. So I leave. You have a family Shepsul?"

"We foster Yo'sef. He's a fine musician please God he will make *aliyah*."

"To love another's child means in heaven your praise is sung by angels."

"Why aren't you wearing a coat?"

"My kaftan was good as new. The boots were strong. With such boots you start walking out on a revolution, before its too late. I'm standing on a London street not ten minutes, before I took another step a villain threw me to the ground, grabbed my kaftan and ran, animals are better. Another one pulled off my boots. I shuffle in old shoes."

"Oy vey! Don't worry I'm pretty sure a weasel's shop is the place to redeem your clothes."

"The weasel's shop?"

"Pawnbrokers. You're a lucky man, ruffians carry chloroform bottles to knock their victims out. Rarely do they end up in the river, but it has happened."

"Oy!"

---

69   A nobody

"Come Shlomo, there are worse problems. Dosha will wonder where I am. Do you have enough money?"

"Yes, yes, my brother-in-law's cousin paid all he owed me. After *Simchat Torah* his wife's mood changed. She smiled when I was leaving. I suppose with relief."

"Where did the thieves accost you?"

"I'm not too sure of street names. Could be a Commercial Road."

"There are dozens of East-end pawnshops. We'll take a tram, ask a few questions."

"Nah, Shepsul, don't bother. Your time is precious. A modern coat is better, like yours I will get. Nobody here wears a kaftan."

"The old ways are slowly leaving us."

"May all my trouble go with the clothes. Rifka and Reuben do they have a family?"

"They are *gebentsht mit kinder*[70], a half tribe of them. Thank god all the family keeps well. My brother is hobbling about, only Reuben can sprain his ankle whilst *davenen*[71]. Is your wife with you?"

"My Sprintza, *olav ha sholem*[72], died in childbirth. Our daughter was still born. It was *beshert*[73]. I ask the engraver to carve a beautiful fruit-tree in blossom with two white doves flying from its branches to heaven, on their tombstone."

"Childbirth is a killer for many lovely brides. One day you may marry again. It will be different."

"Maybe."

"We're almost at the house. The women are together. In such times its wiser. After this war men will emerge either civilised or savages. Liberty is always near the dungeon. Let's hope the world won't be too uncomfortable. Our duty after all is to life."

"Indeed."

70	Blessed with children	71	Praying
72	Rest In peace	73	Fate

"We could walk across the park, its quicker, but lately a few Jews have been attacked, why take the risk. Victoria Park road is 'round the other side."

"Fine oaks Shepsul."

"London has wonderful trees. I remember your father is a wood merchant."

"Was, *tateh* is no longer with us."

"He was a kind man your father."

"He loved the forests. He understood trees."

"I'm surprised these haven't been used for fuel. Coal is difficult to find. In '16 the shortage caused a crisis. We burned anything. Stop and catch your breath, here's Reuben's house. I'll call through the letter-box. Where is everyone? Open the door its freezing outside. Isaac, is the family asleep? You need a week to open a street-door?"

"*Sha*[74] uncle!"

"What do you mean *sha*? Is this how you greet your uncle, sha, because now you're taller than me?"

"*Sha*, Silky's having kittens, the young ones are excited."

"Come on Shlomo, anyone would think Silky's never had kittens before. The whole community has one from her litters."

"Mama one is all black like Silky."

"I can't see mama."

"I want to keep it."

"Auntie Dosha wants it for a friend, ah Silky is cleaning it."

"*Sha* the poor cat needs quiet let her warm them by the fire. Shepsul where did you come from? I didn't hear a knock, my children are very noisy."

"No matter Rifka, I'm in now with Shlomo, he's just arrived from Scotland where's Reuben?"

"Mama, Cissy promised me a black and white kitten for my own if I cleaned my boots."

74   Shhh

"She promised me first."

"I'll promise you a *potch*[75] each if I hear any more talk about kittens – is this a way to greet a guest to your home? Rifka where did you say Reuben was?"

"I didn't say. Good evening Shlomo a new face is always welcome, go warm yourself in the front room, my husband is there with our *Shammos*[76]."

"Uncle Shepsul I bet you didn't know about king Saul."

"No I bet I didn't, tell me."

"The bones of king Saul and his three sons were burned under a Tamarisk tree."

"How do you know?"

"I know, I know."

"You are clever enough to write your papa's *droshes*[77] for him, he needs a rest."

"Sure."

"Such a brain can only belong to a genius, don't you agree Shlomo?"

"Beyond doubt."

"Does papa know his son Yunkel is a genius?"

"Papa says a big head holds a brain the size of a pea."

"What do you think?"

"Papa's always right. Benjamin can write the *droshes* I'm busy."

"Reuben, Yunkel is a clown."

"All my sons are clowns, it's a living. Sit both of you. Join us with a small glass of schnapps."

"Shlomo's just travelled down from Scotland."

"*Sholem*."

"*Sholem*, our *shammos*, Mr. Zilberstein."

"Sholem."

"Scotland, a few years ago we were there. Terrible poverty, worse than London. Twenty families

---

75   Slap   76   Beadle
77   Sermons

made *aliyah* with the help from our mission, and the Mizrahi."

"*L'chei-m*[78], gentlemen."

"*L'chei-m.*"

"I spent a few months working for my brother-in-law's cousin. Now his factory is given over to war work, night and day. The community don't complain but the language for them is difficult."

"Slowly a foreign tongue comes at our age. For children its as natural as walking, they teach us. How many words do you need to get by? If you want to write a book then learn a few more. Our work for *Eretz* Israel is more difficult."

"I'm a simple man Reuben. I see no visions in the clouds above or signs on the earth below. I want to survive this war, please God, without ruin overpowering me."

"Visions, signs, who is talking of such nonsense. Our mission is to help Jews return to their own land; our land. Strangers have sat beneath our olive trees, drunk from our vines for so long, they forget it is the land of Israel where they live. Shlomo, you are sleep walking."

"Leaving us, Zilberstein? Its early still."

"I don't like the family being alone too long. The bombs have left my wife nervous. I'll think over out talk and discuss it next week."

"No hurry take your time. I'll see you out."

"I'll see myself out. You will come to our schul, Shlomo?"

"Sure, I was there already and after years met Shepsul again."

"I'm pleased to hear it. Good evening."

"Zilberstein is a serious man. Once you know him he lightens up. He's courteous, old fashioned even."

---

78   Good health

"Reuben, when did you last wrestle with Shmuel?"

"Shmuel? Who's he? I wrestle with my sons, they wear me out. A Shmuel I don't need."

"My brother needs a *shvitz bod*[79] to clear his head. If we sat here ten years he still wouldn't recognise Shlomo Zisman, mind you I can't talk because I didn't at first."

"Zisman, the wood merchant, I remember had two sons and many daughters, you are his son?"

"I am his younger son, Shmuel is my brother, your sister was my sister Chaya's friend."

"Why didn't you tell me. Rifka says I am hopeless at knowing faces, my wife, she forgets no-one."

"Your wife didn't know me, but the kittens were more interesting."

"Is Shmuel here?"

"He's a freedom-fighter. I told him dead in a ditch is the thanks for your politics, he shrugged the shoulder, that's my brother – stubborn."

"Israel needs such men. A pity he fights with Bolsheviks. He's past the age to be radical. But they add spice to lives of drudgery with their last pitchfork, peasants sing as they march, if food they don't have, feed them on hope. Shmuel should know better."

"You can keep communists, I doubt in this world I shall see my brother again. Chaya has four children thank god a good husband, a chemist in Warsaw."

"What about your wife?"

"I'm a widower since many years."

"Too bad, you must marry again a man should not live alone."

"Papa diner's ready."

"Ah, Shlomo my son Benjamin."

---

79   Steam bath

"One by one I am meeting your sons."

"To meet my nephews together your head would spin."

"Nah, I love children."

"Join us for a meal. We're lucky to be able to grow a few vegetables in a tiny plot in the back garden. Dosha brings soup to the table – with rationing this helps."

"There is nearly always something for the poor."

"I'm glad you said nearly, if you meet a rich rabbi show him to me I must see him to believe."

"Our stomachs may grumble, not our tongues, a family saying."

"Before the women start shouting the food is cold, lets go eat."

"Can you manage papa?"

"I'm not an invalid, a sprain is not much, Shlomo, I'll show you where to wash your hands. Benjamin tell mama we're coming."

"What's your trade Shlomo?"

"Glass blowing, I've all the burn scars to prove it."

"The glass blowing craft is clever. War work is all they want. We're trying to learn about jewellery."

"You are trying Reuben, I watch you trying. For one day we were cabinet makers."

"A day?"

"Believe me that day was a year, Dosha still laughs about it."

"*Tahkeh*[80]."

Wrapped into her teats, Silky's new litter slept.

The children jostle for the family place with each other and their cousins, their meal taken with their mother and aunts.

The men still talking sit down to eat. Samuel

---

80   Is that so

Itzchok shook hands with Shlomo, Reuben sang a blessing and broke bread, Peshe served the borsht.

By morning the corrosive, vicious fighting, the war of anguish would end. The guns silent. The cruel death folly of war cease and armistice declared to a brave nation.

Eat Well, Light Wine, Smoke in Moderation

Flower-beds were massed with daffodils and tulips in the parks.

Along Regents canal's steep banks, birds dived for insects and minnows.

Swans sat on their nests amid the comfort of brown rushes. Pussy willow tufts were showing on the Thames willows.

Spring in a London at peace after war.

By her parlour window Phoebe sat with Gertie curled-up in Henry's chair beside her.

Only the wagons driving to and fro and cries if market traders were noisy.

An open letter lay on her white apron. She read it many times and stroked the lined paper with her finger as if touching the sender.

Sam would be coming home. Before the outbreak of war he'd married Julie Sachs from New York. He enlisted and didn't see his wife or daughter in four years now at last they were coming home. Tucked inside the letter a single curl of Pearly's hair, 'Look ma our Pearly has gold-white silk for hair.'

Alfie would return from France. Her dear little Alfie 'as big as me thumb'. Sam and Alfie alive from hell., "A' ave[81]".

"Gert I reck'n me boys is nothin' bu' skin-'n-bone, an wha' with rationin' they ain't gonna pu'

---

81   Praise the Lord

much on. Still, we'll cope won' we Gert. Now keep them claws away from Pearly. No scra'ches or out yer goes. Sam an' pa ain't tha' rich. I won'er 'ow Julie will take to Lon'on. Not tha' I can imagine mind yer, not likin' our city. Grand ain't it Gert?

Fatigue seemed to engulf Phoebe. Not for a second would she tell Henry or her daughters how headaches tormented her and her fingers and back ached.

She pulled her sleeves over the wrinkles showing on arms too thin, she knew her face was pale and strained.

"I won'ers Gert 'ow rich women copes with aches un pains. Spoilt rotten tha' lot Gert. Ain't as much as pu' their 'ands in cold wa'er. Wa'ed on 'and un foot by servants, Gert. Do yer know them poor servants sleeps in freezin' attics with 'ardly a rug to cover 'em an' it's more than they dare do to complain, 'cause see they needs their wages. Life ain't fair Gert, an' tha's the sad truth.

Remember Gertie when me gals treated me to a day up west, well we joined the crowds watchin' a march-past of American soldiers goin' orf to the front, didn't we. The troops was reviewed by their majesties. The miserable king wished them 'God's speed' why, 'e could 'ave give 'em a thank-yer fur comin' across the ocean to fight along our boys, but no' a smile from their majesties! Yer think a smile would crack their faces. Anyway it were a day out an' the Queens dress were nice. Them Americans are good people Gert an' as they marched orf with the band playin' loud and clear, a big cheer went up from the crowd. I 'ad a lump in me throat big as a plum."

"Gertie me darlin' cat I'll tell yer a secret, poor Phoebe is growin' old. Yus I am, don' argue with me. Me baby days are long gorn. Babies are jus' like

kittens Gert, 'elpless. Don' know how they scream fit
to 'ave the roof orf when they needs a feed – when
our Esther were born, 'enry though' she were grand,
was proud as a peacock my 'enry was. Now all of a
sudden our Sophie's so tall, me neck aches lookin' up
at 'er. I best no' talk abou' me lov'd ones 'cause an'
evil spirit may pu' bad luck on 'em. You 'ave yer shut-
eye me old duck, whilst I goes an sweeps-up the
straw. I wish the wind would stop blowin' it under
our front door 'bout time them 'orses wore slippers
then noise wouldn't be a bother to no one. It's been
my pleasure talkin' to yer Gert, now I'll change me
apron an' do tea for me gals."

"Does a Mrs Phoebe 'arris live 'ere?"

"Yus, wha' yer want 'oo is it? I'm changin' me
apron, I'll be down in a tick. Sorry to keep yer waitin',
gawd 'elp me, me Alfie's 'ome! No a word to say yer
was comin', where d'ya come from?"

"None of us knew when we'd be orf the ship.
Wha' yer cryin' for, I'm in one piece, dry yer eyes an'
sit down me darlin' I'll pu' me kit in a corner, 'ave a
wash an' brush-up then we'll 'ave a nice tea-po'
between us an' before yer knows, ma, yer eyes will
be brigh' as sunshine an' it will be like I never was
away. Better to arrive with no fuss – I didn't wan' yer
all shook-up waiting' at the door. No more tears now,
yer eyes'a be red."

"On the second shelf I 'ave a seedy cake. Ain't
much in 'cause of rationin'."

"Seedy-cake, now I knows I'm 'ome."

"Seein' me Alfie standin' in the 'allway was
like a piece of 'eaven fallin' in me soup. Why when
yer brother's 'ere it'll be like old times in Cox Street."

"'ow's me pa an' sisters?"

"Thank gawd they're well, pa's feet are bad as
ever, bu' otherwise 'e is in good 'ealth, I asks no more

than tha'. Sam is bringin' 'is family 'ome. On pa's chair there is a le'er from 'im all the way from New York. 'ave a read, whilst I do tea. Pearly, tha's 'is daughter's name. I'm all shaky with joy – welome 'ome son, gawd bless yer."

"I'm righ' grateful for me life ma, many a time I felt me number were up. Cox Street were a sight for me eyes I can tell yer."

"Our Esther 'ad Ruthie. She's lovely red 'air like Sophie an' little Pearly's 'air is real blonde. Solly ain't seen Ruthie yet – Esther must 'ave fallen for 'er just before 'e enlisted. Now if yer don' mind she wants a son. Ain't yer enough to cope with I asks 'er. She says a family needs a son."

"Sounds like Esther."

"Wa' if yer 'ave a daughter I asks 'er. 'I'll keep tryin' till I 'as me son.' Seeing as I 'ave two sons meself I didn't say no more. Esther will make do no matter wah', poor pa an' me lived through terrible 'ard times, bu' I managed to cook me family a nourshin' 'ot dinner every day. Rachel an' Becky 'ave been on war-work, tired-out they are. No doubt it will be 'usbands next for the both of 'em. A nice girl Alfie for yerself please-god, when yer cleared yer mind of these years."

"Nahh ma, don' bank on it. A wife ain't up-me-street. Work an' travel on the high-seas that's me lot from now on."

"Yer change yer mind son, bad times fade, an' a bit of sunshine comes out. Remember Esther's pal Flo?"

"Yus."

"Outside 'er pub buntins is blowin' an' tables an' benches is ou' for a street par'y. Such a knees-up we'll 'ave even yer pa will 'ave a jog. I dare say yer no' up to a par'y son."

"I dare say I'm not ma."

"'ome is best place for a rest Alfie, nothin' like yer own street-door. We 'ad real luck, no bombs fell on Cox Street, some 'ouses 'ad the front right orf."

"War is man's curse."

"Them Germans tryin' to kill us. 'orrible bad lot they are."

"I wan' to surprise pa. So when I see 'im comin' I'll nip upstairs!

"'is face will be a picture, when 'e sees 'is boy 'ome. Ten minutes pa will be 'ere, life is tedious for 'im. It'll be good to see 'im 'appy for a change. Do yer know Alfie, the councils are buildin' 'ouses for 'omeless troops, ain't tha' amazin'."

"Amazin' ain't the word ma. It sounds like a bloody miracle. Must be an election comin' up. 'ow many chaps will 'ave one?"

"Well it's a start, ain't it. Yer never know one day us poor may 'ave a nice new 'ouse."

"Ma, when their army boots wears-ou' I doubt they'll 'ave boots let alone an 'ouse. Sellin' matches in the stree'-corners, thats wha', 'oo cares abou' old soldiers un sailors I ask yer. They'll pawn their medals for an eel-pie an' be forgot soon as the buntins comes down."

"We must 'ope for the best, look forward, eh Alfie boy?"

"Yus ma, yer 'ave always seen the best in everythin'."

"Nah, I jus' 'ad to put-up with it like everyone round 'ere. Nip upstairs pa's 'ere."

"I 'ope I don't kip."

"Don't mat'er if yer do, pa ain't goin' no place. Come down when yer feels like supper."

❁

The 'Threepenny Bit-and-Whistle' had a festive air with buntings and the union flag blowing in the breeze. Flo' Kneebone had with Masie's help polished the horse brasses till their reflections shone back at them. Each glass twinkled, the woodwork polished and the tiles outside scrubbed clean of grime.

"Yus Maisie we Kneebone knows 'ow to pu' on a show for our reg'lars."

"A bit chilly for a street do, ma."

"Now don' put a damper on it – a drink an' a knees-up tha' a warm 'em up, 'sides if it do rain we'll come into the pub, won' we? Pa will be the last soldier 'ome, never been early in 'is life."

"Perhaps 'e's been taken prisoner and locked up in a cell in chains an' rats is eatin' 'im alive an' them Germans won't let 'im out till 'e tells 'em all 'e knows about war secrets an' spies."

"'oo yer been takin' to Maisie? Don't make me laugh. Pa with war secrets, why I wouldn't trust Alf Kneebone with a dish of cockles, 'ed drop the lot. Carry-on like tha' an' yer write a book – your 'ead is full of old bull."

"I don' know why yer married pa, yer never 'ave a kind word fer 'im, an' 'im a soldier fightin' fer us."

"'taint fer yer to know my business keep yer thoughts to yerself. If yer please."

"Well 'es me pa an' I'm proud of 'im see."

"An' 'es me bleedin' 'usband an' ye're a saucy cow. Bring-up two jars of onions sharpish."

"I 'ate goin' down there ma, puts the wind up me."

"Too bad, 'bout time yer grew our tha'

nonsense. We spent enough nights down there, when bombs were droppin'."

"I 'ated it."

"It kept us safe me gal an' there ain't nothin' creepy abou' our cellar, yer 'ave to expect a rat now an' again."

"Ma!"

"Well serves yer right, I 'ope a big black one runs up yer leg."

"Yer wicked ma, always windin' me up. Nan says so an' all."

"Maisie in ten minutes I'm openin'-up, bring them onions or I'll lock yer down there so 'elp me."

"If I dies of plague it'll be yer fault. Comes from rats it do."

"Them rats were smother'd with fleas, our rats are clean."

"Pull the other one, ma. Nan been took bad, all cold and shivery."

"Gorn down with a cold 'as she? Always the same, a right drama-queen she is. Soon as I 'ave somethin' on, ma takes to 'er bed. She'll 'ave to wait for an 'ot toddy, cause I'm givin' a street-do no mat'er wha'."

"Coughin' fit to burst nan is."

"La'er on go an' sit with 'er. Stay over if yer like. I'll pop 'round in the mornin'. Ada Jenks comin' to give us a tune, poor Freddie ain't comin' 'ome. Such a nice boy, Freddie was, played the piano lovely. 'ow 'is family must be grievin'- breaks yer heart it do."

"Them pies smell good ma, fancy all tha' food.

"I 'ad to put me thinkin' cap on, everyone gave me somethin'. A party ain't nothin' without a bite to eat. Maisie I don' want yer going' down with a cold, put warmer clothes on. If Ada turns up whilst I fix me cameo, give 'er a pale ale."

"'allo, I'm Rosie Tilley, Ada sent me over. She's gorn down with a cold, all stuffed-up she is, so if its alrigh' I'll play a few tunes fer yer."

"Come in Rosie, nice to meet yer."

"And you I'm sure."

"Ma will be down soon. Shame abou' Ada, me nan 'as a touch of chill, doin' the rounds ain't it? Pale ale alrigh' then?"

"Ta, very nice of yer."

"Ain't Rosie a pretty name, I'm plain Maisie."

"Nothin' wrong with Maisie, we don' 'ave much say in wha' our ma's call us."

"Ma, this is Rosie Tilley, come to give us a tune she 'as, 'cause Ada's took bad."

"Evenin' Rosie thanks fer helpin' ou'. I 'ope Ada's well quick."

"It's only a cold she'll be fine."

"Me ma's gorn down an' all."

"Maisie was sayin'."

"Now yer sit down Rosie, I'll give yer a potato pie with a lump of cheese la'er, with a pickled onion thrown in."

"I will enjoy tha'. Poor Ada loves a bit of cheese, 'ard to come by ain't it?"

"Yus bu' things will improve."

"I 'ope yer righ' Mrs Kneebone."

"Now call me Flo' an' gives us a tune to welcome me friends – nice an' loud so as we can hear the ivories outside."

Rosie began a medley of music-hall favourites as the regulars arrived.

"Evenin' Flo' an' Maisie, wha' yer doin' 'ere Rosie, this ain't yer neck of the woods?"

"Evenin' Ethel, bein' nosey as usual?"

"Nahh, I ain't, bu' the Tilley's a church family,

ain't they?"

"'ow do I know, Rosie ain't been in before."

"Me folks don' drink – I'm fond of me glass, ma says I'm wicked, am bound to roast in 'ell, a gal 'as to brigh'en up 'er life don' she?"

"Cors she do, now Ethel takes yer tipple outside an' we'll eat la'er."

"Ivy was comin' up Whitechapel, poor Bill is slowin' 'er."

"'allo Violet, darlin', 'ows me Vi?"

"'allo one-un-all, I'm nicely ta, lookin' forward all week to yer party Flo', Vera Chapman's comin' thought yer like to know."

"Gawd I ain't seen sigh' nor sound of Vera since our bust-up. Is it forgive and forget time then?"

"Give over Flo', ain't like yerself to 'old a grudge, Vera's a bit rough, bu' she 'as a good side."

"Which side is tha' back or front? To be truthful I 'ardly remember why we fell out, Vera an' me don' see eye-to-eye, she puts me nerves on edge an' she's a right tea-leaf."

"We can't like everyone, make the best of it eh?"

"For me Vi's sake I'll be all sweet un nice to 'er if she turns up."

"Yer sound like a toffee-apple ma."

"Maisie 'as to 'ave a say, why ain't yer serving Mollie, no wonder she looks fed-up."

"Sorry Moll, wha' yer have?"

"Not to worry Maisie, a cream stout'a be lovely."

"I 'ope yer drawers are pressed Vi, else the knees-up will show yer up terrible."

"Wha' a tease ye're Ethel."

"Ethel won' change will yer Ethel, are yer own drawers fit to be seen?"

"Well yer'll 'ave to wait for an eyeful Flo'."

"Drink up ladies do yerselves a power of good, our best beer."

"'allo one un all, 'oo look at all them pies, been in the go all day Flo', done yerself proud I'd say."

"Evenin' Jess, dolled yerself up in finery."

"Must look me best for a do, don' 'ave much call to wear me best, last time was our Doris's weddin' before the war."

"Well, very smart yer look Vi, an' yer suit a nice blue, don' she?"

"Yes Jess, a bloke will catch yer yet, best watch out."

"Stop jawing gals, take a pie, cheese board an' pickled onions on the side – come on Vi, yer dreamin. Pick yer plate up."

"'allo everyone me an 'enry 'ave come to join the party."

"Pleasure to see yer Phoebe, evenin' 'enry, Maisie a pint of our best for 'enry, what's yours Phoebe?"

"A stout'a do me Flo', Esther's stayin' in with the gals. Ruthie 'as the toothache. Righ' miserable Ruthie, she is, bless 'er!"

"I don' know, wha' with chills un coughs now toothache its like a bleedin' 'ospital in 'ere, play up Rosie for gawds sake."

"Me Alfie's 'ome. Come this mornin', 'e did."

"Glad fer yer Phoebe. Now yer mind will rest easy, Albert ain't arrived, they can't bear to part with 'im."

"'e'll come soon Flo' takes time to sort them soldiers out don' it?"

"Yus it do, bu' there ain't tha' many left standin'."

"Shockin' waste of young life."

"Best not think too much, not tonigh' any rate – 'ave a taste of pie, before they vanish."

"Ta Flo' a grand spread ain't it 'enry."

"Looks delicious Flo' ta."

"Heard the latest on Maudie Brown Phoeb?"

"Nahh, Ethel, wha' she up to?"

"Yer ma's neighbour 'oo's in the know like, says to me Maude 'as a fondness for an opium pipe an' what's more she 'as digs in Chinatown. Wha' d'yer say to that'?"

"Not much I can say Ethel – she's daft enough to try opium."

"Somethin' stuck in me tooth!"

"That's yer tongue, I'm surprised yer teeth are yer own."

"I wasn't talkin' to yerself Vi."

"Give us a taste of pie Mrs."

"Yer saucy bugger go an' ask yer ma."

"I ain't a ma an' me 'ome starves us."

"Yer don' look 'ard done-by to me."

"'ere son, 'ave a piece orf mine."

"Ta Mister."

"Yer 'ave a load of 'em round yer feet now, 'enry."

"The lad's 'ungry."

"Don' let Flo' catch yer, these buggars drives 'er up the wall."

"Gawd 'elp us 'ere the 'oly sisters, no' a minutes peace to 'ave a bit of fun."

"Spare a penny for the black babies, poor African orphans."

"Come on gals, 'and over yer farthin's for the sisters, come on Jess open yer purse."

"God-bless you ladies, goodnight to you all."

"Ah, a bit of the Irish, such soft voices."

"'oo cares 'bout us, I'd like to know Vi, the

order of the poor cows, the likes of us are."

"No radicals if yer please."

"Well Flo' I'm fed up 'avin nothin'"

"Ain't like our Minnie to 'ave the miseries, me beers up to tricks."

"Nahh, 'taint Flo', bu' look at us, we ain't a pair of decent boots between us, makes yer sick it do."

"Yus, bu' yer grandma 'ad no boots, bare foot summer an' winter them days. Our lives 'ave improved."

"New boots 'urt yer feet."

"I wouldn't know would I, I ain't ever 'ad new boots 'enry."

"One day yer ship will come sailin' in Minnie."

"Nahh, Phoeb, I don' believe in fairy tales."

"Just as well Minnie, yer never be disappointed."

The barrel organ was keeping time with Rosie Tilley as she played the old favourites. Chattering, the monkey was trying to beat pigeons for dropped crumbs. A policeman walked his beat. Guiding Bill, Ivy made their way to 'The 'Threepenny-Bit-and-Whistle', his white stick tapped the pavement. The barrel-organ played 'Roses are blooming in Picardy' and Rosie Tilley began to sing as Ivy and Bill came near. Not a dry eye could be seen.

"We're there Ivy, I can hear the old sign creaking."

"Yus love we're there now."

"Stop larkin' abou' Miriam, can't yer see me pattern is fragile an' if yer bog feet tear it tell me where to find the money to buy a new one, gawd I saved and saved to buy this one an' bought it cheap 'cause it were shop soiled."

"If me feet's big I can't 'elp it, can I? I'm a big gal."

"Well so am I, but I'm careful."

"Sophie 'arris yer a moaner."

"Miriam Michaels go 'ome, yer bad for me moods. This is me ma's *Purim* dress or will be if I can move yer feet from orf the pattern."

"I'll 'ave to stay, ma's gorn up west fer a change of air, come on Soph, stop rowin' an' I 'elp ter sort out the material."

"Good, that's what best friends is for, pretty colour ain't it? Ma will look a treat."

"I'd like to make me ma a dress, the money just ain't there – last few weeks our rents been behind an' every penny is needed to pay it orf."

"Don't worry, else yer 'air will turn white, ain't worth it – pa's always behind with somethin' - ma pawns this an' that – we cope some'ow."

"We ain't this or that left to pawn, ma says food comes first sod the rent."

"Yer pa's right, them landlords ain't worth a light. Come with me to our Dinah's shop an' we'll choose a dress fer yer ma."

"Sophie that's a mitzvah!"

"Yus, me 'alo ain't 'alf 'eavy."

"Gawd dress-makin' is 'ard work."

"Miriam we ain't started yet!"

"I was makin' a comment."

"Keep it to yerself yer givin' me an 'eadache. I 'ad the pattern neatly laid out till yer feet walked into it."

"Soph yer so irritable 'ave yer womanly's come over yer?"

"None of yer business, fancy talkin' of such things."

"No one can 'ear us."

"Me brother's in the next room."

"'e's snorin' 'is 'ead orf 'e can't 'ear a word."

"'ow do yer know, know-all. Me poor brother's 'ome from the war ain't 'e. Becky's promised me a second-'and machine one day."

"One day's all we 'ear, 'one day' I 'ate bein' poor."

"Miriam I think I'll make a cuppa tea for us – I can't concentrate an' talk – ma says poor is sleepin' under the arches an' 'avin no shoes or coat or anythin' – we ain't poor, we just 'ave no money."

"Is there a difference?"

"Cors, we make do an' don' grumble ma says grumblin' gives yer a sore throat."

"I enjoy a good moan – me an' me ma moan together an' pa don' 'alf do 'is nut an' then we 'ave a good laugh. Nothin' like a good laugh except an' 'ot cuppa tea."

"Give me a chance I'm looking in me drawer fer a penny fer the gas I'm no' earnin' yet bu' Rachel gave me a bob the other day – jobs ain't easy to find are they?"

"I ain't earnin' either – ma says she'll pack me orf to America is I don' earn me keep."

"She don' mean it, yer the apple of 'er eye."

"I 'ope so, I 'ate the sea an' boats."

"Me brother's a sailor, brave as a lion Alfie."

"I ain't brave an' I love the East-end."

"'ow could yer love this smelly place, I'd leave tomorrow to discover the world."

"Sophie, the world's a disappointment."

"'ow do yer know, if yer ain't left Mile End?"

"I sense it."

"Yer mean yer senseless – sense it indeed yer 'ave to live places, see 'em fer yerself."

"An' be called a dirty Jew everywhere yer step yer foot."

"Not everywhere Miriam, some people are alrigh'. I'll tell yer somethin' the other week I went to speaker's corner with me sisters an' we listened to a Jewish man tellin' the crowd abou' Zion an' Israel our homeland – cors there was those 'oo shouted 'im down, bu' 'e took no notice an' 'e says we must pack up an' go back, the return to Zion, Rachel 'ad big tears in 'er eyes she did."

"Well I ain't goin' I like it 'ere."

"Tha' ain't the point, ah! I found a penny. We can 'ave a cuppa."

An urgent knock startled them – answering the street door a telegram boy called

"Cablegram for a Mrs. 'arris – read it now" Sophie opened the envelope to read

```
- REGRET ILLNESS PREVENTS TRAVEL -
SAM
```

"Any reply miss?"

"Nahh, ta very much."

Feeling uneasy, everyone feared telegrams, she put the cable in her purse.

"What's up Soph 'ad bad news? Yer look worried."

"Our Sammy ain't comin' yet from America, someone 'as been took bad, bu' 'e don' say who. Words cost money – Miriam I'm goin' to Esther's place, I see yer tomorra."

"I un'erstand, Soph, I'll 'elp yer fold the patterns up."

"At this rate I'll never finish the dress."

"Cors yer will an' it will be lovely – any rate I'll nip in tomorra big feet an' all."

"I won' disturb Alfie, 'e needs a good sleep. I'll put me coat on an' come out with yer."

"A bit nippy ou' 'ere I'll be orf Soph tarra."

"Bye Miriam ta fer comin'."

She walked to her sister's place with a heavy feeling inside herself, all was not well.

"'allo Sophie, what's up? Yer look worried fit to bust. Ruthie's gorn to sleep thank gawd, the chemist gave me somethin' to soothe 'er gums, red raw they are."

"I'm glad she feels bet'er – this cable came fer ma an' pa, bu' they're at Flo's do I don' wan' to upset them after a par'y – they don' 'ave much to enjoy."

"Let's 'ave a read. Well it don' say whose ill. Yer right not to upset ma an' pa."

"Esther give us a cuppa I'm all jittery."

"Calm down I'll do Klara's milk at the same time. What yer been up to?"

"Cuttin' ma's pattern for a *Purim* dress. A pretty lavender – I ain't worked all the pattern ou' an' Miriam came over an' jawed an' then the cable boy knocked, so I packed it in fer now."

"I'll 'elp yer with the 'ard bits – I can't imagine you'll make a machinist"

"Bleedin' right I 'ate it. I ain't found work yet."

"There ain't much abou' yer can always 'elp Solly an' old Solomon's bark is worse then 'is bite."

"I'd like tha', Rachel turns material into floor rags – mind yer our Becky's a good needle woman, sewing ain't in Dinah's line either."

"She says Abdul does it fer 'er."

"My Klara's clever, questions, questions, yer've not 'eard the like an' books, she wants books – now where's the money fer books I ask yer – I'll ask me teacher she says, I 'ave a real life with 'er, Klara's too clever fer me."

"There ain't no flies on 'er Esther. How we gonna tell ma Pearly ain't comin' yet?"

"New York ain't over the road, she'll be 'ere and tire ma out."

"Can I stay 'ere tonight?"

"Cors yer can, we tuck up together."

"I can't take Cox Street tonight. I left a note sayin' I might stay over."

Like a willow-the-wisp, silently falling over families. The Spanish Flu they named the vicious cruel infection. Few escaped. After four years of war, when armistice brought relief, the people weakened with years of food shortage, and the poor always hungry, little or no resistance was possible. In every corner of the globe thousands died. Instead of lavender pastel, Phoebe wore mourning dress for Julie and her beloved son. Pearl, orphaned, was brought to London by Julie's sister Martha six months later. The doctors prescribed those who could pay to 'eat well, light wine, smoke in moderation'

In moderation the poor ate their bread and jam and took brown mixture.

Year of Peace 1919

A grey, heavy mist masked the Sound[82].

Gulls declared themselves exhilarated with loud gull-calls as a malevolent wind took their wings above a cold sea.

Reb Abraham Slavinsky stamped his feet on Plymouth's draughty station platform waiting for the London train, already late. Fifteen minutes later he greeted Reuben with a friendly handshake.

"Not a pleasant day Reuben, hold onto your hat."

"My hat and yours have stayed on in worse places."

"Was the journey pleasant?"

"A journey's a journey. Trains send me to sleep. Shepsul reads. Noise, jolts, soot, nothing disturbs my brother, but thank you the journey was comfortable."

"Everyone is looking forward to your talk tomorrow. Some of the community are coming from Cornwall."

"Do many of us live there?"

"Very few, of course Penzance, in the far west, had a thriving community of mostly Sephardim[83]. They left long ago only market Jew street and the 17th-century cemetery remain. Our ancient history here is interesting. After the fall of Israel to the Romans, they brought Jewish slaves to Cornwall to work the mines. For tin and copper I believe."

"Tst, Tst, the foulness of Rome. The Almighty

blessed to be His name must have decreed death, before madness came.

"A short tragic existence."

Any trouble with the local people?"

"They are courteous at a distance, trouble enough with war and Spanish flu to bother us. Vicars try to convert us, with humour we thank them for their time. We can't grumble Reuben in a funny way I think they like our schul in Catherine Street, quite a few come to see inside."

"Aaron, one of my sons, when he was about eight years old asked me, 'papa are Jews important people?'

'Very important.'

'I thought so papa, everyone invites us in.' He'd read the mission to the Jews notices."

"With innocence children are wise, you have many sons haven't you Reuben?"

"Yes too many. I'm always telling friends to help themselves to one. They never take the offer up. Benjamin the eldest is fourteen already. He's learning the jewellery trade. I'm learning too."

"I'm a bookbinder by trade, not as lucrative as diamonds. Reb Sheinrock and his wife will join us for our evening meal."

"I remember him we met in London, he enjoyed Rifka's *kneidlach* he's a good man I'm glad he has a schul."

"He's a shoemaker by trade. He also speaks about nine languages."

"Only nine – I struggle with English. At least if the worst comes to the worst our communities will have diamonds and shoes to wear even a good bound book to read!"

"What more could they ask?"

"They'll think of something. Chava my

daughter wants to be a writer, she's gone shopping with a friend to buy the amazing new scientific unleakable pen. My wife's voice reached the ceiling when she found out , 'You gave our Chava two pounds two shillings for a pen! What kind of price is that. You part with two pounds two shillings. What are we rich all of a sudden? When I was a child a pencil was a miracle and it never leaked. For one-and-a-half pence you will could become a genius. She'd better become a good writer for two pounds two shillings."

"Wives they're all the same, money's a worry for them."

"Chava smiled at me. No doubt the amazing pen will leak all over the place and my wife's voice will again reach the ceiling. How can you refuse a daughter's smile?"

"Impossible. Come Reuben time for schnaps. The sea is high, I believe tonight is a spring tide."

The Rabbonim turned walking into the wind. Their voices faded. What they were laughing about was heard only by the gulls.

<u>Reuben</u> <u>talks</u> <u>to</u> <u>the</u> <u>congregation</u>.

"Shalom,
Such good-looking young Jews.
Sea air is doing you good.
What's the reason a tired, slightly overweight Rabbi from an obscure London schul comes to give a talk to a Plymouth community. What's he up to? Before he opens his mouth you don't trust him. Wondering, how much money he needs for schul

repairs!

Dear people don't worry my schul's in good repair.

Shepsul, my brother is usually with me. Together we've visited our communities over the years from London to Scotland, for our mission, religious Zionism.

The *Mitzrahi*, in now what seems a lifetime ago, chose us to begin their work in Great Britain. To this day, I remember the agony of 'homesickness' and the long wait for our betrothed young women to join us.

Plymouth is a famous, old city. You all have pleasant lives here and two schuls. For more than two centuries Jews have prayed here. May they rest in peace.

Home – such an important word.

All the world's creatures seek their homes. Genesis reminds us we are creatures to the Lord, blessed to be His name. Even the ant was created before us! These creatures shared one quest, to find a home. After all to be thrown out of Eden was no joke.

The hazardous journey into the unknown must have been a terrifying, yet wonderful experience. When it came to Abraham our Patriarch blessed to be his name, to join this saga of searching for a home he took up the challenge without debate with himself. Gathered his hill gods, animals and camp then slowly the caravan moved on. Moving with a strange impulse. Leaving a stable life in Ur to follow the winding river. He knew only his direction like the flowing waters would be onwards.

Over the years Jews have purchased parcels of land in *Eretz* Israel from Turks. Passionate, young, even the elderly, Russian and Poles, men and women, Zionist pioneers of the *kibbutz* movement. Following their ideals, fearing nothing, they toiled and sweated to watch neglected fields slowly began to thrive.

Let us ask ourselves how much work can pioneers achieve without help? The ingathering – a miracle of the great return from exile of world Jewry is not expected, the time is not right. No I am here this evening to ask each one to think of making the journey to join the *kibbutzniks*, turn a clod of soil. Even if you leave at least you can say 'I was a *shoymel*[84]' or 'I'd ploughed, planted saplings, I helped.'

Not all our people were part of the *goluth*[85]. After Roman conquest a surprising number of us stayed in *Eretz* Israel which the Romans named Palestine. Even during Christian occupation and now under Islam, Jews remained on their land.

Where our temple stood a mosque stands. The Ottoman Empire claims our birthright.

We shout from within ourselves, 'enough already.' Patience with our volatile natures is not usually a Jewish virtue, only centuries of persecution have taught us in our yearning for Jerusalem to wait, wait, wait with suppressed anger. Patience gave us our great ally, the power of our thoughts. Judaism has a strength beyond the understanding of most of the Gentile world. Why we cleave to an Almighty, blessed to be His name, who cast us off our land to live with supposed shame and endless gratitude on foreign soils. To be humiliated with pogroms, expelled at the whim of kings, killed by the hatred of Queens. This has been our portion for nearly two thousand years. Blamed for misfortune, merely to be tolerated by host countries.

Jewish features are more than obvious in Europe and elsewhere. Conversion rarely by choice to Christianity or Islam swallowed up thousands of lost

84   Armed night watchman   85   Exile

Jews. Our gathering this evening is a miracle, why? Because against the odds our ancestors survived as Jews. Out of the blue we receive cards from Jews who made *aliyah*. I can't tell you the joy my family feels reading their words. A simple card reads, 'Reuben, Shepsul, shalom. No milk, no honey, blistered hands, sore feet, burnt skin, but a happy heart!'

A happy heart, a pioneer's tribute to an ancient land – our land.

Shall we be thrown out of Eden a third time? No, no, no.

No matter how kind a country may treat us and Great Britain indeed is such a land, we Jews know even after a thousand years a land may become hostile and fracture our lives, too often into oblivion.

Isaiah, blessed be his name, gave his council to our ancestors, 'if a man lean on the reed of Egypt it will go into his hand and pierce it.'

Jews say to me they would like to make *aliyah*, yet feel unable to trust or live with Arabs. Look enmity helps no-one. We'll be on thin ice, we must make sure no cracks appear. Israel has unpleasant problems, snake or scorpion bites or fighting with Arabs nobody wants, yet if we are attacked we'll fight. Strengthen Judaism. Aaron blessed be his name, wasn't too worried about unfriendly tribes. I am confident in my message, I am confident in the Jewish people.

Out of those who go, one or many might stay. Remember this journey is not a *may'se bikhl*[86], the timid will grow strong the strong will be powerful.

If I talk for too long you will become restless, many have to go to Cornwall. Thank you for listening to my talk, thank you *rebbetsin* and reb Slavinsky for inviting me to this beautiful *schul*.

May the Almighty, blessed to be His name,

---

86   Fairy tale

keep you all healthy and in fine spirits.
Shalom."

With the *rebbonim* the congregation sang the
Hatikvah[87] then crowded round Reuben, smiling with
genuine pleasure. Pressing envelopes with money in
his hands. Small gifts, notes with prayers for their
loved ones, all talking at once.

Wishing him a safe journey to London.

After the evening meal, their glasses of
schnapps warming in their hands, the *rabbonim*
relaxed. Reuben picked up a book on a side table
beside his chair. 'Revealer of Secrets' by Yoyef Perl.
I've heard of this book, are you reading it?"

"I've just finished the last chapter of the
version in Yiddish. You know 'Revealer of Secrets' is
the first Hebrew novel written over a century ago.
I've been unable to find a Hebrew copy anywhere."

"How do you have time to read novels?"

"I made a free half hour or so to read Perl. An
American visitor told me he thought the work
amazing."

"Do you agree?"

"Yes, not only for the book's fame as the first
Hebrew novel Perl was a man to respect he spoke
fluent high German although a Yiddish speaker
himself, perfect Hebrew, rare amongst Jewry then. A
good writer, scholar, and a devout Jew."

"What are the secrets?"

"Sheinrock I won't spoil the plot, you might
read the book, I can't loan this copy, its not mine.
Perl hid his identity behind the pseudonym Megalle
Temirin he knew the novel would cause a storm

---

87   National anthem

174

amongst the *Hasids*. The last thing they needed was
a parody against *Hasidism*, a satire on a cultural war
between their beliefs and *Haskala*[88]."

"We gave them a rough time!"

"Yes, from the movements beginnings they
suffered attacks from the *rabbonim*. Anti-Hasidic
tracts were produced by the dozen. The *gaon*[89] of
Vilna issued laws of excommunication. He refused to
meet Rabbi Shneur Zalman the Russian leader of the
Hasids."

"The middle of the eighteenth century was a
fiery time for everyone. *Haskala* threatened *Talmudic*
scholarship and *Hasidism*."

"Correct. Remember Reuben the *Hasids* always
showed respect for Jewish law and Torah scholarship.
Also *Hasidism* with all their problems dominated
most communities in Eastern Europe."

"Why do you think the book is neglected?"

"A few reasons, although a Jewish classic
beyond doubt it's difficult to read at first glance. In
Hebrew only a handful of copies exist. The *Hasids*
hated every word of it not realising the parody Perl
had written against them. The Polish overlords with
their brutal anti-Semitism were always ready to
strike at the Jews without much of a reason. The
nobleman had read 'Revealer of Secrets', roared with
laughter at the *Hasids* and *Tsadikim*[90] they translated
the German into Polish for enjoyment of torment, to
Jews, derided without mercy a people they considered
as uneducated, worse than rabble in their midst. Perl
loved the *Hasids* he was brought up one of them, but
thought their extremes made them figures of ridicule.
The writing is realistic, because Perl understood
them. The *Hasids* believed every word in the book.
Their object of searching for this infamous 'bukh' in
the 'Revealer of Secret' ends with them burning all

88   Enlightenment   89 Religious leader
90   Spiritual leader

copies found. Their search was a frenzy from start to finish."

"First editions must be valuable for Jewish collectors, an elderly bookseller calls by occasionally, a Mr Crown with Yiddish books for the women, I'll ask if he's able to find a Hebrew copy."

"One can imagine the *Hasids* desperation trying to keep the story from the princes and overlords. Our people were only just going towards modernity. *Haskala* wanted to try and understand the Gentiles, *Hasids* felt all aliens sinister, Jew haters."

"They were not exactly wrong!"

"*Haskala* thought to Yiddish merely bad German, which kept them backward in a modern world. *Hasids* treated Yiddish, their *mamaloschen*[91], a loving, warm Hebrew, Polish German tongue their own, in a world where precious little belonged to them. All the Hasids were peasants who adored their rebbe-saints, their religious ecstasy, their strange mystical dreams and folk stories. They detested the *Haskala* with their Hebrew and fluent high German, even French. They also detested *maskilm*[92], but remember this is a novel apart from the parody and satire."

"Did much harm come to the *Hasids* from so much assumed chaos."

"They did seem to decline for a while, nobody really knows the reason."

"They grew tired of becoming invisible."

"You both laugh see how easy mocking them is."

"Well they're still going strong. Rabbi Zalman, back in the middle of the eighteenth century really started a lasting movement."

91 Mother tongue   92 Intellectuals

❧

In a sitting-room Chava was showing her unleakable, scientific pen to her mother and *rebbetsin* Sheinrock.

"You want to become a writer don't you Chava? What kind of books will you write?"

"I'm not good at the frivolous, light-weight or romance novels are not for me. No, I will be a serious writer and with luck find a publisher interested in my work."

"You are young and so pretty to be so serious, time enough to think big thoughts. From the little I know about writing finding a publisher may take years. You mustn't waste your energy. You must cope with rejection and bear loneliness. Writing is a tough, solitary vocation. Persevere Chava and please God may your new pen bring you success."

"Thank you. I don't think mama is very impressed with my pen."

"If there are no leaks when your novel is finished then I'll be impressed."

"Will you go to Israel?"

"I'm not sure, if mama and papa are able to visit one day, then I'd like to go. Alone I'd be scared. We know the land is ours, but the world says its Palestine. Mama can't bear heat, so papa says winter is the best time for us to go. Mama doesn't believe snow falls in winter."

"I'd been there in winter and snowfalls are not rare. You won't notice the climate, to be in your ancestral homeland will thrill you too much to bother about weather."

"Take no notice, she'll marry have a family, settle down. I keep telling her she's young, why so serious?"

"I tell mama back, I may not marry, freedom is precious."

"More precious than a family?"

"No, *rebbetsin*, not more precious just as precious."

"You give your parents books instead of grandchildren?"

"Mama won't mind she hates a mess and papa loves books, if he wasn't a rabbi, I'm sure he'd be a writer."

"I give up I don't understand today's young, your mother's right Chava you're too young for serious books. I always think a novel must have a little craziness, a touch of laughter with a teardrop or two at the end."

"Sounds more like Yiddish theatre than a novel!"

"Isn't a novel theatre on a page?"

"I've never thought about a novel as theatre, the arts I suppose have a togetherness maybe they can't be separated. Poets stand alone."

"More likely my daughter will fall in love with the first smiling *sabra*[93] she meets."

"Mama you're impossible."

"Yes, a sabra will be charmed and ride away across the desert with you."

"*Rebbetsin* Sheinrock you should write romance novels and make lots of money."

"The *reb* would have a fit."

"See I told you freedom is precious."

"Chava stop corrupting the Rebbestin."

"When I was a child I told mama to leave papa, because he shouted too much, then I told papa to leave mama because she shouted too much. Papa joked marriage is a big shout."

---

93   Born in Israel

"My *bube, olav hashalom,* asked the *Beth Din*[94] for a divorce. The rabbi listened to her plea put his arm around my 80 -year-old *bube,* told her to go home and prepare the Shabat *cholent. Bube* was furious with him. 'Since I was seventeen years old all I have done is have children, and prepare the soup prepare the fish, prepare the *cholent.* For a change he can prepare as much as he likes for himself. I will not live under his roof for a day longer."

"*Bube* went to live with one of her daughters."

"Did she go home."

"No, my grandfather, a very angry old man had another daughter take care of him. They ignored each other to the end of their lives."

"I refuse to learn how to cook. If I marry my husband will have to eat in a *kosher* restaurant or cook for himself."

"What will you exist on Chava?"

"Fruit."

Smiling at Chava's ideals the *rebbetsin,* while perhaps secretly agreeing with her, teased her about learning how to keep a *kosher* kitchen.

Removing his hat and coat, pushing his *yarmelkeh*[95] back in place, Reuben settled into a window seat nodding good morning to other passengers.

As the 'Cornishman' gathered speed he was able to see through window-grime, pastures fading gently into brown soil. Then red soils of a lush Devon landscape. His eyes closed in a half doze. Saturn the angel in control of time spun him backwards into childhood.

---

94   Rabbinical court   95   Skullcap

West country scenes disappeared. Birch trees shone white with flaked bark curling gracefully down trunks, with deep snowdrifts piled around their buried roots.

Thousands of sombre, dark green conifers heavy with snow seemed to shudder with cold. The rest of the forest, almost lost in a snowstorm, was silent except for the creak of branches in the wind.

In the distance the village pond became a miniature lake with a diamond shine glittering from frozen water, pecked by geese as crows circled above them flying away with a chorus of a laughing caws.

A stencil of a fragile three-quarters moon showed a touch of palest silver, an ominous grey sky streaked with a mere hint of winter sun.

From the edge of the pond Reuben could just about see the few wooden village houses grouped around small shops and workshops. Soon Rifka would come for her geese, Leba one of her friends chatting beside her, as Rifka scattered a handful of seeds to tempt her birds along. Soon ... soon.

Yakov the butcher's son came to skate calling in his loud overexcited voice,

"Skate Reuben, don't go home, why aren't you skating Reuben, enjoy yourself. Don't tell my papa you've seen me here, he'll whip me. I should be in the shop. Smell the pine Reuben, see the snowdrifts will bury the village. I am going to marry the milkman's daughter Reina, have you seen her beauty, why aren't you skating Reuben, skate Reuben, skate, skate ... such a beauty, Reuben you should only see."

"Shepsul what's in your pocket?"

"My pocket - nothing."

"Nothing makes such a lump? Show me what nothing looks like."

"I'll show you, let me wash my hands for

dinner first."

"Shepsul give me your jacket ... a kitten! –
what am I going to do with you Shepsul?"

"Look Mama, his eyes are barely open, he was
dying without food, thrown in a ditch full of rubbish.
Please let me feed him, please."

"Put him in the scullery and close the door,
take a saucer of milk with tiny pieces of bread. If
papa sees a kitten near food none of us will eat
dinner. Hurry up, then scrub your hands. I think
about the kitten later."

"Don't think too hard mama, because your
brain will hurt, mama, thank you."

"Don't thank me, don't spill the milk."

"Listen Mama, he's purring, he's so happy to be
with us."

"Just like you'll purr cleaning up his mess."

"You won't know he's here, I promise you
Mama he'll be the cleanest cat in the world."

"Just the house will do."

"Reuben, go and make sure your brother closes
the scullery door."

"Shepsul never closes anything, you know that
Mama!"

"I know, I know."

"Peshe, quickly come here I must tell you
something."

"What?"

"Three guesses what's in the scullery?"

"Cooking pots"

"Nope."

"Clean pots."

"Peshe can you only think of cooking pots?"

"A pale to catch drips from the scullery leak."

"Three tries are up! I'll tell you, *Lockschen*[96]."

---

96   Noodle soup

"*Lockschen*! Are you a *shmendrick*[97] today? Mama would never keep food in the scullery."

"Mama told me to put *Lockschen* in there with a saucer of milk."

"Shepsul you're not well, you're going down with fever, I'll tell mama to put you to bed."

"I want my dinner first."

"You must starve a fever, liquids only, and rest."

"Yes, yes Peshe I'll do all you say after dinner."

"Go lie down like a good boy; I must tell mama the *shnorrer* wants a Friday *challah*[98], her money's run out as usual."

"Mama did you know we had nineteen monarchs in Judah in five hundred years. From Rehoboan in 933 and Jehoiachim in 597."

"Very clever Reuben, you learn well. Much good they did us. We ended up in *shtetls* up to our eyes in snow with Russians and Poles loathing us, don't tell me about kings."

"Mama, they didn't throw us into *goluth* the cursed Romans did. Papa says we'll return and the Messiah will make everything lovely again, with figs and grapes and flowers everywhere. Isn't that wonderful mama?"

"Yes, Reuben very wonderful, Peshe why so late you look frozen?"

"Sorry I'm late mama, the *yachner*[99] started talking I couldn't leave her talking to herself. Before I forget the *shnorrer* asked for a Friday challah, her money's run out as usual."

"You're lucky you didn't freeze out there."

"You know what she told me?"

"Am I mind reader!"

"Shlomo the blacksmith beat his wife with a stick and pulled her around the room by her hair. His

---

97   Nincompoop   98   Bread

99   Gossip

wife cursed him to drop dead. The children ran out of the house barely dressed and looked frightened. They were crying, their mother screaming, then I left the *yachneh* standing there covered with snow waiting to tell someone else."

"Funny I heard nothing. Deep snow must have blocked the noise out. I'll take food tomorrow for the children, Yenie, Shlomo's wife must keep out of his way when he's drunk. Vodka turns him into a wild man. The children are miserable, Yenie can't cope with her sorrows. Papa has spoken to him, but his ears don't listen. He blames his wife for his drinking."

"Mama how do you know a husband won't be a drunk?"

"They're sad, weak men, drink is their disease. Don't worry my Peshe your husband will be chosen with care."

"If my husband takes a stick to me I'll come home!"

"Of course you will darling, now come help me clean the vegetables."

"Mama I forgot to tell you, Shepsul has a fever. He's talking nonsense."

"Shepsul, a fever?"

"I told him to lie down till you went up to him. Did you tell him to put lockshen in the scullery?"

"He sounds very sick, I must go upstairs. Peshe stir the soup, dinner mustn't be late a *rabbi* from Lomza will join us. Papa will be home soon."

"Mama, what's amusing you, Shepsul's ill and you're grinning?"

"Maybe I caught fever too!"

Peshe heard scratching at the scullery door. She found not a mouse only a ginger and white kitten mewing for another saucer of milk. Shepsul teased his sister for days by pretending to be light-headed and talking nonsense.

The 'Cornishman' pulled into the station coming to a gradual halt with the usual hissing steam and noise. Still in a half-awake doze Reuben could faintly hear his father's deep voice, 'the degrees of life and death were sealed by God, were sealed, were sealed, were ...'

"Wake up old chap, Paddington."

An embarrassed Reuben thanked the Englishman for waking him.

"Trains always send me to sleep."

"No bother, good day to you."

Putting on his hat and coat, taking his case down from the rack he left the carriage, wiping his damp eyes with the back of his hand, taking his childhood memories into himself.

The Potzloch's Give a Party

Jascha Kahn walked with a limp. His watery, pale blue eyes took every step carefully in case he tripped.

His face gave an expression of extreme dislike, even his smile was sullen. Nearly all the rooms in his house were drab and rented out.

Jascha Kahn lived on the ground floor with uncurtained windows so he could see who was coming in. His tenants had almost no contact with him. They paid their rent and kept out of his way.

Local cats sat on his window-sill, surely not for food, he wasn't known for generosity! Yet cat's favoured his sill and curled their thin shapes against his legs whenever he opened the street door.

About five doors from him lived the Potzloch family. A noisy, happy brood. Shmuel Potzloch worked for Jascha Kahn for ten years. He was also one of his tenants, with never a show of anger in spite of day after day putting up with Jascha Khan's demands in a hard-worked dress factory. He started as a presser, aching toil in an airless room from eight o'clock a.m. until Jascha Kahn's watery blue eyes looked at his gold pocket watch and called 'time.' If an order came in from a good store time was called at ten o'clock p.m or later. Shmuel Potzloch 'pressed' for bare necessities, with most of his wages returned to Jascha Kahn by way of rent.

To grumble imbued the spirit with futile longings, when he became a cutter, a job with better wages, was time enough for longings.

In his pocket his treasured harmonica lay. When his hands stopped aching from heavy irons he played.

Sprintzer Potzloch was a lovable *yachneh*. All the women enjoyed gossip and Sprintzer Potzloch almost daily collected her tales with zeal. She waddled along, her body spreading at every angle, from one side of the pavement to the other. Holding her newest baby, which bounced against Sprintzer Potzloch's massive breasts like a rubber ball. A huge smile on a broad, moon-shaped face.

Summer and winter Sprintzer Potzloch was always the same. Friends with her neighbours, her hair covered with a 'kerchief slipping down, wearing an apron covered with whatever she'd cooked for dinner! Whenever Shmuel Potzloch's harmonica tunes drifted over the rooftops the neighbours had to decide quickly to stay inside or go to the party Sprintzer Potzloch would surely invite them to!

"Rifka darling come, come bring the family. Leave the kitchen, time to sing, to watch our men dance. Come, come before cold weather. Who can enjoy then – none of us. Rifka, spring is here, why waste a lovely day. Bring nothing no, I've such a pile of *nash* eh! You won't need food for a week. You should only taste, already my mouth is watering. I must go tell Yenta, if she misses a party she's ill for a week. Rifka did you hear about her sister? What a disgrace. What can you do with families I ask you, what can you do? Don't ask me where I bought beans, who remembers? Rifka darling may you only be well, don't be late."

The newest Potzloch baby began crying for a

feed. Sprintzer Potzloch waddled to Yenta's place, calling at the top of her voice, "*Yashir koyech*[100], Rifka."

An exhausted Rifka hadn't said a word. Peshe was in her shop and would be home late. Dosha had gone somewhere, she'd forgotten where. When Reuben heard the music he'd know Rifka had taken the younger boys to one of Sprintzer Potzloch spring gatherings.

With their children around them the women sang and clapped their hands in time to Shmuel Potzloch music. Some other men have been laid off work for various reasons danced. Laughter echo'd along Victoria Park Road. The children did handstands on the grass falling over each other. They performed tricks and played games they made up. Dusk shaded the sky, the children grew tired. With *nash* now a few crumbs on an old wooden table, Shmuel Potzlock played favourite Yiddish melodies. The women fell into melancholy. Collecting their children, telling Sprintza Potzloch her parties were marvellous, telling Shmuel Potzloch his playing was marvellous, they walked to their homes.

The men stayed talking.

Shmuel Potzlock wiped spittle from his harmonica placing it with affection in a frayed breast pocket. His hands felt heavy, his eyes full of questions, about struggles and why life came swiftly to an end before a pear tree gave fruit.

Jascha Kahn's crippled leg ached, a sure sign of rain. He loathed noise and shrieking children, and the Potzloch's parties irritated him. He pitied Shmuel

100　May your strength continue

Potzlock for his overlarge wife and too many children. Thinking the man needed more sense as obviously the wife didn't have any. The Myersavitch tribe were even worse. Reuben Myersavitch was often away, Rifka Myersavitch always pregnant and cats everywhere. He blamed these noisy families for his headaches and was glad he hadn't married years ago when given the chance.

Headaches or not bookkeeping, which he did nearing the end of every month made his head throb, his yellow skin more yellow than ever, but he didn't trust anyone else to do the work.

Removing long, thin red ledgers down from a dusty shelf, he then opened a narrow top bureau draw to count ready money in a float kept in a black, enamelled tin box. Jascher Khan gripped the edge of the draw till his knuckles showed white. A vein on the side of his forehead bulged with pressure. His eyes became two angry slits. The float was empty, where at least ten pounds or more should have been held, not even a sixpenny piece!

Cursing under his breath he limped to the street door, where he found his voice. Banging his walking stick hard on the pavement. Rain splashed his gaunt face, and a cry of anguish could be heard from end to end of the street.

"*Vey iz mir*[101]!
Mamzer[102]! *Mamzer*!
Oy! Oy! *Oy vey*!
Ganof[103], may your hands drop off –
May you be whipped day and night,
Police, call the police!
Behind bars I'll see you,
Do you hear *mamzer*!
Behind bars. Thief! Thief!

---

101   Woe is me   102 Bastard
103   Opportunist

Lobus[104]! *Vey iz mir*!
You should break your neck better!
Police, police!"

Nobody who was at home took notice of Jascher Khan's tirade, thinking a tenant had run off without paying rent. Jascher Khan became nearly hysterical at least once a month.

Limping into Victoria Park he found a policeman on duty. With this hands shaking with anger he demanded a policeman arrest the thief, who'd stolen his petty cash. Somewhat amused at the sight of a lopsided little foreign man's disturb ramblings in broken English.

"Now, now I don't arrest anyone one, two three. Calm down old Guv an' slowly tell me yer trouble. What's missin', what time did yer miss what's gorn missin', what's yer name, address an' age. Now address first."

Jascher Khan took the policeman to his house, the policeman examined the empty black, enamelled tin box he circled the room looking at the decayed window frame.

"Keepin' money in a tin box haint good business Mr Khan. This is a poor neighbourhood yer have no curtains an' a window a child could break into with 'is eyes shut. If they smell money them will nick the lot. Who lives in this 'ouse?"

The policeman took down the tenants' names, asked about people who lived in houses near his and closed the report book. The shaken, silent Jascher Khan limped the policeman to the door.

"Fix yer windows Mr Khan, the report will go

104 Low life, wild boy

to the station, yer'll hear from us, good day to yer!"

The next morning the policeman whose name was Constable Brown, went from house-to-house asking questions from anyone in. Mostly women with small children and out of work lodgers. Women at home all day saw and heard things others missed. Constable Brown listened carefully, wrote in his report book, then with a glass shattering knock arrived at Reuben's door.

Reuben was equally amazed to see a policeman standing, where he expected to see a known face. With politeness he showed Constable Brown into the front room and offered him tea. Showing respect for the rabbi, Constable Brown told Reuben ten pounds had been stolen from a Mr Khan's house. He asked the ages of Reuben's sons. Requesting the five eldest should be questioned by him, if they were at home. Benjamin came first, telling his name and age.

"Do yer go to work yet Benjamin?"

"Yes sir, I'm apprentice to a Hatten Garden jeweller."

"I see, 'ow do yer spend yer wages?"

"I give mama all my money. She gives me pocket-money. I save two shillings and keep a few pence for things."

"Did yer work today?"

"No sir, Hatten Garden closes for the *Passover.*"

Reuben, listening to his son with a certain pride knew Benjamin would do well in life. Benjamin always gave a good impression. Constable Brown noticed Benjamin's good looks, his height and broad shoulders. Amos, Reuben's second son came to be questioned. He too told constable Brown his name and age.

"Are yer still at school Amos?"

"Yes sir."

"Are yer a truant?"

"No sir."

"Do yer know Mr Khan?"

"Yes sir."

"Do yer like Mr Khan?"

"No Sir, Mr Khan hates us. He threatens us with his stick, only cats like Mr Khan."

Reuben, smiled at Amos. Amos always pleased his father with his brand of honesty. Constable Brown took note of the boy's good looks, his height and broad shoulders. Yankel came next to be questioned. A big smile on his face, sunshine followed Yankel, a joke was better than a scowl. Constable Brown asked if he thought stealing money was a joke.

"If papa lost money, that is terrible for mama, if Mr Khan loses money, who cares! Mr Khan is rich and nasty."

"Are yer a truant Yankel?"

"No sir, I like school."

The Constable notice Yankel didn't have his brothers' good looks. His body was thin with broad shoulders and he grinned all the time. Reuben thought Yankel puts both feet in his mouth the moment he opens it even though he was a clever boy. He was glad when constable Brown asked to see his fourth son. In came Lazarus who clowned around more than Yankel. Together they were impossible. He was bursting with humour, good intentions, loving and helpful, and completely useless! Rifka always said of Lazarus, 'that son of ours of either join the circus or a madhouse.' Constable Brown took down his name and age, asking the same questions his brothers were asked, except for one or two different ones.

"Did yer know Mr Khan 'ad a loose windowpane, which opened easily, Lazarus?"

"No sir, I've not been a Mr Khan's house ever."

"That's all Lazarus."

He notice the boy's good looks and blonde hair with blue eyes. Like the third son or was it the second son.

"Send in yer brother the fifth I think."

He also took note of his broad shoulders and height remarking to Reuben his sons were 'well built lads.' Reuben knew Lazarus wouldn't let him down. His Hebrew was good and he understood and loved Torah study. Reuben's secret hope was this son would become a *Reb* Myersavitch in the future. Lastly Abraham came into the front room, a confident boy with blue-black hair and apple rosy cheeks.

"Do yer enjoy school, Abraham?"

"Yes sir."

"What's yer favourite lesson?"

"I'm good at arithmetic, but I like English best."

"Do yer ever play truant?"

"Sometimes, if I'm bored."

"Where do yer go."

"To see London. London's beautiful with the river and boats."

"Did yer attend school today?"

"No sir, I have toothache. Mama said stay at home. She took me to the dentist."

"Ye ate too many sweets?"

"Yes sir."

"Do yer share sweets with yer brothers?"

"If they want some, papa says we must share everything with each other."

"Do yer buy sweets for them?"

"For Cissy my sister because I love her."

"That must cost yer pocket money?"

"Yes sir, sometimes."

"No more questions Abraham thank you."

Constable Brown noticed Abraham was small for a ten-year-old, with broad shoulders and expressive soulful eyes. A fine face, the boy had a personality like a child-actor, showing in the young boy's voice and manner.

Reuben watched and listened to his son. He wondered why Abraham was asked so many questions. Of all his children Abraham touched his heart with a kind of loving pity he didn't understand. Abraham was heroic, very brave even at ten years old. Rifka caught him her 'little poet'. Constable Brown collected his hat, placed his report book in a large pocket and noting the time on his pocket-watch he asked Reuben how much time he spent with his sons.

"I travel with my brother to other communities to preach of give talks."

"And Mrs Myersavitch does she have anyone with her, a sister perhaps?"

"My widowed sister Peshe lives with us, she runs her small dress shop. My sister-in-law often comes to us."

"So most of the time yer wife is alone with the children?"

"Yes."

"I see, that is the end of this routine inquiry, rabbi, thank yer."

With relief Reuben saw Constable Brown out. He felt concerned about his sons. Memories of police in Russia never left an emigrant Jewish family. When trouble was in the air and they hoped like the soon to be celebrated *Passover*, it would pass over them.

The Passover 1919 Pasach - The Seder Night

Londoners on their way home after work, were cheered on their way by clusters of pink almond and cherry blossom, delicate pink softened with fragile, white apple blossom, and front gardens scented by flowers.

The merest breeze left blossom petals along pavements like a shower of confetti from a thousand bridal gowns, as petals floated hither and thither.

On such a springtime evening Reuben preparing for prayers draped his *tallis*[105] over his shoulders. An uneasy shudder went through his body. For the last month he'd suffered from bad headaches and giddiness. He was plagued with moments of ill-ease he couldn't understand, thinking tiredness and the beginning of middle age were the cause. Rifka, soon to give birth knew none of this. Reuben hoped all would pass.

Shepsul, with several other Jews was *davening*. Looking across the *schul* at his brother comforted Reuben. He sighed with relief as the men intoned Hebrew prayers and women silently prayed.

After the evening service the brothers joined everybody, wishing each other 'good *yom tov*'.

The whole family gathered for *Pesach*, Rifka with Peshe and Dosha were preparing the special meal. Cissy was allowed to hard-boil the eggs. Rifka

---

105   Prayer shawl

chopped herbs from those which grew in little pots of earth, kept on the kitchen window sill. The fragrance of roasting lamb began to seep through the house.

"A pinch more salt in the soup Mama."

"Cissy too much salt ruins soup, let me taste ... um you're right, no more than a pinch! "

"Where's the wine?"

"In the cupboard under the stairs, don't bang your head Dosha, the cupboard's very low."

"Here Cissy take the *matzos*, cover them with the folded napkin where papa sits, Peshe and I will bring in the herbs and eggs."

Samuel Itzchok was discussing the *Haggadah* with Lazarus. The younger brothers were listening and asking questions.

"I'm glad the Egyptian soldiers drowned – we're nobody's slaves."

"Yossel nobody should ever he owned by another person. Really everyone in Egypt was owned by Pharaoh. The soldiers were ordered to chase the Hebrew slaves and kill them. You must never be glad someone drowned."

"If the red Sea hadn't parted to allow us to walk to freedom, we wouldn't celebrate the *Passover*."

"No, history would tell a different story."

"Why do people hate us?"

"I'm sure Jacob, some people like us, but we Jews to not honour their gods. We are resented and sometimes this all turns into hatred. Hate becomes a bad habit."

"You're wise uncle Samuel."

"No, no, I'm just an old man. My *tateh* taught me when children called me a 'dirty Jew', the Lord our God, blessed be his name, put those words into the Russian boys' mouths, to make me a better Jew."

"We're always called names and they throw

stones at us."

"They're ignorant, all they know is abuse, feel sorry for them. To be born a Jew is a great blessing."

Coming into the dining-room Rifka told her sons to hurry up and dress.

"I must also change."

"There's plenty of hot water Samuel, the boiler has been on all day."

She took the candles from a drawer putting each one carefully into the silver candlesticks that were betrothal gifts from her parents. They had belonged to her grandparents. Such a treasure from her *shtetl*. In the brightly polished silver she saw her distorted reflection, thinking how ridiculous she looked. All protruding in front heavy with pregnancy. She looked away. She'd always disliked wearing an ugly *shteitel*. Never before questioning why orthodox women cut their hair and wore wigs. Peshe and Dosha covered their hair with pretty blue 'kerchiefs, each corner embroidered with tiny flowers. They looked as women should look, feminine. Slowly she would release herself from the *sheitel*, and cover her hair with pretty 'kerchiefs. She remembered her mother's headaches on warm days when the wig felt tight against her head. Rifka knew the feeling well. Her unborn baby kicked inside her pushing her loose blouse up. She sighed deeply, engulfed by sadness, her youth vanished like a rainbow. Cissy's face held the memory of her own young face. She hoped the newborn baby would be another daughter as lovely as Cissy.

On the sideboard a small stack of unopened letters for Reuben needed to be attended to, on *yom tov* Reuben would not read the post. Rifka, briefly looked at the letters and forgot about them.

Dosha came in with the wine. The kindled

candlelight in twilight would play patterns on the glass and the wine glasses would glitter. The whole family in their best clothes waited for Reuben and Shepsul. Samuel Itzchok always sat nearest the door. He was so myopic if he walked around the table he'd knock chairs down, falling over his own feet.

Posies of violets scented the air. In a corner Yosef propped his violin case up, he would play tranquil music at the evening's end. At a separate table the children sat with the women, the men wearing velvet *yarmelkehs*. Dosha thought how handsome Yosef had become, Peshe tidied her son's hair, Rifka looked at the family grouped around the table with pride. Samuel Itzchok loved all of them. To the family he was *neshomeleh*, a sweet soul.

A wine glass in his hand to begin the *seder*[106], Reuben rose from his chair. He mouthed words, but no sound came from him. The family waited. Rifka thought her husband was praying for a few seconds.

Reuben gripped to the side of his chair, then his legs weakened beneath him, he was able to sit down before he collapsed, his body sliding to the floor.

Shepsul and Samuel Itzchok rushed to aid him both realising something terrible might have happened to Reuben.

Rifka, almost too shocked to move, quickly took hold of herself and went to her sick husband's side.

Cissy burst into tears, Dosha and Peshe each comforted the boys. Yosef watched the scene feeling helpless.

"Don't crowd round him, he needs air, Cissy stop crying, fetch a blanket to cover your father."

Cissy immediately obeyed her uncle, with tears running down her cheeks.

---

106   Passover diner

Samuel Itzchok was a strong man and together he and Shepsul carried Reuben up to his bedroom.

"Rifka he'll be all right, many people have these types of attacks, he's been over-doing things, now he must take life a little slower, you'll see, the doctor will agree with me."

Rifka wanted to believe Shepsul, he looked on the bright side always, doubt showed in her eyes. Her beloved Reuben was ill! Shepsul trickled drops of wine on his brother's lips, his forehead was cool, he seemed to be asleep. Benjamin went with Amos to ask a doctor who lived about ten minutes away if he would attend to their father.

After he examined Reuben, Dr FitzGerald told Rifka and Shepsul Rabbi Myersavitch needed complete bed-rest. He gave Rifka several packets of white powder to be given in warm milk.

"They will relax and soothe him. I will call to see him in the morning. He should be a little improved by then. On no account can he leave the bedroom. His bowels and urine have to be seen to up here. Not too pleasant but necessary."

When Dr FitzGerald left, Shepsul began the *seder*.

"Wipe your tears away Cissy no harm will come to papa."

A heaviness clung to the atmosphere. The meal had become cold. Shepsul reminded the family of Hebrew slaves a long time ago whose *tsores* passed over them.

Jacob, Rifka's younger son opened the street door to let the angel in.

The gentle purring of a cat beneath the table, the scent of violets and candlelight gave a tranquil ending to a difficult evening.

Rifka, unable to sleep, tidied her under clothes

in the chest of drawers. A familiar sharp pain gripped her womb, she didn't expect labour to begin for at least three weeks. She lay down, hoping the early contractions would cease if she remained still. An hour later contractions became painful and fast.

Rifka put on a dressing gown and went to wake Peshe.

"Don't worry Rifka darling I see the midwife comes soon, if you're not too uncomfortable sit in a chair whilst I prepare your bed. One of the boys will go with Shepsul for Reina Levi, please god she's not attending another birth."

With an armful of brown paper and a large rubber sheet Peshe came back and stripped the bed, she spread the rubber sheet over the mattress then covered it with brown paper. Cissy, used to her mother giving birth, brought in a jug of boiling water and a white enamel bowl.

"I'll fetch the towels next, the boiler is full of coal for hot water auntie."

Dosha made up the crib beside Rifka's bed. A hard small mattress with warm covers awaited the newborn.

"The doctor was sensible to say Reuben should sleep alone, Samuel is sleeping on the couch, poor Samuel's legs are so long they're on a chair. He never complains."

"I've upset the whole family!"

"Nonsense, we're not in labour, Cissy's forgotten the soap I'll bring a large bar up and send Cissy back to bed."

Reina Levi arrived, her midwife's bags almost bigger than her.

"I'd told Nathan I'd be called tonight I had a feeling." She followed Cissy upstairs to her mother's bedroom. Taking the kettle of boiling water from her.

"I'll take the kettle Cissy, you're a good girl, ah, Rifka what a surprise! The little one can't wait, yes, yes baby's head is engaged."

Rifka sobbed, "Reuben is ill, Reina."

"I know, nothing to fret about. Rest and a light diet with good soup, he'll be on his feet. My concern is you and baby."

Rifka's labour was quick and harsh. Almost before Reina Levi had shaved Rifka's pubic hair and swabbed her legs with warm soapy water, Rifka's waters broke. She screamed.

"Now, now, calm mother, calm. Push Rifka, pushed hard we don't want a suffocated baby, push."

The baby's head appeared and Reina Levi gently eased then pulled the wrinkled little body from Rifka's dilated womb.

"*Mazeltov* Rifka, you have a son."

After she'd cut the umbilical cord dangling and attached to his mother in her capable hands, Reina Levi slapped his bottom and the first cries were heard from the newborn Myersavitch.

Reina Levi bathed the newborn with special care for his mouth and nostrils. Covered him in a flannelette baby sheet and placed him in his mother's arms. She then pressed down hard on Rifka's stomach to release the afterbirth.

"If I'm not mistaken Rifka you have a redhead."

"My father is a redhead, I so wanted a daughter."

"Be grateful for a healthy, beautiful boy. Now I think we deserve a cup of tea."

Reina Levi lay the newborn in a crib next to Rifka's bed. She scrubbed her hands and washed, then settled Rifka. Peshe brought soothing glasses of tea. Rifka sipped hers with tired eyes, saying not a word. Peshe gazed at the baby with sadness, she would never again give birth.

"He's just beautiful Rifka." Rifka smiled, looking down at her new son,

"He looks like my father, Lieb, Peshe, Lieb shall be his name."

A queue was outside the bedroom door, all the children wanted to see their brother. Reina Levi, told them they'd have to wait till the morning, their mother needed to sleep. She let Dosha in to tie a red, silk ribbon around Lieb's tiny wrist, an ancient tradition for newborn babies. Dosha kissed Rifka and thanked Reina Levi for a safe delivery.

Almost time for the dawn chorus after an unforgettable night the exhausted family slept. Later on in the morning Peshe went to Rifka's bedroom, she open windows, made up Rifka's bed with clean sheets, puffed up her pillows. Cissy brought hot water and a bowl for her mother to wash and clean her teeth. Loss of blood had weakened Rifka, she wanted to sleep and sleep. Peshe bathed and changed Lieb before Rifka put him to her breast.

"See Cissy he will suck and milk will begin to flow for him – in a day or two."

"A day or two, he'll starve mama."

"No, another liquid is there for him till then."

"Don't tire mama Cissy, she needs to rest."

"I know, but Lieb is so beautiful I long to hold him."

"You will soon enough, now we must bring mama's breakfast."

Shepsul bathed Reuben making him comfortable and spoon feeding him with oatmeal and warm milk, he was disturbed by his brother's collapse, hoping Reuben had just worked too hard and no sinister sickness would strike him. He'd never known Reuben ill or inactive.

Nearly all the community called to wish Reuben better, saying *mazeltov* for Lieb's birth, bringing fruits and flowers.

Dosha took over running the house, cooking and going with Cissy to The Lane Sunday morning for shopping. They enjoyed mugs of tea and biscuits at a *kosher* café, talked to everyone they knew and enjoyed the bustle of market life. Telling Peshe all the gossip, Dosha showed her remnants of material bought to make curtains. Cissy gave the boys their sweets, taking a pretty box of Turkish delight upstairs to her mother.

Peshe brought Lieb to the bedroom, lying the newborn next to his father.

"*Mazeltov* Reuben, your son Lieb."

Reuben stroked his son's head as Dr FitzGerald arrived to visit his patient.

"Well if that's not a miracle I've never seen one!"

The first laughter in forty-eight hours was heard in the house.

'*Straighten out the branch*
Of a tree when it is soft,
For when it hardens you will not
Be able to make it straight.'

The Talmud

"Dosha, I've decided to rent a holiday house in Bournemouth for two weeks. Rifka will be up soon and Reuben is much better. The sea air will do us good."

"Two weeks at the seaside, can we afford such

a luxury?"

"Money is not an issue. With seven miles of beaches, we'll be spoiled for choice."

"I'll tell Rifka, she'll have something to look forward to. Peshe will moan about money, she always does."

"She'll have to moan, because I'm not changing my mind. I'm going home for a few hours to air our rooms."

"Shepsul, before you leave, what's happening about Reuben's post?"

"I'll open the letters. Rifka can't read English, I'm not bothering Reuben with bills or trivia."

He sat at the dining-room table and opened the letters. He put bills to one side to be dealt with, he noticed an official envelope with 'On His Majesty's Service'. Reading the document enclosed, a summons for Reuben to appear at nine o'clock the following Monday with his son Abraham Myersavitch aged ten years, to answer charges of theft from Mr Jascha Kahn before the Bench.

Shepsul read and reread the court order. He was shocked and angry that Jascha Kahn was small-minded enough to do such miserable thing to Reuben. He gave Dosha the summons to read.

"To go before a magistrate, Abe, why what's he done wrong?"

"A police constable came to see Reuben and asked to question his five older sons – a routine enquiry he told Reuben."

"Why didn't you tell me?"

"With Reuben's collapse and Rifka in labour I completely forgot, Reuben didn't think the boys' questioning meant more than a routine enquiry."

"I'll come with you to court a woman should be with Abe."

"No, no, I'll carefully explain the charge to Abe, he's only ten years old. I don't want him frightened."

"We must go to a solicitor, Arnold Goldberg is good you know him, he's the very tall man who towers above everyone in *schul.*"

"Yes I know Arnold, there is no time for a solicitor we don't need one, I'll speak for Reuben. I'll also talk to Jascha Kahn, maybe I persuade him to drop charges. I'll offer him the lost money."

"He's a mean-spirited sour creature, Abe might not be guilty, why waste money on such a man."

"I can only try."

"Koppel Ginsberg left a tiny parcel for Rifka I must go and give it to her. Stay there darling, I'll make a glass of tea. All this trouble will make us ill. Men like Jascha Kahn always cause aggravation their money is a curse."

Sunday morning after breakfast Shepsul told Abraham to go to the sitting-room he wanted to have a talk with him.

"Come and sit next to me Abe. I want to talk to you about a letter papa received about you."

"About me, why?"

"Do you know what a summons is?"

"No uncle."

"A summons is issued by the law courts to people about all sorts of problems. They might owe too much rent or they owe someone money they refuse to pay back so they ask the court to summons and they soon pay up."

"I don't owe money, I'm a boy still."

"Of course you are Abe, only a summons is also issued for more serious offences like fighting with a knife or stealing. Do you remember a constable asking questions about Jascha Kahn ?"

"Yes."

"Now the magistrate who sits on what's called the Bench, wants to ask you questions as well. Tomorrow morning we go to the court. Do you understand Abe?" Abraham didn't say a word

"*Nu*[107]."

"Yes uncle, I think I understand."

"Good boy. A long age ago Abe, when we Jews lived under our own laws in *Eretz* Israel, a son was allowed by the Torah to steal to help his father in times of need. We live Abe as exiles in other people's land and we must obey their laws." Shepsul hugged his nephew, not showing how upset he felt.

An emigrant is an easy target for suspicion when crimes occur, hardly speaking a new language, unable to afford a solicitor and living in already run down districts emigrant families stand out in a country not overfond of foreigners. They have large families, too often children go astray if parents lose their control. A life of crime usually has a simple beginning such as a small boy stealing from house or shop. He is then taken through all the dark tunnels of low life. Few escape the octopus tentacle of arrest and punishment.

Outside the magistrate court the usual crowd of gawpers waited to go in and listen to cases up before the Bench. Sinister, shadowy men and women also watched and waited. Any innocent girl falling to their clutches will begin the life of a streetwalker with no chance of escape.

Shepsul held Abraham's hand, when proceedings began. They sat with London's choice villains. Pickpockets, drunks, procurers of children and whores. They sat for over an hour listening to their lurid stories and claimed innocence. Abraham at the age of ten years whispered to his uncle,

107   Well

"They were all liars."

"*Schutm*[108], Abe."

At last a voice boomed,

"Call Abraham Myersavitch," and again, "Call Abraham Myersavitch."

Shepsul told Abraham to stand before the magistrate. A severe man with iron grey hair and thick glass lenses in even thicker frames. The clerk of the court read the charge brought against the boy. Every word spoken was written down by a scribe. The magistrate's knew Shepsul was there in Reuben's place, Reuben Myersavitch being ill. He told Abraham to remain standing and Shepsul to remain seated. The charges against the boy were repeated by the clerk of the court.

'Call the first witness! '

Constable Brown entered the witness box to read his reports to the court.

"On the morning of twenty second of April 1919, the lad Abraham Myersavitch was seen by a neighbour climbing through the ground-floor window of one Jascha Kahn's house at 46 Victoria Park Road. Walking my beat that evening at about 7.30 p.m. the same Jascha Kahn came and told me of the theft of ten pounds from his black tin petty cash box had taken place. He was much disturbed by the discovery. Bearin' in mind wha' the neighbour described to me when I questioned her along with others, I concluded the lad Abraham Myersavitch was the thief. I also questioned his four older brothers yer 'onour."

"Thank you constable Brown, you may step down."

A signed affidavit from the unnamed neighbour was read by the magistrate.

"Abraham Myersavitch how do you plead,

---

108   Be quiet

guilty or not guilty." In a clear to voice Abraham answered,

"Guilty your honour."

The magistrate, somewhat taken aback by the boys honesty, then asked him why he'd stolen the sum of ten pounds from Jascha Kahn.

"My brotherly Yankel told me papa needed money for a debt and I was small enough to crawl through the window."

"How old is your brother?"

"Almost twelve, your honour."

There followed a period of silence except for coughs and shuffling feet. The magistrate looked up from his notes and in a voice of utter indifference he spoke to Abraham.

"Abraham Myersavitch, under English law a child of ten years is considered able to tell right from wrong. You have committed the crime of left. A thief is an unpleasant person, a pest to society. You must therefore learn right from wrong the harsh way. A son cannot steal to help his father for any reason. As your father did not teach you how you must regard another's property, the State must teach you instead. You will now be sent for no less than five years to a Reformatory school to improve and discipline your unruly nature. You may step down."

The magistrate rose, taking no notice of Shepsul shouting,

"He's only a boy of ten!"

Or even the gawpers stamping their feet to cries of,

"Shame! Shame!" A voice boomed,

"Clear the court."

The crowd wandered onto the street.

A formidable unsmiling woman in a stiff, high collared black uniform told Abraham to follow her.

"Uncle Shepsul. Uncle Shepsul."

All Shepsul heard was the lost voice of his nephew as he left the courtroom. Shepsul gave a broken sob, as he too left the court.

School of Correction 1919

A high stone wall with pieces of jagged green glass, edged along the top like weird knives, surrounded a dirty building. Dark trees almost hid from view an iron gate, opened by a watchman. He sat in a small lodge with heavy keys hanging from a chain on his jacket. All day he smoked a pipe. From barred windows white-faced boys stared into nothing

Callers clanged a large rusty bell at the building's entrance. Sounds of banging doors and keys turning locks could be heard. In the white-tiled hallway, staircases led to many landings. Harsh voices crashed into cold rooms like showers of hailstones. A strong smell of carbolic and boiled cabbage clung to stale air. If houses held a sense of peace or unease, those who entered this house breathed silent misery. Goodness didn't reverberate within these walls. The staring eyes of boys at the barred windows showed defiance and fear. This building was Reading Reformatory School for boys.

An apprehensive Abraham Myersavitch arrived at Reading Reformatory School with the uniformed stiff-faced woman who'd collected him from the London court. She handed over the tired, hungry boy to a nurse. He was immediately taken to a washroom. On a wooden trellis table, a collection of enamel bowls, soap and thin cotton towels were laid out next to a cold water tap over a sink. Nurse filled a bowl with cold water telling Abraham to wash his hands and face. This done she weighed him, inspected his teeth and nails looked to see if his ears were clean and roughly ran a flea-comb through his blue black hair. Lastly she wrote a brief report on Abraham Myersavitch, aged ten years. 'Religion Jew. General health seems good, although pallid and small stature for his age. Teeth good no nits, no scabs or sores.'

Nurse handed Abraham a navy-blue sack with a draw string top. In this went a vest and long pants, a navy blue shirt, a shapeless coarse material navy blue jacket, a pair of matching trousers, a pair of heavy black socks and after she measured his feet a pair of second-hand black boots. In red stitches on the shirt and jacket was Reading Reformatory School. A flannel nightshirt and a toothbrush made up the kit.

"You will wear this uniform from tomorrow morning – every two weeks your shirt will be washed you will polish your boots and keep the uniform clean."

Giving him a label with his name on it she told him to tie it on the sack.

"Tomorrow the uniform will be marked with a number 9. You have to earn the right to be called by your name."

She then took the boy to the kitchen, which also had a dining section. The uniformed cook looked at him with obvious dislike. He was just another unpleasant package to deal with, the reformatory was full of them!

Two thin slices of bread spread with what smelled like rancid butter, a mug of unsweetened cocoa were placed on a long wooden table.

"Sit down number 9 and eat your food."

From the day he been weaned from his mother's

milk, Abraham had only eaten kosher food. His mouth was dry, all day he'd had no food. In a small voice he asked for a drink of water. She handed him a tin mug and told him to fetch the water himself. Eating the bread, trying not to taste the rancid butter and drinking the bitter cocoa Abraham felt an intense loathing for these harsh women and their orders. Everywhere he dared look in this terrible house he saw their forbidding eyes waiting to strike him. The brief meal finished, he was told to wash and dry the plate and mugs. He was then taken up a flight of stairs to the first landing. Entering a long, narrow dormitory with barred windows. Rows of iron beds were covered with grey blankets and one pillow. Grey cotton covers had Reading Reformatory School printed across the tops.

"This is your bed number 9. Each morning, you will empty your slop bucket in the latrines and rinse it out."

A straight-backed man marched a line of white-faced boys all of Abraham's age into the dormitory. The nurse told him Abraham's name and number. He glanced at the boy, leaving the dormitory would the order,

"Prepare for bed."

The white face boys collected their thin cotton towels and toothbrushes, waiting to be marched first to the dining section of the kitchen, then to clean their teeth and wash in the washroom. Mr. Phelps, an ex-army man had an unsmiling face, a clipped moustache. Mousey hair didn't add much to his charm. As he walked he banged a cane against his hip, even when still he swung the cane to and fro. He barked orders at the boys with a sharp terrier sound. His personality lacked authority, oppressive discipline with his cane was his only means of expression.

Tin mugs were placed on the table where Abraham had eaten his meagre tea. Each mug was painted with a number. The boys sat at their mug, which was filled with unsweetened cocoa drinking it in total silence. Cocoa finished they collected their slop bucket's and brushed their teeth with tooth-powder. They were always hungry. Lack of good nourishment kept their bodies restless, sores didn't heal, they caught colds easily and coughed continually.

Mr. Phelps, nicknamed 'bootface' by the boys marched them back to the dormitory for evening prayers. His eyes watchful for trouble, his hand itching to bend his cane against bare legs. Red welts showed on several boys hands and legs, often bleeding. Mr. Phelps left the dormitory. The door was locked by morbid sounding keys.

"Seen the ba'k of bootface fer tonigh', Sow Cow'll come next ta see if 'er li'tle darlin's are tucked-up nice an' safe. 'ow I 'ates the bleeders. Archie Biggins me name come from Poplar, I do. If ever tha' lot come near Poplar me pa'll take their bleedin' 'eads orf, so gawd 'elp us 'e 'ill."

"I'm Abraham, Abraham Myersavitch my family live at Victoria Park Road"

"Toffs are yer, nice up tha' way, wat yer doin' 'ere, sell yer pa's silver tea-set?"

"No, we are quite poor."

"Poor, me pa's skint as a chick'n with no fevers. Me ma shoplif's, she ain't 'alf good never bin pinch'd she ain't. Foreign are yer?"

Abraham didn't reply.

Archie Biggins had red scabs around his mouth like many others at the reformatory school. From birth he was ill-nourished. Thin with bandy legs, broken front teeth and bitten nails. Abraham had only known English boys from a distance. Usually when with his brothers they were taunted with name calling for being Jews.

"Seeing' as I like yer face, I'll be yer mate in 'ere, if yer want ta."

"Call me Abe. Friends would be nice."

Boys isolated behind barred windows whispered to each other. Occasional laughing broke out reminding them they were after all children. Too poor with no champions to fight for their rights, too young to know the meaning of regret, their sullen faces took on the strain of their lives.

Rebels waiting to strike back at an unfair world lingered in every one of them.

"Have you been here long Archie?"

"Seems long, longer then yerself any rate."

"Why did they send you here?"

"Cors I 'ave to learn ta be good as gold. Same as we all do in 'ere. I 'elped me bruvver do a ware'ouse job, and the bleeders nabb'd us, me ma kept some stuff an' they search'd our 'ouse an' found it – me bruvver went down fer five years 'ard labour."

"I stole ten pounds to help my papa, he would have paid the money back, but the constable told the court I was a thief."

"Never mind Abe, we'll show the bleeders, see if we don't, 'ow come yer speak posh?"

"I didn't know I spoke posh, must be from school. I listened to my teachers. Mama can't speak English and papa speaks it badly."

"Why do yer go the school yer won't learn noffin', them places. A waste of good shopliftin' time me ma says, I ain't ever bin ta school. Round our way if yer 'ave teef yer a sissy same if yer goes to school."

"I like learning things, can you read Archie?"

"Cors not, readin' don't buy nuffin'."

"The food here is horrible."

"Don't bovver me, I ain't used to dinners. I pinch'd stuff orf stalls, didn't I, pa took money fer booze an' ma never fed us more un bread un jam, pa took orf years ago an' ma boozes when she ain't thievin'."

The boys were quietened when the uniformed women came into the dormitory. Miss. Green was tall, stick thin with a long sour face. The boys nicknamed her 'snake', because she looked at them, ready to poison them. In a thin reed-like voice that went with her face she called,

"Prayers."

The boys knelt down on bare floorboards as she read a verse from St. Mark, and with her they said the Lord's Prayer. Abraham knelt down, saying nothing.

At the top of the house an attic was used for solitary confinement. Older wayward boys were locked-up in the attic on bread and water punishment after being caned. Older boys were also separated from the younger ones by a partitioned section of the house.

The 'snake' left the dormitory with the usual noisy key turning that dominated the boys lives along with constantly on yellow lights casting sinister shadows on the green painted walls.

A group of talkative ruffians circled Abraham's bed. Abraham felt threatened.

"Wat's yer name nine?"

"Lost yer tongue 'ave yer?"

"Wat's in yer drawer, smuggled sweets in did yer?"

"We wan 'em see."

They tipped up the draw and threw Abraham's

kitbag across the dormitory. As he bent down to pick up his uniform he was kicked in the shins.

"Clear orf yer scum, leave 'im alone."

"Shut yer gob Archie Biggins or we'll do yer, won't we?"

A chorus of,

"Yus, Archie Biggins we'll do yer," echoed from the others. Archie Biggins grabbed a handful of hair pulling hard.

"Let go me 'air let go me 'air."

"By the time I lets go yer 'air will be on the floor Arfer 'icks."

Arthur Hicks scratched, kicked-out and roared with abandon. The others joined the fight. Slop buckets when flying, gashing the cheeks of a boy who was cheering the fight on. Blood marked his cheeks. He wiped his hand over his face making a grotesque red stain.

Amid the din they didn't hear Mr. Phelps come into the dormitory. For a few seconds he half watched the brawl with anger and fascination. Too much of this kind of nonsense, he could well lose his position. One of the boys shouted 'Bootface' and the brawlers untangled themselves, restless energy had been released with kicking, biting, scratching and bloody knees. Almost as if they knew the routine by heart they stood in line. Mr. Phelps brought the cane down heavily on each boy's open palm. One boy named Freddie Smith began to cry. He stuttered, was often bullied and the fighting had overwhelmed him, standing by his bed he'd not joined the fighting. This didn't stop Mr. Phelps caning him and taking pleasure from the boy's distress. He ordered every corner of the cold dormitory to be cleaned up with not a trace of mess in the morning. With sore hands they started cleaning up.

With kicked shins, angry red, raised welts on his right-palm, Abraham Myersavitch, a tired, miserable boy climbed into the narrow bed. He watched as boys turned to each other for comfort stroking penises, tossing and turning in hunger and pain.

Abraham turned his face away from the yellow light to see outside the sky was light blue, a summertime sky. He wanted to go home, he wanted to be free.

The first day at Reading Reformatory School ended. All through the night keys would turn, doors would bang and older boys behind the partition would shout abuse and fight.

Get-up time with loud bell clanging at six thirty in the morning with 'Bootface', his red-rimmed morning eyes vigilant to every movement, his cane freshly polished, timed the boys to the second. Marched in line to the washroom and back to the dormitory, damp if you were too slow.

Overalls with Reading Reformatory School written across the bib with the usual red thread, were worn to empty slop-buckets, mop the landing, the dormitory floor and the staircase. After airing, beds were made. No orders about problem bed-wetters were given to staff by the authorities. The 'snake' made these boys as miserable as she was able, which made their habit worse. Their mattresses stained and stinking were never covered with rubber sheets and nighttime to them was a trauma of nerves.

Toothache took two boys to nurse who did nothing to ease their pain. She wrote out a chit for the teeth to be pulled by a visiting dentist.

A suspected chickenpox case was quarantined. She dabbed green, foul-smelling ointment on rashes and brown liquid on mouth sores. A poor boy with fits was left in a locked room alone with a mattress on the floor. Porridge, two thin slices of bread and a mug of tea was breakfast for all of them.

Sunday breakfast was an egg with a single rasher and a mug of tea.

Lack of good food hardly nourished growing limbs. Inadequate portions with no fruit and few vegetables increased nervous problems suffered by these young people. Lack of proper care towards their obvious tensions increased their hostility and future violence. Food became a tyranny organised without sympathy by law and order.

Monday to Friday two hours of lessons were given. Two boys to a desk, in a large cold room with a blackboard and easel and a Miss. Coxford always holding a piece of white chalk, which she pointed at the class like a sword. Not used to the discipline of learning boys hated these lessons. Reading, writing and arithmetic meant nothing to them. They shifted uneasily at their desks, biting their nails and listening to nothing. Nicknamed 'cocky', Miss. Coxford took these classes dressed in black, never smiling. Talking to the boys in a flat, distant voice, she was a perfect funeral guest. The boys dislike of her was mutual. She loathed what she called, the 'mess of our back-streets'.

At the far end of Reading Reformatory School, a playing field and an exercise yard offered a small freedom to the offenders. Every day they were allowed the yard for half an hour, sometimes an hour to seem a little normal. Abraham though dreaded the yard. To the bullies he was different. He could read and write. He wasn't one of their kind. They kicked and taunted him the moment a chance came, a guard dressed like a constable didn't come to his aid. Only Archie Biggins defended him and ended up being punched and kicked.

Once weekly woodwork was taught to 'safe' offenders. Again, watched by a guard. For some reason they were not taught painting, just paper hanging. They were not allowed near scissors or any type of blade or knife for personal use. Their nails on hands and feet were cut by a nurse. Only tin mugs were given for drinking. Glass considered too dangerous near unstable boys. All dinner meats were already cut in pieces or minced. Their hair was cropped, shaved if nits were found.

Considering their young ages the treatment at Reading Reformatory School was almost as harsh as adult prisoners receive. They were 'little' thugs and thieves sent to reformatory school to be taught a harsh reality, that 'wrong-doing' will be punished and they had a debt to pay to society.

Bedtime and sleep let childhood dreams show those without nightmares, a brief glimpse of fairyland. Abraham closed his eyes away from the, hated yellow-glowing light, he closed his ears to night-time whispering and to himself prayed the prayer learned at his mother's knee.

In the name of The Lord.
Our God of Israel.
May Gabriel be on my right side.
Michael on my left side.
Before me Uriel
Behind me Raphael.
And above my head
The Divine Presence
Of the Lord our God
Amen

Sunday morning church service was taken by a local vicar in the draughty hall. The sermon brought on coughing bouts and the guard didn't report the boys poking their tongues out of the vicar's back. No respect was shown to clergy and the vicar was glad to leave the moment prayers ended.

Clean kit was handed out on Sundays. Boots were polished and the 'snake' inspected their lockers. Disturbed boys of ten ripped their clothes, some slashed their arms and legs with stones. Severe cases were sent to hospital.

During the night banging and shouting wasn't unusual from older boys. The 'snake' going off duty didn't take much notice when a noisy group began a chorus of swear words. Suddenly as she was collecting her things an unpleasant crash made her jump and she felt uneasy enough to go for a guard. Boys were screaming and tearing their dormitory apart. A fifteen year-old boy who was tall and heavily built managed to shatter the window-glass with a piece of hardwood from a broken locker. Through the jagged crack they threw bed-sheets out to the ground below. Slop buckets were poured down and smashed lockers and kit went down with everything else. Two night guards rushed in, but found the riot difficult to control, calm was impossible. In a wild frenzy of pent-up frustrations several boys were almost knocked out. By the time more help arrived a boy pushing his bedding through the cracked window-pane screamed as he slashed his arm on the jagged glass. Blood oozed over his hands staining his clothes. From shock at the sight of blood and near exhaustion from frenzy some boys began to sob, others swore obscenities at the guards.

With a ripped pillow-slip binding his arm to try to stop the bleeding the injured boy was hurried from the dormitory. An ambulance was heard coming up the drive of Reading Reformatory School. The eyes of most boys were showing swelling from punches and blood dripped from noses.

A kind of order returned with the worst trouble-makers being separated and locked in secure units. The rest were taken to an empty dormitory. No bedding was given to them and no treatment for gashes or bloody eyes and noses. They were locked in and left. The Governor would deal with their iniquitous behaviour in the morning.

Younger boys whispered lurid tales to each other about the night's 'going-on', going to the extremes of their imagination. The 'snake' was chucked out the window, when she was pushed through the bars her legs came off. 'Bootface' was tied up and left with a slop-bucket over his head and his cane tied to his hands behind his back. Archie Biggins told Abraham, the boy taken to the ambulance was dead. Abraham listened half with excitement and half with horror.

"A bit a ja'ged glass did 'is throat in, bled to death didn't 'e. Those bleeders killed 'im for sure, with me own eyes I seen 'is coffin, and 'is face all green."

Their thoughts held within their silence, the black-suited men approached the iron-railings and large iron gates. The watchman, a cigarette stuck to his lips slightly opened the gate when the bell was clanged. Saying that they were, the black-suited men asked to speak with the Governor and the gates were opened wide. The watchman pointed the way to the main entrance of Reading Reformatory School. The rusty bell was clanged and a uniform woman opened the door. She too asked their business, and a request to talk to the Governor was asked for.

"Do you have an appointment?"

"No"

"The Governor rarely sees anyone without an appointment. Please wait I will ask him. May I have your name and reason to visit."

"My name is Myersavitch, Rabbi Reuben Myersavitch. My brother is Rabbi Shepsul Myersavitch. I wish to discuss my son."

Realising he had a boy at the reformatory she gave both brothers a dismissive look.

"Please wait. Mr. Myer ... please wait."

The smell of carbolic and stale badly cooked food touched the rabbi's nostrils. Reuben felt an oppressive gloom spread over him. He was tired, his face pale and drawn from his illness. Shepsul mirrored his brother's emotion, both knowing Abraham was locked up in this prison-house.

"Please follow me, Mr. er ... the Governor will see you now."

"Good morning gentlemen, what can I do for you?"

"I've come to talk about my son Abraham Myersavitch sent here by the court. My brother and I would like to see him."

"I'm sorry gentlemen, you've had a wasted journey, we don't allow the offender a visitor for six months if their behaviour has caused no problems, your son may receive a visit. Now would unsettle him – we cannot allow new boys to become disturbed as a strict regime has to be learnt. I'm surprised all this information was not sent to you by post."

"No letter has been received about my son."

Reuben placed a blue velvet bag on the desk.

"I've brought my son's prayer-shawl and his prayer-book. His head must be covered with his *yarmulke.*"

"Mr. Meyersavitch your son is an inmate of Reading Reformatory School. He may have none of these things. May I remind you this is a Christian school of reform."

"May I remind you my son is a Jew, the son of a Rabbi."

"Such a pity Rabbi, he became a thief."

Shepsul put his hand on his brother's shoulder,

"My brother is recovering from recent illness. I do not want him provoked by you."

The Governor, Mr. Terence Hopkins-Richford, a red-faced rather obese man with a voice used for order and discipline – a voice with no kindness. A rules and regulations voice – an abrupt civil service man, gave both brothers a disdainful glance that could have withered a plant. He rang a hand-bell. The woman in a black uniform came in.

"Show the gentlemen out Miss Hughes."

Reuben looked at the Governor would eyes of scorn.

"You will never be a wise man, you use your little government power with offensive authority, my son will overcome this experience but men like you lessen England – to treat children badly for whatever reason is a sin. You should not be in charge of these unfortunate young boys. Their crimes are small compared to yours, a few moments in your company was enough to see your whole character."

As the main gates close behind them, Reuben looked up at the high wall covered with jagged-glass. He muttered to himself,

"The abyss, the abyss."

Shepsul his eyes tearful for Abraham and Reuben, was quiet. Once more the black suited men walked in silence towards the railway station.

Kitty's Wedding

"Come on me angel, give us the old one-two. Yer not made of wood Klara pick them feet up. Think of the parents who look forward to the school show. They like a sing-song an' yer terns. Don't stand like a dummy, give us yer best. Yer singin' a song about yer garden – move yer eyes as if yer gazin' at a view.

"Ma."

"'ow many times 'ave I told yer not ta call me ma!"

"Ma – mummy I can't remem'er all tha' about a silly song."

"Cors yer can. Now try the song the way I told yer."

"Oh it really is a werry pretty garden,
An' the soap works from the 'ouse tops could be seen,
If I got a rope an' pulley
Yer'd enjoy the breeze more fully
If it wasn't for the 'ouses in between."

"Give 'er a clap Phoebe, good gal, Klara, yer 'ad real style. I told yer, yer do it right."

"Why did Miss Margolis choose me. I 'ate singin' I ain't no good at songs."

"If Miss Margolis chose me Klara ta sing, me Klara will sing. Durin' the week we'll take a bus ride ta auntie Dinah's place. Yer cousin Becky will 'elp yer with singin'. She sings lovely in the *schul* choir. Stop moanin', yer temperament is as bad as a prima donna."

"I ain't a voice for singin'."

"'ere she goes moanin' again Mummy. I'm doin' a poem. I like poems best."

"Let's 'ear yer poem then, my Phoebe."

"Bed Time – A Poem.
Ta bed, ta bed, said Sleepy 'ead
Tarry awhile, said Slow
Put on the pan said Greedy Nan
We'll sup before we go!"

"We'll make a star of me gal yet."

"Phoebe's stupid, tha' ain't a real poem."

"Don't upset yer sister Klara, 'cause yer fed up. Phoebe does 'er best. Don't yer dolly?"

"Yus Klara I do's me best."

"Stupid, stupid school show, stupid Phoebe, stupid poem. I 'ate school. Miss Margolis is 'orrible."

"Klara that's enough, till we go ta auntie Dinah put the song in a drawer, else I'll 'ave an 'eadache with this carry-on. An yer'll 'ave a dose of brown mixture. Tha' soon sort yer mood out. Right now it wouldn't be a bad idea if yer both tidied up yer things before Pa comes 'ome. The lino's covered with pencils and drawin' paper. I thought yer loved yer doll Phoebe."

"I do love 'er."

"Then don't leave 'er with 'er pretty face in the coal-scuttle. I want everythin' ship-shape by the time Mr Levy comes for yer piana lessons. Wash them 'ands spotless. I can't 'ave sticky, dirty fingers on me ivories."

"Mummy, 'ave yer bought the stuff fer our

dresses?"

"Not yet, auntie Kitty 'asn't decided what colour or kind of stuff 'er bridesmaids will wear. Just as well as I'm a bit short this month. Pa didn't make much last week. Things 'ave been very quiet in the markets. The weddin' ain't fer a few months. Yer'll 'ave yer outfits by then. 'er temperament's as bad as yer own Klara if not worse. She'll change 'er mind a dozen times before she tells me the stuff ta buy."

"I 'ope its pink, pink's me favourite."

"I favour a nice peach or lavender organdie, pink's wishy-washy. Yer both suits peach or lavender better."

"What's organdie?"

"Questions, questions, a cotton muslin, very fine and stiffened. Its translucent, which means yer can see through it. Lit'le gals look pretty wearin' party frocks of organdie."

"Tra ... l ...ain't no good mummy our drawers will show!"

"Don't be daft yer 'ave white petticoats, won't yer! Grown up gals wear a silk called organza, that's very posh."

"Do their drawers show?"

"Cors not, they wear silk slips from France."

"When I'm big I'm gonna wear silk slips all day, 'an be very posh."

"I ain't gonna be posh like Klara. I like livin' with mummy an' me things."

"Ta very much Phoebe, now I know wha' yer think of me."

David Mendoza was doing his father's accounts.

The Mendoza's were a good family highly thought of, Kitty had done herself proud. They lived in a large Victorian, beautifully furnished house off Hackney Downs. From a stall in The Lane, their business had grown to three shops each managed by one of Raphael Mendoza's three sons. Raphael Mendoza had every reason to be proud of his achievement. He sold cutlery from cheap everyday use knives, forks and spoons to silver sets for occasions. Good crockery in the latest designs, down to basic household ware like buckets, mops, brooms, coal scuttles and bread-bins. Window shoppers might be tempted to buy the new gadgets from America, very cheap goods from Hong Kong and fragile china tea-sets from Japan. Festivals were not forgotten with fine linen tablecloths or oil cloths for kitchen tables. Beautiful glass in dazzling colours was displayed next to Italian pottery and British stoneware bought for strength. Large white cups and saucers which were cheap in times when money was scarce which in the East-end was always, were to be found in almost every house or rented rooms.

David Mendoza was a good looking man in an understated way. He was reserved, but not shy. In fact he was stern in his life-views. He'd certainly stand no nonsense from Kitty.

Sadly Raphael Mendoza had been a widower since his sons were small boys. He'd never remarried, Marie his sister helped him raise the boys.

Behind closed doors relatives and friends gossiped together about the betrothal.

"Amazin' ain't it, Kitty being wed. She must 'ave slipped a spoonful of love potion in 'is teacup."

"Don't be mean Rachel, Kitty's not as bad as she's painted."

"Nah, she's worse, 'er sour face's enough ta

curdle milk."

"David Mendoza could 'ave done worse believe me."

"'ark at ma, yer'v 'ad more bust-ups with Kitty then the lot of us!"

"Be fair, it ain't nice or right to talk about a gal just going to stand 'neath the *chuppah*[109]. 'ow would yer feel if yer own weddin' was mocked?"

"Chance would be a fine thing ma!"

"Don't worry, both of yers will find good 'usbands, Dinah saw weddings in 'er tea-cups."

"Findin' a man ain't me problem, gettin' 'im to the *schul* is a different story."

"Yer 'ave to learn to be subtle, don't yer, no man will willingly take on a wife, even less likely just after a war, yer 'ave to learn all the funny ways ta 'is 'eart, make 'im feel important an' clever even though 'e ain't none of them things. Coax 'im up the aisle."

"Cor ma, yer sound like an agony aunt in the romance magazines. If I 'ave ta take all that trouble ta make meself a bride forget it – no man's worth me learnin' the 'idden arts of love ta please 'im."

"Well as I said our Dinah is a true teller of tea-leaves, same with 'er dreamin' right every time, a weddin's comin' ta Cox Street before so many moons. I don't remember 'ow many moons mind yer. I 'ave ta ask 'er again."

"Poor Sarah must be so 'appy, ta be gettin' Kitty orf 'er 'ands. Wha' a dance she's led 'er ma fer years. Old Solly will put on a good show, 'e won't lose face in front of the Mendozas."

"Cost 'im a good 'andful of sovereigns this do will. The bride's family always pays fer a weddin', tradition ain't it."

"Did yer 'ear tha' pa, yer'll 'ave ta fork out fer

---

109   Wedding canopy

our nuptials."

"Please God only find 'usbands both of yers, an' ma will do yer a nice plate of cheese an' pickled onions on 'ot fresh rolls, with a slice of bread puddin' thrown in."

"Pa!"

"Don't laugh Rachel, pa means it!"

"Don't matter nothin' wrong with a tasty bit of cheddar in Flo's back room at the 'Three-Penny-Bit-and-Whistle'. She'll give us a medium fer alf-a-crown."

"Yer 'ave low standards Rachel, Flo's back room indeed, I ain't 'aving me weddin' party ruined in such a dump. Fer me a good 'otel ballroom, with gleamin' chandeliers an' violins an' delicious food an' pastries an'..."

"Better marry rich not poor Becky, else a big disappointment's on the cards."

A dozen or so streets away old Solomon was complaining about the reception costs.

"Kitty will ruin us Sarah. I won't 'ave a penny fer the 'orse's 'ay."

"Solomon Starr do yer want ta show us up in front of our guests? Would yer be 'appy to serve up salt-'errings? Be proud our daughter's marryin' David Mendoza. I thought she'd never find a man let alone Raphael Mendoza's son."

"There's more to Kitty then you ever give 'er credit fer. Still I'd still like to eat fer the rest of the year."

"Stop moanin', yer won't go short."

"Sarah, 'ave yer ever in yer life seen such prices. The war didn't cost the treasury as much as they want ta bake a weddin' cake. I ask yer Sarah four pounds, five and six fer a fancy bit of decoration. A bouquet of lilies two pounds ten, button 'oles eight

pounds fer dozen. Bleedin' robbery. Fer one-and-six
the gypsies will sell yer carnation ta fill a vase an'
throw in a 'wish' into the bargain. Madam wants the
schul choir if yer don't mind, then there's loads of
candles to pay fer plus the *schul* donations, wine an'
more flowers fer the tables, add tha' lot up Sarah, just
ta marry Kitty orf!"

"I ain't takin' a blind bit of notice, our
daugh'er's 'avin' a grand weddin' ta remember an' I'm
havin' a huge framed photograph to 'ang up over the
fireplace. Remember our shabby turn-out Solomon.
Cake an' a pot of tea in yer ma's place, the tea was
cold an' our relatives 'ardly able to move in 'er small
parlour. Remember I cried meself to sleep in yer ma's
back bedroom an' you slept on the settee because the
bed wasn't big enough fer both of us. Yer want our
Kitty ta suffer such humiliation?"

"Be reasonable Sarah, me ma did 'er best bless
'er, but them were 'ard times. I've made good fer yer
since – I know Kitty's a modern gal an' we'll give 'er
a grand weddin', don't mean ta say the prices are fair.
They're all money grabbers when it comes ta
weddin's. We still 'ave to count our pennies."

"While yer countin' Solomon add on the cost
of weddin' outfits an' our clothes. I ain't wearin' me
faded black silk an' yer shoes are scuffed."

Sarah called the collies into the scullery for
their dinner leaving old Solomon to his calculations.
The more he added up the longer his face grew, he
mumbled mild curses under his breath, thinking
what a terrible waste of money weddings were. Even
the *schul* dowry aggravated him.

"She'll give all the money ta 'er new 'usband.
Sarah an' me won't see as much as a brass farthin'!"

Kitty arrived home with a face as long as her
father's. Sarah gave one glance at her and sensed

trouble. Kitty had her 'I'm in a black mood' face!'

"What's up gal?"

"I need a cup of tea me stomach 'urts."

"I'll make yer a glass of warm milk with honey an' a peck of ginger. Tea ain't no good fer belly-ache. Young brides 'ave all sorts ta cope with, aches an' pains fer no reason, cry their eyes out they do, then the moment a gold band's gleamin' on their fingers they don't 'arf cheer up."

"Some of 'em can't stand the sight of their 'usbands."

"Serve 'em right fer marryin' fer reasons an' not fer love. 'taint worth it – leads ta misery all round."

"Love don't last ma, what then?"

"Then don't mat'er, love's a good start – marriage is 'ard if yer poor but love 'elps, at least love 'as a nice 'onest feel, marryin' fer reasons don't."

"Good ta know yer married pa fer love of 'im an' not 'is 'andsome face an' big wallet!"

"'taint none of yer business why I married pa."

"Stop embarrassing yer ma Kitty."

"Truth is embarrassing sometimes, I'll give ma the benefit of the doubt. Fer two pins I'd call the 'hole thing orf with David. I dunno what I'm lettin' meself in fer, do I – 'ow do I know I'll like livin' with 'im or he'll like livin' with me!"

"New wives don't know the future, no more than old wives did – leavin' 'ome will be just as 'ard fer David as yerself. Pa will be only too 'appy to give yer two pins to call it orf, 'es havin' 'eart palpitations over the cost of things!"

"Trust pa, 'e don't do anything with a good 'eart."

"God job 'e's just gorn out, pa thinks he's the soul of 'uman kindness. Just the same don't be mean about yer pa, 'e enjoys a good grouse same as you. By the way Bella popped round this mornin', yer next fittin' is 2.30 pm next Thursday. She was pleased with the material, wild silk an' lace is lovely, an' the dress already looks wonderful 'arf done."

"So it should do she charges enough."

"Bet'er write down the appointment, yer 'ave a lot ta remember, 'ere take yer 'ot milk an' 'oney. Lucky to 'ave a peck of ginger. Ain't been none since the war. I think it was old stock. Solly's treatin' Esther to a gown by Bella. My Solly's a good 'usband shares every penny with 'er. I couldn't wish fer a nicer daughter-in-law than Esther. She 'ad terrible guts-ache before 'er weddin', like you. She was green. Nerves – all nerves."

"I'm gonna 'ave a lie down ma."

"Yus. That's right, sip yer milk slowly dolly – too much excitement, simply too much excitement."

David Mendoza was giving his wedding outfit a good airing – no moths were flying about the bedroom light bulb, he didn't need new evening shoes, perhaps he'd buy a brocade waistcoat, not flash. Good quality and well tailored, he needed a dress-shirt and silk black socks. He thought he'd look quite the dandy.

"Yer doin' a runner David, clothes all over the bed?"

"They're ready fer a good airing – don't leave yours till the last minute. Tuesday afternoon I'm buying silk socks an' cologne an' a silk handkerchief fer me jacket pocket. Yer bound ta need odds an' ends, come with me."

"Gawd we'll be dressed up like nancy boys. Why can't we wear dark suits?"

"Dressing correctly fer yer weddin' is important – the women will be dressed up to the nines. Can't let 'em steal the show – the suits will end up moth eaten if we don't wear 'em. Don't wear too much rouge Jonathan an' yer won't pass fer a nancy."

"Weddin's, why do yer want ta marry Kitty Starr, she ain't yer type. Yer've always run a mile from gals like 'er."

"That's true, but I like 'er spirit, she don't stand no nonsense. She's alright, 'er temper will calm down an' I think she'll be a good mother. She knows the value of money, why go 'untin' fer a wife, when she's on me doorstep. Solly and me get along and Esther's one-in-a-million. I thought abou' askin' her sister Rachel out but she's a bit young fer me – an' Kitty seemed right fer me. I don't think I've made a mistake.

"Well brother sooner or later we're gonna find out. I bet yer five quid a win she'll drive yer round the bend."

"Yer on – an' yer better pay up. By the way according ta pa's books yer down on takin's."

"Not my fault, customer's are thin on the ground. They buy the odd cup an' saucer when old cups are too cracked ta use – ignore fancy goods, even mops aren't sellin' they're using rags to clean floors – yer can't blame 'em. Pa would do bet'er ta fill the shelves with tea, sugar and fresh but'er – food an' drink that's what they need – war an' flu's taken the guts out if most of 'em – in fact I'm thinkin' of branching orf from pa an' startin' a grocer's. Food stores David, big style, full of food an' fruit, food stores, that's the future, pa should advertise, something about adverts people like an' remember – gettin' back ta Kitty, I don't think yer 'ave been starstruck with 'er – ever – now Elisa Bamberg she 'ad the works – both of us 'ad weak knees lookin' at Elisa."

"Moonin' over a gal and choosin' a wife have no connection – Kitty an' me ain't in love – our union will be a partnership, to share our lives – I'm stable – Kitty likes that, the buildin' blocks of marriage are not made of piles of love-letters."

"Sod bricks – I want sweet pastries – where did pa get yer from – yer sound like a robot. I dare say yer argument's sound enough an' much *mazel* to yer, but give me Elisa – a chap needs a bit of glamour ta wake up next ta 'im – we're old an' ugly soon enough."

"Your Elisa will cost yer – she'll want such a diamond ta make all the Whitechapel Becky's eyes pop out, such dresses yer'll need six wardrobes, no Cliftonville or Margate only the Riviera will do fer madam – think about it!"

"I am, ah the bliss of watchin' me Elisa put all them dresses on – and take 'em orf, an' I fancy a walk around the Riviera meself."

Kitty lay on her bed staring at the ceiling going over and over events in her mind.

"I'm twenty-nine years old if I don't watch out fer meself I'll be too old to 'ave a family. I 'ave me doubts about David a real torment they are, just when I think I'm not makin' a mistake, a big doubt jumps at me shoutin' 'yes yer are gal', and I come all over miserable with the whole weddin' circus. Me trouble is I'm impulsive I get meself in daft situations and 'ave ta wriggle me way out like an eel caught in a drain. Yer'd think at twenty-nine I 'ave more sense. I suppose a lot of gals are so thrilled to be on a receivin' end of a proposal, they says yes, that's why yer see some really odd couples 'cause she was taken by surprise an' 'e wants a wife ta take care of 'im. I'm fond of David Mendoza but I'm fond of loads of things ain't I. We don't 'ave a romance, maybe thats wha' I'm searchin' fer – then again 'ow many gals 'ave I seen breakin' their 'earts over romance, dozens! Ma's 'appy as a lark about David Mendoza, pa's fed up listen' to 'er go on about the weddin', am I weird or somethin' I 'ave doubts. I ain't no one ta ask that's me problem me galfriends are such silly cows when a man's in the picture. 'Give 'im ta us if yer don't want 'im Kitty!', that sums 'em up. Brains like sieves they 'ave, a serious discussion to them is the colour of their winter coats an' goin' 'up West' fer dinner. No I'll 'ave ta sort me doubts all by meself. Gawd one kiss an' a bunch of sweet violets an' I order a weddin' dress. I love this old 'ouse an' ma an' pa – I 'ate the thought of livin' with strangers next door. I've grown up with our neighbours they're like me own family – an' me bedroom, every problem I've 'ad, since ma gave me, me own room when me periods started an' she told me with such a serious face 'ow babies 'appen (bless 'er) an' I 'ad to guard me precious 'womanhood', I sorted out, lookin' up at the ceilin'. Why I know every stain and crack up there, pa's no good at gettin' repairs done quick. Poor ma would 'ave thrown a fit if I told 'er I've known where babies come from an' 'ow gals make 'em since I was ten an' Hetty Michaels told me 'ow she'd watched through the keyhole 'er ma an' pa makin' babies – 'orrible it was gave 'er such a fright she kept away from keyholes an' 'as never married, just shows yer. Michael an' Jonathan will be nice brothers-in-law, Marie's not bad not sociable mind yer, just as well I ain't too fond of relatives. Now if yer don' mind David wants ta move to Chingford. Well I ain't movin' there – I like it here. Why should I upset me parents ta please 'im. David says we 'ave ta bet'er ourselves an' raise our children right – do me a favour – he's already lumber'd me with a 'ouse I don't want an' children – 'e sounded like a solicitor askin' me to sign me will! Then doubts started comin' real quick – ma thinks yer 'ave ta be subtle with a man – well I ain't subtle an' I'm not dancing ta the Mendoza's tune fer the rest of me life – I'm sorry 'e ever asked me out – an' I ain't goin' through with the weddin', gawd I feel bet'er already – ma will be disappointed an' I'll 'ang the weddin' gown up in me wardrobe and won't take it out till I'm sure I 'ave no doubts."

"'ere Kitty 'ave yer dinner on a tray, no wonder yer 'ead aches there ain't a breath of air in 'ere."

"Ta fer the tray ma, I feel much bet'er I needed a few minutes to relax."

"Are ya goin' ta the club?"

"I dunno, what's the time?"

"7.30 pm, yer friends will already be there, will do yer good ta 'ave a night out."

"David don't want me goin' there no more once we're married, clubs ain't dignified places fer married women."

"Why, yer grown up with the crowd who goes there – a bit of light relief don't 'arm no-one."

"Them Mendoza's are a very grand lot ma."

"Too grand if yer asks me Kitty,"

Lou Moss arrived at the club same time as Kitty, to play snooker. A group of girls stood in a circle watching the game. Harry Moss, Lou's father ran a barber's shop off Commercial Road, Lou worked for his father as Harry had worked for his, in the same shop. Smart men used Harry's barber shop, even West end actors liked him to cut their hair. Faces were shaved and cleansed with hot white towels, their moustaches trimmed even waxed. Some types liked their nails manicured, all were splashed with cologne before leaving, were fussed over, gossiped with, while buying the secret things men buy at the barbers. Each man felt an Adonis unto himself.

You can see someone many times not taking any interest in them. Suddenly they step out of a grey background, coming froward like important figures in a painting. Kitty saw Lou Moss a smiling man with a dimpled chin and glossy black hair. A thrill went up and down her spine as she watched him. Thin-air took all her doubts away. Yes, a barber like Lou would suit her fine. She knew all that would become dear to her was in his face. The club lights were dimmed at ten-thirty pm. Harvey Goldman the manager called,

"Collect yer coats please, 'ope yerv enjoyed yerselves. Go 'ome safe now an' be'ave yerselves."

Saying goodnight to Harvey, Kitty collected her coat from the cloakroom – to walk home with her girlfriends. Lou Moss came up behind her,

"Fancy a walk 'ome Kitty?"

"Sure Lou, don't mind if I do."

"Ma yer goin' to look grand in turquoise silk with one or two tucks 'ere an' there, a light iron an' lo an' be'old yer be dressed ta go to the ball."

"I was in luck Miriam 'ad choice remnants goin' cheap, wha' she only stocks, its worth goin' ta her shop just ta look 'round. Sequins in silver an' gold, beads of every size, feathers, find yer anything Miriam will – "ere Phoebe,' she says, 'make-up lovely fer a weddin', take the silk outside an' see the colour in daylight.' Miriam sells yer stuff yer didn't know yer needed! 'er daugh'er's expectin' any day now, Miriam is over the moon, she's knitted enough baby clothes ta start a business."

"I'm glad she showed yer the turquoise, 'bout time yer 'ad a change of colour. Black an' more black been yer motto fer years. Esther calls us the Chinese silk road queens, funny 'ow we all chose sensual silk."

"Mind yer language Rachel."

"Ma, don't be narrow minded, we ain't Victorians. Silk is sensual, same as velvet."

"Well I'm proud ta be a Victorian an' our Sophie's too young fer such talk in front of 'er."

"No I ain't ma, I enjoy listening ta me sisters, that's learnin', ta listen an' remember things."

"I'll give yer, 'no I ain't!' I says in Cox Street yer is."

"I 'ear bad things down the markets when I 'elp pa. Pa don't say I must block me ears up an' not listen!"

"I ain't yer pa, an' 'e's too busy trying ta make a livin' an' so 'e don't realise what yer can 'ear goin' on. Yer 'ave ta respect yer 'ome, cos if yer don't know-one else will – set an example Sophie, set an example."

"Keep still Soph, unless yer'd like a bum stuck over with pins like a pin-cushion."

"I'm so excited Becky, I ain't ever 'ad such a divine dress in me 'ole life, I truly ain't!"

"If yer keep movin' yer still won't 'ave a divine dress cos it won't be finished in time. Wait till yer see

Klara an' Ruthie an' Phoebe ma, adorable ain't the word – yer won't take yer eyes orf 'em. Their bridesmaids dresses are palest lavender organdie covered with deep violet velvet polka dots, over white silk petticoats. Their bonnets are smothered with tiny white and pink rosebuds an' their slippers are soft violet leather with gold buckles. We know 'ow ta put on a show of style when the fancy takes us, we'll look so gorgeous no-one will know who the bride is."

"That will just suit Kitty, she'll scratch our eyes out. I still can't imagine Kitty as a wife let alone a ma."

"Stranger things 'ave 'appened, odd types marry. Where they 'oney-moonin'?"

"Big secret that one, Kitty ain't sayin' – don't forget the rice, we'll smother 'em."

"Yer the milk of 'uman kindness Rachel, a right cruel streak runs in yer veins."

"Well I can't pretend to like Kitty, I'm only goin' cos I enjoy a weddin' an' I don't want ta upset ma, an' Kate ain't goin' 'cause she can't leave 'er business,"

"Well I ain't wastin' our food, rice indeed, cut-out paper shapes an' colour 'em in – after all confetti only lands on the pavement – why we could be arrested fer wastin' food."

"Nah, ma don't be daft, I ain't such a thick 'ead as ta get us nabbed am I, weddin' is a weddin' after all – cheers up everybody."

"Take yer 'alf-'our if the three of yers does paper confetti, 'cause yer ain't 'avin me rice, so stop naggin'."

"Come on ma, be a sport a few grains of rice won't be missed, I'll give up me dinner portion."

"So will I."

"An' me."

"I don't know where you three came from why can't yer be sensible like yer brothers – yer can 'ave a bag full, but no rice with yer baked potato's next week."

"Ta ma, one bag will do nicely."

Sarah went with Kitty to order the wedding invitations from Meisel's the printers. Kitty had taken care to write all the names of relatives and friends clearly, so no-one was forgotten – Sarah was worried the arrangements would go wrong – there has already been a big enough upset with the Mendoza's, Sarah didn't wish for anymore.

"Stop worryin' ma, I'm a good organiser."

"There's so much ta remember, if one of the family was left out, think of the aggravation, the feud would go on fer years."

"No one will be left out, anyway that will be no loss, yer see 'em once a year if yer lucky, I'm bein' polite invitin' 'em ta our weddin'. Yer'll be a wreck if yer don't stop worryin'. Remember what pa said after our Solly's weddin', 'e'd never go ta another family weddin with yer. From day one yer were impossible. And why ma, a weddin' is a joyful occasion. This time ain't no different. Yer all nerves an' worry – for the 'undreth time let yer 'air down. Enjoy yerself fer once."

"I know I'm a worrier, but I ain't slap-dash like you an' pa. I'm conscientious."

"Now about the invitations, I want gold borders – an' gold print, silver is too boring – gold is elegant. 'ere's Meisels lets go in an' ask what's on offer."

At various addresses when the gold bordered invitations arrived in the morning post, the exclamation was the same – 'well I never!'

SARAH AND SOLOMON STARR
INVITE YOU WITH GREAT PLEASURE
TO CELEBRATE THE WEDDING
OF THEIR DAUGHTER KITTY,
TO LOU MOSS SON OF
JESSIE AND HARRY MOSS AT 4.30 PM
BEVIS MARKS SYNAGOGUE
SUNDAY 22ND JUNE
RECEPTION
AT
THE CORNER HOUSE
PICCADILLY
7.30PM TO 11.30 PM
DANCING TO
MAXI LEVINE'S BAND

rsvp SOLOMON STARR

Sunshine shone through the bedroom curtains waking Kitty after a restless night. Small nervous spasms in the pit of her stomach gave an edgy start to her morning. Thoughts of Lou came into her mind, wondering if she would find his nakedness embarrassing and if he would like her body. Their sense of humour would help any odd moments, they both enjoyed a good laugh and both of them undressed would be as funny as fair-ground 'funny mirrors'.

Before rising she prayed. Taking comfort in Hebrew words.

Sharp at seven-thirty am, Sarah came into the bedroom with a morning cup of tea and a plate of

biscuits. Kitty watched her mother draw the curtains
and open the window, a ritual that hadn't changed
since Kitty's childhood.

"Ma yer shouldn't wait on me, I should bring
you an' pa tea in the morning."

"'appy the bride the sun shines on. What a
lovely day its gonna be. Drink yer tea. I'll make
breakfast after yer bath."

"Bring yer tea in 'ere ma, sit with me awhile, I
won't 'ave the biscuits, I ain't cleaned me teeth,"

Sarah fetched her tea and relaxed in kitty's
bedroom chair.

"Won't 'alf be quiet 'ere when yer gone an I
'ave two empty bedrooms on me 'ands."

"Yerv always wanted a sewin' room ma, an'
'ated yer machine in the corner of our parlour, now
yerl 'ave one – Solly's old room or mine."

"Pa makes such a face when I use me machine
– 'e 'ates the treadle noise, mind yer 'e don't grouse if
I'm repairin' a shirt of 'is."

"I 'ope Lou don't turn into a pa – people change
after a few years, sometimes for the worse."

"Don't be daft, no-one could turn into a 'pa',
'e's a one orf. The collies will miss yer terrible. An' in
'is way so will pa – but 'e don't show it – ain't manly
'e says ta show feelin's."

"Gawd 'elp us ma, I ain't sailin' ta Australia.
I'll be round the corner."

"Ain't the same as bein' at 'ome, when yer
family goes their own way, ain't the same no more."

Big tears moistened Sarah's eyes and bigger
tears splashed down Kitty's cheeks, onto her chin.

"Ma leave orf, yer know I always cry when yer
upset. I meant ta be bleedin' radiant today, not red-
eyed with swollen lids. No wonder brides cover their
faces with veils – they've cried their eyes out all

night."

"I'm sorry Kitty, I didn't mean ta cry did I – but well ... I'll run yer bath, blow yer nose an' clear yer 'ead."

"I love yer ma."

"An' I love my Kitty."

Solly took his mother, Esther and the children ahead of Solomon who would escort Kitty to Bevis Marks Schul.

Jessie and Harry Moss had taken their place beneath the canopy and were joined by Lou. A *minyan* of ten men were present, the choir were softly singing Hebrew songs, friends and family members were arriving. All men wore the prayer shawl draped over their shoulders, their heads covered with velvet *yarmulkas*.

Sarah's nerves had been quietened with a tot of brandy. Wearing a dove-grey gown with a corsage of tiny lily-like flowers, her hair covered with a dove-grey 'kerchief and a tiny lily tucked into her bun at the nape of her neck she looked every inch the proud mother of the bride everyone was longing to see. Before she left home Solomon had squeezed his wife's hand – this from him was tremendous affection!

Bevis Marks Schul always kindled candles for weddings, which with the exotic perfumes in the air gave a glow of romance to the wedding ceremony. Dinah, Becky and Rachel arrived, smiling with pleasure and sure of their beauty. Becky, Dinah's daughter, looked pretty in pink muslin with silver stars sewn around her waist. Sophie believing she would faint with the splendour of it all wore her dress like a princess, although all the morning she'd fretted about her freckles. Phoebe in her turquoise felt a lump in her throat, looking at her daughters and granddaughter all dressed up, knowing Henry's feet were bothering him, she sat him down, before she joined women guests on the balcony. Dinah's husband Monty, was late and Alfie arrived just before the bride. All Lou's friends and relatives were there watching kitty's family with interest as they didn't know them very well.

Just before a special event the strange hush of expectation lulls a gathering, suddenly the mood lifts as the awaited moment is upon them. The bride with her father was coming before the canopy followed by two small fairy-bridesmaids – dressed to delight all who saw them. Klara and Phoebe holding Kitty's lace train, their violet posies clutched in their hands and their wrists showing the coral bangles their new uncle Lou had given them.

Followed by Esther, tall and lovely in a deep violet taffeta gown. Strands of gold thread wound through her hair the same thread of gold falling from her waist to the folds of her gown. Esther too, like her children carried a posy of violets. Ruthie wide-eyed up in the balcony with Phoebe and her aunts.

Kitty looked very beautiful – her dress of wild silk covered with ivory lace, her delicate headdress of tiny white and pink roses, her bouquet of white and pink roses, her jet black long hair brushed loosely lay long and lovely almost to her breasts.

> *'Blessed be he that cometh in the name of the Lord. We bless you out of the house of the Lord.*
> *O, come, let us worship and bow down;*

let us kneel before the Lord our maker.
Serve the Lord with joy, come before him
with exulting.'

With the two families being joined by marriage,
a psalm of thanksgiving is recited by relatives and
friends.

'Shout for joy unto the Lord, all ye lands.
Serve the Lord with joy; come before Him
with exulting. Know ye that the Lord He
is God. He hath made us and we are His
people and sheep of His pasture. Enter
into His gates with thanksgiving and
into His courts with praise. Give thanks
unto Him, bless His name for the Lord is
good, His loving kindness is everlasting
and His faithfulness from generation to
generation. He who is might, blessed and
great above all beings, may He bless the
bridegroom and bride.

Prayer of Address

Blessed art Thou, oh lord our God, king
of the universe, who createst the fruit of
the vine.
Blessed art thou, O Lord our god, king of
the universe, who hath sanctified us by
the commandments and hast given us
command concerning forbidden
marriages; who hast disallowed unto us
those that are betrothed, but hast
sanctioned unto us such as are wedded to

us by the rite of the canopy and sacred
covenant of wedlock.
Blessed art thou, O Lord, who sanctified
thy people Israel by the rite of the canopy
and the sacred covenant of wedlock.'

Lou took Kitty's right hand and placed upon
her forefinger a band of gold.

"Behold though art consecrated unto me by
this ring, according to the law of Moses and Israel."

The Hebrew marriage contract is read by the
celebrant. The seven benedictions are said.

'Blessed art Thou, O Lord our God, king
of the universe who createst the fruit of
the vine.
Blessed art Thou, O Lord our God, king of
the universe who hast created all things
to Thy glory.
Blessed art Thou, O Lord our God, king of
the universe creator of Man.
May she who was barren (Zion) be
exceeding glad and exult, when her
children are gathered within her joy.
Blessed art Thou, O Lord who makest
Zion joyful through her children. O make
these loved companions rejoice, even as
of old Thou didst gladden Thy creatures
in the Garden of Eden.
Blessed art Thou, O Lord who makest
bridegroom and bride rejoice.
Blessed art thou, O Lord our God, king of
the universe who hast created joy and
gladness, bridegroom and bride, mirth

and exultation, pleasure and delight,
love, brotherhood, peace and fellowship.
Soon may there be heard in the cities of
Judah and in the streets if Jerusalem, the
voice of joy and gladness. The voice of
the bridegroom and the voice of the
bride, the jubilant voices of bridegrooms
from their canopies and of youths from
their feasts of song.
Blessed art Thou, O Lord who makest the
bridegroom to rejoice with the bride.

The two families joined by marriage sip wine
from a shared glass. The glass is broken by the
bridegroom, *mazeltov, mazeltov, mazeltov* is shouted
by the gathering of relatives and friends.

The Celebrant Pronounces The Benediction
Psalm 90:

Praise ye the Lord, praise God in His
sanctuary
Praise Him in the firmament of His power
Praise Him for his mighty acts
Praise Him according to His abundant
greatness
Praise Him with the blast of the horn
Praise Him with the harp and the lyre
Praise Him with the timbrel and the
dance
Praise Him with stringed instruments
and the pipe.
Praise Him with the clear-toned cymbals
Praise Him with the loud-sounding

cymbals
Let everything that hath breath praise
the Lord.
Praise ye the Lord.
Blessed be the Lord forever more. Amen
and amen.
Blessed be the Lord out of Zion, who
dwelleth in Jerusalem. Praise ye the
Lord. Blessed be the Lord God, the God of
Israel, who alone doeth wondrous things
and blessed be His glorious name for ever
and let the whole earth be filled with His
glory.
Amen and amen.

Lou kissed his wife gently.

Sarah and Jessie both mothers, their eyes wet with tears left the *chuppah*. Henry and Harry clasped hands and the celebrant shook hands with all of them wishing the bride and groom a long, prosperous married life.

Klara and Phoebe carefully lifted the delicate lace train and with Esther behind them followed the bride with her groom to the entrance of Bevis Marks.

Everyone crowded around them throwing sweets, rice and coloured paper over them with clapping and laughter.

As the wedding photographs were taken a chimney sweep (hired by Jessie) came out of the small crowd of cockney's waiting to see the bride calling,

"Best of sweep's luck ta yer missus."

A cockney shouted,

"Keep yer rollin' pin 'andy an' bash 'im one if 'e plays yer up."

Banter went back and forth and cockney children stuffed the fallen sweets in their mouths.

Kitty threw her bouquet high in the air and Rachel caught it. Lou looked down on Kitty's face.

"I love yer Mrs. Moss."

Kitty could only smile her heart was so full of joy.

Sophie had the last word as the wedding party went home to rest before the reception.

"Cor ma, me life will never be the same, never I tell yer, never ma. I ain't ever felt so rich."

1921
Let's Bob Our Hair and Dance the Charleston

Waiting for the removal waggon to arrive at the new house in Narford Road, Hackney, Reuben with Amos and Lazarus were discussing Darwin's 'Origin of the Species.' All the Myersavitch family had loud, pleasant voices resonant, like most East Europeans. They didn't hear the waggon pull-up at the front.

"'ere guv, are these 'ere yer goods?"

"Yes, yes, thank-you. One second I'll open the front door."

Soon after the furniture arrived Peshe came to help Reuben sort things in as much order as is possible on moving day. Dosha was a great re-arranger of furniture. Shepsul often called her 'Mrs Re-arranger' or 'Mrs Where's-my-chair-gone?' Peshe was glad Dosha hadn't come, she could work on without a fuss. Reuben stood watching the men carry the contents in. Some items mysteriously vanished off these waggons, so being a wise, careful soul Reuben kept his eyes on things.

Amos and Lazarus were still in discussion. Reuben taught all his children from childhood the difference between a discussion and an argument. Never-the-less voices in the garden sounded agitated, a cockney with a cane-basket on his head balanced with one hand, shouted,

"'ere you two sounds like a bleedin' punch-up. Come an' give yer pa an 'and."

Carrying an end each of a chest of drawers upstairs Lazarus told Amos he was a soul-sick pagan. Amos called Lazarus a foolish believer in fables, worse than the 'long black coats'.[110]

Religion and science clashed head on as Lazarus the believer almost dropped the chest on Amos the scoffer's foot. Amos tried to have the last word calling his brother a believer in fantasy-mist full of mad prophets and weird threats from heaven.

"Amos, did Darwin ever say he was an unbeliever? Evolution only means gradual changes in animals over millions of years, that too may be ordained by God. To believe is much harder than not to believe."

"Science is the future Lazarus, stop wasting your life on myths."

"Ei! Ei! Where did you come from?"

A grey and white thin cat was gently purring by Reuben's leg.

"You've moved in and demand food well perhaps I can find you a saucer of milk."

As Reuben opened the pint bottle of milk they'd brought with them, the thin grey and white young stray, purred louder. Another cat would make Rifka smile.

The waggon load was scattered over various rooms. Amos found a broom and brushed the stairs down. All the windows were opened to air the house – Peshe was searching boxes for bed linen, and blankets were shaken out in the garden.

An elder tree hung with tiny black pearl-like fruit, swayed with the autumn breeze – sparrows pecked at the clusters dropping berries, which

---

110   Hasidics

everyone trod on, leaving a rich juice stain patch on the grass.

The removal men were each given a tip and thanked Reuben with a salute from their caps.

"Mama will be happier here papa."

"I hope so, she grieves for Abraham, we all do, but his mother hurts in another way. A change of scene may ease her mind."

The gasman arrived to turn on the gas, showing them where the safety taps were and costing a sixpence in the meter an hour. Peshe couldn't wait to find a sixpence, she'd unpacked and rinsed cups and they clapped when the kettle 'whistled' *mazel tov*. The strange rather ghostly odour in the cellar where the metres and safety taps were, lingered in the hallway. Peshe was glad there was an electric light down there. Cellars were always unwelcoming places, with omens in dark corners.

Dr Michael Kavitz had known Reuben since childhood. His father had for many years fund-raised for the *schul*. Even when his family moved to north London, his father still fund raised for the community.

"Rifka is low spirited, very sad and distant from us at home – I'm unable to reach her, to ask her what's wrong – she seems damaged, Michae. Our older children are concerned for their mother's health."

"Reuben we show stress in our own way. In the correct amount stress is good for us, making the body aware that action is needed. Our bodies otherwise could be in danger. Stress is the danger signal we carry with us from early mankind's fight for survival. Gloom has overtaken Rifka. She is hurting for Abraham's sake."

"We have other children who need her!"

"True, but they are at home. The family's there

for their needs. Abraham has no-one. Boys in reformatory school are helpless. Rifka reaches out to him with silent sadness. Depression manifests as an illness and indeed may become so, which often leads to suicide. Rifka is simply passing through a dark period. Since your early life together she has given birth nearly every year. Fatigue has weakened her body – she is anxious, tired and unhappy for her son, the last thing she wants to do is talk or smile at anyone. She needs to cry herself out, make her feel sorry for herself Reuben, being too strong is not such a good thing for these problems. Stroke her hair, talk about her family in Eastern Europe, touch a nerve release some of her tension. Medicine is useless for Rifka's sorrow, a little loving-kindness goes further.

You must also realise she is nearing the time of life, when a woman's body begins to show signs of change.

Over the next five years or so Rifka may experience difficult times. Men do not respond to their wives suffering and problems, men appear callous. She will be tearful, have headaches and bone-pain and face apathy and nervous traumas. Her life will seem useless to her. Some women go through none of this bodily chaos, they're the lucky ones. Let's hope Rifka is such a one!

For Rifka and the family this change will cease as she reaches her fifties, please God all will be bright again.By the way, how's the diamond trade?"

"Benjamin has a quick eye, he finds a blemish in a stone before me. I enjoy the business."

"I'm a doctor without a trade!"

"Michael a doctor won't ever need one, thank you for our talk I feel less worried now."

"Take care of yourself Reuben. In a few months I'd like to check you over, don't forget."

"I'll come but I feel fit enough these days, thank God."

For years Shmuel Potzloch needed a reason to hand in his notice to Jascha Kahn and at the same time move to a new district. His low wage packet and the disgust he felt about Abraham Myersavitch's detention decided his mind into action. First he found a job as a cutter, with Irving Julius Limited., a well known dress firm. Then he rented a house in Hackney, a few streets away from Narford Road. Only then did he tell his wife they were leaving Victoria Park Road.

Sprintza Potzloch thought poor Abraham Myersavitch being taken away was a cruel act. By nature she was inclined to let unpleasantness pass her by. The fuss of moving was a nuisance. She knew her husband was right. Jascha Kahn could easily accuse one of their sons of stealing. She was pleased to be going near to Rifka Myersavitch, and accepted her husband's decision without complaint.

As Sprintza Potzloch handed Jascha Kahn the rent book, she told him for what he did to Abraham Myersavitch for a few paltry pounds he should '*se zul dir grihmen in boych!*[111]'

Jascha Kahn became known in Victoria Park Road as 'the nasty man with a limp who has small boys locked up'.

Ignored by neighbours, Jascha Kahn's existence was as isolated as ever, only the stray cats on his window-sill offered him companionship.

---

111   You should get stomach cramp every day

Ida Sirkes walked a little slower although she still worked hard for Jewish causes, she was growing old. She heard about Rifka's depression and made her way to Narford Road. An autumn day when wistful memories rustle through thoughts like dry leaves rustle over shoes. Ida had no idea she was a healer, wherever she went on visits to the needy, they improved, her gentle voice moved mountains for situations that were stale and forgotten by those whose careless standards caused endless problems and delays.

Ida's autumn remembering took her back to the first meeting with the Myersavitch family. How homesick they were in a strange country. Tears gathered into tiny pools at their nose tips and Friday night dinner was ruined. They rented a wreck of a house where Rifka and Dosha fought a battle everyday with floorboard fleas and nightly with bedbugs. Peshe sewed skirts by hand in the top landing room until she'd sold enough at Petticoat Lane's Sunday market, to afford a sewing machine. Jacob her son was raised with his cousins Myersavitch, like his father he will be a *cantor*. Reuben and Shepsul founded their *schul* and worked tirelessly for their mission, the *Mizrahi*.

Ida felt warm affection for all of them, but knowing the police attitude for emigrant families even those of long residence, she wasn't surprised at little Abraham's arrest.

Monty was disturbed the Government had never passed a bill concerning the harsh treatment of child-arrests.

"What's more important than a nation's children, I'd like to know."

"The nation's rich pa, touch money and you've had it, better to give someone a beating than touch 'sacred-cow' money."

"One of our own people had Abraham sent to reformatory school, Monty."

"Makes me sick the whole dirty business – Rifka and Reuben have such a huge family, one of them was sure to kop trouble. They'd be wise to leave London, London breeds villains."

"Monty don't be foolish, where don't boys find trouble. Maybe Abraham will learn a lesson and behave."

"Doubt it, he'll be scarred for life."

"He's a child he'll overcome the experience, you'll see."

"Ida darling, wait, I bet I'm right – borstal will be 'round the corner."

⚜

"Ida, come in I'm so glad to see you, give me your coat, come, sit by the fire, today there's a chill in the air."

"I wanted to wish you *mazel* for the new house, and to see Lieb."

"My Lieb, he's two already, Cissy's taken him to the park to collect conkers. They won't be long."

"Ah, he's an English boy now."

"Lieb much knows a conker from a stone, the walk will do him good, he's a bit chesty, moving dust has upset him. Cissy ruins him, every minute when she's at home, its 'mama see Lieb's red curls in the sunlight they look golden.' 'See Lieb smile like papa.' 'Listen to Lieb learning a rhyme. Mama he knows *aleph,beit*[12].' She's so maternal, I tell you Cissy will have more babies then me. Is everyone well Ida?"

"Thank god my small family's in one piece.

112   Alphabet

You know Monty closed the shop."

"I heard."

"After the war Eli didn't want to work at butchering. The sight of blood upset him and the loss of his arm didn't help. We all worried about him for a while."

"So how do you make a living?"

"Monty bought Eli the lease of a fish and chip restaurant. Monty handles the business side, and his wife runs the restaurant at Southend. At Monty's age the paper work is enough for him and Eli is doing a job he enjoys. We live simply Rifka, we're content. In the summer come down for the day. The restaurant is pretty, tables with red and white check tablecloths, even tables outside. All kosher with hot soups and rolls, I love going there. Here before I forget!"

"Lovely, Peshe's favourite madeira cake, she could eat cake all day."

"Peshe's lucky cake doesn't show on her hips. One slice I gain a pound."

"Nonsense Ida. you look wonderful, plump suits you – you want to look like a stick."

"Don't put any sugar in my tea."

"You want a slice of lemon one or two are beginning to come to the market."

"Please Rifka, a slice of lemon no milk. You know Shmuel Potzloch moved his family a few streets from Narford Road?"

"*Oy vey,* Sprinza will drive me mad, funny how we can never get rid of some people!"

"Sprinza won't change, we all put up with her. I like it here, the house is pleasant."

"Ida don't ever move. Moving is a nightmare we can't find anything and when we do dust chokes us – Reuben put on a pair of Samuel's socks the other day and Samuel's feet are huge. Reuben couldn't understand why his feet hurt – and they were odd socks that's the state we're in."

"Don't worry a few more weeks the house will be fine. What news of Chontche?"

"Can you believe Ida she lives in Kent – I write to her and say Chontche my childhood friend like a sister to me comes to England and where does she settle down – Kent – miles from me, can you believe, she writes, come and visit us as if I can go to Kent one, two, three."

"Rifka my angel Kent is not the world's end. Trains go there every day – and they're comfortable, you must visit her, what does her husband do?"

"Baruch's opened a shoe-shop, as if he couldn't do that here. A community should stay close by each other, moving around the country is not good for us."

"We've begun to go out of London – Jews mustn't live in a ghetto Rifka, those awful times haunted out ancestors enough."

"I don't agree with you Ida, we break apart become isolated, then comes mixed marriages and problems, problems – we should do our best to avoid these things. Reuben says in fifty-years if we're not careful hardly a Jew will attend *schul* or know one festival from another."

"Such a bleak picture, lets pray we won't be lost, around the world for centuries Jews have married out and they said we'd all vanish, but we're still here. Be hopeful Rifka for the future. There's bound to be change after a war. The young have different expectations, change is energising."

"So is a brisk walk, you'll see Ida we'll be lucky to escape damaging Jewry."

"God forbid – when is the baby due?"

"Please god, six weeks."

"I haven't seen Dosha for ages, how is she?"

"She's well and working with Peshe in the shop. Peshe thinks she's an excellent saleslady, shifting stock Peshe can't sell in a couple of days. I doubt if our Dosha will be a mama."

"She's still young, wives sometimes wait years, then are thrilled to find themselves pregnant. Yosef, what's he doing these days?"

"Yosef is becoming known, next week he's off to New York and then Chicago to give recitals at charity fund raising functions. The violin sings in his hands."

"He's sure to settle across the Atlantic, the dollar is such a temptation."

"Dosha and Shepsul will be sad, yet happy for his success. His poor mother died a year ago, his father came out of prison, and simply disappeared from Yosef's life. We are his family, he belongs."

"I must go with Monty to hear him make music; mind you not everybody enjoys classical music, concert halls can be boring, hot places, obscure composers are beyond me, just a noise to my ears. Jews breath opera. I can't stand it. Monty calls me a philistine."

"If you don't like so what, are we sheep we have to follow the same likes. Anyway next time Yosef performs here I'll give you tickets."

"Rifka I need a favour. I'd appreciate your help in the Jewish centre at Stepney Green, for the last year Jewish ex-soldiers have come to the centre for refuge with problems they are finding too difficult to cope with. I'm asking my friends to visit our boys, so they see as many friendly faces as possible. They're a mixed group. Some come only occasionally to chat to comrades, others have serious wound trauma, mental and physical problems. Life now is difficult to adjust to, ordinary living is a hurdle for them, we have shell-shocked victims who might take years to heal if ever, they are all scarred with war. Will you come?"

"How could I refuse."

"You'll be upset."

"I only have to see, they have to bear. Tomorrow please God I'll come about two o'clock and we'll catch a bus to Stepney Green – the centre is a short walk."

With baskets of fruit, sweets, cigarettes and pipe tobacco they arrived as volunteers were clearing away lunch dishes. Some of the men were still eating their soup – all food was given by families and local Jewish shops. If one or two hungry Cockneys came at hot-soup time they were never turned away. Leaning up against an upright piano several men in a haze of smoke were listening to a handsome man playing old, favourite tunes. Rifka soon realised, after going over to the group to say hello, the handsome pianist was blind. Ida came to introduce the *rebbetsin* and the men were pleased that she had come to visit them.

"They haven't had a *rabbi* come yet, maybe Reuben of Shepsul could manage a visit – the boys would be glad to welcome either of them."

"Sure Reuben will be only too happy to spend time with them. I'm surprised a *rabbi* hasn't been to see the men before now, I'll tell Shepsul to come as well."

The pianist played a tune Rifka had never heard,

"I'm curious Ida what's he playing?"

"That's the latest dance craze, the young and just about everybody else dance at every chance, its called the Charleston. Quite ridiculous and wears shoes out. The craze began in America, here the flappers kick their feet sideways up and down and sing like idiots, proving the young are wild and the old are even wilder! Hyman did your horse romp home yesterday?"

"With my luck Ida what yer think?"

"I think you came out evens."

"At least I came out, Birtie didn't make it."

Hyman's mind wandered to a battlefield, in lucid moments he's pick up a racing news and back a couple of horses for a few bob.

"You must talk as if all is normal – simple day-to-day things Rifka. Hyman give me a tip for tomorrow."

"Trixie Sweetheart, 2.30 Kempton park – don't blame me if your money goes west."

"Would I do that Hyman?"

"Nah, Ida, right through yer a real gem."

A volunteer arrived with a tea-urn, white cups and sliced, homemade cake, a huge plate of sandwiches and a large bag of apples given by a local coster.

Rifka poured tea, Ida served sandwiches, a nurse helped a sufferer with shaking hands hold his cup of tea, dipping the cake into the tea, making it soft for him to eat. Ida took a plate of food and fruit to a quiet man sitting in a corner playing the *dreidl*.

"How are you today Irving?"

For a second he stared at her, then with a half smile on his face almost a grimace, he spun the dreidel, only his hand moved. Ida spoke tenderly to him like a mother,

"Irving this is *rebbetsin* Myersavitch come to visit you and wish you well."

"Hallo Irving, I've brought you cigarettes and sweets. My children play the *dreidl* just like you, come eat your sandwich its good for you."

Irving sat watching his *dreidl* as if the moment he stopped spinning the world would end.

"Last week for a joke one of the chaps hid the *dreidl*, Irving cried like a baby – his mother comes every day at five o'clock when the market closes. She too cries. Eastenders bring in knitted scarves and gloves, even socks, such good people and things are far from rosy for them. A gypsy came the other day, "ere Missus a charm to 'ang up, good luck missus, good omens.'

"Did you hang it up Ida?"

"Sure, why not, she meant well, I'm not throwing luck away for these boys, they need all the luck I can throw at them. Over there on the wall by the window. Sammy Goldman, the boy in the wheelchair went and sat under it, calling 'look Ida, a miracle my legs are moving.' My heart hurts for them. What a disgrace we grumble about shortages.

Suddenly to everyone's surprise Irving started speaking to himself.

"Round and round, the shells spun round, his head spun round and round only his head. Screeching, screaming, burning, round and round. A blood-shot eye went round and round, only an eye. Mud, thick brown curdled with blood buried the dead, buried the living and we went round and round."

A morbid silence touched them, as they listened to Irving's lament. The blind pianist broke the moment with the piano music from the film 'The Sheik' staring the Italian film-star women loved Rudolph Valentino.

"Will he ever be well Ida?"

"Only God knows. Shell-shocked victims can't bear loud noises, we have to be careful with them, to think Irving spoke is an encouraging sign. Our pianist Sol Eisenberg, has a place in a blind school to go to. These schools are wonderful Rifka, they teach them to be able in time to care for themselves. Most of our boys will find work when they are fit enough."

"Futile, all so futile meaningless war. No matter what our leaders tell us looking at these poor soldiers tells a different story."

"Evil must be fought, man has no other way to protect what is right."

"Do you believe Ida this sight of broken bodies is right, no, but its called sacrifice to defend a country against monsters who'd put us in chains at least these boys are alive, millions are in mud pits with no tomorrow."

Whilst talking Rifka felt a warm liquid on her thigh, she asked Ida where the lavatory was,

"Come I'll show you". As she stood up a familiar pain stabbed her back and a second later she had a contraction.

"Ida, Ida! help me, I'm in labour."

"*Ei! Ei!* I must get an ambulance *Oy vey* Reuben will blame me for asking you out."

"Don't worry about Reuben, just get an ambulance quickly Ida, please find help I can't give birth in front of these men God forbid."

The London hospital at Whitechapel was a stone's throw away from the Jewish Centre and Rifka was rushed to the maternity ward and left with a midwife.

Ida was so shocked she needed a cup of tea, but instead took a bus home. Monty to her relief had just come in.

"Monty even if you're tired you must go to Narford road to tell Reuben, Rifka's in the London hospital maternity ward."

"Rifka's where?"

"I can't explain now, she's being confined, Reuben must be told."

"Calm down Ida you'll wear yourself out, I'll

go when I've had a warm drink – Rifka's in the right place. If please God the baby's arrived, Reuben will be happy, otherwise he'll walk up and down for an hour. Darling Ida put the kettle on, relax and we'll both go to Narford Road."

"Yes, you're right Monty. I need to sit for a while."

Later that evening Rifka was able to hold her daughter. Reuben was allowed a mere five minutes with his wife not quite believing the events of the day. The maternity sister came and whisked the baby away before Reuben had hardly gazed at his newborn second daughter. Visiting time ended and Reuben kissed Rifka's forehead. She didn't say a word. Before leaving the London hospital Reuben asked a midwife if his wife was well. In a broad Irish accent she told him his wife was grand and still shocked at nearly giving birth on a floor, his little lass was healthy with a great thatch of black hair.

The maternity ward-sister was as ferocious as a terrier. Reuben felt uncomfortable in this kingdom of dominant women. Rifka has always been confined in her own bedroom with a Jewish midwife.

Sharing an evening meal with Ida and Monty they hardly spoke. The outcome of the day had left them slightly tongue-tied.

"Did you see your baby Reuben?"

"Only her hair. Five minutes was all I was allowed with Rifka. They are very severe in the hospital."

"They have to be the new born are a responsibility. Visitors may bring infection into the wards. Women like Rifka who've many babies often give birth unexpectedly. Thank god all went well. Have you chosen a name for her?"

"Ida tonight I almost forgot my own name. Let

Rifka and baby rest awhile. It is said before we are born our names are known to the Lord our God of Israel, blessed be His name. Tonight she has her red ribbon on her wrist to protect and greet her birth."

Sitting on the end of the hospital bed Cissy was longing to see her sister.

"Mama its just like a prison in here."

"Our babies have just had a feed and now the nurses burp them and change their napkins. Then the babies sleep. I wish she was next to me, I feel uneasy with my baby in the nursery. A poor mother last night lost her son and she has cried and cried. They come to expel the milk from her breasts. She is stricken with grief. Now we all feel sad for her. I'll be glad to be home."

"Mama what a miserable story! What happened to her baby boy?"

"We don't know, but the mother's think the baby was suffocated."

"How shocking, I shall never have a baby in a hospital."

"Darling tragedy may happen anywhere. The flowers are so pretty Cissy, Ida and Monty brought me such an armful they're all 'round the ward."

Rifka noticed with amazement Cissy's hair. For a second she didn't say a word then,

"Cissy what have you done with your hair? Have you gone crazy or something?"

"Mama all the young girls in London have bobbed their hair."

"Bobbed your hair? Why?"

"Short hair is the vogue, I don't want to look like *bube* Cohen."

"You're beautiful hair Cissy, how could you?"

"You'll love it soon mama."

"I have too much to become used too, all this

change, next you'll be dancing the Charleston."

"How did you know about the Charleston?"

"I know more than you think."

A nurse called,

"Will visitors please leave."

Cissy cuddled her mother, "Thank you for my sister mama."

"I'm sorry you waited so long."

"Come home soon we miss you. Without you mama the house is not the same.

Four weeks later after their daughter had been named Aviva, meaning 'springtime' Rifka went to *schul* to give thanks for a safe delivery.

Her hair was covered with a blue kerchief. Reuben was talking to the beadle Nathan Davidson and only glimpsed Rifka from the corner of his eye going up to the woman's balcony.

The morning service over, Nathan Davidson was waiting to close the *schul* Reuben was waiting for Rifka to end her prayers.

"Come Rifka we'll walk a little before we catch a bus. Nathan told me the *schul* has a damp patch on a wall, I must call a man to give an estimate of costs, damp is serious."

"Will it cost much?"

"Probably, building repairs are expensive. Shepsul will sort it out when he returns from Manchester. I can't have the community catching cold from damp."

"Always something to worry you."

"Can't be helped, repairs are needed in buildings. I just hope we don't need to ask for funds from the congregation."

"They'll give."

"I know but I don't want to ask too much of them. Rifka do you have a headache?"

"No."

"Why aren't you wearing your *sheitl*?"

"Reuben I'm not *bube* Cohen."

Reuben didn't say a word.

Archie Biggins

Two years of stringent discipline passed since Abraham Myersavitch was sent to reformatory school by a London magistrate. The latent gifts he possessed could not be nurtured in an institution, nor an education for a meaningful career be given. Bullies enjoyed tormenting smaller boys and Abraham Myersavitch's bravery was often tested, for not only was he small he was also a Jew. Becoming wary of the strength of his broad shoulders and bored with blooded noses from his fists the bullies gradually left him alone, except for shouting 'maggot' and 'Jew boy' at his face.

Children who live within the hardship of routine discipline without a vestige of kindness in their young lives, jump to commands with glints of hatred on their faces. Even tough boys jump with the same quick movements of nervous energy, they feel hostile, some even violent. Their laughter has a hint of torment, as if any second an order will come to blow them away, because they are unwanted.

There is a line below sorrow.

These children do not play in the sunshine of summer days, a forsaken liberty is theirs. A progress of unshed tears.

Roger Dortman, a new officer at the reformatory school for the last six months, was a tall, stick-thin man with a long, unhealthy face. On his obviously thin legs black trousers flapped against his ankles and big feet stuck out in a comical way. On nervous hands long bony fingers constantly picked dust specks off his black jacket. He appeared uncomfortable with himself and no happier than the wilful boys in his charge. His frustrated life he vented against them. He was ineffectual and looked older than his thirty-five years.

The boys decided such an odd man must be made of thin wire stripes, calling him 'Oddy Rogye'.

Roger Dortman's eyes had a weird expression, a kind of dismay mixed with meanness.

Tom Carter a nasty minded bully who enjoyed hurting animals, liked to edge Roger Dortman into corners on the dormitory landing near the stairs. Without much effort he might have pushed him down stairs and broken his neck. The officer was well aware of the hazards he faced dealing with these disturbed children and did his best in trying to avoid them.

The unfortunate skin infection scabies came to the reformatory school, when a ten year old boy arrived covered with itchy, red scabs. His arm pits were bleeding from the poor child's constant scratching. Nurse was furious a boy had been sent there in such an infectious state. Fleas were bad enough to cope with and he had them too. Everyone from cook to the Governor was treated with foul smelling lotion and needed nightly hot baths. A rare luxury for the offenders only used to tepid water in a grimy washroom.

"Gor bli'me we stink worse than Ma 'ickey's knockin' shop."

"Ma who Archie?"

"Ma 'ickey stank see, yer'd be 'ard beat ta find a more cunnin fence I can tell yer. Died easter last didn't she. Well seein' 'ow never a spit of wa'er came

b'tween 'er, 'er dir'y clothes an 'er stink, the law let
'er be most times any rate. They was put orf wat they
was searchin' fer cause 'er 'orrible stink turn'd their
guts over. Me ma made a few quid from old Ma 'ickey,
'don't let a stink put yer out of pocket Archie son, she
pays well do Ma 'ckey.' Just as well she pays out else
they'd do 'er in!"

"They might like her Archie."

"Don't be daft Abe, those that live down our
way don't like no-one, 'sides the poor old cow's dead
now."

"Archie, what's a fence?"

"Where yer bin 'alf yer life? They buy our loot
don't they. Never pay what the stuff's worth mind
yer. That's business Abe."

Abraham Myersavitch didn't think 'business'
was the right word.

"I like listening to your takes Archie, I hate
morning coming, at least at night they leave us alone.
Your tales add a bit of cheer to the day."

"Glad to oblige, Abe. Me bruver was 'ere, much
good it did 'im, 'e's inside, went down fer five years
'ard didn't 'e. Going straight yer starve, no eel pie,
nufink, mugs goes 'ungry, Archie Biggins like's 'is
eel pie."

Listening to the tale Abraham Myersavitch
thought about home. He was born one of the sons of
a brilliant Torah scholar. He could hear the family
singing *zmires*[113], his father's warm slavic voice
filling the room with a vibrant belief. His mother
dipping her finger into a glass of wine for her newest
baby to taste. Inside himself he called, 'Mama, Papa,
where are you?'

There was no reply.

---

113   Sabbath songs

❧

On a bitterly cold winter's morning, window panes were patterned with lacey-frost icicle hung from window ledges, drain pipes dripped. Tiny birds fell off branches as they died of cold. On this raw day a Government inspector came to the reformatory school for a yearly inspection. With mops and buckets of freezing water the boys washed landings and stairs, breaking ice with mop handles. Silently they stood in line, hands behind their backs, their noses red with cold, their lips cracked, their hands chapped and their toes itching from split, painful chilblains.

Roger Dortman agitated and yellow-skinned failed to notice crude swear words scratched into the frosted window-panes. A greeting to the inspector who walked into the dormitory with a stern expression as if his tight shirt collar was choking him.

The boys stared straight ahead taking no notice of Roger Dortman or the Government inspector who asked unfortunate Freddie Smith in a loud voice to state his name and age. Poor Freddie Smith whom a moth would startle couldn't find a word in reply.

"I asked your name are you deaf or insolent?"

"F ... F ... Freddie Sm ... Sm ..."

With a disgruntled scowl, a stamp of his foot ignoring the line of boys and poor Freddie Smith trying to finish a sentence the inspector left the dormitory thin lipped and dripping with authority, rather like an icicle.

Denis Holder with bright red hair, protruding front teeth and fleshy wet lips kicked the boy next to him,

"Wakey wakey 'e's pi's'd orf, gawd knows wat

'e came in 'ere fer, ain't nuffin ta please the likes of 'im."

"'e 'oped ta find yer stash of gold an' if yer kick me shins agen carrots yerl 'ave a nice shiner where yer eye was."

"Aw shut yer face 'arse'ole, else yerl 'ave a thick-lip."

Welsh Owen Thomas tried to goad the snarling pair to fight,

"Land 'im one fer me boyo."

A chorus shouted,

"Aw go back up yer moun'ain taffy, mind yer own bleedin' bus'ness."

A cold, sad Abraham Myersavitch gave a wry smile to Archie Biggins, as they sat on the ends of their ugly beds listening to the boys cussing at each other.

"Just like me 'appy 'ome them two rowin'."

"Never mind Archie, nothing last forever. One day we'll be free."

"'ow right yer is Abe mate. Stick close ta Archie 'cause I 'ave a plot up me sleeve."

"A plot, you're dreaming Archie Biggins."

"Yerl see Abe, yerl see."

Silenced by Roger Dortman turning the lock, entering the dormitory and swinging keys in a threatening way. He ordered Dick Betts, a tall, quiet boy with acne scars etched down his cheeks to scrape the offensive swear words off the window panes. Dangerous implements were forbidden so Dick Betts did the best he could with a wooden ruler. Roger Dortman waited for the boy to finish and hand the ruler back to him.

"Supper is forfeit also a week's exercise, to try to teach each of you to respect the authorities. Contempt for social values will not help the struggles to be faced outside these gates. I suggest as delinquents with records of misdeeds, start to improve yourselves."

With every word he swung heavy keys in the faces of hungry boys. His own yellow face almost red with anger. Picking off invisible fluff from his ill-fitting jacket. He then locked them in until the morning bell.

Dick Betts cussing trying to warm his numb fingers,

"Old git, if I sees 'im outside I'll kick 'is balls in!"

"Could 'ave done wiv me cocoa, we ain't spoilt fer grub in 'ere. An' 'im stuffin' 'is face wiv din'er. I 'ope 'e chok's. Over me dead body will they lock me up agen in a pig-'ouse."

Abraham Myersavitch felt a sensation of doom at Archie Biggins' words. A feeling of terrible tragedy.

Nearing Christmas the officers were sent into near turmoil. The security of double checks for dormitory door locks was the duty of the night officer, who on this night was Mr. Hylton, returned from leave.

Rain lashed rattling window panes, an unfriendly wind became a gale, ice and snow were reduced to slush puddles and a ghostly whine echoed through the trees. Every two hours Mr Hylton climbed the stairs to the landings in his charge, watching through spy holes for trouble makers in the dormitories, beating his cane with amorous thumps against his thigh. He felt the draughts and was glad in the officers' sitting room a pleasant fire was lit. Satisfied the rogues were too cold to leave their beds and give him problems on such a raw night, he went downstairs and settled into an armchair with a glass of brandy. Not being a bookish man he sat in the glow or bright flames and thought of nothing.

Suddenly he felt uncomfortable wondering if the brandy had gone to his head. He went over to the fireplace to see if the high wind was causing a down draught. Only when he began coughing and choking did he realise there must be a fire somewhere in the reformatory school.

Forgetting his cane, knocking the glass of brandy off the side-table, he threw himself out of the sitting room in a wild rush of fear to ring the fire alarm bell in the hallway. Yelling,

"Fire, Fire! Wake up, wake up for god's sake."

Ringing the bell so hard his arm felt as if it was breaking. The black horror of boys being harmed brought out a sweat as he ran faster than he had in years taking stairs two at a time. In as much control as possible he unlocked doors, ordering them up and out. Thankfully a night security guard came to his aid and the boys didn't dare cause even more problems for Mr. Hylton.

Miss. Coxford, a light sleeper awaked by the slightest sound, tore downstairs in a long, heavy white nightgown, her tartan dressing gown half falling off. Her shoulders, her face pallid with shock. Miss. Coxford was also myopic and in panic to leave her bed sitting room left her spectacles behind. Calling,

"Where's the smoke coming from? Do something, do something. Save us! Save us, where am I?"

"Calm yourself Miss. Coxford, please you will send the entire reformatory into panic."

A ridiculous, mournful Roger Dortman appeared clutching an empty bucket, wearing a night shirt up to his knees and beige leather carpet slippers.

Clanging bells were heard nearing the drive. In seconds firemen pushed ladders up as high as the attic-windows. Inside their long hoses soaked every corner downstairs to lay the smoke. Coming from cook's attic bed sitting room the source of the fire was found to the relief of everyone. Cook's sentimental affection for candle light and dislike of electricity, calling such inventions 'black magic' had almost burnt the reformatory school down.

Cook had left a candle kindled in a brass candlestick on her chest of drawers. A powerful draught knocked both candle and candlestick over, the still lighted wick did the rest. The attic bed-sitting room was gutted and cook was dismissed in disgrace without references.

Gradually a kind of order took over amid the sooty mess.

The Governor stood in the soaked hall wearing one soggy black boot and coughing, his face like all the staff and offenders smudged with black streaks. Miss Coxford was in no state to help anyone and vowed to resign the moment she found her spectacles. Then she fainted falling heavily onto Roger Dortman's foot. He too lost a slipper, was soaked to his skin and looked as if any second he would burst into tears.

The Governor ordered two fifteen year olds to,

"Prop-up that idiotic hysteric against a wall until she comes round. Women have no place in an institution such as this Dortman, why the Home Office allows such nonsense is beyond common-sense. A domestic has almost burned us alive in our beds and Miss. Coxford is made of jelly. What an example for unruly youth to follow."

Roger Dortman managed a subdued,

"Quite so sir."

The Governor glared at him with an unspoken,

'why doesn't that insipid creature shut-up'.

Sleepy boys were marched to the kitchen for hot cocoa then marched up to the dormitories. Mr. Hylton told them to dry themselves change in dry nightshirts, make the most of discomfort and be thankful the kitchen could be used for their hot drinks. The boys not used to much comfort anyway settled down for what remained of the night.

If a single boy spoke a word about the near disaster the blizzard tuned it out in favour of the storm's deafening wind.

The officers' sitting room was a sorry sight but the exhausted men slumped into damp armchairs, swigged brandy and fell into a troubled doze.

Miss. Coxford pulled herself together and climbed the stairs in a daze to her bed-sitting room, half wondering why the door was ajar. She felt her bed for damp, tried to bear the smell of acrid smoke and shut the windows. Disconsolate, overwrought and alone she sat on the bed and wept.

A week after the fire the Governor held a meeting of officers. During the emergency certain orders of discipline had not been carried out. Miss. Coxford was named a culprit. In her haste to leave her bed-sitting room she ran leaving the door open. Not only dangerous in a fire alert, but breaching a major rule in an institution. She had shown pathetic weakness in the eyes of the men. Clearly she was considered unfit to continue with her post at the reformatory school. The Governor stressed he felt sorry for the work-load the officers had to endure. The staff shortages were of course due to the enormous loss of men during the Great War. Miss. Coxford was advised to have more control of herself during times of anxiety.

Roger Dortman wasn't cowardly, yet lacked

any kind of leadership quality.

Mr.Hylton was thanked for remaining calm on a distressing night. Miss. Coxford sent her letter of resignation to the Home Office. Roger Dortman didn't resign much to the Governor's surprise who considered the man incapable of knowing his own mind.

Archie Biggins' mother, Minnie, taught him to thieve almost before he could walk. His father trained him to know by heart certain East-end streets, alleyways and crowded markets. By ten years old he could run faster than a blink of an eyelid or seemed to by a stall holder straining his lungs trying to catch him. Arche Biggins could crawl through a small gap in a garden fence to rob a house, and lick the head off a glass of beer before a man paid for his drink. He'd pickpocket whilst eating stolen fruits, he was a fearless yet lovable street boy who knew no better. Minnie took orders from safe customers who asked no questions about a cheap bargain.

"'ere ma if yer ain't drunk," a valuable fob-watch left Archie Biggins' grimy hand for his mother's grasping fingers. Funny enough a shattered window in a local shop took him off to reformatory school. Poor Archie Biggins was blamed for another tyke's crime. The constable thought the streets needed a tidy-up and the magistrate agreed with him.

In the rush to follow Mr Hylton down to the hallway, Archie Biggins saw Miss. Coxford's bed-sitting room door was open. He lagged behind the scared boys until they were gone, then he was in Miss. Coxford's room. Her briefcase on a desk chair was open, there with personal correspondence, paper work, a diary and her spectacles Archie Biggins saw what he'd hoped to find, a bunch of heavy keys. Keys to open or lock the main reformatory doors including the lodge gates. Oblivious to the fire alert Archie Biggins grabbed the keys, kissed then with a 'ta ducks'. Leaving Miss. Coxford's bed-sitting room as he'd found it, with the door open.

In a corner of the landing stood a large ugly glazed pot, where a neglected aspidistra grew in hard, caked soil adding no charm to the dismal surrounds. Without causing too much disturbance for someone to notice he dug the bunch of keys as deep into the soil as possible. His already chapped fingers were now grazed from the hard soil and the thickening smoke was making him cough.

He fell into a heap at the top of the stairs where Mr. Hylton found him as he marched the boys up to the dormitory after the hot cocoa.

"He's drenched to the skin, but thank heaven not dead. Shock I should think, must have been overcome by smoke."

"The soaking saved his life."

"No doubt the soaking saved all of us, Dortman, better help me to the clinic with him, I believe its reasonably dry there."

The wet tired officers dried Archie Biggins, put a nightshirt on him, placed a stone hot water bottle in bed next to his feet to warm him up and left him for nurse to attend to in the morning. Pleased with his night of mischief Archie Biggins no longer had to play half-dead although his chest hurt him, placing his cold feet firmly on the warm stone bottle, trying to think up the rest of his plot, falling instead fast asleep.

Roger Dortman went early to the clinic and was amazed to see Archie Biggins out of bed.

"How is the boy nurse?"

"He'll survive Mr. Dortman, a good dose of

'hold yer nose and swollow' is the best of medicine. Nothing like brown mixtures for making 'em move."

A puzzled Roger Dortman returned a pale, coughing Archie Biggins to the dormitory.

Nurse who didn't trust one of the boy inmates put the bottle of brown mixture back in the medicine cupboard.

Christmas 1921

A heavy snowfall cast an eerie quiet over the procession walking to the early morning Christmas service.

Sprays of festive holly with an abundance of scarlet berries relieved a sombre, Spartan chapel as officers and boys entered behind the Governor. Wearing reformatory winter coats either too small or too long the boys took their places in pews watched over by a guard.

The Governor allowed this attendance at an outside service to discover if the boy inmates were responding to discipline. In a low almost humble tone the vicar led congregation with '*We Three Kings From Orient Are*'. Roger Dortman played the upright piano, his face a picture of rare enjoyment while the Governor's over loud boom completely silenced Mr. Hylton. Miss. Coxford's tinny soprano was expected of her.

Abraham Myersavitch stood silently with his hands behind his back. The rest of the boys were nearly all suffering colds, sniffed and coughed in time to Roger Dortman's music-making.

Calling for prayers the vicar then greeted the good news sent to mankind. A stern eye and a brief moral lecture was directed at the young offenders.

Reminding them on this Christmas morning they were wrong-doers who had deeply hurt god. Who with loving mercy sent his dearly beloved son to save all sinners. They must mend their ways and show respect to the officers and Governor.

He gave thanks to god for the safe delivery of everyone on the night of the fire. After the *'Our Father'* he wished the congregation a joyous Christmas. Roger Dortman played them out of the chapel with a thumping *'Onward Christian Soldiers'*.

The Governor led the procession back to the reformatory school. A faint whiff of brandy fumes lingered in the cold air as he breathed in and out. Mr. Hylton found walking a straight line rather difficult and a glassy eyed Miss. Coxford giggled.

A snowball battle began when a boy couldn't resist bending down to scoop up a fistful of snow. Taking aim at a boy's back. To the utter astonishment of the Governor. Mr. Hylton's shout of 'single file at once,' fell on deaf ears. Roger Dortman catching up with the snow splattered procession and hit by a hard flying missile whilst humming *'Once In Royal David's City'*, was reduced into nervously picking melting snowflakes off his long winter tweed coat. Miss. Coxford's spectacles were wet and she was frantic to find a handkerchief to dry them. Opening her handbag a fast disappearing snowball fell in and soaked the contents. The Governor clouted the boy nearest him. The others surrendered their snowballs to the snow. The procession went on to the reformatory school.

Back at the school Mr. Hylton was told to take the young philistines for breakfast, also because this was Christmas day no punishments were to be given for the snow battle.

Besides each breakfast plate lay an orange and

a small chocolate bar. Although reading skills verged towards illiterates a religious tract was handed to each boy as he took his place.

They were allowed to receive small parcels but none arrived.

Tom Carter a born bully threatened to bash into Welsh Owen Thomas if he didn't pass his chocolate bar over, taking no notice Owen Thomas shoved the bar into his mouth with obvious relish.

Underneath the table long legged Dick Betts kicked Tom Carter in the spirit of a birthday party game. All their teeth were smeared with chocolate. David Holder wondered if they'd have Christmas pudding then cook demanded silence as the rest of breakfast was served.

Watching from his office window a ballet of gentle snowflakes float to the ground, the Governor remembered his long ago boyhood. Snow fights that brought some masters to their knees as snowballs became weapons. Boys were expelled for hiding stones inside snowballs and he was caned when his cold, hard snowball hit the headmaster who was in no mood for a mouthful of snow.

The fine line between harsh public school and a reformatory school is fine indeed.

Before leaving to spend Christmas with his family he tidied away papers on his desk, mostly rules and regulations. Leaving out a memo to ask Miss. Coxford to return her keys only to him. He knew by nature he wasn't an over-kind man, he also realised 'there but for the grace of God', he too might have been a reformatory lad. His usual rigid expression relaxed a little to show a middle-aged weary man.

❀

Miss. Coxford dressed in her usual morning clothes left the bleak building never to return. Her cases were sent on to her new address in advance except for the aspidistra plant she has bought to liven up a dull corner by her bed sitting door. After Christmas she'd decided would be time enough to write to the Governor about the lost keys.

A boy gazing out of a dormitory window no doubt thinking about his lost freedom spotted Miss. Coxford walking to a waiting car in the drive.

"Now ain't that a sight fer sore eyes old Cocky's leavin' with 'er aspidistra under 'er arm. A grand music 'all song I calls it."

Archie Biggins was the only boy not laughing.

Spring 1922

Unknowingly Miss. Coxford wrecked Archie Biggins' plot. He was now forever parted from the precious keys he'd hidden in her aspidistra pot.

Mr Herbert George Aston's last position was sports master at a severe boys school. A powerfully built man with a no-nonsense approach who was known as H.G.A, although a tough man he didn't believe a smile was unnatural or treat poor Freddie Smith as a freak. Mr. Hylton hated him on sight thinking H.G.A's attitude would undo his own methods of dealing with wayward boys. His habit of polishing his pocket-watch by rubbing it against his chest then shaking and listening to the tick at his ear earned him the nickname 'tick-tock'

He discussed with the Governor the possibility of allowing him to introduce to the boys the sport of football. The Governor was favourable towards the idea as long a mayhem wasn't the final score.

"Remember Aston these are young rogues."

"I am aware sir of their status."

The boys were so conditioned to whispering during exercise when H.G.A gave them permission to talk they barely raised their voices. The buzz of secret whispers between them walking across the field sounded not unlike spring bumble bees flying in and out of a pink flowered ribes shrub.

Tom Carter started his usual torment by kicking Owen Thomas until he fell over in pain. H.G.A. tweaked Tom Carter's right ear then tweaked his left ear. Boys standing in line to leave the field clapped as a pathetic wail came from Tom Carter who gave a defiant glare to H.G.A.

"Remember this Carter I detest a bully. You will cease your favourite pass-time or answer to me, fall in line."

Tom Carter spat on the ground as H.G.A. turned his back on him. At the far end of the field a group of boys were listening to Archie Biggins talking to Abraham Myersavitch.

"See them flow'rs Abe?"

"Where?"

"Be'ind yer."

"What about them?"

"Smell like cat's pi'dle, 'ave a sniff."

"Cat's piddle Archie."

"Told yer."

The others had a sniff to a song of 'cat's piddle, cat's piddle.' H.G.A. blowing his whistle for them to hurry up wondered if they had a touch of spring madness.

"Come on Archie we'd better run back or we'll be in trouble."

Archie Biggins' quick eye spotted a gap in the hedge hidden by the spreading branches of the ribes shrub in full bloom. The field not protected by the high wall of the main building led to open country. Why this had been overlooked by the Governor and officers wasn't a worry for Archie Biggins.

"Stick close Abe." A furtive murmur Abraham Myersavitch only just heard on the run to fall in line.

Archie Biggins devious brain juggled the if's and are's of a breakout. Once he'd overheard his brother telling a con how to breakout without too much trouble.

"Keep yer plot simple, catch 'em by surprise, yer'l forgit 'alf a plan before yer big toe's outside the gates an' be in solitary 'olding yer dry bread. Simple see. Keep runnin' if yer ain't sprung an' don't look back, yerl come over chic'en. Don't go 'ome, first place them bug'ars go ta find yer. Don't carry a weapon an' never trust a tart, she'll turn yer in fer a tanner!"

Being twelve years old his brother's prison advice wasn't much good to him and the only place Archie Biggins could go to were the two threadbare rooms he called home. The hedge gap would not longer be hidden when the ribes flowers faded away, so by next field day him and Abraham Myersavitch must scarper. Abraham Myersavitch pieced together Archie Biggins' snatched bits of jigsaw puzzle whispers. He realised he was taking a risk and being foolhardy but he wouldn't desert Archie Biggins. A promise is a promise. Rebellious cords were pulling at his own impulsive nature. He was restless to be gone.

A week passed. The two boys saved their bread, Archie Biggins pick-pocketed a few pennies from an officer's jacket, out of pure devilment. Most of the dormitory had colds,

"Nothing like fresh air for bunged up noses, fall in line to collect coats."

A blustery wind quickened their pace. Twice round the field and back in line for routine exercises. On the repeat twice round the field Archie Biggins gave Abraham Myersavitch an eye signal.

From where H.G.A. was standing fast moving boys in navy blue coats became a blur. Not thinking for a moment anything amiss was happening he wasn't too observant. Ginger-haired David Holder's broad shoulders were able to almost eclipse two smaller boys with mere seconds to leap through a hedgerow gap.

Brambles tore their flesh, petals stuck in their hair. The hard, stony field certainly didn't cushion their landing. A sense of shocked awe at their daring gripped them almost to a standstill. Adrenalin fuelled energy returned their courage. They ran and ran pushing their thin bodies through more hedgerows. Abrupt suddenness led them almost falling at a dusty dirt track.

A sinister hawk cast an unpleasant omen as it circled overhead.

"'effin thorns scra'ched ta buggery I is."

"They pull at clothes and these coats are heavy, shows how tough brambles are, your scratches won't smart for too long Archie, take a deep breath, we must run on, they be after us by now."

"Shame we 'ad to wear coats, 'cause we goes ta ch'pel in 'em they ain't got refo'm sch'ol inside, don't look nice do it Abe?"

"Suppose not Archie."

"Where do yer reck'n this 'ere leads?"

"Maybe a farm, we won't find out gawping, we must move on."

"Still odd ain't nuffin like 'oove prints 'orses do."

"Archie what do you think of tick-tock?"

"Them geezers is all the same, bastards."

"He's kinder than Bootface."

"I 'ates the sight of 'em."

"Over there Archie, a roof, rest of the house can't be seen till we get nearer, seem as if we're out for a stroll in case we've been spotted."

"Them lot knows them tha' lives round 'ere."

"Listen barking."

"Bleedin' dogs don't miss a trick 'ear yer miles orf. A good thief strangles 'em."

"You're not that cruel Archie."

"Ain't got time ta be kind Abe."

"On the count of three start running, one ... two ... three!" A cloud of dust veiled them as they took off.

A narrow stream meandered alongside the not much used bridle path the boys called a lane, which ended outside a village a mile or two further on. The pair of runaways were hungry,

"We'd better keep going Archie, we're far from safe, there's sure to be some cover we can hide and eat a slice of bread."

"I ain't bothered too much. Next 'ouse I sees I'll thieve us a bite ta eat."

"Characters in books always follow rivers to find places, so we'll follow the little stream."

"Cor we might end up by the seaside. Wen me ma weren't on the beer she'd take me to Soufend, we'd 'ave a plate of cockles and a paddle, nice them days was."

"Before a stream joins the sea Archie it becomes a river then flows to the sea."

"I don't know nuffin like yerself Abe, yer'v 'ad

schoolin'."

"I read books, books are full of knowledge. Do you know what philosophy is Archie?"

"Na I ain't never 'ad good food."

"Philosophy's not food, philosophy's a belief."

"Wha' yer need tha' fer?"

"To help you understand what life is about. Help you reason things out and seek truth."

"Abe yer won't 'alf get the 'eadache if yer read tha' stuff, if yer can't thieve an' flog it ain't worth fussin' with."

"Archie you learn to understand the meaning of life."

"Jist as yer say Abe, jist as yer say."

"We'll hide in the wood."

"Yer won't git me in them, woods is full of bad spirits an witch's fly on broomsticks into 'ouses an' cast evil black magic spells."

"Archie!"

"Na I tell ya, wha' me nan says ta me I believ's. Come on Abe, I ain't stayin', all them eyes is watchin' us an' castin' the evil eye on our 'eads."

"You win Archie, you're enough to frighten the life out of anyone. We'd better find shelter before dusk."

Eventually they sat behind the trunk of a massive hawthorn tree heavy with blossom, nibbling their bread like woodland mice.

In melancholy silence they aired their blistered feet. By habit their shoes and socks lay tidily on the grass.

Neither would admit to be scared. The tranquil

countryside at dusk became ominous with cawing crows flying to roosts. Strange shapes danced near them, phantoms of dark shadows faded into nothing.

"This is as good a spot as any, we're out of sight and bone dry grass isn't too bad to bed down on. No sense traipsing over fields at night."

"Good we're used ta bein' 'ungry an' cold."

"First light we'll try to find a railway station, we may be lucky to catch a train, they sometimes stop at villages. Cheer-up Archie you'll be in London yet.

Darkness obscured a starless sky. Two lonely boys pulled their coat collars up to keep warm glad of each other's company.

From her cornfield nest the small, brown skylark soared in an almost vertical line high into the sky, singing a perfect song. The ravenous pair trembled in the cold dawn, damp with dew they made for the stream to sloosh their faces.

"Bet our breaths stinks."

"Don't mat'er."

Shaking drips off their scratched hands with sore, blistered heels they walked towards the village.

"I 'ave the rheuma'ics I 'ave."

"Me too, stiff as a post."

"Bout all yer gets in Lon'on fer nuffink is the rheuma'ics.

"We'll feel better if the sun comes out."

"Feel even bet'er with a bite ta eat."

"Don't stray into the centre of a field, they'll see us for miles."

"Can't walk in 'alf of 'em the corn's too 'igh."

"That's true."

Climbing over a farm gate they saw a low growing crop sprouting green tops.

"Have you seen this vegetable before?"

"Na, only knows cabbage bleedin' earth's rock 'ard."

"Might be cattle food."

"No cow's shit 'round 'ere."

"Anyway Archie whatever they are we can't budge 'em."

Archie Biggins kicked the plants with aggravation. A bit further on loose root-vegetables lay along the margins of the field. Archie Biggins pounced on them like a hungry cat.

Aware of the food laws he'd been raised with Abraham Myersavitch held back. He ate the awful reformatory meals to stop starving away. The round yellowish vegetable splattered with soil didn't seem edible without boiling, he contented himself with chewing a bitter green top.

"Archie you'll break your teeth biting into a raw vegetable."

Archie Biggins wouldn't listen, he ate every morsel. He sat back on the grass only too pleased to have eaten at last. Once again they moved on, hoping to find a railway station.

"Never in me life did I see nuffink but fields."

"We're bound to see a farmhouse soon, must be a rich farmer owns all this land."

"Me ma says 'taint right the king owns most land an' us poor ain't given a blade-a grass. Yer can't argue with the king can yer Abe."

"No Archie, you can't argue with the king."

"When we gits ta Lon'on will yer still be me mate Abe? I only asks 'cause they say Jews 'ave 'orns, but 'taint true an' I'll tell 'em different."

"Thanks Archie. I'll always be your friend whatever they say."

"Ta I'll look out fer yer Abe I'll do them that does yer 'arm."

The two boys became solemn after their declaration of friendship until Archie Biggins stopped and held the side of his stomach.

"I've got guts ache."

"You wouldn't listen Archie I told you raw food is hard to digest, we'll stop for a while, feelin' any better?"

"Na I ..."

Archie Biggins double over in pain began coughing, his face twisted with discomfort. Abraham Myersavitch thought any second Archie would throw-up. Archie Biggins began to choke, wildly clutching the air. His face turned from pale white to a deathly blue as he collapsed into a small unconscious heap.

Abraham Myersavitch stared in disbelief at the still body of his friend. In frightened dismay and panic he began running to find someone to help Archie Biggins. Half blinded with tears he shouted,

"Please help us, help us, please help us."

Farmer Clayton was entering the stable to see if the new stable boy was mucking-out. When he saw a boy running and shouting for help with a tear stained face.

"Wha' in the name of saints 'ave I 'ere?" He stood waiting for the boy to come nearer then walked towards him. Abraham Myersavitch with relief at seeing the hugely tall man, cried even more.

"Well lad when yer done blubbering what 'ave yer to say for yerself. Running loose on me land at this early 'our. 'ave gypsies abandoned yer?"

"No sir, its Archie my friend Archie Biggins."

Abraham Myersavitch wiped his hand across his tears, "Archie's lying in the field he's very ill."

"Show me where lad."

Abraham Myersavitch took farmer Clayton to where he left poor Archie Biggins lying amid the loose vegetables. The farmer bent low to touch the boys cheek. Deeply shocked he told Abraham Myersavitch his friend Archie wasn't unconscious he was dead. Dead in his turnip field.

"Best come back ta 'ouse, the police will sort this business out soon enough.

The exhausted boy his face streaked with dirt from tears followed him.

"Tom, what's this about then?"

"Couple of runaways, I'm phoning the police."

"Why the police, vicar will 'andle them just as well Tom, no problem too big for 'im."

"Not this mornin' Betsie."

"Why ever not?"

"'cause me dear other lads dead in yonder turnip field. I seeded a few swedes mixed in."

"My dear soul! What are yer sayin' Tom?"

"Dead Betsie, dead and gone."

"Poor lad what d'yer think he died from?"

"Well I 'ope weren't our turnips. I be 'ard put ta git me price fer 'em."

"Scullery's left 'and door go an' wash yer 'ands an' face an' I'll give yer a plate of breakfast, no doubt 'ungers gnawing at yer."

"That's very kind of you."

"Only my Christian duty. Fine state yer in an' yer speak nice. Silly ta run orf they always gits yer back an' to be sure they thrash the daylights out of yer."

Abraham Myersavitch kept silent. He didn't care what happened to him, he could only see his

friend lying quiet and still and alone on the hard
earth, his hands clenched with pain he felt as he
died.

The police arrived with a loud knock at the
farmhouse door. Mrs Clayton took the two constables
into the huge kitchen where Abraham Myersavitch
was eating a boiled egg with a plate of bread.

"Yer'll let the lad eat his breakfast constable?"

"Yes, be quick lad we haven't all day ta waste."

Abraham Myersavitch didn't shift his gaze
from the brown egg in a yellow eggcup and the bread
spread with real butter. He ate till the last crumbs
then he stood up and walked over to the farmer's
wife.

"Thank you for giving me food. I am sorry for
the trouble this morning."

"Don't bother to show us out Mrs Clayton we'll
let ourselves out, good morning to yer."

"Good morning constables."

"Can't think Tom what he did ta put 'im in
reformatory. A good lookin' lad and so well spoken."

"He's in fer a well deserved good hiding. Yer
too soft Betsie Clayton, too soft, standin' there with
watery eyes over a little crook an' a dead mite on our
land in the midst of harvest if yer don't mind."

H.G.A. needed a large dose of Dutch courage as
he told the Governor, a difficult man at his best, two
boys under his supervision were absconders.

"At lunch time head count I realised Archie
Biggins and Abraham Myersavitch were missing sir."

"Runaways usually follow a pattern Ashton,
running like mad at the start, slowing down, hunger

sets in, run off again feeling lost, worried with no sense of direction. Shorn hair and reformatory clothes are known for miles. The police will pick them up and I deal with them. I'll write up your report for the Home Office. Aston pull your socks up dear boy, or open a village shop and keep racing pigeons."

H.G.A. was taken back by the Governor's reaction to the missing pair, but he was relieved to be the other side of the door. In the officers' sitting-room he opened The Times, turning to 'situations vacant'.

The nurse flinched as the birch rod came down on the boy's bare back, she flinched when again the birch rod came down on the boy's backside. His hands with upturned palms had already felt the stinging cut of the spiteful lash. Abraham Myersavitch didn't cry out once. Only when the room began to spin and his eyes glazed over did the ghastly punishment cease.

The nurse then led the crumpled, bleeding boy to the clinic to pour luke-warm water over the red welts and put the boy to bed.

The night-duty nurse felt the boy's pulse, read a brief note on his condition from the day nurse.

'The birch rod should be outlawed, its bad enough watching the beating even worse the look of enjoyment on the Governor's face as the birch rod came down (tear this note up please.)'

Abraham Myersavitch was delirious the night nurse placed a cold wet flannel on his forehead. She couldn't understand the words that came from his

cracked lips,
> "Tatenuti, tatenuti."
> The loving Hebrew word for 'papa'.

October 1925

'If you are not for yourself
Who will be for you?'

Wearing a mismatched grey suit with black thin soled, walking shoes, Abraham Myersavitch was taken by H.G.A. to the Governor's office.

"At ease Myersa ... a ... I won't keep you long, before and inmate leaves custody the Governor says a few words to him. You are now considered as a fifteen year old able to travel to your home unaccompanied by a parent or guardian. Your father hasn't been notified of your release date, we do not encourage emotional reunions that may disturb young offenders, the officers and I hope the discipline required of you during detention will lead to good conduct beyond these walls. Do not sacrifice yourself as a ne'er-do-well. Keep away from those who seek to cause infraction. You will be given a single third class train ticket to Paddington station and two separate shillings by officer Aston. Good luck for your future Myersa ...a ...."

The Governor leaned forward across his desk to offer a handshake to the fifteen year old youth.

Abrham Mysersavicth ignored the hand, turned his back on the Governor and followed H.G.A. from the room. Clutching a small brown paper parcel of clothes he'd worn to the reformatory school in 1919, Abraham Myersavitch walked with H.G.A. to the lodge gates, which the keeper unlocked.

"Goodbye to you Myersavitch, keep out of trouble and happy landings."

"Goodbye sir."

A slow October drizzle wet Abraham Myersavitch's head as if a baptism for his freedom. Before walking away he glanced up. His eyes didn't betray his contempt for the high stone wall with sinister, jagged green glass jutting from the top. His contempt for the harsh experience of correction hidden by those lumps of piercing green, uncontrolled thoughts leapt to his mind like teasing imps, he was slightly on edge wondering if the family would be pleased to see him, after all he'd brought shame on his father's name. How would he cope with his brothers. Sharing a confined space with delinquents had given a raw quality to his personality. Would he be able to control a quick temper. The monologue with himself continued on the train. What kind of work could he expect. Nobody would trust him. He hadn't as much as a hawker's trade to his name. Apprehensive but unafraid the optimist in his nature rescued the fifteen year old youth from a hundred doubts. From being locked-up he couldn't sit in his carriage. A claustrophobic near-panic caused a sick-turning in his stomach and he stood in the corridor until the train steamed into Paddington station.

Able to take his time with a long walk to Hackney, as no-one was expecting him. His father had written the family had moved to Narford road. He stopped for a mug of tea and buttered roll from a stall on a narrow side street.

"Walkin' 'ome son?"

"Yes. Saves money. I'm surprised by the number of cars on the road though."

"Yus, toffs showin' orf their toys - an' a right

problem them 'eadlights is with dazzle, a right lot them toffs. Don't care 'ow much trouble them cars causes. Just as well we 'ates the sights of the bleeders."

"What the cars?"

"Nah the toffs. Let out today was yer?"

Abraham Myersavitch nodded.

"Not that I'm being nosey like, I seen yer parcel an' shillin' piece an' wot wiv yer 'aircut, well I says to meself this little geezer's bin payin' fer 'is sins. Nothin' ta be ashamed of, mind yer in my day they only give us two tanners ta git by. Still 'twere bet'er than a good-'iding."

Abraham Myersavitch noticed years of open-air work had given the tea-seller watery eyes and a weather-beaten, brown genial face.

"I'll be on my way; you make a good mug of tea."

"'ere son I don't 'ave much trade this time o' day."

"I was going to buy another roll."

"Nah keep your pence. I only throws stale uns to the pigeons. Mind 'ow yer go, walk with purpose, they'll nab yer if yer dawdle."

He walked on as the swirl and silvery to dull Thames flowed with the strange, hypnotic power of waters. Outside a bookshop a selection of second hand books were displayed on a rickety table. A card in a cracked saucer read,

Any Book 3d

Abraham Myersavitch bought a pocket book of Shakespeare sonnets.

His energy wasn't keeping up with his enthusiastic walk to Hackney, with six miles to go, at the docks he leaned against a stack of Indian tea chests. He watched dockers shifting cargo into massive warehouses, the smell of their sweat mingled with the beery scent of breweries. An oily damp from the river cast a Victorian image of fugitive ships slipping silently towards the sea with mysterious passengers and crafty, hungry rats. A cold breeze blew an eerie shudder through his thin suit. He moved on with a stray at his heel.

"Excuse me you wouldn't happen to know the Myersavitch house?"

"Sure I'm visiting a couple of doors down. Are you one of the family?"

"I'm Abe."

"I'm Minah Kosminski, when we were small our families were neighbours. My *bube* drove everyone mad."

"I vaguely remember her."

"How could you forget her, she rowed with Chayah my mother from morning till night. So tell me how is it you don't know your own house?"

"I've been away, we used to live at Victoria Park Road ... satisfied?"

"More or less. Your's is the one with a large bush in the front garden!"

"Thanks Minah."

"You're welcome."

The street door was ajar. He bent down to stroke a tortoiseshell cat curled upon a frayed doormat. She stretched, arched her back and curled up without opening her eyes. Running up the path a boy with red-gold hair gave Abraham Myersavitch a quizzical once over, pushing the street door with his foot he called over his shoulder,

"Ma leaves the door unlocked when Jim's inside."

In the narrow hall he noticed an untidy assortment of coats and scarves slung over the bannisters belonging to his brothers. The stray sniffed the air finding the kitchen in a leap. A small fire was lit in a grate with an iron fireguard surround hung with airing socks. Late autumn wasps buzzed over a dish of ripe apples, a jeweller's loupe lay on the table next to some black leather bound Hebrew books as always the *mizrach* hung in the east wall showing the direction a Jew should pray. The familiar smells of home reminded him of being a child. He was drained of childhood, tired and exhausted. Suppressed anguish ached within him could he learn to become normal again or would the ugliness of an institution cover him like a hair shirt.

His desolate thoughts ended when Jim the old *fire-goyah* and general help chased the stray up from the cellar.

"You belong 'ere mister?"

"I'm Abe, I've been away."

"This your mutt then?"

"Yes. He's a friendly stray, followed me from the docks."

"Well I dunno missus likes 'er cats she do."

"He won't hurt the cats, he needs a kind home."

"Funny I doesn't remem'er you, me back 'alf kills me come mornin', trenches bone ache, evenin' drawin' in time to fill scut'le, best mind mutt. I dunno wha' missus will say, I really don't.

"Leave your galoshers on the step, I'll bring them in later."

"Ma I like walking through leaves, they sing. Do you think ma they mind me kicking them up?"

"Why should they mind, they fall down so Aviva can find, what's those brown things called you search for?"

"Conkers ma."

"Don't ever eat them like nuts, they're

poisonous, now wash your hands and face and give your hair a brush over."

"Ma, come quickly, we've got a dog."

"*Oy vey* we've got a dog!"

"He's friendly, needs a home."

"Abe you've come back to us. Danken got!"

"Who is he ma?"

"Abe your brother."

"Abe my brother!"

"Go and wash Aviva, no dog upstairs."

If Abraham's eyes were tear-brimmed, his mother's were overflowing.

Slithering on a scaly belly with the head of a Komodo dragon fascism brought Mussolini to dictatorship in Italy. The spirit of Locarno symbolized hopes for an era of international peace and goodwill. In the dark forests of Austria and Germany the Locarno Pact 1925 were treaties writ on tissue paper blown in the wind.

In Romania a Jewish cemetery was desecrated, synagogues and Jewish schools were looted. Behind the Komodo dragon crawled the anti-Semite.

In England a Roman mosaic was uncovered in Colchester, Malcolm Campbell breaks the world land speed record and P.G Woodhouse published his second Bertie Wooster, 'Carrym on Jeeves.'

Outside Bow street a few hundred people sang 'The Red Flag ' when two leading communists were charged under the Incitement To Mutiny Act. Anarchists and Zionists were obvious hate targets of the British Fascisti, a movement started by a colonel's Empire loving daughter in 1923. Foreigners were to be treated with scorn and suspicion.

Jewish shops in the East-end were daubed with racist slogans, windows were smashed with bricks and ignorant youth wallowed in Jew-hatred. The myth of Jews gold – *kick a Jew and gold will fall out of his ears* – was their favourite theme.

The Protocols of the Elders of Zion was widely distributed.

Bad housing, bad wages, poor health care, did nothing to ease racism. Many families migrated to Canada, New Zealand and Australia and South Africa. For a better life.

In the best English he could manage Koppel Ginsberg wrote to the Home Office concerning Jewry. He was gravely alarmed when a clairvoyant warned him extreme racists were knee-deep in plots to rid their green and pleasant land if Jews who schemed to rule the world.

He received a card in reply stating the Home Office took the security of His Majesty's subjects very seriously. Groups of men gathered after the morning service to talk together,

"The British will never accept fascism, they're royalists."

"That does not mean we will be protected."

"True, true, we must protect ourselves."

"Don't listen to Koppel Ginsberg he talks through his *toches*[114], he's *mushugganah*."

"How do you know it won't turn nasty?"

"Indeed events may prove nasty."

"*Nit heint, nit morgen*[115], but one day."

"Never, trust me, never"

"He thinks he's Prime Minister, all the Getzel family are the same big know-alls."

"Give punch for punch, kick for kick."

"At my age I should kick and punch, a spit is

---

114 Buttock   115 Not today but tomorrow

too much energy."

"What will happen?"

"*Nor got vaist[116].*"

"Zion, a land of our own, why live amongst hate-mongers! Zion I tell you."

In the Ethics of our Fathers, Rabbi Chanina, the vice-high priest said, 'pray for the welfare of the Government, since but for the fear there, men would swallow each other alive.'

The men departed for their day's work, satisfied enough had been said.

Before arranging his book display of second-hand Yiddish books in a stall he rented in Roman road market at Bow, Amos swept the autumn leaves into the gutter. He also sold *yarmulke* and *mezuzoth*, homilies of favourite *rabbonim* and Hebrew tracts. Abe was with him. The brothers were discussing the Romantics and their love of Milton.

A group of Jewish people showing interest in the books were reading homilies out loud. Pushing through the crowd Abe saw obvious trouble makers coming towards the stall. A gang of scowling fascist youth prowled, sneered and mocked the Jews.

"'effing yids up wiv the lot boys."

Throwing books and Hebrew tracts in the gutter. Seeing a *mezuzoth* trampled underfoot a boiling rage gripped Abe.

"I've had enough of you lousy scum touch another thing, I'll break you apart one-at-a-time."

Abuse twisted the anti-Semite faces with ugliness. The Jews were threatened with death if they came back to Roman road market. Screaming

116 Only God Knows

'yids out, yids out' and the insult '*shundicknicks*[117]'
in their ears the fascists moved off when the shout of
'police' went up. Before the attack Amos sold a book
for a shilling.

"Toss you for it Abe."

"Keep it Amos that's for a hard morning's
grind."

A smokey haze drifted lazily across a late
autumn sky, coke burned scarlet on braziers tended
by night-watchmen. Peshe locked up her dress shop
wondering what she'd find in the morning. Today
had been difficult. She's arrived for work to read
'yids out', 'kill a yid' painted in a white-wash scrawl
over the shop windows. Typical of her, with patience
she fetched a bucket of warm water from a near-by
café and cleaned the offensive words off the glass
after all a brick might have been thrown or red paint
daubed over the shop front.

She wanted to hurry home to read a letter from
New York. She hoped America would offer Ezra a
good life. Ezra called himself an atheist. She knew in
her heart he was an observant Jew. His father's spirit
shone in his eyes, how could it be otherwise! Peshe
sighed, memories of youth are sad and deep. Her
silver-streaked hair was testimony to middle-age. For
an unknown reason she thought of *tishe b'av*, the
Sabbath of comfort. Could there be comfort for the
destruction of the Temple?

Peshe believed the vast universe could be
concealed in the nucleus if a small prayer, and she
could hold the Temple in the palm of her hand.

Last week she'd listened to a sermon by a
visiting Rabbi, Julius Marks, on *devekut*[118].
Afterwards she asked Shepsul,

"How can one cleave to a nebulous God?"
Shepsul stroked his beard and smiled.

117   Pimps   118   Cleaving to god

"You can only understand *devekut* with your eyes closed."

A cacophony of voices touched the roof and bounced off the garden gate. The Myersavitch brothers were talking together around the kitchen table. A question being asked by many Jews was, 'would Zionism exist without anti-Semitism?'

The Brother's Debate

"Before Genesis anti-Semites were teaching their children to hate Jews - its born in 'em."

"No facetious comments please."

"They hate us so much they have stolen our ethics, prophets and a born Jew for a God."

"Even Roman Tacitus called us vile."

"We refused to bend the knee towards Rome."

"Brothers may we now debate the question,"

"To say Zionism wouldn't exist without anti-Semitism is untrue."

"Why untrue?"

"We said next year in Jerusalem long before the Black One Hundred."

"The energy to create Judah again comes from our fight just to survive."

"No it comes from our belief in God's destiny for us."

"Did the Lord our God of Israel blessed be His name, destine us to be exiled?"

"Don't you appreciate home more for being away?"

"You leave by your own freewill and we will return by our own freewill."

"So are you saying God is not in Zionism?"

"Zionists are fleeing Russia. If the Russians

didn't attack Jews they would not leave."

"So are you saying God and Zionism are in us?"

"Then maybe God is behind the attacks."

"To kill the chosen people Israel is not the Lord's way."

"Come now we were holy under Judah Maccabee and the Greeks slaughtered those resting on the *shabbat*, only when we fought as and when we had to, did we win."

"The Greeks were idol worshippers and anti-Semites."

"And the Romans after them."

"And the Egyptians before them."

"But we have only just become Zionist."

"Because we've only just learned we must fight to live."

"Then Zionism is the answer to anti-Semitism."

"Herzel would say so. At the first Zionist Congress in Basel did he not say so?"

"He was looking for an answer to slaughter."

"He knew we would not be allowed to assimilate unless we converted."

"Zionism has a political agenda."

"So does anti-Semitism."

"Anti-semitism?"

"Of course. Leaders across the world use it as a way of blaming us for their bad decisions."

"I agree, look at Dreyfus."

"The French are anti-Semites."

"Is anyone not an anti-Semite to you?"

"Is any Jew not a Zionist?"

"Many are not."

"Then many individuals are not anti-Semitic but all countries are."

"You mean the rabble in Europe?"

"I mean countries are; anti-Semitism is a political tool, and Zionism is a political necessity to achieve a religious aspiration."

"Next year in Jerusalem."

"Amen!

Birth and Death

Minnie Biggins had taken to going to the 'Threepenny Bit and Whistle'. The last traces of health showed in her face. A once beautiful woman betrayed by poverty. Blue-violet eyes now scared with blood-shot whites, sunken cheeks, bad teeth. Her lips might have charmed the fates if the dirt-poor hadn't claimed her birthright.

"They killed my Archie, they did for 'im, them that took 'im 'orf me motherly care. Never, I swear on me life, my boy 'urt no-one. So wat 'e thieved, bet'er than starvin', they picked 'im up stiff an' cold. Twelve year old 'e were, I ask yer, twelve year old. My Archie, I ain't nuffink now, me arver boy's inside, I ain't me own flesh un blood. They took 'em 'orf me. Buy me a drink dearie."

"Wat yer need Minnie is a fancy man buy all the booze goin' fer yer, he would."

"Nah, past it ain't I, they'd want change 'orf me fer half-a-crown, 'sides me 'usband were no good but he were me 'usband."

"Then stop moanin' gal, I lorst my boy in the Great War, yer 'ave to learn to live without them yer loves an' don't yer pretend your Archie were an angel 'cause we knows differ'nt, biggest tea-leaf fer miles the lot of yers."

Minnie Biggins turned her head away from the small group of regulars, which over the years had become even smaller. Flo Kneebone rarely stood at the bar these days. She suffered from sciatica, ('all them cold war days and nights in the cellar' Flo told one and all. 'There's a lot of it about' was always the response.) Maisie, much to Flo's surprise, was a good barmaid. She was 'walking out' with Jimmy Deagan. Alf Kneebone made many a remark about Irish trouble in the family.

"Can't be more trouble than yerself Alf Kneebone."

"An' what's more pa, the Irish fix things, you ain't knocked a nail in an 'ole fer years."

"They fix things my gal, wait till the other side blow the bleedin' pub up."

"Look on the bright side Alf, they ain't wed yet. She may git tired of goin' to wakes an' masses."

"To think a child of mine goes to mass."

"She'll grow out of the novelty don't yer worry."

"The sooner the bet'er Flo."

A terrible scream echo'd a chilled voice through the 'Threepenny Bit and Whistle'. For a split second Maisie at the bar and the regulars were too stunned to move, then in one movement they rushed into the street. Cars came screeching to halt behind a car, skidded half way onto the pavement, a pedestrian lay sprawled into unconsciousness. Blood seeped to the cold stones.

"Gawd almighty wat a sight."

"Bleedin' cars ban 'em I says."

"'oo is it?"

"Dunno looks like a woman from 'ere."

Two policemen arrived, standing over the victim, a young woman of about thirty years old. Waiting for an ambulance and holding her handbag in case of theft the police cleared the crowd away."

"Glad it weren't a child."

"Yus, 'urt lit'le-uns is worse."

"Gawd 'elp us, can't be much worse than tha' poor cow."

"She's dun fer I thinks."

"What a thing eh? Lousy cars!"

"May as well finish our brown ale, can't 'elp standin' gawpin'."

Their clothes rent to part them from the dead, the small family group in stark black surrounded Becky Harris' coffin as she was laid to rest. Aunts, uncles, cousins and friends with respect stood apart. All were grieving in a sombre silence heavy with tears. Phoebe and Henry held each other close. Esther held on to Solly. Sophie was nub with sorrow. Katie, Rachel and Alfie held each other's hands. Dinah and Monty stood close.

There were no children.

Light rain was falling, a slight rainbow arched the sky, a sunbeam's ray touched the new grave.

"Our gal's watchin' over us 'enry."

"Cors she is Phoebe, cors she is."

Esther Starr, now a matronly thirty-eight, soon to give birth to her fourth child, she fervently wished for a son. The end of 1925 had brought tragedy to the Harris family. Birth meant new life, new hope. When she went to Cox Street these days ma was lost in mourning, she had shrunk into herself and would sit quietly in Becky's room upstairs remembering her daughter's life.

"Yer too thin ma, I bet 'alf yer dinner goes to the cat."

"Don't worry Esther, I've always bin a lit'le 'un. Gerty's an old gal like me, she's such a faithful puss, I don't begrudge 'er a bit extra. I 'opes yer takin' care of yerself Esther. Yer gettin' on a bit fer the baby lark."

"Not likely ma, women are strong 'ave 'em at all ages they do. 'sides a new grandchild is just the sunshine yer need. Solly put a quid on us 'avin' a son."

"Just like 'im to throw money about."

"If 'e wins 'e'll treat us to a salt beef supper."

"Very nice I'm sure."

"Put the ket'le on ma an' we'll 'ave a taste of a new biscuit just come out."

"Wats new in 'em?"

"Chocolate ma, McVitie's Chocolate Digestive. Look I bought half-a-pound.

"Save some fer pa, 'e likes a taste of chocolate."

"'Fancy that, wat will they think of next,' 'e'll say, then e'll 'ave chocolate over 'is 'tashe!"

"I told Klara to come 'ere with Phoebe and Ruthie after school an' not ta bother Solly in the shop. They think 'avin' a business is a joke."

"'ow's 'e doin'?"

"Alright ma, ended last month with thirty quid profit came 'ome pleased as punch 'e did. So I says where's me wages then, 'wages ain't fer family. Yer 'ave ta give time fer free ta make yer business grow.' Oh yes? well in that case I'll work in the afternoons for old Joey Isaacs an' e'll pay me fer me labour."

"Don't be daft Esther the labour yer in fer won't give yer time to work fer Joey the slave driver, I can see yer face when 'is 'and goes up yer skirt."

"'e thinks e's Selfridges me husband."

"Well in a way 'e's right Esther, if yer spend yer takin's yer won't do well."

"I don't see why I should stand there sellin' fer 'im, e's mean just like 'is pa. I'm 'avin' a stall of me own with me own money."

"'e's yer 'usband."

"I've got the needle to 'im anyway, Klara's teacher spoke ta me about 'ow clever our Klara is an she should go to a good 'igh school an' college, fancy ma, our Klara at college, an' all 'e says was, 'no', right out. 'She'll 'ave a brain storm, bet'er she stays workin'-class.'

"Shame 'e thinks like that, men 'ate us women gettin' on in life, our fault Esther we ruin 'em."

"I'm fed up with Solly, some days I could walk out fer good an' all."

"That's yer condition Esther nothin' else, by now with yer fourth yer know we go up an' down like a see-saw."

"I'd be bet'er orf on me own."

"Left it a bit late gal to changer yer mind."

"Marriage is a trap, men 'ave the best of the bargain, I truly loved Solly, but after 'e came back from the war, something went stale. Four years is a long time ta be left alone. The feelings were gone ma. Not all couples are like yerself an' Pa, some of us ain't cut-out ta be Darby and Joan."

"Yer pa's a good man, so are me gals 'usbands, Monty leaves too much ta Dinah, she don't complain, Katie seems 'appy with 'er lot an' our Rachel ain't wed.

"I bet Sophie stays single, I admire 'er spirit."

With a clatter of boots Klara, Phoebe and Ruthie rushed into their granny's small parlour, instantly smothering her with kisses.

"'old out yer 'and and close yer eyes and I'll give yers a big surprise."

"Oh, biscuits with chocolate over 'em!"

"Now don't make crumbs an' don't talk with apple in yer mouths."

"Ruthie give granny yer drawin'"

Ruthie produced a crinkled brightly smudged painting of 'Gerty Cat Fer Gran by Ruthie.'

"Well ain't that grand – give us a kiss."

"Friday next week I 'ave to go to 'ollerway, I've an appointment at Marie Stopes clinic thought yer might come with me."

"Esther they'll 'ave a laugh when yer walks in."

"Let 'em laugh, I want to learn 'about birth-control, Marie Stopes is very clever, not before time someone gave real 'elp to us poor cows."

"Cors I'll come, I won't tell pa 'e's too straight laced fer Marie Stopes."

"Time ta go 'ome an' do Mr.Starr's supper, 'e's cack-'anded in the kitchen, kiss Pa fer me when 'e comes in, come on me lov'ly daugh'ers leave granny in peace. See yer later in the week Ma."

"Mind 'ow yer go Esther, put yer legs up yer ankles are a bit swollen."

On the walk home Esther told her girls to look up and see the beautiful evening star, brightly shining in the twilight sky.

"Like a diamond mummy."

"More lovely by far than a diamond."

"I ain't ever seen one."

"Just as well Phoebe, crooks only pinch 'em. God put the stars up there for poor-orfs to gaze on an' dream."

"Of bein' rich."

"If yer like Ruthie or bein' all sorts in yer 'ead,

don't cost ta dream."

"I'm gonna make a wish."

"So am I."

"Me too."

"Altogether, look up, bu' keep quiet, if yer tells yer wishes, they'll be lorst."

They were almost at their street door when Phoebe put a rather faded photograph into Esther's hand without saying a word in front of her sisters."

"Wat's this Phoebe?"

"I asked pa if I could 'ave a tanner fer school notebooks an' 'e says sure dolly see wat's in me jacket pocket on the back of the chair, an' I found the picture of 'er. I knew she weren't an aunt. I puts 'er in me school-bag to give ta yer."

Esther Starr didn't answer Phoebe when she asked who the lady was. She took the gals in and for a few minutes stood in the landing outside. She made out a faded message on the bottom of the photograph, 'My own Sol from Mavis'. Talking to herself inside her head with,

'Keep a grip on yerself, don't upset the gals. 'taint the end of the world. So Solly 'as a fancy woman, well that's men, ain't bleedin' saints are they. Me an Solly 'aven't bin close fer a while now. Not lovin' as 'is right fer a marriage, must be me own fault, me love goes ta our gals an' I sort of forgot Solly, now 'e 'as forgot me, daft I never saw what was 'appenin' under the roof, still 'e'll never marry a shiksa[119].'

Esther Starr looked up at the evening star, her hands on her belly, her proud face stern, her eyes sorrowful. She knew Solly would be late for dinner, being late had become a habit.

"So much to do at the shop," was as good an excuse as any. At the back of the old wardrobe, an

119   Non-Jewess

even older dusty suitcase would do for Solly's bit-and-pieces, a couple of suits, two pairs of shoes, his winter coat, freshly laundered shirts. Esther packed them neatly. When the girls were asleep, going to the front door on hearing his footsteps, before he'd a chance to say a word, she placed the case at his feet.

"Piss-orf Solly Starr ta yer fancy woman."

She banged and bolted the door. Esther Starr felt a weak contraction in her womb with a show of blood. A stabbing pain in her lower back was enough to convince her moving a heavy wardrobe wasn't a good idea, her labour had begun.

"Gawd son don't come ta night, I've 'ad enough fer one day."

By the morning the pains were stronger.

"Klara I'm takin' meself orf ta the lying-in-rooms, dress yerself darlin' an' 'elp yer sisters dress, then the three of yers go straigh' to granny."

"Mummy yer can't manage alone."

"Cors I can. Phoebe and Ruthie are more important, don't fret. I'll be fine."

"I love yer mummy."

"Bless yer Klara me angel, yer won't let me down will yer?"

"Never, never!"

Esther Starr just reached the London Hospital. She collapsed on the steps. A nurse found her double-up in agony. Calling orderlies to fetch a stretcher Esther Starr was carried to a delivery room. Siddi Starr was born without too much fuss half-an-hour later. Leaving the children with their grandpa Phoebe Harris walked to the lying-in-rooms at Commercial Road to be told a Mrs.Starr wasn't there.

"Not 'ere, wat yer mean not 'ere! My gal's in labour and left me a mes'age to say she was goin' ta Commercial Road lying-in-rooms."

"She's most certainly not here. I suggest you walk to the London Hospital, they sometimes help mothers who can't wait to deliver."

"Ta very much, I 'opes she's there."

"I am sure mother and baby are doing well so don't upset yourself grandmother."

On making her way towards the London Hospital, Phoebe Harris stopped to catch her breath buying a penny bunch of sweet violets for Esther and a bag of mixed humbugs. Her relief as being told Mrs.Esther Starr was in the maternity ward when she arrived at the hospital was matched only by the smile of utter delight when for a minute or two she was allowed to gaze art her first grandson, held by a nurse; baby Starr.

"Well me Esther yer 'ave a son, may 'e live fer an' 'undered years. A nice nurse let me tie a red silken ribbon on 'is wrist, bu' she put 'er foot down when I tried ta place a bit of silver in 'is 'and. Ain't 'alf strict in 'ere', I says, 'nursie 'cause of yerself me grandson will be poor 'is whole life.'

'Rules grandma', she says,'rules' and marches orf with our blessed boy."

"It ain't the layin'-in-rooms Ma, 'ospitals are careful 'cause babies come over queer if too many relatives breathe over 'em."

"I 'ave a right. I'm 'is gran 'an I come over queer if too many relatives breathes on me. I wonder wat's keeping Solly ain't like 'im to dawdle at a time like this."

"I don't suppose 'e know I'm 'ere."

Esther Starr didn't wish to upset her mother with Solly's goings-on. The ward sister called visitors to 'please leave the ward'.

"Best be orf Ma, I'll be 'ome soon please gawd."

"Yus I'll be on me way. Wat a find boy Esther,

I right proud of 'im."

The Circumcision

*'Those present at the ceremony rise and
say,
Blessed be he that commeth,'*
On a soft white pillow baby Siddi lay. Solly
held the pillow and in a low voice spoke the Hebrew
words for his son to be initiated into the covenant of
Abraham.

*'I am here ready to perform the
affirmative precept to circumcise my
son, even as the Creator blessed be He,
hath commanded us, as it is written in
the law, and he that is eight days old
shall be circumcised among you, every
male throughout your generations.'*

The *Mohel* takes the child

*'This is the throne of Elijah, may he be
remembered for good.'*

After the *Mohel's* prayers those present
respond.

*'Oh let us be satisfied with the goodness
of Thy House, Thy Holy Temple.'*

The Mohel places the child upon the knees of
the Godfather, and prays before performing the

circumcision. The Mohel and those present continue to pray.

The Godfather drinks of the wine.

A few drops are given to the infant.

And the cup of blessing being sent to the mother, she also partakes thereof.

Merry-Go-Round of a Day

A sense of merriment pervaded the afternoon. Jobless men managed wan smiles watching children share a ha'p'orth bag of peanuts with pigeons.

A playful breeze lifted young girls' skirts. The elderly dozed on park benches. People drifted by and noble swans floated on the Serpentine like white water lilies.

A ranting northern voice gave discord to the rhythm of the hour. A small crowd stood listening to a hard-bitten character standing on his soapbox, wearing a cheap black stained suit with a flat cap and muffler, a pointed finger darting the air, he tried to stir the crowd up with a loud harangue.

"'appy with yer lot, 'nice' 'ouses, bellies full?"

"Bread slice wiv lard an' mug o'tea most days," came a voice from the back.

"Rid our land of blood suckers, work'ouse will rot yer bones else, like me poor mam's, yer'l creep along them cold stone floors bent with shame, work'ouse will break yer spirit, kill yer 'orf. I tell yer friends 'old yer 'eads 'igh, politicians with their 'umbug let them walk in shame at our 'unger."

"Red propaganda," a belligerent Londoner shouted, "bleedin' Red go 'ome ta Barnsley."

"Wat yer doin' on yer soapbox ta 'elp us?"

"I'm tellin' yer ta vote with yer bellies, fer change, stamp on them that crush you."

"Yer can't fool us mate, no-one 'elps the likes o'

us, never 'as, never will."

"Join a union, unions will fight for the labour force, fight for workers."

"Wat union? Wat job?"

"Answer that one northerner!"

Before walking away a middle-aged man told them not to listen to rebellion jargon, a woman called,

"I come out fer a bit o' fresh air, an' yer give me an 'eadache."

"Can't 'elp that Mrs, yer won't 'ave change by whisperin'."

"Bleedin' radical."

"'e's right, we deserve bet'er."

"'e ain't right, jus' an agitator come ta cause trouble."

"Ooh, 'ark at the big words, go ta 'igh school did yer?"

"Up an 'igh 'ill, tha' was 'is schoolin'."

"Let the man 'ave 'is say, shut yer norf un souf."

"Come my dear, this is not for young ears."

"Ask yerselves, 'oo built them fine 'ouses toffs live in, 'oo waits on 'em 'and an' foot be'ind them wall'd gardens? Yerv gorn quiet on me, touch'd a nerve 'ave I?"

"Yer tell 'em mate, let 'em do their own dirty work."

"We 'ave ta set'le wiv wat we got, makes do an' mend, 'sides I don't wanna go 'untin' an' shootin' all day. That ain't a life."

The northerner ranted on, stamp on landowners, stamp, stamp, stamp!

"Stanley Baldwin will sort things out, a national government, best for all!"

A small gathering of Roman Catholics were kneeling saying their beads oblivious to the grand ideas at Speaker's Corner. Riff-raff were not to be ignored on this afternoon of merriment, chanting 'effin' yids out' their derelict brains hot with hatred. Ah! The plausible reasons, the invisible rebellion marching in the sky.

The street-door of a narrow anonymous house closed behind the *rabbonim*. Briefly they talked, shook hands and walked in opposite directions. Shepsul Myersavitch was glad to be in the fresh air, musty meeting rooms and cigarette smoke always gave him a slight headache.

Trams rattled past him, noisy, draughty cumbersome monsters with a side-to-side sway along a track. Incongruous and comical. He noticed they were going to Victoria Embankment, having a hopeless sense of direction often finding himself in places he didn't mean to go to, he thought a long walk to Holborn would be pleasant. Rabbi's rarely walk streets alone. Shepsul Myersavitch rather wished Reuben or one of his nephews was with him, but there he was alone. With his lack of direction and much to think about morbid fears of London streets were banished. The afternoon was light with unusual freshness, even the less than eau de parfum smell coming up from Thames mud didn't put him off his walk. Dosha always praised mud with being health restoring, as good as the sea.

Thinking about Dosha, Shepsul Myersavitch went over in thought the big question, 'how was he going to tell her the outcome of his meeting today with *Mizrahi rabbonim* from Jerusalem?'

'We'll sit with a glass of wine, a slice of *strudel*, talk together. I'll cut another slice of *strudel*. Dosha's look means save *strudel* for tomorrow. Who can resist? I'll tell her my news if Dosha is difficult I will be stern

'This is *bashert*! There can be no argument!'
Dosha will then argue for an hour. Oy!'

He'd walked almost two miles coming to a
billboard for 'bile beans to keep reg'lar' and Charring
Cross Station, quite forgetting why he was going to
Holborn. Shepsul Myersavitch bought a ticket to
Aldgate East.

What a strange afternoon, a storm was bound
to follow. He mustn't be late for evening prayers.

"Chance controls the universe." Tychism's
theory was most unlikely to mean overmuch to
fastidious George Sugg, small time crook, albeit not
a very good one. Nevertheless by chance George
Sugg's muddy shoes didn't go with his perfectly
creased trousers, showing just the correct amount of
sock. His twice ironed short and smart jacket, his
straight flaxen hair combed flat and sprayed with
Macassar oil. George Sugg took no chances with his
sense of fashion.

By chance Joey (alias 'The Nark') Sims had set
himself up on a corner as a shoeblack, George Sugg
was walking round.

"Wat's up Joey? This ain't yer usual line o'
work?"

"Keep yer foot still an' shut yer cake'ole. A
certain party I knows of is on the look out fer able
bodied low-lives, if yer inclined ta be curious, nod.
Redman's Road, Bartholomew's iron wheeled cart-
yard. Tall thin geezer with a cock-eye. Drop 'im a
pony, ask fer Cheng."

George Sugg flicked a note into Joey Sims tray,
gazed at himself in a shop window before heading

for Newley's Club, called over his shoulder,

"I hopes yer not settin' me up Joey Sims."

"Now would I George, perish the thought."

By chance Shorty Boyd, a bookies runner was touting for business at Newley's Club when George Sugg arrived.

"Now 'ere's a thing, if it ain't pretty George Sugg."

"Alright Shorty cut the wise cracks. Wat's the gen on a tall, thin geezer Bartholomew's iron wheeled cart-yard?"

"Bleedin' funny question."

"Come on Shorty, Redman's Road."

"Nah can't say I 'ave gen on such a geezer."

Slowly George Sugg waved a white note under Shorty's Boyd's nose.

"'old on I tell a lie, next ta Bartholomew's yard, or there abouts, is a couple of roomin' 'ouses, I ain't sure, I think they was whore 'ouses. Mind yer I only knows from 'ear-say don't frequent them meself, live an let live eh George, fancy a bet for the ..."

George Sugg wandered over to the billiard table thinking 'why would Joey Simms send 'im ta a tart joint? 'e 'ad enough trouble keepin' Gloria 'appy and why pay out fer wat 'e got fer niffink!'

No pleasantries were overheard at Newley's Club. Rough street voices exchanged awkward, untrusting monosyllabic grunts. Long flexes dangled shabby, green lampshades over card tables. A fog of cigarette and cigar smoke veiled players. Grim faced men with nervous tics. A flash of silver blade razored a cheek. Smoke curdled into blood no one moved. Knock, knock, knock from billiard balls the only sound.

'Hear no evil, see no evil', a code of wilful defiance, society's axioms dust to be swept away with spit. George Sugg was in no mood for razor shenanigans. According to safe breakers *spielers*[120] were the least respectable of villains. Before leaving Newley's Club he glimpsed a silhouette caught in daylight from an open door. A red silk cheongsam clung to the sleek beautiful shape of a Chinese girl. Like a spectre, she faded into the smoky den. George Sugg's endearing vows of fidelity to Gloria met a swift demise. An irritable loser pushed him,

"Da yer mind if I gets out."

"Sorry gov'na, no sweat, know the red dress?"

"Nah just a skinny Chinese dame, same old gubby face, loads of 'em 'round 'ere."

"She can initiate me in Chinatown's rituals anytime."

"Rather you than me. I likes me women well sprung, well padded, if she's in Newley's Club she's no bet'er than she should be."

The day of merriment wasn't finished with George Sugg. Bartholomew's iron wheeled cart-yard was heard before he found the entrance, furious barking from several loose terriers, a large black cross bred was tied-up with a dirty rope. The underfed dogs didn't inspire confidence. Leaning over a rusty, iron wheel a thin shape took on the appearance of a squint-eyed man.

"Oi guv, do me a favour, call yer bleedin' mutts orf."

"Wat's yer business 'ere, where's yer cart?"

"Do I looks like a carter?"

A whistle brought the terriers to heel. George Sugg, slippery burglar and racketeer, knew only too well the bites these dogs could inflict so stayed put not moving a step further into the yard.

"I was told Cheng lived 'ere-abouts."

"'oo told yer?"

120   Gamblers

"Joey 'The Nark.'"

"Well, well I'll 'ave words with 'im. Sendin' Tom, Dick an' 'arry ta me yard. Now Cheng migh' live 'ere, on the uvar 'and 'e migh' not."

"I ain't got time ta play games guv, tell Mr Cheng me name's Sugg, find me at Newley's Club Saturday night. Ta fer yer trouble. George Sugg left a pony by the yard gate. He'd walked a step or two when running behind him a young Chinese boy panted out a message.

"Cheng velly sowy not in, now Cheng in. You come Cheng say. Good deal, velly good."

George Sugg stared down at the messenger and walked on, not feeling obliged to meet Mr.Cheng.

The Chinese flew after him, with sword like arm movements to George Sugg's legs brought him to his knees.

"Up pees, no fuss, Cheng no like kep wait."

Slowly George Sugg stood up, cursing Joey 'The Nark' for his penny worth of trouble. Brushed down his trousers, looked to see if his shoes were cuffed, then with a faint whistle aimed a surprised left, leaving the Chinese sprawled on the pavement.

Cheng seated on an oversized chair his obese bulk bolstered with scarlet silk cushions, his small feet clad in black Chinese slippers resting on a low Peking table. Cheng with long sensual strokes fondled two highly polished, beautiful jade pieces, once the jade eyes, stolen from a Chinese temple Buddha.

Cheng rarely spoke, from his overuse of chewing mescal buttons. A South American hallucinogenic drug, his voice had been badly affected. He also drank mescal liquor. Apart from caged finches on the Peking table there was no Chinoiserie in the business-like, cold, empty room. A monotonous tweet, tweet sang the caged finches as Cheng removed a tray from the bottom of the cage. He placed with care the priceless jade in a white tissue diamond wrapper and replaced the tray and wrapper in the cage.

With closed eyes a satisfied look cast his face with a grimace-like smile. Two Chinese men entered the room with the beautiful girl last seen walking through Newley's Club. In silence the men helped Cheng remove his obese shape from the chair. The beautiful girl took the bird-cage slowly they went down the not very stable stairs their black Chinese slippers making no sound.

Cheng was placed with some difficulty on the back seat of a black car, behind which a small van was parked. The men returned to the room to remove the oversized chair and Peking table and silk pillows. Nobody took any notice of this strange group, Chinatown wasn't far off and Londoners were used to them.

By chance Abraham Myersavitch was walking passed with Morris Gonbrect a gambler who wanted to marry Cissy and as time will tell could bring her no happiness.

Abraham Myersavitch had learned to smell out crooks from two paces, his eyes followed the car with van following and he heard the desolate tweet, tweet from little finches.

The tall, thin man with a squint went up to the empty room to see all was in order, the terriers as his heel – to let out the smell of mescal liquor he opened a window. He asked no questions. The room was let by the hour. The police asked questions he made a living by not being nosey.

The afternoon of merriment faded into early evening,

"Funny old day by any account," a passer-by called to a neighbour.

"Just weather," came a reply.

Twilight played patterns on the choppy, small river waves. A black Chinese slipper bobbed up and down. Had the green eyes of rare jade caught their victim and their revenge.

Massacre 1929

Excessively hot, windy air blasted the camels with quick painful whips of sand. Sand fringed their twitching nostrils. They swayed with half-closed eyed across the desert trail.

Heavily shrouded Beduin faces showing only blood-shot, dark, irritable eyes goaded and cursed exploited, poor beasts. In spring and summer's end the south-easterly Arabian desert winds blow their dry, hot air temperatures, which rise to 122 degrees Fahrenheit, when sand becomes almost a weapon, people become anxious, ill-tempered even violent. Such is the desert khamsin.

Violence has no moral principle –
No honourable reasons –
Violence is a simply written prescription,
Kill, kill, kill.

Minor disputes between Jews and Arabs became serious towards the end of 1928. The Arabs raged about the Jewish right to pray as the 'Wailing Wall', the Western wall in Jerusalem, the only remaining piece if the Temple king David's gift to his God and his people, destroyed by the Romans.

The Mufti of Jerusalem Hajamin Al-Husseini fuelled Arab hatred by accusing the Jews of endangering Mosques and holy Islamic sites. Husseini called Arabs to 'Itbach al-Yahud', slaughter the Jews.

On August 22nd – 17th Av – 1929 the leaders

of the *yishuv*[121] met with the British deputy High Commissioner to alert him of their fears of a large Arab riot. The British officials assured them that the Government was in control of the situation.

The Jewish agency for Palestine was formed early in 1929 and the following day after the orthodox Jews had met with the British, the riots of 1929 erupted. Throughout the Palestine Mandate lasting for seven blood-thirsty days. In the old city of Jerusalem the *khamsin* winds became Israel's '*sharav*'.

Ancient narrow streets became tunnels of fierce winds and burning sun. Slowly the arguments between Arabs and Jews turned nasty. From Arab's brooding, assumed wrongs to their holy grounds and the Jewish rights to pray at their Western Wall the British proved fruitless.

Jerusalem was badly hit as was Hebron, Safed, Jaffa and many other parts of the country. Further attacks were repulsed when the *Haganah*[122] was able to mount a defence. The Jerusalem violence generated rumours, fabricated accounts of Jewish attempts to defile Muslim holy paces inflamed Arabs. Villages were plundered and destroyed by Arab mobs. Jewish defences in Tel Aviv and Haifa were thwarted. In Hebron sixty-seven Jewish men, women and children were slaughtered. In Safed eighteen Jews were killed, one hundred and thirty three deaths were recorded and three hundred wounded.

The Arab violence in Hebron was one of the worst atrocities in modern history of Israel. The Arabs were unmolested by the British authorities as Hebron the ancient Jewish quarter was destroyed, and the Jews exiled from their own homes in their own land. A Commission of Inquiry was announced by Lord Passfield which began an investigation of

---

121   Jewish nation   122   Defence

the riots in September 1929.

Commissions of Inquiry cannot bring back the dead. More than one thousand Arab terrorists massacred unarmed Jews even blowing one hundred and fifty Jews to pieces as they slept in their beds in Ben Yehuda Street in the centre of Jerusalem. Unarmed doctors and nurses were savaged on their way to Haddasah hospital. Yet in the midst of carnage in the dust of pain and tears great Torah scholars, some in their eighties, would keep asking questions, argue together into the sorrows of the night and brush the flies off their sacred scrolls.

Lazarus Myersavitch lay almost beyond shock on the blood stained *Yeshiveh* floor. His legs were shaking too much to bear his weight if he'd tried to stand. Grit dug into his eyes as blood seeped from his left shoulder. He was light headed, not caring about his wounds, not understanding how he survived such an attack. Surely he would find his obituary beside him, surely he was dead – but no he lived.

'Their knives must have been blunt by the time my turn came,' went through the broken thoughts in his head.

The morning began well, the *sharav* was blowing with a ferocity that energised him. He enjoyed the tempest, the wild spirit from the skies, the heated air, nature pushing man's ego into a corner.

Then a rush of evil came, knives slashed the living to death. In a frenzy if chanting 'slaughter the Jews', 'Allah is merciful' and pissing over the dead. The poor Yemenite Jew he was discussing *mitzvot*[123]

---

123   Commandments

with, was dead at his feet, his death mask seemed to ask 'why such hate?'

"I will bury you with tears my friend, you came to *Eretz* Israel with hope and belief, I will go on believing for you I will not forget."

Lazarus Mysersavtich blacked out.

"If you keep blaming yourself for Lazarus's wounds you'll give yourself a peptic ulcer. Our son is where he wants to be. He knew a Jerusalem *yeshiveh* wasn't the world's safest place the risks from desert marauders was always there. Death may be inevitable for many Jews, but defeat never."

Reuben Myersavitch lay in silence next to his wife. A surge of anger at the massacre of Jews in *Eretz* Israel brought on a headache. He took the onus for young dying Jews in his own shoulders. For more than twenty years he and Shepsul had preached *aliyah* but Arabs preached violence. Palestine was their land. In his throbbing head Reuben Myersavitch asked himself, 'where in all the Holy Books is the word Palestine? Moses blessed be his name didn't know such a name for his people Israel.'

Jerusalem
August 1929

My dear family,

By now the 'massacre news' must have reached you. I was wounded. Thank God my shoulder is healing slowly, I'm lucky to be alive, we lost many good Jews. We live in pernicious times, what's new? A gloom has descended, for years to come an ugly stain will cover us like a table cloth where the bad mannered have left a mess for someone else to clear up!

This letter reads like the 'meditations of the poor Jew Lazarus'. To brighter things – Being a yeshiveh student and no great catch I needed courage to ask a young Sabra called Hadassah Bat Begun to marry me – her parents are medics. Hadassah is strong, capable and loving, like the women of our household. She has a sister called Simcha who hopes to become a psychiatrist, I'm sure any quirks of mine will soon be sorted out between them!

Every day is uncertain here. Resilience in our community is vital. Despite the strain I believe one day if I am blessed with children they will grow up beneath our own flag – please God may Hadassah and I stand under the chuppah, till then we keep our spirits high.

I miss and love you all

Lazarus

Abraham Myersavitch folded his brother's letter and across the kitchen table gave his mother a comforting smile.

"There ma Lazarus is on the mend and a *Sabra* is joining our family."

"I'm happy he can share the *shabbos* candles with good people, Hadassah sounds just right for him, but Abe he's gone. They will never live here."

"They'll visit."

"Nah, I doubt very much that will happen. Perhaps once. I'm thankful he's alive. Do you think the British treat us well out there?"

"We are a pain in their sides. The British are no lovers of foreigners, they used to hurl bricks at the Dutch and French who settled here. I'm pretty sure they'll aim a few bricks at Jews before they quit."

"Do you think they'll go?"

"Sure ma, they'll go. Don't give yourself a brain-storm worrying about politics. Political animals are dodgy characters that's how the world turns round. Now mama mine how about a glass of hot, sweet lemon tea."

"I received another letter from Chontche the other day. Her cousin wrote from Radzilow telling her lots of news."

"Such as ma?"

"Well in 1922 electricity cables arrived, she didn't say if they could switch on yet."

"Ma we're almost in 1930!"

"I know, but our news takes ages to go the rounds. You know Abe my stomach always feels uneasy when I hear those names. For years Papa and Shepsul have tried to convince the old folk to leave, they're so stubborn. Now in their eighties they won't budge. I wish everyone would leave."

"People put up with conditions they're used to. Change scares them. When you came the Governor and uncle Shepsul had reasons, a mission."

In high spirits, giggling Aviva came into the kitchen.

"Guess what ma."

"You're top of your class."

"Nope teacher says I'm erratic. I looked up erratic, I'm inconsistent. Do you think so Abe?"

"Yes, try improving."

"Can't be bothered anyway erratic is a good solid word makes me feel important, at least I'm something. You still haven't guessed ma."

"Tell me."

"Morris Graubert is *schmoozing* Cissy by the gate. I watched them kissing."

"Aviva stop spying on your sister."

"Well aren't you going to go hysterical?"

"Why should I go hysterical?"

"Ma, if I was *schmoozing* a boy at our gate you would go hysterical!"

"Aviva you are not a young woman. Cissy is with her future *chossen*, maybe they got a little carried away. Everyone always hoped Cissy would marry a cantor, but there you are she has chosen Maurice Graubert."

"How could she bear to kiss a man with a moustache, they're awful."

"Aviva your Papa has a moustache."

"The governor is a rabbi, that's different and parents never kiss."

A smiling Rifka was just going to say something when the kitchen became overcrowded with her sons all speaking at once.

"Abe have you heard the news? Wall Street Crashed today."

"Yossel joked,

"I've lost my millions I'm going into the Thames."

"Well leave your overcoat here we'll need to share wearing the only overcoat in the house!"

No Job - No Bread

Resplendent in his commissionaire's uniform, Great War medals pinned to his chest, stiff-backed and proud, opening car-doors for the rich and famous, his white gloved hands politely accepting tips for holding an umbrella high over the 'satin and furs'. No raindrops could mark the ladies' satin dancing shoes as they arrived to stomp the night away at the Savoy.

A stone's throw from opulence, grey faced men stood in line clutching bread-coupons. A hand-out of a dry crust. Others waited their turn in night-time soup kitchens.

The Great Depression gathering force since the late Twenties now like a terrible storm, rained misery down on the poor. Nineteen-thirty for them had one symbol, the dole queue. Pawn brokers and ragged clothes the poor were no strangers to; the claws of near starvation dug deep into their anger. A sad torpor spread amongst a usually vibrant people. Hope for better times to come helped their miserable plight. Men marched from up north for bread. Married women were not allowed to work. jobs were for men, if they could find one that is.

Across the Atlantic Americans too were going hungry. Suicidal poverty turned able bodied men into tramps. Overnight, hideous 'dollar-a-dance' dance halls opened. Couples danced non-stop for hours to win prize money. Death stalked the dancers as the music played on and on ... .

Stressful lives knowing tomorrow would be just the same. The author John Steinbeck cast hope aside in his masterpiece 'The Grapes of Wrath'. The poet's English voice called out,

"The poor are fast forgotten."

"Gawd 'elp us Kneebones, we can't breathe for pottles."

"Stop moanin' Alf Kneebone, since when was one Pottle, 'pottles' I should like ta know!"

"Yer auntie Florrie is all yer pottles roll'd inta one Pottle, an' don't give me 'she's frail an' old' bit, she'll run the lot of us inta the ground before she buggers-orf believe yer me. See us all out that old piss-pot. ain't yer got enough ta do Flo without cleanin' up 'er piss, bleedin' pottles I ask yer, wat a disgrace."

"Speak-up wat yer say?"

"Good job she's deaf Alf Kneebone. She'd give yer a good earful. Do a good turn when yer can Alf Kneebone, just like yer ma ain't yer - mean. They don't come much meaner."

"Leave me ma alone Flo, she ain't pissin' over the place, worse than a lamp-post this pub smells, an' dogs stink bad enough."

"Gits on me wick 'e do."

"'oo do auntie Florrie?"

"'e do, gits on me wick, a right 'hore son if ever I seen one and 'is wife a silly cow scared of 'er own shadow. 'ow they stands each uver I don't know. I could tell yer things Ada makes yer 'air turn green. Bad blood, bad blood. Seedy 'hore son gits on me nerves!"

"Ada, Ada, where she gorn now?"

"'oo's Ada when she's at 'ome ma?"

"I don't know Maisie, Auntie Florrie goes back

in 'er 'ead don't she. Ada must be family died years ago."

"'opes I don't go backwards when I'm old!"

"Sometimes she says funny things. I 'ave a good laugh ta meself I do. Pa can't stand 'er but yer don't see yer own on the streets do yer Maisie - 'cors no."

"Takin's is down Ma, last night I were glad ta call time. An 'andful comes in, sat like stone statues, not a word between 'em. Drink up I says, yer beer will evap'rate. They didn't even look up."

"Comin' ta somethin' a Cockney as ta dig deep fer half a pint best bitt'r. Why in the Great War we was pack'd out. The 'Threepenny-Bit-an'-Whistle' kept our spirits up."

"In more ways than one ma."

"Maisie I've been thinkin' with yerself in the family way we should close at half-time. Pa an' me have a few bob in our nest egg no Kneebone will stand in line fer free soup. Barney Tooks is a good geezer. Li'tle uns goes 'round back yard at 'is eel an' pie – 'e 'ands out left overs like sweets. Take my advice Maisie gal git yerself ta Marie Stopes. Jimmy Deagan won't care 'ow many yer drop. Yer would 'ave 'im with 'is racing card in one 'and an' the aver up yer lace frock. I dare say 'e's at the nags right now."

"Well I dare say ma 'e ain't. 'e's gorn ta bash up black-shirts down docks.

Esther Starr put on her coat over the leather money-pouch she wore around her waist. Trade was low on the ground. Even in better times East-end market stallholders suffered more bad days than good.

"All packed up Ernie bring the cart over."

"Give us ten minutes Esther."

Esther Starr went half-rental with Ernie Waters (who did lines of all sorts of cheap goods), for cart hire.

"Fancy goin' ta the pitchers Esther?"

"Nahh, ta fer askin'."

"Yer too good fer Solly Starr Esther, a fine lookin' woman like yerself could do much be'ter - too good be far I says."

"Load up Ernie Waters this 'andsome creature wants ta go 'ome."

"Well the of'er still goes if yer change yer mind."

"Don't drop me jar of red ca'bage my Siddi loves 'is red ca'bage with a saveloy."

"Beef I 'opes. I liked a nice saveloy meself. Then I can't rightly remem'er 'oo told me the Frogs made 'em with pig brains. I ain't n'ver 'ad one from that day ta this."

"Are yer a Frenchy all of a sudden?"

"Nah, but yer never knows!"

The first one home from work was Ruthie Starr, she was learning a trade as a finisher in tailoring. Ruthie Starr was completely beautiful, fifteen years old with not only a lovely face, her nature was soft, smiling and uncomplaining even though her young, delicate hands were already showing signs of pricked fingers from sharp needles, and small but obvious callouses on the sides. Her eyes were red and watery by early evening and she couldn't leave if the tailor worked late, which was usual.

Klara lay on her bed with half-closed eyes. An obvious headache grimace on her pale face. Headaches were the family curse. All the Starr family suffered. A tin of headache balm was in all their cupboards. She had met Sydney Myers in the market. Standing outside her father's new shop with its bright, red 'Sale' sign her father swore he would never take down.

Sydney had looked in need of a good meal. She felt sorry for him. So many men were hungry. He drank strong tea. She could see he was doing whatever he could to make money to eat. Her headache worsened.

"Fancy ferget'in' yer balm I can't find any!"

"It's a bad un."

"Yer get'in' too many me gal. What yer got on yer mind?"

"Leave 'er alone. Can yer eat anything me angel?"

"No ma, ta."

They left her and padded around the house aware of the misery she was going through.

The Elopement

Alice had prepared a simple wedding breakfast. A big smile all over her face.

"I don't know what you look so happy about, you hated every day of your marriage. For a start you can put the pickled onions away and the drink - Jews don't drink."

It was time to wake the couple.

Klara wore a simple navy-blue and white dress and he was as pale as a bag of flour. Off they went to the registry office and were married. It was too precious for anyone to throw rice. They came back to a simple meal and he couldn't thank Esther enough. Abraham Myersavitch, now Sidney Myers, was a husband and would soon be a father.

Constantly on her mind, Klara worried about the police. He sat in the clubs and he was marking the cards. She didn't believe that he was not up other things. Anything to make a few bob.

A watchfulness seeped through the atmosphere of the dingy club, everybody watching everybody. Then it seemed to be time to go. A man stood up and grabbed hold of Sidney Myers and said,

"Right, you're under arrest."

He had to empty all his pockets which were empty but for his Craven 'A' cigarettes. He had the sum total of sixpence.

"Ah well," he thought, "it's a fair cop."

❀

Shepsul walked proudly through his front door and thoughtfully scratched his beard. Dosha had been very quiet when he broke the news. She had nodded in her wise, patient way. Emigrating once in a lifetime to start a new life in a strange country was an upheaval, now the *Mizrahi* wanted Shepsul her husband to go to America.

Reuben received the news from rabbi Shlomsky an hour before Shepsul came to talk to him. No one knew how the Potzlock's found out but parting words were offered. Even Koppel Ginsberg was welcomed to bid them farewell.

"I will miss you."

"I will write Peshe. Look after Rifka."

"Rifka looks after me. No matter how much you write I will miss you."

"When we are settled come for a visit."

"When are we ever settled?"

"Are you excited auntie?"

"Well Aviva, yes and no."

"That's two answers and no answer auntie!"

"Why are you complaining do you want another one?"

Dosha held her cup in her hands and smiled at her husband.

"I will miss the family."

"So will I."

"At least we have a while to get ready."

Rachel ransacked the second hand shops for two strong suitcases. Rifka persuaded Reuben to have a photograph taken for the emigrant couple to keep. The brothers spent long hours together before the journey. They knew they would never see each other again. Rabbi Myersavitch said a special prayer for Shepsul in the *schul* and privately at every meal before their departure date.

It was a drab, drizzling day when the party arrived in Southampton. The Aurania was in dock. Shepsul stood with Dosha and Sidney, who seemed more at ease travelling around England than his brothers. His voice carried no trace of a yiddish accent.

"Two Aurania's have gone down."

"Third time lucky," Sidney told Dosha. "Better than the onion boat you came to London in."

"Stay out of trouble," Shepsul told him.

"I can't. The coppers all know I'm a reformatory school boy."

"Perhaps you should leave London."

"Stop crying," Sidney told him. Shepsul patted Docks, who since following him home had become Sydney's shadow. Peshe preferred cats and remained unsure of dogs.

"Learn the diamond trade from Reuben."

They passed the signs to the newly opened Gravling Dock. They came up to the Aurania.

"If only our future home were as big," said Shepsul as they stood before the passenger walkway. They hugged. Shepsul's pockets still filled with parting gifts including three small diamonds his brother had given to him.

"Better than money and I am out of dollars," joked Reuben

"We are going to make another new home."

"Well," smiled his brother, "it's good to keep in practice."

They had hugged the breath out of each other, the bear-hug remembered from their father. For the first time in their lives they understood the melancholy he felt when they left for England, that made him silent at their final parting.

The narrow-faced crewman checked their ticket and looked at the two travellers.

"Other gangplank," he told them, "this is first class only."

Shepsul and Dosha climbed the walkway and turned to wave goodbye to Sidney. He was crying. Crying because of separation, because of distance, because of loss. Dosha was crying because she was suddenly sad. Only Shepsul did not cry. Docks wagged his tail.

This was not an escape. The grey clouds refused to move before the ship left port.

Reuben put on his glasses to read all the letters Dosha sent them. They were filled with work, new people and Dosha telling them about New York.

"Look at this," he read, "they have found the Shulmarks. Joseph's father was our cantor in Poland. They emigrated in '23, a year before they first got electricity."

In her third letter she told them she was pregnant. Their son was born in a third floor room of a large tenement overlooking a busy, busy street. Looking like the babies in their family had looked for thousands of years. She called him Izaak because she was 42, when they had given up all hope of having a child.

"At her age ... a miracle," said Cissy.

"Must be the air over there."

Rifka thought it had taken Koppel's amulet a long time to work.

Reuben, who missed his brother, sipped his tea

and said,
     "God, blessed be His name, gave them a going away present after all."

Fever

Cissy, Sydney's favourite sister, who was giving birth to her second child was the only one who saw he was a part and yet separate from his brothers.

Cissy gave birth to her second daughter, Madeleine and exhausted from her labour fell asleep. Her elder daughter Evelyn looked at the baby and cuddled her father.

Cissy woke up with a growing fever. She was soon running a temperature over one hundred and one Fahrenheit. Her back hurt and she had a pain in her abdomen. Her husband was with a blonde dancer as the pain worsened. After ten hours she was bleeding and listless. After a day she was dying. Sidney found her husband and dragged him to the hospital.

They stood by her bed as she died. Puerperal fever. A piece of the placenta had been left inside her uterus.

Sidney did not move. He did not feel the tears rolling down his face. When his brothers brought Rabbi Myersavitch to the room, he heard *Kaddish*[124] being sung he became aware of them. He couldn't feel his hands.

The funeral was held on a very foggy morning and Sidney, who seemed to know the shrouded streets, as he seemed to know all things about England, better than his brothers, led the cortège to

124   Funeral prayer

the cemetery. Evelyn crying and Madeleine wrapped up warm, stayed with the women in the house. Rifka cut their dresses crying,

"My darlink Cissy –"

As the coffin was lowered into the muddy ground no one needed Sammy the Weeper to cry. The cantor's voice rose above the tears. Sidney softly recited Longfellow to himself, one of his favourite poems.

> *Tell me not, in mournful numbers,*
> *Life is but an empty dream!*
> *For the soul is dead that slumbers,*
> *And things are not what they seem.*

> *Life is real! Life is earnest!*
> *And the grave is not its goal;*
> *Dust thou art, to dust returnest,*
> *Was not spoken of the soul.*

> *Not enjoyment, and not sorrow,*
> *Is our destined end or way;*
> *But to act, that each to-morrow*
> *Find us farther than to-day.*

The next day Sidney and his brother Benjamin walked to the grave and laid stones on it.

"I remember how I used to tease her and undo her aprons when she tried to read us stories," his brother said.

"Mother will tell Dosha in her next letter."

Sidney reached into his pocket and felt something he had forgotten about. He took out the neatly folded paper.

"Got some stones I see," said Benjamin.

"Yes, a few diamonds. I'm making them up into rings with father."

"Who for?"

"Just business. Nothing big. Puts bread on the table."

Cissy had been a brief flower after all. They walked back to the gates.

They left the cemetery to the tears from the clouds. Sidney went a few miles east and visited another grave. Minnie Biggins was buried near Archie.

Before you weave the cloth, you must make the loom.

Sidney did the work with his father and sold five of the rings. Sidney Myers disliked the way Cheng shortened his name to 'Sid' but the money helped him buy his first, small car to drive his new family around. He was putting the reformatory school behind him.

Sidney bought Klara a new coat to keep her warm as she was heavily pregnant with their first child.

The thought of new life filled him with wonder. Sometimes as he looked at his Klara he felt he was almost floating.

Klara did not have bad headaches carrying her first child. But she had to get used to sleeping with the light on as Sidney could not bear the dark.

A Pillow-Case

Klara felt better than she had done since she married. She worked in the market in her father's shop. Sidney had been quiet since Cissy's death but as the birth of their first child drew nearer he seemed contented. He had recited every poem he knew to her as they cuddled up in bed, talked about Shakespeare and all the books he had read in the library at the reformatory.

Rachel, their daughter was born on a Tuesday in May. She had the Myersavitch body and the beauty of her Starr ancestors. Sidney came into London Hospital to see them and brought with him all her clothes. Just as Klara had asked. Her grandmother had knitted a pink frock baby-coat. It looked fetching against the red string she had tied around her wrist.

Two weeks later Klara was back in her flat and Sidney was working with his father. He did not visit Cheng anymore and when a Chinese man knocked on her door Klara let out such a scream he ran away.

At six weeks old they took Rachel's father away. Because of a pillow case that had been stolen and 'found' in his new car. They could prove nothing - yet they proved everything with two, paid witnesses. He was sentenced to eighteen months. Once a thief, always a thief, they said. The reformatory school would never leave Abraham Myersavitch alone.

Rachel lived with her grandmother Esther

whilst her mother worked.

"I'll keep the gal with me at the market in the day," said Esther.

"They put 'im away for eigh'een months!"

"It'll pass."

"Fer nothin' 'e ever did."

"You got to see ta Rachel."

"I can't take her with me ma, the fact'ry owner says it's not allow'd."

"Don't you worry about our Rachel, she'll be safe an' all."

She loved her grandmother so much it hurt when she had to go back to live with her mother again. It was never the same. She was never close to her mother. This cycle would repeat itself, torturing her early life.

Esther kept the baby basket with her all the time and looked down on her granddaughter with pride. Klara had to take tea breaks to empty the milk from aching, swollen breasts in the communal lavatories. Once a week she gave a man with a broken nose some money for Sidney's cigarettes inside prison.

She visited. The bleakness of the prison began three streets before the huge iron gates. He smoked too much. He had a cut over his eye from a fight.

"Ma's seeing to Rachel, she keeps her at the market during the day."

"Your mother's good that way."

"We should leave London."

"Can't leave everything you know."

"Your uncle's in New York."

"Maybe one day, but we need a bit of money behind us."

"She'll be walkin' by the time yur 'ome."

"I'm sorry luv."

"Your dad says he has some diamonds for you to sell when you get 'ome. Set you up again in 'atton Gardens like your brothers."

"I'll go see him straight away when I get out. You managing?"

"I'm getting by. Saving a bit for you so you 'ave more than sixpence in your pocket."

Klara collected Rachel and walked home. In her mind she walked over the police with contempt. She was walking through the gates of hell.

The sign to the 'Threepenny-Bit-And-Whistle' fell at her feet. And the gypsy flower woman said,

"You buy violets today?"

Klara looked at her daughter and said,

"Today is not a violet day."

The End

Glossary

A

Achi Nabbich 18
Aleichem Sholem 143
aliyah 145

B

Babyla 13
badchan 101
bashert 325
Bevis Marks Schul 247
Bimah 29
Black One Hundred 308
borsht 152
bube 15

C

cantor 11
chedder-boys 100
chedder-class 100
cholent 14, 23, 74
chossen 337
chuppah 16, 69
Chuppah 36

D

davenen 146
devekut 308
droshes 148

T

V

Y

Z

Also by Shänne Sands

During the 1950s Shänne Sands lived between England and India. This evocative, beautifully written prose work brings gods to life, populates streets with breath and takes you into the world of many religions, wandering their path on unsteady legs through the vibrant seasons and the reasons people give for living.

Paperback: 204 pages

48 colour photographs

ISBN: 978-1908867018

"This book has the most lyrical prose that I have ever read."

Anna Mills, Amazon.

"... she is the most accomplished Poet of our times."

Dr Butler Brewton,
South Carolina

5 volume series of selected poems by Shänne Sands:

Volume 1 :-Fidelity is for Swans 978-0-9566349-4-8
Volume 2 :-The Silver Hooves 978-0-9566349-7-9
Volume 3 :-Moonlight on Words 978-0-9566349-8-6
Volume 4 :-Night Song 978-0-9566349-9-3
Volume 5 :-Fragments of Desire 978-0-9566349-6-2

www.ingramcontent.com/pod-product-compliance
Lightning Source LLC
Chambersburg PA
CBHW072115250626
47159CB00007B/2451